A Complementary Connection

ESKAY KABBA

4 Horsemen
Publications, Inc.

A Complementary Connection
Copyright © 2024 Eskay Kabba. All rights reserved.

Published By: 4 Horsemen Publications, Inc.

4 Horsemen Publications, Inc.
PO Box 417
Sylva, NC 28779
4horsemenpublications.com
info@4horsemenpublications.com

Cover by J. Kotick and Autumn Skye
Typesetting by Autumn Skye
Edited by Jen Paquette

All rights to the work within are reserved to the author and publisher. No part of this publication may be reproduced, stored in a retrieval system, or transmitted in any form or by any means, electronic, mechanical, photocopying, recording, scanning, or otherwise, except as permitted under Section 107 or 108 of the 1976 International Copyright Act, without prior written permission except in brief quotations embodied in critical articles and reviews. Please contact either the Publisher or Author to gain permission.

All characters, organizations, and events portrayed in this novel are either products of the author's imagination or are used fictitiously.

All brands, quotes, and cited work respectfully belongs to the original rights holders and bear no affiliation to the authors or publisher.

Library of Congress Control Number: 2024947566

Paperback ISBN-13: 979-8-8232-0394-4
Hardcover ISBN-13: 979-8-8232-0395-1
Audiobook ISBN-13: 979-8-8232-0690-7
Ebook ISBN-13: 979-8-8232-0393-7

DEDICATION

T. Browne: A Complementary Connection

Content warning: Explicit Langauge,
Explicit Sexual Situations, and Drug Use.

Table of Contents

Epilogue

I, Nicholas Elliot Highton, verbally dictate this last will and testament before my attorney group, Jacobsen, Pomeroy, and Jacobsen, my most trusted advisor and personal assistant, Zoey Rachel Huffnagle, my senior executive Marcel Cyrille Delacoux, and secondary witness and signature of this will, my sister Emma May Highton, Attorney at Law and CEO of Highton Optimum Holdings. I am of sound mind and body, and my current medical and psychological evaluation is placed with these documents.

To my loved ones: If you are reading this, I am either unexpectedly dead or about to be, and I apologize for the trouble I've caused. But it is extremely important to me that my last wishes be followed without interference from any members of my family. It is my life, it is my career, and it is my money to do as I see fit.

In the matters of Highton Media and Publications, I leave it in the hands of Parker Kenneth Madison of Parker Madison, Incorporated, as acting President, with Rion Daniel Matthews as acting Vice President, and Marcel Cyrille Delacoux as Chief Operational Officer, a title he should have been given a long time ago. Parker and Rion's salary will stay the same, but Marcel's title comes with a starting salary of six hundred thousand dollars ($600,000), one hundred (100) shares in the company, and an employment contract for ten (10) years. Between the three of them, my company will be in good hands until my nephew, Robert Emerson Highton-Dorado, is prepared to take over as the President and Chief Executive Officer. Then a new executive team with Robert at the helm will be brought together. Under his leadership, young mind, and fresh ideas, HMP will flourish for the next couple of decades. The Highton legacy will continue.

In the matter of my financial affairs, I currently have no children to bequeath to, known or unknown, and I have no plans to have children of my own. Therefore, my four personal savings accounts and three checking accounts will be combined and split among all my nieces and nephews: Arlow Socrate Highton, Angus Giancarlo Highton, Maddox Leonardo Highton, Robert Emerson Highton-Dorado, Blair Gisella Highton-Dorado, Maurese Hollingsworth, Jeffery Hollingsworth, Katelyn Hollingsworth, Morgan Grant Navarro, and the unnamed firstborn child of Avalon Santos Mathews. At the current time, the contents of these accounts contain approximately two hundred and eighty million dollars ($280,000,000). Any subsequent nieces or nephews will obtain one hundred (100) shares in Highton Media and Publications upon their birth.

To Zoey Rachel Huffnagle, you have been more than my personal assistant; you have been my best friend and confidante. To you, I leave two hundred and fifty million dollars ($250,000,000), tax free, and ten (10) acres of land in Augusta, Georgia, where your family is from, so you can officially retire. It is nowhere near what you deserve, but it's a start.

And to Rion Daniel Matthews, who made it very clear from the beginning that he never wanted a cent of my money: To you, I leave you no dollars or cents, as you wished. Instead, I leave you with assets. The apartment in New York City at 60 Riverside Drive, the apartment in Denmark, and the home in East London that we bought together are all yours. So you'll always have a place to lay your head. And if my mother, Madeline Highton, ever releases her hold on Highton Estates at Sea Cliff Manor, the deed will immediately be transferred to you. All my vehicles belong to Saving Grayce except for the Toyota Camry, which is in Rion Daniel Matthews's name, without his prior knowledge. Sorry, Rion. I lied about the car. I bought it, and it's been yours. Please ensure that the cars are sold off at auction by Saving Grayce, the organization run by Penelope Benson, and Saving Grayce receive one hundred percent (100%) of the profits. It is the least I could do for her.

And one more asset: My entire stock of Highton Optimum Holdings is to be transferred to your name, Rion Daniel Matthews. You, along with my siblings, Emma and Brian, hold one-third of all of Highton Optimum shares, stocks, and bonds. I'm sorry I made you ridiculously, filthy rich. Deal with it. In the event that my demise included the demise of Rion Daniel Matthews, my shares are to be given to his sister, Gabrielle Hernandez-Navarro, along with her husband, Gael Navarro. She is the next best thing.

To Rion, if you are reading or listening to this, you are probably frustrated and annoyed with these decisions to include you and your family in my will. I don't care. Your family is my family too. Because you, Ree, are the greatest gift in all the world that money could never buy. My heart began to beat the day I met you. And I will forever be grateful to the universe for seating us next to each other on that red-eye flight that first day of June. No matter where I am, in life or in death, Nicky Will Always Want Ree.

Whatever is left of my assets outside of what I have mentioned will be returned to the primary account of Niles Clark Highton or, upon his demise, transferred to his firstborn son, Brian Niles Highton or, upon his demise, transferred to his firstborn sons, Arlow and Angus Highton, and so on noted.

This concludes the final will and testament of Nicholas Elliot Highton.

1

Rion woke right as the sun was rising, but he did not open his eyes just yet. He listened. He listened to the sound of the birds right outside his window. He listened to the soft whistle of the wind coming through a crack in the windowpane in the master bathroom. He listened to Nicholas's slow breaths, strong but not exactly a snore. He knew Nick must be lying on his back. Rion reached over to test his theory, and he felt Nick's chest hair. He ran his hands farther down to his abs and felt Nick's hand. Rion left his fingers next to Nick's and fell back asleep for another ten minutes.

The second time Rion woke up, he opened his eyes fully and sat up. Nick was still deep in sleep. Rion went into the bathroom to relieve himself, brushed his teeth, washed his face, and went over to his side of the closet. He grabbed a pair of jeans, a t-shirt, and his favorite hoodie, a yellow one that said "California, the Sunshine State" on it, and got dressed. He gingerly walked around the room to gather his laptop and his camera, threw both straps over his shoulder, and silently closed the bedroom door.

On the second landing, he noticed his sister Avalon's room door was open, so he peeped in. Her bed was unmade, but she was not there. He wondered if that meant she left last night or in the middle of the night. Rion went down to the first floor of the flat and walked into the galley kitchen. As expected, Izzy floated in after him. He gave her a few chin rubs while he started a pot of coffee, then opened up a can of Friskies and fed her breakfast. Afterward, he added coffee to his thermal and left the pot on warm. Then Rion stepped out into the bright morning sunshine and looked around the quiet St. Katharine's and Wapping neighborhood before he walked up the street and rented a Santander Cycle.

As Rion rode the bike toward the city, he pressed the button of his right EarPod and said, "Call Ava."

The phone rang four times before she picked up. "Hello," she said groggily.

"Top of the morning to you!" he teased.

"I don't start work until noon, Ree," she said, and he heard her plopping back down on the bed.

"You're with Kaleb?"

"Yes." She paused, then said, "I am fine."

"Okay. Just checking on you. You were home last night but not this morning, so..."

"She's fine, mate," he heard Kaleb say in the background. "I'm taking care of her."

Rion smiled. "Alright. I'll see you both later for dinner."

"Yup, cheers," Kaleb said, taking the phone from his girlfriend and hanging up on his friend.

Rion kept riding until he made it to Hyde Park. He found a quiet spot under a tree, opened up his laptop, and put on Spotify, syncing it to his headphones. Then he began to write.

Three hours later, Rion was walking back to the house when suddenly three people were behind him: a reporter with a mic, a cameraman, and a photographer. Rion kept walking, ignoring them. Then they got in front of him to snap a picture and put the camera in his face.

"Ken Willis, TMZ," the reporter introduced himself. "How are Ryan D. Ryder and Mr. Deep Strokez doing? Still going strong?" Rion smiled and kept walking. "Do you like it here in London? Are you ever planning on moving back to the States?"

Rion gave them no response. He opened up the small gate, and the men followed him up his walkway. "C'mon Rion, give us something," said Ken. "You posted two pictures over a year and a half ago, and no other pictures of the two of you together. At least Nicholas Highton would post a picture of the two of you here and there when you traveled. Now you don't even leave the house at the same time. Are you actually a couple or not?"

Rion put the key in the door, but it opened on him. He looked up at Nick standing there, hairy chest and full set of abs on display. He must have thrown on the first pair of linen pants to come to the door because he obviously had no underwear on; the outline of his lax penis was visible. Nick reached his hands up to hold onto the top of the doorway, showing all the muscles in his shoulders and arms. Even Rion had to admit it was a beautiful sight. Being ridiculously wealthy and ridiculously handsome at the same time was Nicholas Highton's burden in life. The photographer went crazy, snapping pictures of Nick at every angle. Rion stepped slightly to the right to avoid getting in the pics with him.

"Good morning, gentlemen. I just want to remind you that once you've crossed that gate, you're officially trespassing," said Nick kindly.

"Sorry, Mr. Highton," Reporter Willis said as the cameraman zoomed in. "You're obviously still a pair, but the world wants to know, how is the relationship going between the two of you? We just want you to give us something, innit."

Rion scoffed with a smile and tapped Nick's waist to step inside. But as he crossed the threshold, Nick stopped him from walking with a touch on his arm. "Here's something."

Nick turned Rion's face to him and kissed him on the lips, right in the doorway. Rion opened his mouth and sucked his bottom lip. Nick put his tongue in Rion's mouth, and Rion could not help the moan that escaped. For a few moments, they kissed with the flashes of the photographer and the camera zooming in on their faces. Nick ended it first, leaving Rion pink-faced and shiny-lipped. They both turned to the camera, smiling.

"You have five seconds to get off my property, or I'm calling the police. Good day, gentlemen," Nick said with a smile. He pulled Rion from the doorway and closed the door.

Rion laughed. "I can't believe you did that. Zoey is going to have kittens when she sees it on TMZ."

Nick smiled. "It was fun though." He ran his fingers through Rion's curls. "Hey, babe. Want breakfast? I just scrambled eggs."

"Sure, babe."

Nick went into the kitchen, and Rion went to the living room to turn on the TV. "Ava's with Kaleb? I didn't see her this morning."

"Yeah, she's over in Brixton with him."

"Is that official yet? Or are we all still pretending that they're not sleeping together?" Nick asked.

"I'm going to ask them about it tonight," said Rion. "Another soccer game is on, but it's Chelsea, so we're watching it." Rion had discovered he was a Chelsea fan in the year they had been living in England.

"Okay," Nick called out. Then said, "Also, it's football. Not soccer. We live here now, so get used to it."

Rion laughed. "Yeah, okay." He walked over to the table as Nick came to the table with two plates of scrambled eggs, avocado, and wheat toast. "Coffee?"

"I had coffee already. OJ?"

"Sure."

Nick went back into the kitchen and poured Rion a cup of orange juice. They sat next to each other at the table, legs turned toward the other as they ate. They could hear the reporters still outside, but they both consciously ignored them.

"What time do you start today?" Rion asked.

"In an hour. I have three meetings: one with the finance team, one with the editors, and one with Nguyen. You?"

"Just the book review meeting at 3 today. The meeting with my publisher is tomorrow evening."

"Parker is coming by too. We have a quick meeting."

"Okay. So you'll be done by 6, right? Because Sonny and Lennox are coming by for dinner."

"Yup. Parker is my last meeting of the day." Nick's phone rang. He looked at it and smiled before he put it on speaker. "Good morning, Zoey."

"God dammit, Boss! Didn't I tell you to warn me when you do this shit!? My phone is blowing up at 7 a.m. with reporters wanting an official statement, so I had to dragged myself out of bed to find out what the fuck they were talking about!"

"Sorry," said Nick with a smile. "It was spontaneous on my part."

"Obviously," she said in a mocking English accent. "Poor Rion looked like a cute casualty in the shots you fired at the media."

Rion's face flushed again. "Complete collateral damage," he said.

Zoey tsked. "Any other media make-out sessions I should know about?"

"Just the one," Nick said as he buttered his toast. "I figured one every other year or so should keep them wanting."

"He's kidding, Zoey," Rion called out before Zoey started cursing again.

"He better be," Nick's personal assistant warned playfully.

"I'll see you in a few weeks," said Nick. "Enjoy the rest of your day."

Zoey had been flying out to London for three days every month since they settled in the city to check in with Nick. She had just left last week. "See you next month, Boss," she said.

Nick hung up and looked at Rion's smile. "What?" Nick said, stuffing his mouth with eggs.

"Nothing. Just love you," Rion responded. Nick smiled back.

After their shared meal, Nick went into his home office on the first floor to start his 12 o'clock Teams meeting, which was 7 a.m. back in New York City where his company, Deep Strokez Publications, was. Thanks to Marcel, he did not need to fly back and forth often, as his executive assistant continued to run the office as a tight ship. So Nick spent most of his afternoons and evenings working alongside his staff remotely and went back once a quarter to be in person for an all-staff meeting.

Rion had not been back to the States since they left over a year and a half ago for a Buddhist retreat in Thailand, and neither had his sister, Ava. Rion swore it was not because he still had a fear of flying—after traveling to ten different countries in five months, he was mostly over it... kind of—but because he simply had nothing to go back to. His life was wherever Nicholas was. And Ava felt the same, having been clean and sober for the last eighteen months and feeling like her life was falling into place. So when Rion suggested they buy a house and stay in London a year ago, Ava happily jumped at the chance to stay with them, also having no desire to go back to the life she had.

Rion went to his own office on the second floor, the bedroom turned into his personal space right next to the meditation room that all three of them used at different intervals throughout the day. He reread his work, saving and proofreading. While he was meeting with the book review team, he heard Nick's steps and the door close in the meditation room, so he slid on his headphones so he wouldn't disturb his partner's midday meditation. Once done, Rion checked his email and saw his editors sent him the rewrites for his current novel, so he worked on that for an hour or two before he ended his day. Since his office faced the back of the house overlooking the garden, he had not heard the commotion outside until he started going down the stairs. Rion peeked out the front window and saw more reporters had gathered right outside of the gate. He shook his head and went to the kitchen, glancing at Nick's closed door only once.

After 5 p.m., he heard the chime of the front door opening. "Hey!" Ava called out.

"In here," Rion called back. She and Kaleb came in together.

"That smells smashing," Kaleb said, coming closer. He attempted to stick his finger in Rion's onion-and-mushroom gravy, but Rion poked his finger with a fork instead. Kaleb pretended to be hurt and sucked on his finger. "You could have just said no."

"No," Rion said. "Dinner will be ready in an hour. You're staying?"

"Yup. Rilianne and Laurence are on their way too." Kaleb left the kitchen and asked, "You catch the match today? Chelsea's really looking good, innit?"

"Only caught the first half," Rion called out.

Ava walked up and kissed his cheek. "Hey, baby bro. Your other half is still working?"

"Yup. He'll be done at 6. At least he better be done at 6," Rion said, more to himself.

Nicholas was a self-proclaimed workaholic, but they managed to balance each other out, working hard to make sure they took breaks and spent quiet time with one other when possible.

"He caused quite a stir with that passionate kiss you too did," said Kaleb, taking him out of his thoughts. "The wolves are swarming, and they are hungry for more. We barely got in here; they were hounding me for questions about the two of you." Rion smiled but did not respond.

Nick opened up his office door. "Ree?" he called out.

"Yeah?"

"Parker's on his way and confirmed he's staying for dinner."

"Okay." Rion pulled two more steaks to season as Nick closed his door again. Ava silently began to help by seasoning the meat.

Sonny and Lennox arrived next, hand in hand. Ava gave them both hugs and put out a small spread of cheese, grapes, and wine. She and Kaleb entertained their guests while Rion finished up dinner. The doorbell rang again, and Kaleb opened it for Parker Madison, Nicholas's best friend and company investor. The short man already had an attitude, speaking loudly without greeting anyone.

"Christ, you would have thought Harry and Meghan were living here. The bloody fuck is going on!? Why are the paparazzi in front of your door?"

"Because Nick decided to give TMZ a show, so the wolves are howling again," Rion teased as they shook hands. He had just placed the pasta salad on the table.

Ava opened up her phone and showed it to Parker as he entered the living room. He watched it with his eyebrows scrunched in and eventually chuckled.

"Well, well, well. Nick certainly knows how to perform for the masses, doesn't he?" Rion smiled as he went back into the kitchen. "I have Hanson out there with a cricket bat, making sure they stay off the sidewalk and don't disturb the neighbors. Now, where is he?"

"Still in his office," Rion called out, "but he should be done soon. He promised we would eat dinner at a decent hour tonight."

"Bollocks. I'll get him out." Parker stormed off to Nick's office, opened the door without knocking, and walked in, closing the door behind him.

Rion shook his head as Lennox came over to him and wrapped her arms around him from the back. "You American, you. Just can't help yourself, throwing it all in our faces, can you?"

Rion smiled and patted her hands. "Well, you and Sonny don't seem to be shy yourselves, smooching every five seconds."

She squeezed his midsection again. "I know. It's so good what we have. Who knew falling in love with your friend was just what I needed? What we both needed."

Rion turned around and linked his arm around her waist. "The marketing job is going well?" he asked as they walked back into the living room.

"Yes, actually," she said excitedly. "I love being able to come up with ideas to help clients be their best selves." She looked over at the other couple. "Ava seems to be doing so well. Thanks to Kaleb." She winked.

"Yeah..." Rion trailed off as he also watched the two of them.

They orbited around each other, one never too far, eyes always looking at the other. The office door opened, taking Rion out of his thoughts of his sister and friend being in a relationship. Nick and Parker stepped out, laughing. It made Rion smile. He loved seeing his partner happy. He was equally happy to see that Nick made it on time for dinner, thanks to Parker.

"Let's eat, everyone," Rion announced just as the doorbell rang again.

Nick went to open the door, and Laurence pushed Rilianne inside. The flashes went crazy with a small glimpse of Nick. "Hey, Loverboy," Rilianne mused as she kissed his cheek.

"Made any more sex tapes today?" Laurence joked. "Because that kiss sure looked like the beginning of one." Nick laughed and steered them inside.

One by one, they made it to the dining room with Parker commenting, "If I knew we were coupling it up this evening, I would have bought a date!"

Nick slid over to the seat next to Rion, still talking with Parker. But he placed one hand on Rion's thigh and squeezed. Rion looked at him, waiting for him to finish his joke, making Parker laugh loudly. Nick turned to him, his eyes twinkling. Rion gave him a small smile.

Nick leaned over and kissed his cheek, then said softly, "Thanks for making dinner." Rion nodded slowly. Nick squeezed his leg again and turned to Lennox to say something quirky.

They dug in, conversation flowing as easily as the wine. Afterward, the nine of them played Pictionary, with Parker happy to host the evening, keeping score and teasing the bad drawings and equally bad answers. More wine was passed around as they settled in the living room discussing UK politics, comparing it to what was happening in the United States. Sonny fell asleep, his head in Lennox's lap as she stroked his black hair. Laurence and Rilianne left first, having another event to go to.

"It's getting late, and I have an early day tomorrow," said Parker after they left, glancing around. "We're not all still on American time a year later." He stood up. "I think I'll leave Hanson here for the night and call a car service. Just to make sure no one is sneaking into your garden for a peek at your undies."

"Thanks, Parker," Nick said sincerely.

Rion tapped Sonny awake, who wiped the drool off his chin and off Lennox's bare thigh. Parker offered to drop them off, and Sonny and Lennox agreed, happy that they got a ride somewhere. But when the car arrived and Parker went to open the front door, the cameras immediately flashed. And the crowd had gotten bigger.

"My apologies," Parker said loudly. "No nipple shots right now. Unless you want to see mine."

The 5'7" hairy man playfully lifted up his shirt to his belly button and actually got a laugh out of a few of the reporters. That gave Sonny and Lennox a moment to sneak past and jump in the car.

Ava laughed from the couch, hearing Parker's declaration. "That Parker is a mess. But Nicholas loves the attention."

"He's just really good at playing it up for the media," said Rion, watching Nick clear the dining room table. "They both are, in different ways."

"Tell me about it." She opened up her phone to the TMZ website and handed it to her brother. "I know you haven't watched it yet. The kiss is spectacular."

Rion also grinned looking at it, especially afterward when his lips were all shiny, his face was pink, and he had a goofy grin for the cameras. As Nick came back into the living room, Rion gave Nick Ava's phone so he could see too. He also grinned as he sat next to Ava.

"Speaking of kisses," Rion said casually. He stared at his sister, then his friend. They looked at each other, then back at Rion. "I just want to know the deal. That's all."

"We both do," said Nick, handing Ava back the phone.

Kaleb spoke first. "Well, I've fallen hard for this lady, but I think the both of you already knew that."

"We know," said Nick. "From that first dinner in London, you've been a little lovesick."

"And I asked you to back off and let her get her feet under her," Rion reminded him. "Ava needs a lot of stability right now. She's still so early in her recovery."

"Please don't talk about me like I'm not here," said Ava. She reached over and took Kaleb's hand.

"We're not trying to do that," said Nick. "But you aren't supposed to be in a relationship for at least two years."

"Well I'm in recovery with her," said Kaleb. "So we're working the steps together."

"What?" Nick asked before Rion could. "You're not in N/A."

"No, but I do have a drinking problem," said Kaleb, trying to convince them. "Well, I did. So now I'm in the program with her, and we're supporting each other."

"That's not how it works, K," said Rion. "If you're in recovery too, then you definitely do not need to be in a relationship."

"He's not actually in recovery," Ava said, sending him a scolding look. "But he did stop drinking and has discovered how hard it is to live without a vice you've been so casually living with for so long. And working the steps is helping him understand what I'm going through, and he's encouraging me. Kaleb is my rock right now."

Rion sighed. "Guys, I can see you're in this state of new love and blissfulness right now. I get it, trust me. I've been there, literally. But if this goes bad—"

"It's not going to go bad," they chorused together.

Nick smiled at them. "So you've discussed it?"

Kaleb sat forward a little more and said, "We talk every day about it. We do a check in weekly to make sure we're on the same page. We want to maintain this friendship more than anything because that's what she needs, mate. Stability in her life, like you said. And if we ever feel like we're moving in different directions, we end it amicably, and I stay in her life so she never feels abandoned by me. So whether it's as her boyfriend or her friend, she's got me for life." He nodded at her. She nodded back.

Nick looked at Rion. He could see that Rion was still worried about their relationship, but Rion said, "Okay."

"I'm headed back over to Kaleb's," Ava said. "I just wanted you both to know that I'm okay."

Kaleb stood up and stretched. "Yeah, I want to make a quick stop at my mum's, so let's head out."

The rest stood up and Nick walked them to the door. He opened it widely. The photographers went crazy with flashes again. He pretended they were not there as he gave Kaleb a dap and brotherly hug and hugged Ava tightly. He waved goodnight to them, then closed the door.

Rion was waiting in the hallway. "You're nothing but a showman."

"That's why my 138 million fans love me," he said smugly, kissing Rion on the lips as he walked past him, taking Rion's hand.

Rion let Nick lead him into their bedroom. Nick went straight to the bathroom, turning on the shower. Rion stripped and hopped in with him. The men didn't talk as they quietly washed and rinsed the other off. After drying off in the bedroom, Nick fell into the bed backward, taking Rion with him. They kissed sweetly, grinding against each other. Nick reached down first, grabbing Rion's length and tugging. Rion let out a moan and fell to his side, sucking Nick's neck. Nick used his other hand to give Rion the lube. Rion gave him a sly smile, acknowledging Nick's request.

He used one hand to prepare and tease him, and Nick quickly forgot about Rion and grabbed his own anatomy. Rion readjusted his body until he was between Nick's legs and entered him. Over the last two years, Rion and Nick discovered the best positions to ensure Nick had maximum pleasure, and Rion was determined to give it to him. Nick kept his knees up and his feet flat as Rion hovered and thrust at a steady pace. Nick held on to Rion's bottom, encouraging him to move faster, press harder. It made Rion smile.

Nick began moaning, toes curling so tightly they were grabbing the sheets. He reached down again and slowly stroked his cock, moaning, "Yeah... Yeah... God yeah..."

Rion felt his body tense up from inside and knew Nick was close. He also knew to stay focused before he came too. It was one of Rion's favorite things, being inside of his partner, making him cum in that way, knowing that he was the only one who had ever done so. He watched Nick's face contort, his head thrashing back on the pillow, until his head froze to the left, his mouth opened, and a deep groan escaped his throat. Nick continued to stroke himself as cum shot out of him, melting into his dirty blond chest hair.

"Jesus, Nicky," Rion said quietly.

He reached down and lifted up Nick's legs until his bottom was off the bed and his knees were in his chest, then began to move at warp speed, slapping his thighs against Nick's bottom roughly. Nick, who had not fully come down from the high of his orgasm, quickly built back up. Nick put one hand on Rion's bottom, the other on the back of his neck, and held on. Nick's body flushed, and he released again. Rion stopped moving, let go of Nick's legs, and grabbed his face, pushing his tongue in Nick's mouth. Nick moaned and ran his hands through Rion's hair as they kissed for a long time. Rion pulled his face back first and smiled. Nick, having climaxed twice, gave him a lazy smile back. Rion began to move his hips again, putting his face in Nick's neck, his hands in Nick's hair. Nick held his bottom once more with one hand, encouraging him, while caressing Rion's back with his other.

They stayed in that position for a while until Rion came, whispering his lover's name, "Nicky..."

Nick's heart melted. "I love you too," Nick whispered.

Once Rion could move, he kissed Nick again, slowly, sensually, pulling out but staying in the moment with him. Nick began to chuckle.

"What?" Rion asked softly.

"If someone would have told me three years ago that I would have enjoyed sex this way as much as I do, I would have laughed in their face."

Rion smiled and put his face on Nick's right pec. "Well if someone would have told me that I would be fucking a wealthy, infamous, hot as sin, former playboy in a ten million dollar London townhome that I own too, I would have also laughed in their face."

Nick chuckled and played with Rion's hair, content with his life and heart.

They laid head to foot on the long couch, both reading their individual novels that quiet Sunday afternoon. Their phones were right next to each other on the low coffee table when Nick's phone rang. He reached for it with one hand and said, "Good morning, Emma."

"Good afternoon, Nicholas. I come with upsetting news."

Nick put his book down and sat up. Rion looked up in confusion. "What's wrong?" Nick asked.

"Father had a stroke."

"A stroke!?" Nick yelled. "Is he okay!?"

Rion also put his book down and sat up, immediately coming to Nick's side so he could hear what was going on. Nick put the phone on speaker as his sister explained.

"Yes, he is fine. I'm so sorry. I should have led with that. It was a mild stroke, and it was at the office, so they caught it immediately and took him into the hospital. It was two days ago. I wasn't there. I was in Texas with the Dorados when it happened. But

Mother didn't tell Brian or me until last night. Father is already home and resting. He's out of work for the next six weeks at least."

Nick shook his head. "Why would she keep something like that from us?"

"I think she didn't want us to worry. But of course we're all worried. But Nicholas, that's not the end of the upsetting part." She let a moment pass and said, "Mother is calling a family gathering tomorrow at dinner. The whole family will be there, and she is demanding your presence. Expect to stay for a few days."

Nick sighed. "It's fine. Rion and I will get on the plane and head right over to Rochester. We'll—"

"No, Nicholas," Emma said, cutting him off. Rion already knew what she was going to say, not understanding why Nick didn't expect it. "Rion cannot come."

Nick's eyes narrowed at the phone. "Rion is my family." Rion put his hand on Nick's shoulder and gave him a gentle squeeze to calm him down.

"Yes, Nicholas, I know that," said Emma. "Rion is family to all of us."

"So then he's coming," said Nick.

Rion shook his head. "Nick—"

"Don't be stubborn, Nicholas," his sister said.

"Is Gary going to be there?"

"Of course."

"Will Lia be there?"

"Maybe, but—"

"Then Rion will be there," said Nick stubbornly.

"I'm not," Rion broke in. Nick looked at Rion in frustration. "I'm not going, Nick. I'll come back to the

States with you but not to Rochester. You need to be there for your father."

They stared at each other as Emma spoke again. "I think she wants to discuss future plans for the company and the estate. The pre-will reading. Rion is not a Highton, and you're not married yet. He cannot be there."

"It's fine, Emma," Rion said, squeezing Nick's shoulder again. "Nick will be in Rochester by tomorrow evening. I will head home to the apartment in the city."

"Thank you, Rion. As usual, the voice of reason."

Nick sat back in his seat. Rion asked, "Is Niles really okay?"

"Yes, he is, thank you for asking. He has a bit of recovery to do, but he is walking and talking and has his full faculties. We are very thankful."

"I'm so glad to hear that," said Rion. "I know he's not a spring chicken, so now is a good time to have the conversation of putting his affairs in order."

"He's eighty-one, Rion. So yes, it's the right time."

"And how is Madeline handling it? Even if they didn't have a loving relationship, being with one person for over forty years counts for something."

"Madeline would never show weakness. If this is affecting her personally, I wouldn't know. But the fact that she is calling this meeting tells me she has some worry about his health and longevity."

Rion nodded. "We'll get in touch with Zoey and get a flight out by tomorrow morning."

"Thank you, Rion. And Nicholas?" she called out.

"Yes?"

"Please be on your best behavior. Whatever snarky comments she makes about your life or relationship, just let it roll off. We all saw the kiss and it was lovely. But I know she saw it too, which, I suspect, is why she is pulling us all together now and especially wants you there in person. So come prepared but don't engage."

Nick scowled. "Fine."

"I'll see you tomorrow, my dear brother. And I will see you soon, Rion." Emma hung up the phone.

Nick was still slumped on the chair. "We had birthday dinner plans."

Rion threw his leg over and straddled Nick's body. "We don't have to leave tonight, Nicky, so we can still go to dinner and celebrate your birthday early. We can leave tomorrow and have you there just in time for the family dinner. Also," he kissed his forehead, then lifted up Nick's chin to kiss him, "we knew this was coming at some point. Madeline was not going to let you go so easily, so whatever they have planned, we just have to stay strong and not let them come between us, okay?" He kissed Nick's lips one more time.

Nick nodded. "I won't let them. Especially her," he said seriously. "I promised to protect you in my world, and I meant it."

"And I believe you," said Rion with another gentle kiss. He reached behind him, took Nick's phone, and placed it in Nick's hands. "Call Zoey and make the flight arrangements. And prepare her for battle too."

Rion had gotten used to flying on Nicholas's private plane. When they first began traveling, they would still fly on regular flights. But the first one from Thailand to India was bombarded with their new fans a month after they came out as a couple on all social media platforms. By the second flight to Singapore, it was maddening in the airport alone, as if people were somehow getting their flight information and following them. When they started traveling closer to Europe, Zoey put a stop to it right away, sending Nicholas's private jet that he rarely used to get them from Dubai. And she hired a pilot that Rion had met once and trusted, imploring them to "stop traveling with the people before you get murdered." She also made sure that it was always stocked with Cool Ranch Doritos and Hershey's Kisses.

The marble floors and soft leather seating was throughout, leading to a bedroom with a bed on one side and full bathroom on the other. The closet was stocked with suits for both of them, although Rion still preferred jeans, short-sleeved shirts, and hooded sweaters, so he always packed for himself. The long plane rides gave him the space to write too. He started a travel blog of his adventures, which had a steady stream of followers. It was completely separate from Nick, and he barely mentioned him there.

Rion settled in his seat and began writing on his laptop before the plane took off. His fingers moved quickly, letting the words and story consume him so he wouldn't have to think about the plane going up in the air. He secretly still hated flying, at least the takeoff and landing times. But things were so much easier with Nick by his side. Nick was quiet most of the ride as they sat side by side, both on their laptops, only pausing when lunch was served.

As they were finishing up their meals, Nick suddenly looked up in alarm. "I didn't meditate this morning." Rion also looked up at him. "I slept through my typical morning hour, then Ava was in there, and I figured I would go back at some point before we got on the plane, but I just realized that I never made it back into the room."

"You can meditate now. Chant before you get there."

"No. I'm too amped up, and I won't be able to focus. The closer we get to Rochester, the more I feel like turning the plane around."

Rion closed his laptop. "How can I help you become less anxious?"

"You know you can't, Ree," said Nick moodily. "I just know you're going to be brought up in some way, and it's going to piss me off. But I won't come off as angry and emotional. I refuse to let them see that side of me." He sighed. "I'll be fine."

Rion studied Nick's face for a moment. "It's our anniversary tomorrow."

Nick turned to him with his eyes scrunched in confusion, then smiled. "The day we met on the plane."

"And here we are, three years later on a plane together. This time going the opposite direction, from London to JFK." Rion grinned.

"You know I don't consider this our anniversary," said Nick with a small smile. "And you know why." He raised one eyebrow.

Rion rolled his eyes and looked away. "It was a minor five-month bump in the road for us. We were still in each other's hearts."

Nick turned Rion's head to him and kissed his lips. "Yes, we were."

They kissed again, deeper with need. Then Rion said, "Let's take a shower."

Nick grinned. "We took showers at home." Rion grinned too. "You just want to use those hooks I had installed."

"Well that's one way to calm you down," said Rion standing up. "And we have," he looked at his watch, "two hours and twelve more minutes in the air." He held out his hand and Nicholas took it.

After stripping and preparing himself, Rion stepped under the rain showerhead first. He leaned his head back and ran his hands through the curls on his head, which elongated when wet and stuck to his forehead and neck. Nick stood there admiring the way the water fell onto his lover's lean and toned body, getting caught in the brown hairs everywhere. He looked at Rion's chest, the mound of his pecs, as soap and water trickled down and through his body hair, getting caught in the ridges of his abdominal muscles. Nick's eyes traveled to the curve of his bottom attached to his long legs that put him at 6'1", just three inches shorter than himself. Rion's cock wasn't hard, not yet. It laid against his round testicles, slightly darker than the rest of his body, nestled in the middle of his curly brown forest.

"Are you going to keep staring, or are you going to come in?" Rion said with his eyes closed while rinsing himself off.

Nick smiled and stepped into the shower behind him, closing the door. He pulled their bodies close, his cock resting on Rion's bottom, and wrapped his arms around him. "I love you," he said softly.

Rion cocked his head to the side, exposing his neck. "Show me," he said.

Nick wasted no time, sucking and kissing on Rion's jugular vein, moving one hand down to his penis to wake him up. Rion rose and grew in his hand, and Rion put his hand over Nick's to help stroke himself. Suddenly, Rion turned around, stepped back, and dropped to his knees. Nick entered Rion's mouth slowly, meaningfully, and Rion's cheeks tightened with every thrust. Then Rion held onto Nick's hips to stop him from thrusting and bobbed with intention, hitting the back of his throat a few times before he held himself steady and paused, keeping Nick there. The tightness was overwhelming, and he involuntarily twitched a few times, rushing too close to the edge too soon.

But then Rion pulled back and let him go with a gasp. Nick's cock head was purple and angry, the rest of him hard as steel, standing straight up. Rion stood and smiled. Nick growled at him and pushed their faces together aggressively, making Rion giggle between kisses. Then Rion stepped farther back against the wall. He looked to his left and wrapped his left hand around the metal hook near his head. He looked to the right and did the same. Then he looked at Nick, no longer smiling. Nick walked right into him and grabbed his bottom. Rion lifted his legs and wrapped them around Nick. Nick adjusted himself so that Rion's pucker was aimed at the right place.

"You okay?" Nick asked softly. Rion nodded, staring deep into Nick's eyes. They were full of desire. And trust. "Okay. Hold on." Nick lowered his knees slightly and thrusted upward, completely sinking himself inside of Rion.

"Hoooooly shit," Rion moaned as Nick filled him up. Nick did it again, and again, watching Rion become undone in this position. Rion began to tremble, the pressure on his internal g-spot never ending as Nick lived up to his name, stroking it deeply. His fingers began to slip, so Nick moved closer, putting Rion's back against the wall. Rion carefully let go of one hook, wrapping it on Nick's shoulder, then moved the other in between them, stroking himself. Nick moved faster, bouncing Rion against him. Rion moaned and called out his name over and over again until his cum rutted out.

Nicholas did not stop. Rion held on to him with both hands, and Nick drilled into him. Nick hitched, then growled, pumping shallow pumps until he was completely empty and Rion was full of him. They held each other tightly without speaking, only the sound of the water rushing over their bodies.

"Feeling better?" Rion asked softly.

The couple laid together in their robes, open in the front so their legs were connected. The plane rocked slightly, but neither noticed.

Nick kissed up Rion's pen tattoo on his forearm and continued kissing until he reached Rion's shoulder. "It was a good reminder, that's for sure."

"Reminder of?" Rion asked, his brown eyes never leaving Nick's blue ones.

"Why I'm going to fight so hard. Because I'm going to fight for you, Rion. For us. I didn't go to war with my family for Trixie, but I will burn the entire empire down for you."

Rion sighed. He didn't want that. He just wanted to live his happily ever after with the love of his life. But he knew how Nicholas felt about his parents meddling in his life, especially his love life, and how they had succeeded in the past to ruin his romantic connections. So Rion let it go.

"It was a good twenty months, wasn't it?" Rion said instead. "Seeing all those different countries and cultures. Hiding from the paparazzi."

Nick chuckled. "Yeah. But just living with you in London this last year was my favorite. It felt different than when we were in the apartment in New York. Like we had all the time in the world. Just being together, like the first time we were in London."

"It's the home we bought together," Rion reminded him, running his hands through Nick's dirty blond chest hair. "Every piece of furniture, appliance, artwork, we bought together. So yes, it was different. And we'll be back. Soon."

"I hope so," said Nick. "But you knew we'd have to come back to the States at some point. I'd have to face my mother. And you'd have to face yours."

Rion froze and turned his face away. After finding out that his mother, Roslyn Matthews, lied to him his entire life about who his father was, Rion cut her off completely. But he missed his two other sisters terribly. He was glad to have the chance to have seen Gabby in January with her fiancé, Gael, celebrating his niece's ninth birthday in Disneyland. Nicholas promised Morgan a Disney trip for her birthday, and he delivered, bringing the whole family to Paris. The only one he hadn't seen in a while was his sister, Muriel, but he avoided Muriel for many reasons. His oldest sister, whom he loved dearly, reminded him of his mother's taboo secret, her lies and betrayal.

Nick pulled Rion closer to his body, and Rion melted into his chest. He knew not to say another thing about Rion's mother. Instead, he ran his hands all over the hardness of Rion's body and soft curve of his bottom. Rion began to do the same, kneading his fingers into Nick's back, pushing their bodies against the other. They both had strong erections, but sex wasn't what either wanted. It was the closeness, the sensuality, the connection, concentrating on every touch, every breath, every soft groan, being in the moment with each other.

They touched until they heard the announcement from Pilot Pete: "Gentlemen, the plane will be landing in thirty minutes. Please return to your seats."

Rion lifted up so they were lying face-to-face. "I'll wait up for you. You're coming home tonight, right?"

Nick kissed him. "Nothing is going to keep me from your arms tonight. Nothing."

After a seven-hour flight and making love to Rion, then another hour-long flight, Nicholas was thoroughly exhausted. But he put on a brave face as the car entered the iron gate and brought him up the mile-long driveway to the Highton-Marigold Estate and Compound. He took a deep breath, straightened out his Stefano Ricci silk tie, and walked up the stone steps. A new staff member he did not know opened the front door and greeted him with a smile.

"Good evening, Nicholas Highton. We have been expecting you."

Nick nodded at the man about the same age as him and walked into the building that never felt like home to him. He noticed the floors were a different color quartz than he remembered, but it had been over two years since he was there. He looked up at the steps, also quartz, and considered looking at his old bedroom but decided against it. Another staff member greeted him with a glass of chardonnay as he walked down the foyer to the main room, a large open space where parties were held. He looked up at the oversized chandelier, all glass and diamonds sending sparkling prisms all around. His eyes traveled to his brother, Brian, who was standing on the left side of the room staring at a contemporary style painting. Nick went over to stand next to him, also staring at it.

They stood side by side in comfortable silence, drinking out of their respective glasses. "It's a Liu Xiaodong original," Brian finally said. "How Mother managed to get her hands on it is beyond me."

"It's exquisite," said Nick.

"It's haunting," Brian retorted. "Such harsh strokes of the city behind the man's face. And is it a man? I can't tell. It's leaving me confused and wanting, but I can't take my eyes off it."

Nick smiled. "Now who's the sensitive one?"

Brian finally looked at his younger brother. "You look good, Nicholas. Happy."

He gave a slight nod. "Thank you. I am."

"You're ready for tonight?"

Nick shrugged. "As ready as I'll ever be."

Brian nodded back. "Emma said you wanted to bring Rion."

"I should have, just to throw my happiness in her face. Maybe it will make her melt into a puddle of green goo."

Brian chuckled and downed the rest of his bourbon. "I did not bring Lia." Nick looked at him in surprise. "What?" Brian responded. "Lia doesn't have any part of the Highton wealth. She has her own family wealth and the prenup will make her an absurdly wealthy woman if she ever decides to divorce me, so she doesn't need to be here."

"I bet you Gary is here though," Nick said bitterly, thinking of his sister's husband. "He'll be the first one in line with his hand out."

"He's been by Father's side since his stroke. And, I'm sure, hinting along the way that he is a Highton by extension," Brian confirmed.

"Dick," Nick responded before he too finished his glass of wine.

Brian smiled. "We're the disappointments, you and I. With me not going into the family business, and you going into ... Rion."

Nick grinned. "Shut up."

A woman silently came by with a tray to take the empty glasses and offer more wine. Both the Highton men declined. "I miss you being around," said Brian. "I miss my brother."

"Oh *nooow* you want a brother?" Nick said sarcastically.

Brian laughed out loud, and Nick chuckled. Then he heard his mother's voice from across the room, and it was like ice water had dripped down his spine.

"Nicholas."

They both abruptly stopped laughing. Brian raised an eyebrow at his brother before he turned around. Nick sighed and turned around too. "Mother."

The same attendant immediately went over to her and offered a glass of wine. She took it without glancing at the help. Madeline instead put it to her lips, staring at him. Nick stared back.

"Come closer, my son," she said. "The last time I saw you, you left in tears, like a spoiled child."

Nick glared at his mother, but he did as he instructed, coming toward her. He bent down for her air kiss and a touch on his shoulders, then stepped back. Madeline took another sip and looked at him.

"So. Have you found what you've been looking for? Did you find it in the mountains of Thailand or the slums of India? How was Mumbai for those three weeks you were there? Maybe you found it in that Singapore high-rise you stayed in or the Dubai one? Or the farmlands of Budapest? Maybe it was in Italy at the Mercurio Villa in Tuscany or skiing in the Swiss Alps or that adorable two-bedroom flat on Vetergage Street in Denmark that you ended up buying, right across from the café you went to every morning. Or since you've settled in the East End part of London, six months prior to your week at Disneyland Paris with that nine-year-old Hispanic girl and her family that was celebrating her birthday, maybe that was where you needed to go to find what you were looking for. You and your ... *project*. And his pet that followed the two of you everywhere. You know? The former prostitute? Or maybe she's a current one. It's hard to keep up with your ... *desires* lately. Nevertheless, I'm sure that having them both in that way made your time away ... invaluable."

Anger spread through Nick's veins at his mother's words, her snooping in his life, and her insinuations. Before Nick could respond, Brian stood between them.

"You've made your point, Mother; there is nowhere on earth that Nicholas could go that you wouldn't know about." Brian turned to Nick. "Come. Let's go see Father."

He took his brother's arm to lead Nick away, but Nick turned around and said with a smile, "Yes, Mother. I did. I found what I was looking for in all of

those places with the most amazing man at my side. His name is Rion Matthews. And I'm going to marry that man."

Nick turned away before his mother could respond and followed his brother out of the great room to their father's den.

Dinner was just as much of a nuisance as Nicholas thought it would be. Niles was happy to have his family together again and greeted his youngest son with a hug and kiss on the cheek, things that Nick would classify as a no-no in their family. He continued to ask Nick about his travels and his work with Deep Strokez Publications without once bringing up Rion's name. His siblings noticed but also did not bring him up. That was extremely frustrating to him. But he smiled, nodded, and answered questions about his time away from his family. Unfortunately, when Rion was finally mentioned, it was his asshole brother-in-law who did so to stir the very low simmering pot that was the Hightons.

"So, Nick," Gary called out in his booming voice as dessert was being passed out by the wait staff, "how's Rion, the kick-with-a-dick?" Then Gary laughed out loud before slobbering wine down his expensive shirt.

Brian smirked in his plate. Emma scowled at him. Madeline pretended she did not hear. But Niles looked up expectantly, as if he was waiting for someone else to bring up Nick's partner.

Nick smiled at Gary. "Thank you for asking," he replied politely. "Rion is fine. Great in fact. We had a great time traveling and exploring the world, and now he is home at the apartment in the city."

"So *your* home, then?" Gary said with a smirk. "Because the kid seems to just follow you around and live in all your properties. When is he ever going to stand on his own instead of mooching off your money?"

Nick immediately frowned. "Gary, you went from mooching off your parents' money to mooching off my sister's trust fund. When are *you* going to stand on your own two feet?"

"Nick, you wouldn't even begin to understand what it means to make something a real success with your own hands. All that little magazine is doing is feeding your boyfriend's mother's drug habit."

"Gary!" Emma scolded.

"Gary, dear, please do not bring up contemptible conversations at the dinner table," Madeline said in a bored manner.

But Nicholas was filled with rage at Gary's comment. He shot daggers at him from across the table. "Remind me to punch you in the face before I leave tonight for that one, aye, Gary?"

Gary smiled, feeling like he won the sparring match.

"I think it's a good time for us all to retire to the family den, yes?" Niles said as he stood up slowly. Gary jumped out of his seat and practically ran over to grab his arm. Niles smiled and patted Gary's arm. "I'm fine, son."

"I know you are, Niles. You're as strong as a bull. I'm just here to help you along."

Brian rolled his eyes and looked at his sister. Emma shrugged helplessly and followed their parents out of the dining room. Brian rose and left the room too. Nick was last to leave the dining room.

Niles's personal assistant, Ian McCully, was already waiting in the den. Niles surprisingly chose a seat in front of the big desk in the room instead of behind it and waited until his three children and son-in-law were seated in the various chairs in front of him. Nick chose an armchair near the corner of the room, crossed his legs, and folded his hands in his lap. Madeline chose a high back chair right next to her husband. She watched Nicholas curiously, gave a sly smile, then turned away. Nick did not like that at all.

"As with Highton tradition," Niles began, "the pre-reading of the will is so that there are no surprises in the event of an untimely death. Yes, I am eighty-two this year, but I had no intention of doing this any time soon. It was arrogant and foolish of me not to do this sooner. But it seems like life has a way of making a person step back and look at everything with clear eyes. Even an important man like me. So here we are."

Ian quietly handed Niles the blue folder as he spoke. "All tangible money—checking, savings—and related assets associated with me will go to Mrs. Madeline Marigold-Highton as agreed upon when we first were engaged forty-four years ago. At this time, the total number is around $2.6 billion. As expected, the Highton assets will be divided. Stocks, bonds, and the financial portfolio is divided among my three children equally. Ian has made sure of it. As far as company assets, Emma," he turned to her first, "the one who will carry on the Highton legacy. You have never disappointed me, and I have always been so proud of you." Then he began to read his will.

"To you, my daughter, the company is yours. You will be made President and CEO starting tomorrow.

Any accounts associated with the Highton Optimum Holdings are being transferred to your name as we speak, and I am officially scaling back any involvement in the company. I am there in name only, and you will run it completely moving forward. I have handpicked the board over the last five years to ensure that the vote will be made unanimously. Not that you had anything to worry about; you have already gained the confidence of the executive team, and there are no concerns with your leadership capabilities. However, as tradition would allow, a person with a Highton last name must take the helm. Nothing against Robert; he will have as high a stake in the company as a Dorado, much like the Marigolds, the Benningtons, and the Mercurios. But as we discussed at his birth, being a Dorado, your son simply can't be named CEO. You will continue to take Brian's children, Arlow and Angus, under your wing, and when you decide to retire, you will pass along the torch to them. They are the future of Highton Optimum, the next generation of Highton men. Until such time, with you at the helm and Gary by your side, the company will flourish, I have no doubt."

She nodded respectfully. "Thank you, Father. I will do you proud and honor your wishes always." Gary grinned happily at the Dorados being tied to the Highton legacy.

Niles smiled and turned to Brian. "To my son, who has disappointed me," Brian rolled his eyes playfully, "I thought I would never forgive you for abandoning your duty as the eldest son to carry on the Highton name in business and finance. And yet, every single achievement you have accomplished gives me a tremendous amount of joy and pride. You have made your own way in this world and carved out a new legacy for Hightons in medicine. I couldn't have asked for a more formidable son as my firstborn."

Brian was a little speechless. It was probably the nicest thing his father had ever said to him. "Thank you, Father."

Niles looked down at his papers again. "Now, I would not have done something so foolish as to give you a stake in the company. You have earned the right to not have anything to do with Highton Optimum. Instead, all twelve vintage cars and all personal homes are being transferred into you and Idalia's name as we speak: the two on the island, Highton Margo Largo, Highton-Mercurio Tuscany Villa, Highton Plaza, and Highton-Marigold Estate here in Rochester. As I promised her father all those years ago, Lia will have equal partnership with you in the real estate venture. All the residential properties are yours to pass down to your children when they are ready." He looked at his son, leaned in a little, and said, "I trust you not to kick your mother out before she greets me in the afterlife."

Brian smiled. "I think I can manage that, Father."

Niles turned to Nicholas. "And for my last son, the one who constantly defies my wishes and carves his own turbulent path, and who forces everyone to either fall in line and accept it or get out of his way. My emotional, sensitive, little boy who is never satisfied with anything, as your mother says. The one I did not expect to have..." Nick waited for it, his face stoic. Niles smiled at him. "And so grateful that I did."

Nick finally met his father's eyes, allowing him to continue. "If Brian has fortitude, your determination comes with endurance. And for that, I admire you the most, Nicholas. And I support all of your endeavors. To show you that I do, I've put together a separate portfolio named Highton Media and Publications and named you Founder, President, and CEO. You will carry out the Highton legacy by doing exactly what you've been doing but on a much grander scale."

Nick sat up straighter. "Father, that is..." He was thoughtful. "What's the catch?"

Niles smiled. "Two things. One, you have to move back to the States. I want my son close to me at the end of my life. And a very small caveat: Deep Strokez cannot be your only publication. I want you to bring Deep Strokez Media under it but build other sources of media: print media, textbooks, film, TV shows, create social media outlets, whatever you want. You have full creative reign, and I will not step in. Neither are demands or a request. It is an ask from an old man who wants to see you expand your empire and wants you to come home so I can spend time with you. Can you do that for me?"

Nicholas nodded. "I'll talk to Rion, but yes, it's doable."

Niles nodded back. He continued, "The headquarters is located in the Bay Area, and you can use your current office in New York as a satellite location. You can start tomorrow if you want. There is already a manor purchased on Sea Cliff, also in your name. Tomorrow, I am sending the details for both Highton Media and Highton Estates at Sea Cliff to Ms. Huffnagle to add to your personal portfolio. Both are yours if you want it."

Nick stared at his father with his mouth slightly open. His siblings looked at him, also in shock. His mother was impassive.

"Just to clarify," Brian said, "why San Francisco exactly?"

Emma shot her oldest brother a look. But Niles turned to Nick and said, "Because Rion Matthews has family there, and that should make the move an easier decision for him. As I said, I support all of your endeavors. I look forward to meeting Mr. Matthews one day."

"Oh," said Brian, nodding his head. "Oh, okay." He turned to Nick and gave him a nod of approval.

"So?" His father looked at Nicholas expectantly.

"I do want it. Both the company and the property," Nick confirmed. "And I do want to spend time with you. Thank you, Father."

Niles gave him a grateful smile. "Of course. I just want you to come home so I can get to know you better, Nicholas Highton the man."

Warmth settled in Nick's chest, and he gave his father a genuine smile. "I would really like that."

"Then it's settled." His father rose and said, "Emma, Gary, a word."

They watched their father slowly stand up, and once again, Gary was by his side. Ian was right behind them. The Highton siblings all stood at the same time, and both Nick's brother and sister embraced him.

"Like I said, Rion is family," Emma said gently. She left the room to meet with her father and husband.

"It would be good to see Rion at family events from now on." Brian patted him on the back. "Gotta make some phone calls, first to Lia, then to Kara."

Nick looked around, and it was him and his mother in the room. Nick walked over to her and sat next to her on a nearby couch.

"Thank you, Mother. I know that Father would not have made these decisions without your input. I know we haven't always seen eye to eye, and I am sorry that I hurt your feelings the last time we spoke. I'm just glad we can turn a new page, and I can finally have the relationship with my parents that I've always wanted."

Madeline smiled. "It was absolutely my idea to create Highton Media and Publications. We should have done it a long time ago, brought your work and your talent back into the Highton fold. You will do well leading the company and being a key figure on the Highton executive team." Nick smiled. "But the new estate was not in the plans. And you will not move into that house with that boy and any members of his degenerate family. That will never happen. I will burn it to the ground first."

Nick's smile faded. "What the fuck is your problem, Mother?"

"You are my problem, Nicholas," she said, her fake smile also fading. "You can never just be a Highton. You always find the most depraved way of doing things and must be reigned back in. This is me reigning you back in."

Madeline stood up, towering over her son. "We're moving into the house in Napeague. The sea air and calm living will do well for his condition. And I need to keep closer tabs on you. You will come by at least once a week to sit with him. Everyone else has an actual job to do, Nicholas. Brian simply cannot do it with his schedule. Emma is running the company. I am running his personal affairs. And I'm sick of Gary's stench around my husband. This will be your job. You will move back into your one-bedroom apartment in the city and manage Highton Media and Publications from there and take care of your father, and that is all you will do until he dies, never meeting that vagabond of yours. Highton Estates at Sea Cliff is in escrow and will stay that way indefinitely. I've already made sure of that with a couple of favors with the state senator. Your place is here in New York, and that is the last I will ever hear about the Matthews boy or San Francisco ever again."

"And if I refuse?" he said angrily. "If I decide to just get back on a plane and head to London with Rion, never to return again?"

Madeline grabbed his chin roughly but spoke in a false sweet voice. "Who do you think gave your father the idea of Highton Media and to give you praise for all your hard work and accomplishments? The thought to acknowledge you and want to get to know you, Nicholas Highton the man? You've already made promises to your father tonight. If you back out now, you'll break his heart. You wouldn't want to be responsible for the death of your own father, would you?"

Nick shook his head out of her hand. "You're such a bitch."

Madeline laughed cruelly. "The fact that you thought for a second that I was going to let you settle away in another country, satisfying your carnal appetite and your need for attention, is laughable."

"You literally told me to do that, remember?" he sneered at her. "You said Harry and Meghan did it. I could leave too."

"I also said you could give back the money that you despised so much," Madeline sneered back. "Speaking of money, don't even think about marrying that boy. Prenup or not, if I get so much as a whiff of a secret backwoods wedding in the hidden jungles of Thailand, I don't give a shit what your father wrote in his will, you will get one third of nothing. I will bury your little magazine project and everyone that works for it and will tear that boy and his entire family apart, one by one."

"Fuck you," Nick said, standing up. "There is nothing you could do to harm them or me." He started walking away from her.

"Do you know how easy it is to plant child pornography on someone's computer, Nicholas?" she called out. Nick slowly turned around to her. "All it takes is a virus to spread like wildfire through your company network and land on a couple of your employees' computers, at home and at the office. Eddie, your reporter, or Barry, the accountant, or even that nice Mrs. Anne that sits at the front desk who loves to read erotica. Even yours. What would that do to the reputation if Nicholas 'Deep Strokez' Highton actually likes to deep stroke children?"

"You wouldn't," he said. "You couldn't. My team is—"

"Nguyen is good. But my contacts are darker than his," she said simply. "Do you know how inexpensive it is to pay people to plant drugs pretty much anywhere I want? At your apartment or in one of your cars? At Safeway Supermarket? At the Princess Diner? At the Post Office on Lansdowne Street? Hell, I can have coke planted in little Morgan's backpack or in

Maurese's locker at Teleevo High School. How would social services respond to that?"

Nick's mouth opened again as she mentioned the workplaces of Rion's family members and brought up Rion's niece and nephew. He walked quickly up to her and put his hand on her throat, willing himself not to squeeze.

"You do anything like that, and I will literally kill you with my bare hands, Madeline," he growled.

She looked up at him impassively. "But the damage would already be done. They will lose everything. And you will lose him."

Every time Nicholas thought he could not hate his mother more, she made moves that sank his hatred for her even further. But he knew that her reach was strong, so he had to play her game until he could figure another way out of it. He let her go and stepped back.

"I'm taking the company. I'm moving back to New York. And Rion and Father will never meet. Anything else?"

"And you will never marry," Madeline reminded him. "Because he will never have access to the Highton fortune. He doesn't get to have millions of dollars just because he knows how to suck your cock."

"You didn't seem to have a problem with it when Father was giving millions of dollars away to his mistresses for doing the same thing over the last forty-four years."

Madeline slapped him. Nick was startled, as she had never laid a hand on him. But he didn't have time to react before she reached up and grabbed his chin again, this time digging her nails into his skin until it bled.

"Let me make this very clear for you," Madeline said coldly. "You will not eat, shit, or think without getting permission from me from this moment forward. You will do exactly what I tell you to do and behave accordingly, or I will make you regret the day you were born. Just as I have for the last thirty years."

Nicholas again thought of how easy it would be to wrap his fingers around his mother's throat and end her life, right then and there. But knowing his mother, she had a contingency plan for her untimely death too. So he opted not to chance it. That was the only thing keeping him from killing her that night.

She let him go and walked away, saying, "You are not to leave tonight, Nicholas. You are to stay the night, just like Emma and Brian, and we will have breakfast in the morning as a family. The Highton family. You'll head back to the city with Brian in the morning on the private jet. And you will not breathe a word of this to your siblings or to your father."

Madeline stopped at the door and turned to him one last time. "Oh. And happy birthday, my son." She walked out of the room.

Nick stood there in his family den as angry tears slid down his cheeks. How she knew his first instinct was to get in a car and drive the six hours back into Rion's arms, he didn't know, but she even took that from him. After he was able to compose himself, Nick straightened out his tie and walked out of the den heading to the bedroom he had not stepped foot in since he left for college.

"Hey, Nick," he heard his brother's voice, "Gary and I are stepping out to the club for drinks. Coming with?" Nick turned around to see Gary and Brian coming down the hall together.

Brian took one look at Nick's face and asked, "What happened? What did she do?"

Before Nick could answer, Gary said smugly, "My guess is that mommy dearest let it be known that Mr. Matthews will not, in fact, be a part of the Highton family any time soon." Gary smirked.

An angry tear accidentally slid out again. Nick wiped his face. "Yeah, she did," he said, casually walking toward them.

But before Brian could ask more questions, Nick swung his right fist and hit Gary on the mouth. The hard punch knocked Gary off his feet. He immediately grabbed his bleeding lip.

"Muthefucher," he yelled from the ground.

He tried to get up and lunge for Nick, but Brian was already there, holding Gary back as Nick made his way upstairs to his childhood bedroom.

4

Rion heard the key in the lock and got up from the couch, grabbed the glass of Monnet he had sitting on the island, and walked to the door. He had not heard from Nick except for a text to say he was staying the night and would be home in the morning. When he tried to press about why, he didn't get a response. He didn't know if that was a good thing or a bad one, and it worried him all night. But Nick would not respond to any other texts from him.

As Nick opened the door, he saw Rion standing there holding out the glass. Nick paused and looked at it. He looked at Rion, then at the glass again. Nicholas closed the door and took the glass from him. He swallowed it whole as Rion smiled. Then Nick threw the glass against the nearest wall in anger. It shattered into pieces.

Rion frowned immediately. "That bad, huh?"

Nick pushed Rion against the opposite wall and kissed him hard. "My father offered me a job, a CEO title, status, and to get to know me as his son and as a man. And he wants to get to know you. All I have to do is move back."

"Oh," Rion said, confused. "That doesn't sound—"

Nick kissed him again, pushing his tongue in Rion's mouth. "Then my mother threatened to destroy me, my business, my employees, you, and your entire family if I don't fall in line."

"Ohhh," said Rion in understanding. "Well we can—"

Nick kissed him again and, this time, grabbed his cock. "No more talking."

Nick lifted Rion off his feet and held onto his bottom. Rion yelped and held on, wrapping his arms around Nick's neck. He carried Rion to the couch and gently placed him down. Nick trailed his lips across Rion's neck, lifted his t-shirt, and kissed every inch of his torso. He yanked Rion's shirt off and roughly turned him onto his stomach. Nick kissed all down Rion's back and pulled his house pants down. Holding his cheeks open with both hands, Nick began to lick and kiss Rion in his sensitive area.

Rion moaned. "Oooooh fuck. Lube," Rion said breathlessly. "Under the couch. I expected—"

But he was cut off with a hard slap to his ass cheek. "Jesus, Nicky!" Rion yelled out. He quickly forgave him when Nick's tongue made it to his center, making him moan again.

Nick moved back up to kiss Rion's mouth while he ran his hand under the couch and found the lube. Then he kissed his way back down to Rion's tunnel. After Rion was prepared, Nick took off his clothes and positioned Rion on all fours on his leather couch, facing the Hudson River, and showed no mercy. He thrusted and pounded and jackhammered into Rion, who hollered and clawed on the edge of the couch. Nick came but was still hard; all the anger, frustration, and adrenaline from holding it together still consumed him from the inside out. Rion came, hands free, shortly afterward, but it did not stop Nick from pushing him flat onto the couch.

Rion stopped Nick from re-entering him. He turned all the way around and laid flat on his back. "Come here, babe," Rion said softly, his kind brown eyes full of concern.

Nick connected himself to Rion again and began to move. He slowed down, but his cock was still steel, and he needed to release one more time. He laid on top of his lover. Rion grabbed his hands, laced their fingers together, and called his name softly and sweetly.

"It's okay, Nicky babe. It's gonna be okay, love."

Nick couldn't help it. His eyes sprouted tears, and he let them come. He felt the pressure build up in his midsection again and choked out a sob as he came a second time. Nick buried his face in Rion's neck. Rion gently caressed his back, allowing him to silently cry. They laid that way for a few moments until the sniffles stopped.

"You have twelve hours to feel everything you're feeling," Rion said softly. "Then you tell me everything."

"It's deeper than you and me," Nick said sadly. "She doesn't just want to destroy you and your family; she wants to destroy me. She wants to take away everything I've built and everyone—"

"No more talking," said Rion. "Today, you rest. Tomorrow, we'll bring everyone that needs to know to the table. And we protect you and everyone around you from the cruel Madeline Highton."

Nicholas sighed. "Okay," he said softly.

Rion felt Nicholas's body melt on him. Nick was heavy, but Rion didn't mind. "Sleep, babe. I'll be here when you wake up."

Nicholas closed his eyes and allowed his mind to rest.

Nick finally stopped talking and looked at the four faces in the room: Zoey, Marcel, Nguyen, and Rion. Even their siblings on the videocall were quiet: Brian, Emma, Muriel, Ava, and Gabby.

"So I'm just going to say what everyone here is thinking," Muriel said. "What the fuck is her problem?"

"Madeline Highton is a control freak and a supreme bitch," said Zoey, "who must be stopped once and for all."

Nick nodded in agreement. "So? What do we do?"

"Emma," Brian volunteered her. "How do we stop her, Emma?"

"Why me?" Emma retorted, almost frightened. She was the least known for standing up to her mother.

"Because you are the most powerful Highton right now," Brian reminded her. "Your reach can surpass hers. You can circumvent all she has done without her even knowing. You know you can."

Emma was still in disbelief at all her mother had said to Nicholas and tried to collect her thoughts. "I honestly do not know. I don't even know where to start. The threats against Nick's company? The threats against Rion's family? The house in San Francisco?

Manipulating Father so if Nick backs out of any of it, it will be a slap in the face to him? It's like she's thought of every angle to make Nick's life a living hell."

"That will never happen," Zoey said right away. "I will end her if she tries to destroy what Nick has built with his own hands."

"I won't let that happen either," said Emma. "None of us will. We'll all protect everything that's Nick's from his assets to his home to Rion and all of Rion's family members."

"Okay, Emma, but where do we start?" said Brian again. "Nick can play the long game but only for so long. Zoey's right. It's time to officially put Mother in her place."

"I just want to say," Nguyen chimed in, "that I am honored to be mentioned by name by the great Madeline Highton as someone she feels worthy enough to destroy." He smiled. Marcel reached over and playfully hit him on the head.

"But you're right, Nguyen," said Emma. "She mentioned you for a reason. And that comment about her contacts being darker than yours. What does she know that we don't?"

"Okay," Nguyen started as he folded one leg over the other. "I sorta, kinda deal on the dark web. And I'm sorta, kinda connected with some pretty badass hackers. Because I sorta, kinda used to be one before I got the job with Nick."

Marcel's mouth dropped. "I need to do a better job at vetting employees." Nguyen smiled again.

"How deep?" Rion asked. "Like, can you protect every computer associated with Deep Strokez?"

"I could..." Nguyen was thoughtful. "I have a friend that's working on a reversed virus. So like, if anyone tried to hack into a system, they get the virus instead. It's like Covid for computers. Stay six feet away or you run the risk of getting sick. It's a sure-fire way to protect the system. But it's risky. It hasn't been tested in the field yet. Certainly not at this magnitude."

"Do it," Nick said. "And don't tell me any details. Just do it and protect every single employee, even Mrs. Anne. And give everyone the option of putting it on their personal computers."

"And put it on my computer too," Ava spoke up. "Mine and my sisters."

"That's a great idea," said Rion. "We'll pay your hacker friend whatever he wants."

Nguyen had already taken out his phone and was texting. "Done," he said.

"What about protecting us physically?" Gabby said worriedly. "Drugs in Morgan's backpack? With our family history, I'll lose my only daughter!"

"I won't let that happen," Zoey said seriously. She turned to her boss. "Nick, I'm calling in Nightwatch."

Nick nodded. Rion asked, "What's Nightwatch?"

"A private security group we use from time to time to protect our interests," said Brian. "They blend in and infiltrate neighborhoods and communities to keep an eye out for us. That's most likely how Mother knew everywhere you were in the last two years, Nick."

"So how can you be so sure they will protect my family?" said Rion. "If they are answering to Madeline too..."

"Different branch offices do different things, and they don't speak to each other," said Nick. "They're mostly ex-military men. They live by a code, and honor means more to them than money."

"Okay, so what do we do?" Muriel asked.

"Nothing," said Nick. "Zoey will make the call. You just continue living your lives as usual. You won't even know they are there."

"I'm going to dig into the finances, Nicholas," said Emma. "I want to make sure that the company Father built for you is actually for you, no loopholes. And I'll find out about the house in San Francisco. Muriel, it would be nice for you and I to meet when I head out there."

"Just tell me when and where," Muriel said. "I'll make myself available for you."

"And I'll come out in a few weeks too, Rel," said Rion. "It's been a while since I've seen you, so it will be good to catch up."

"Excellent," Emma said. "Zoey, you'll come with me. We'll tour the two properties together, the one that will house Highton Media and Sea Cliff."

"Of course," said Zoey. "Sea Cliff belongs to Nicholas and Rion—"

"Leave it," Rion said, cutting her off. "We don't want the house. We have a house in London, and if worse comes to worst, we leave the country and never come back."

Nick looked at him and saw the determination in Rion's eyes. "Okay, Ree." He turned back to the screen and said to his sister, "Let's meet one day this week to go over the books together before you leave for California. Parker can help."

"Okay. In the meantime, you have to take the company, Nick," said Emma. "And you also have to be there for Father. I know he doesn't know any of this. And you don't want to trigger any portion of her threats to come to life, so you can't tell him. Do exactly what she wants you to do so we can put protections in place right under her nose. Which also means that, Rion, you won't be meeting Father any time soon. I'm sorry."

Rion nodded. "That's okay. Like Brian said, we're playing the long game here."

"And I'm going to give Madeline a bit of a distraction for the next couple of months so she'll take her eyes off you and focus on me," said Brian. "Kara is pregnant."

"Oh noooo," Zoey said and hung her head.

"Brian, you didn't!" Emma yelled at her older brother.

"Holy shit, Brian. Mother and Father are going to have your head on a stake for this one," Nick said.

"Who's Kara?" Muriel asked from the video.

"My brother's mistress," said Emma.

"Don't call her that," Brian said sternly. "She's my partner and the absolute love of my life. And Father already knows; I told him my plans before we started trying."

"You planned it!?" Nick and Emma both exclaimed.

"Of course we did," said Brian. "Kara deserves to have a family. And I've already put contingencies in place for her and my fourth child."

"Whew, this is going to be juicer than a Lifetime movie," Ava joked.

"And Lia?" Nick asked. "Your *wife*? Or did you forget?"

"Lia knows as well," said Brian. "I could never keep something so huge from her."

"And your wife just accepted that you're having another woman's baby?" Muriel asked.

"It was always the plan," Brian said simply. "Kara and I have been together for ten years. Kara doesn't want my money or my status. She just wants a piece of me. And now her life is complete."

"Well, that's certainly going to distract Mother," Emma said. "She'll turn her sights to destroying Kara instead of Rion. Wonderful."

Brian's smile was a sneer. "I would like to see her try."

"So we all have a role to play," said Nick. "Brian, you'll distract her, get her focus off me. Nguyen, you protect Deep Strokez Publications. Get Barry and Eddie involved since she named them too, and protect the company. Emma, you, me, and Parker will dig a little deeper into the finances and protect my assets. Zoey, pull Muriel in with a codeword and set up Nightwatch for the next twelve months, then we'll reevaluate. Marcel and Rion, you're coming aboard Highton Media, Marcel as head of operations and Rion as my VP."

"I can't be a part of any of it, remember?" Rion said.

"No, she didn't say that. She said we can't get married, you can't meet Father, and we can't move to Sea Cliff Manor. She didn't say that I couldn't hire you. Plus, with all the time I'm going to be spending with my father, someone needs to actually run the company. You and Marcel will do just fine."

Rion shook his head but didn't respond.

"What do me and Gabby do?" Ava asked.

"You live your lives," Zoey said. "And just know that someone will always be there to protect you. Once I set it up, Muriel will give you the codeword if you're ever in doubt."

"Should we tell Mama?" Gabby asked. "Shouldn't she know too?"

"Roslyn will be just fine," Rion responded. He stood up and went to sit next to Nick on the couch, taking his hand. "I just want to thank you, all of you, for standing by us. We know we come from very different worlds and, for all intents and purposes, we shouldn't be a thing. But we are. And Nicky and I are going to be together, no matter what, until the end of time."

"Niion Lites Forever," Emma said softly.

"Niion Lites Forever," everyone responded in chorus.

Nicholas and Rion looked at each other and kissed.

It was a stunned silence, then the uproar began. Nick grinned, watching his employees hug and congratulate each other after he told them about Highton Media and Publications and them all moving into the big leagues with a twenty percent raise in salary across all departments, better equipment, and a larger space since Nick bought the floor below them out. After everyone settled down, he told them the other part:

"I'm still President and CEO, and I'm pulling Rion in as Vice President of Highton Media. So you'll be hearing from him more than you'll hear from me. Marcel is no longer my executive assistant. I'm bumping him up to Deep Strokez Publications Senior Executive of Operations, and he will continue to manage the day-to-day here. But don't worry. I'm still signing the checks."

"Yeah, twenty percent more money in our checks!" Dion screamed.

"Yeeeeeeaaaaahhh!" Edgar screamed behind him, making the uproar and high fives happen all over again.

Marcel rolled his eyes, but Rion looked over at Nick and grinned. Nick grinned back. When it died down, he passed the meeting to Nguyen.

"Everyone is getting a new laptop," the IT Manager said. "We have new malware protections for everyone, and as a courtesy, you can add the same top of the market protections on your personal computer at no cost."

Nguyen began explaining the new software and how the protections would be rolled out. Then Nick discussed the plans for Deep Strokez, essentially keeping the online magazine the same, but that Aspen and Carli were working on a separate online magazine with other content, and Eddie was going to be the Senior Managing Editor in that department. Eddie discussed his vision for the unnamed platform at length, answering questions and gathering ideas. Marcel ended the meeting by discussing next steps in operations as the sandwiches came to the office for lunch.

When everyone else was occupied, Nick tapped Rion, Marcel, Barry, Nguyen, and Eddie to follow him downstairs one floor. "This is our new office space," he said as the doors opened. They stepped out into an open space surrounded by windows. Offices had not been built out yet, but the entire space was carpeted.

"Four corner offices," he said. "One for you, Eddie, and another for Marcel. Rion and I will maintain the space upstairs with the administrative offices: Finance, HR, and IT. Once we move everyone down here, there will be so much space to organize."

"I will never say no to a corner office!" Eddie said excitedly. "Will it have a couch?"

Nick put his arm around his number one reporter, now his Senior Managing Editor. "You can put two couches and no desks. It's whatever you want it to be."

Eddie grinned at him. They heard the elevator ding, and all looked over at it. Nick's nephew Robby was coming toward them, his brown leather satchel half slung on his shoulder. "Hey, Uncle Nick. Sorry I'm late, but I'm here now."

"Robby, good that you came." He brought his nephew over to the others. "So here is my other plan that I haven't told anyone about yet. Robby is going to apprentice with me this summer and every summer until he gets his degree. Because he's a Dorado, not a Highton, he can't be CEO of Highton Optimum Holdings—"

"Pfft," Robby scoffed. "As if I would want that anyway."

Nick smiled. "But he's talented, quick-witted, and creative. And I want to make sure he gets a big slice of the Highton pie, so he's going to be my protégé. And eventually my VP once he graduates college with his bachelor's in communications and will take over as CEO in ten years. I plan to be retired in my forties."

"That's fucking awesome," Rion said, nodding his head in approval. "That's the best idea, and I'm happy to be a part of helping you take over the company."

"Even if it means I'll be your boss as CEO?" Robby said smugly with a wink.

But Rion walked up to him to give him a dap. "I'll follow your lead anywhere," Rion said sincerely. Robby grinned happily.

"Okay, so this is it," Nick said, looking around. "This right here is my executive team for Highton Media and Publications or HMP."

"Also known as Hump," Eddie said with a straight face.

Marcel reached out and playfully popped him on the back of his neck. The rest of them giggled. But then Nick got serious again.

"Essentially, here's what I want to do: I want to collect smaller companies that are already doing the work in media, give them the Highton name, bankroll them with Highton money so they can do what they do on an even greater scale, and make a profit. They don't necessarily have to change their name, but they have to sign a contract with HMP, and we'll be the umbrella company."

"So you're replicating Highton Optimum Holdings but on the entertainment side," said Robby.

"Sort of," said Nick. "But I'm not breaking up any companies. Whoever is the CEO of that company is becoming the Senior Vice President of their company and part of this executive team of HMP. And the executive team has a collective final say on what gets put out into the world of entertainment. I'm looking for ten companies to start. A combination of movie production companies, social media production skits that could work for TV, and at least one record label."

He looked at Rion. "I'm looking to you to take care of Deep Strokez full time. Until we build the executive team fully, you'll have a dual role as VP of HMP and as the Senior Executive Director of Deep Strokez."

He turned to his nephew. "Robby, I want you to handle all acquisitions, the ones you scout yourself and the ones brought to you by others. You'll vet the companies, work closely with Barry on the risk management, and bring it to the executive team if you want to make them the offer. We'll go into detail about what the contract will look like. Eddie will work alongside you. But you'll answer to me.

"Nguyen and Marcel, you know your role in all this: Protect Deep Strokez at all costs." They both nodded.

Nick looked around and said, "I can see it. Six thousand square feet of desks filled with people working all toward one goal."

"To make you more money?" Robby said with a smile.

Nick threw his arm around his nephew. "No. I have enough money. The goal is to put quality, meaningful stories out there to make the world feel something again."

"Well with a name like Hump, you're definitely going to feel it," Nguyen deadpanned.

Barry laughed out loud. Eddie started humping the air, and Marcel smacked him on the back of his head again.

Nick said goodbye to his team, and Rion followed him out of the building. "So, we both know you're not going to retire."

"What do you mean?" Nick asked.

"You're a workaholic," Rion said plainly. "Everyone knows that you're not going to stop working, even if you do pass the baton to Robby."

"I don't know," Nick said with a shrug. "Maybe I want to work really hard for the next ten years, then pass the baton so I can spend the rest of my days making love to you in every city in this world." He held the front door open for him.

Rion smiled and walked through it. "There's only one city I want to get back to—"

But he was cut off by a man approaching him. "Mr. Matthews?"

Rion stopped cold, and Nick stopped behind him. "Yes?" said Rion cautiously.

The man held out a clipboard. "Sign here, please."

"For?" Rion asked with his eyebrow raised.

"Uh, I can sign it," Nick said evasively, stepping around him. He grabbed the clipboard and signed the paper as Rion looked at Nick curiously.

He watched the man hand his boyfriend a key fob and say, "Enjoy." The man walked away.

Nick walked up to the curb and turned around with his arms spread wide and a big grin. "Surprise!"

Rion stared at him. "Explain."

Nick pretended to be exasperated. He stepped two feet to the right and waved both hands in front of the car. "It's a Midnight Blue Toyota Camry!" he said excitedly. "And it's yours."

Rion continued to stare at him. "No." He started walking down the block toward the A train.

"Oh, c'mon!" Nick yelled. He ran up to Rion and jumped in front of him. "It's a lease," he said. "I leased it for a year because that's how long we're going to be here."

"Why would you need to lease a car, Nicholas?" Rion asked him calmly. "You have six cars in the parking garage. An Audi A8 Spyder. A Cadillac Celestiq. A Tesla Model X. An Aston Martin Superleggera. A Maserati GranTurismo. And a Lamborghini Sián Roadster. Why would you need a seventh car to drive while we're here in the city?"

"For you, not me. I figured you'd want something less conspicuous to drive around in," he said with a shrug.

"So you leased it in my name?" Rion asked.

"Well, yeah," said Nick in an obvious way. "I don't need a car, and I'm certainly not putting my name on a Toyota. I'm Nick fucking Highton."

Rion laughed at Nick's attempt to be smug. "Just say you wanted to buy me a car and this is your underhanded way of doing so."

"What do you mean?" Nick said, feigning innocence. He took Rion's arm and turned him around to walk back over to the car. "I leased a Toyota so we'll have a regular car to drive while we're here. That's all."

Rion stood in front of the car. "Have you looked at this thing? There is nothing inconspicuous about it. It looks like a Toyota from the future."

"That's because it is," Nick said with a smile. Rion looked up at him. "It's a model two years into the future."

Rion shook his head. "Holy, holy shit. You can't even buy a regular car. Even your fucking Toyota runs on a flux capacitor."

Nick laughed out loud. He pressed the button on the car to unlock it and said, "Come on. Doc. Let's check out the new DeLorean." He hopped into the passenger side. Rion sighed and went to the driver's side.

Rion put his finger on the starter, and the car came alive. The screen came on with the words, "Hello, Rion" on it. Rion cut his eyes to Nick, who laughed out loud.

"So cool," Nick muttered more to himself.

Rion put his signal on and pulled out of the space. Even he had to admit how smooth the ride was. It was quiet, a hybrid, and energy efficient. "This thing has eleven miles on it," Rion commented.

"Literally from the dock to the showroom to right in front of the office building," said Nick. After a few blocks, Nick said, "Okay, Dad, let's pick up the pace here."

"I'm not gunning it on the streets of Manhattan."

"Then cross the bridge and gun it on the streets of Jersey," Nick said seriously. Rion laughed. "I'm serious, Ree. I know you know how to; I've been in your BlueBird."

Rion smiled, remembering driving Nick around San Francisco in his Jeep Wrangler Rubicon. "I miss my BlueBird."

"Well, her name is BlueBird 2," said Nick. "And she's yours if you want her."

"God dammit, Nicky," Rion exclaimed, hitting the steering wheel. "I told you—"

"*If* you want her," Nick said, talking over Rion's frustration. "It's a lease with the option to buy after one year. If you don't want her, she goes back on the shelf for the next two years."

"Nicky," Rion groaned.

"The entrance to the bridge is right there," Nick said, pointing to the ramp off Amsterdam Ave.

Rion crossed the George Washington Bridge and followed the road down to the New Jersey Turnpike.

Nick put the chair back and fiddled with the screen to connect his Bluetooth playlist. They listened to music and talked about Nick's plans for HMP, laughing at how internally they would call it Hump. Rion found that he liked driving on I-95 in New Jersey. The speed limit was already 65 with most drivers doing 75, and while there were some curves, it was mostly a straight route down to Delaware, which allowed him to drive comfortably at 80, fifteen miles over the speed limit. He also noticed that the closer they got to Philadelphia, the clearer the road. So he started driving twenty miles over the speed limit.

"You know you want to," Nick said, taunting him.

"Shut up," Rion said without looking at him, then pressed his foot on the gas, and the engine roared from 85 to 100 almost immediately.

Nick rolled down the window and screamed, "Woooooo hooooo!!" as Rion sped down the turnpike, weaving around cars that were moving slower than he was.

"This shit is fire," Rion said, impressed with how the Camry handled itself.

"I told you!" Nick yelled excitedly.

Suddenly, there were flashing blue-and-red lights behind him. "Fuck!" Rion yelled.

But Nick laughed loudly. "Oh shit! Do you even have your license on you?"

"Doesn't matter. I'm giving them your name. You're Nick fucking Highton," Rion said smugly, making Nick laugh again. He slowed down and came to the shoulder to stop.

The state trooper practically stomped out of his vehicle and angrily came to their car. Rion pulled his window down and said innocently, "Good evening, officer."

"Do you know how fast you were going!?" the cop yelled at him.

"Erm... What did you clock me at?"

Nick snickered. But the officer was not amused. "102."

Rion nodded. "Yeah, that sounds about right," he said. Nick snickered again.

"You think this is funny!?" the officer scolded. "You could have killed someone on this road."

"I'm very sorry," Rion said sincerely. "I fell into peer pressure. It will never happen again."

"Yeah, it will," Nick said. And Rion accidentally let out a smile.

The officer was beside himself with anger. "Are you two drinking? On drugs?"

"No, sir," they chorused.

Then Rion said, "Wait... Did I take a gummy today?" He turned to Nicholas.

"No, but you did yesterday morning," said Nick.

"Ah." He turned back to the officer. "Not since yesterday morning."

"Get out of the car," the officer growled at them. "Both of you."

They did as they were told and were forced to sit on the side of the road while another police vehicle showed up. Then a third.

"Oooh, we're in so much trouble," Nick said with a grin. Rion opened up his phone and pressed the TikTok app. "What are you doing?" Nick asked curiously.

"Going live," he said. Then he set up the phone and held it up.

"Hey Lite-heads. That's what I call all you followers of Niion Lites. So, here's what happened. Nick bought me a car—"

"I did not buy him a car," Nick said from the background. "It's a lease with the option to buy."

Rion narrowed his eyes and made a face to the camera. "He thinks I'm an idiot. If he hasn't bought me the car yet, he's planning on it. Anyway, after literally years of telling this ridiculously rich boyfriend of mine to *not* buy me shit, especially expensive shit like a car, he leases a car in my name that's, like, not even on the market yet—"

"And it runs on a flux capacitor," Nick yelled out again.

Rion looked at him and grinned. By that time, the hearts were steadily coming onto the screen, and the comments were out of control, mostly of how cute they were when they argued.

Rion turned back to the camera. "So, back to this situation my boyfriend got me in. So he convinces me to drive it. Cool. Then suggests we leave the city so we have more space to drive it on an open road. We end up on the freeway—"

"We call them highways over here!"

"Whatev. Same shit. Anyway, we're on a ... turnpike?" He turned to Nick and asked.

"The New Jersey Turnpike," Nick clarified.

Rion turned back to the camera. "And he dares me to gun it. And at first I refuse, then then I'm like, 'Fuck it. There's like ten cars on the road.' So I hit the gas and I'm doing, like, 110 when..."

He turned the camera around to show four state troopers digging into the car, trying to find the drugs they were convinced Rion and Nick had taken.

"Don't let him fool you," Nick called out again. "There is no other place in the world he'd rather be than sitting on this dusty turnpike right next to me."

"Yeah, right," Rion said and turned back to the camera. "So that's it, y'all. I'm going to jail, and it's all Nicky's fault."

"No one's going to jail," Nick said. "I'm Nick fucking Highton. I'm above the law."

Rion looked back at the camera and rolled his eyes. "See how the One Percent live? They truly believe they are above the law."

"Don't put it on me. You could have said no. You broke the law—not me."

Rion turned to him. "Yes, but I would not have broken the law if it wasn't for you pressuring me." He turned back to the camera. "I follow the rules of the road all the time. And even if I don't, I'm at least being safe. Speaking of which, shout out to all the state troopers out there, saving the world from assholes like me who think it's okay to do a hundred on a public road." Rion saluted them.

"No, you don't follow the rules of the road," Nick said loudly. "Remember that time you gave me a blow job while I was driving on the Southern State Parkway?"

Rion's mouth dropped. He shoved Nick's arm saying, "What the fuck, Nick!? We're live!"

Nicholas laughed heartily. Rion glanced at the comments that were coming in quick, everything from laughing emojis to eggplants. "Jesus, Nicky... I'm logging off now."

"Wait!" Nick said. He came closer into the camera view and kissed Rion's lips. "Now you can log off."

Rion's entire face went red. The eggplants went to hearts. Rion smiled at the camera. "I'm not keeping the car but ... I think I'll keep him." Then he logged off.

He moved closer and put his head on Nick's shoulder, watching the officers continue to search the car. "No other place I'd rather be," Rion said softly.

6

Nick opted to drive himself the three hours out to Napeague in the new Toyota. He left early, around 5 a.m., to beat the traffic and arrived just as his father was sitting down for breakfast.

"Ah, right on time," Niles said joyfully. "Come, sit."

"Good morning, Father." Nick dutifully sat at the other end of the table. Breakfast was placed in front of him. "Where is Mother?"

Niles gave him a curious look. "That simply will not do. Anastacia, please place Nicholas's plate beside mine."

The housekeeper smiled politely as she lifted up his plate and brought it down three chairs to place it next to his father's. Nick stood up and walked over to sit down next to his father as well.

"That's better." Niles smiled at him. "Your mother planned to make herself scarce on the days of your arrival. She said that she wanted to give us some time to bond as men. She's with her cousin Rhoda, just about thirty minutes away, and will be there until the evening."

"Hm," Nick responded.

His mother always had an agenda, so he wasn't sure if it was a good thing or a bad thing. He wouldn't be surprised if she had installed closed-captioned cameras around the house and was watching them right now.

"So," his father started, cutting into his eggs Benedict, "have you informed your staff yet?"

"I have, just last week," Nick replied, also picking up his fork.

"I'm sure they were excited to hear how you are expanding the company."

Nick smiled, remembering their roar. "They certainly are. And they've already started throwing around ideas on how to take Highton Media forward."

"That's wonderful. It's a shame that they all won't be there to see it flourish."

Nick paused eating and gave him a pointed look. "What do you mean?"

"Nicholas, now is the time to purge and bring aboard new people," Niles said, putting his fork down. "More experienced journalists, analysts, and editors. Build out an A&R team to scout talent for you. Start looking at those already successfully in the business and see who they recommend as talented writers, producers, and directors. Acquire smaller media companies as your own, break them apart and build them into your empire. There is much work to be done."

Nick was still frowning. "I have twenty-six loyal employees. I'm not getting rid of any of them. And I'm definitely not buying grassroots media companies, stealing their ideas, firing their employees, and hiring a bunch of Harvard and Yale legacies or unvetted children of other media moguls to fill their place. I will never do business like that, Father."

Niles gave him a disappointed look. "Your heart is too good, Nicholas. You won't get far in this business without having to make the tough decisions."

Nick was getting annoyed, already feeling like these father-son visits were getting off to a bad start. "I can make tough decisions, Father. What I won't do is be cutthroat because it suits me or makes me richer. I am going to build my empire that will be filled with loyal, hardworking, untapped, extremely talented individuals that want to build with me."

"You cannot bring new people with new ideas into your team and not prune some of your current team members. Especially those who are solely focused on sex-related media."

"Because I've asked them to focus on sex-related media," Nick countered. "But now I've asked them to focus on all kinds of content, from documentaries to sitcoms, from music to major films. Even creating a social media outlet to rival Instagram and TikTok. And they have already begun putting together new ideas. I have an amazing, very dedicated, very talented team. Unless someone tells me they want to walk, they are all coming with me, Father."

"But the headquarters will be in California," Niles countered back. "Are you planning on relocating twenty-six people?"

Oh right, Nick thought sadly. *He thinks we're moving to San Francisco.*

Nick chose his words carefully. "For now, we're staying here in New York. At least for the next year. I know you already have space in the Bay Area, but I have acquired space in my current building on Columbus Circle, one floor below, and am going to expand here first. And most likely I won't close the New York office; I will make it a smaller, satellite branch office. The goal is to build from what we have and acquire new talent. Then when the time is right, we'll expand across the coast. And," Nicholas gave his father a loving look, "I plan to be here for you for a while."

Niles smiled at his youngest son. "You're right. And I don't want us to spend our days talking business. But I do want to hear how you got started. All I know is that you stopped speaking to us because of ... well ... you know. You graduated from Harvard, moved to New York City, and suddenly you had this thriving magazine, almost overnight. You must have built up a following at some point."

Nick smiled. He told his father how he, his roommate Lionel Degrassi, and Parker Madison, who was at Harvard as an exchange student in their sophomore year and became his best friend, started their sex gossip pamphlet in college anonymously. How he and Lionel almost got caught a couple of times but maintained it through all their years at Harvard. That led to more stories of how the three of them would get into trouble, mostly because of Parker. Niles commented with his own college stories at Dartmouth and the things Nolan, his younger brother of fourteen months, would get him into. Nick found himself happy to hear about a younger Niles and how they were similar as they ate together.

Niles threw down his cloth napkin and stood up. "Let's take a walk, son."

"Should you be walking long, Father?" Nick asked with concern.

Niles smiled at him. "I promise you, I am fine. I put on pretenses for Madeline so she would take pity on me. But my heart, lungs, and legs are still strong." He patted his bulging stomach. "But I have to walk off some of this meal, or I will get heartburn. Join me?"

"Of course."

They switched to flip flops and walked out the back door together and down the ramp. It was a mid-June day, nice enough for the sun to peek its head through the clouds but still had a chill in the air. The water was too cold to walk along, they quickly discovered, so they walked a few yards above, enjoying the warm sand underneath their toes.

As they walked, Nick asked, "So it wasn't a stroke?"

"No, it was a stroke but a very mild one," Niles confirmed. "But Madeline took it seriously and made me go to the hospital. They told me it was important that I begin to look to the future for my children at my age."

"Is that why you had the will reading, Father?"

"Well, I knew that's what Madeline wanted. In all these years, I had never shown her my will, so what better way than to prompt it to all come out about who gets what? I'm sure she wanted to ensure that she received her payout as promised."

"Wow," was all Nick said in response.

"She told me that you told her that you did not want to be a Highton," Niles said. "That you despised the life we live."

Nick sighed. "That's not exactly what I said. But you have to understand how hard it was for me growing up. I was shipped off to boarding school by age five and watched my friends go home on the weekends, wondering why Mother never gave me permission to come home. I spent more time with Sparta, the housekeeper, than with my own parents. Except when we had a dinner party or a gala or event to go to. Then suddenly I had two parents who dressed me up as a doll and made sure I was seen and photographed. It was depressing and lonely. I didn't care which alma mater I went to, Harvard, which was hers, or Dartmouth, which was yours. I was just happy to get away from that large, lonely house."

"You know, my upbringing was very much like yours," said Niles. "My father was consumed with all things Highton, and I barely saw him. I spent more time with the old man as he was in bed dying of cancer than the first thirty-nine years of my life. But I too grew up in a big and lonely home. My best friends were Contessa, my nanny, and my brother. I lost my virginity to the housekeeper's daughter. There was literally no one else around." Niles began to laugh.

"But I didn't even have that," Nick cut in. "My siblings are much older than me, so I didn't have that relationship. I was utterly alone."

Niles didn't comment, and they continued to walk along the beach in silence. Suddenly, his father stopped walking and bent down to pick up a broken plastic toy bucket. He turned to his son.

"Have you ever made a sandcastle, Nicholas?"

Nick looked at his father in confusion. "I don't think so."

"Well, my favorite thing to do when I was a child was to build sandcastles with Contessa. I haven't done it since I was a boy." His blue eyes lit up.

But Nick's eyes narrowed. "Surely you aren't suggesting..." He gestured around him.

"Well? Why not?" Niles moved away from him, closer to the water. "You have something better to do today?"

Nicholas actually did. He had a meeting with Marcel scheduled at 10 a.m., a meeting with Robby at 12:30 p.m. on the small playwright company in Tennessee that he wanted to meet up with, and was hoping to be on the road by 2:30 p.m. so he could be back home in time for dinner. But he watched his father happily gather water and rush it back over to where he was standing as it leaked from a crack on the bottom. Niles promptly got on his knees and started making a moat. Nick sighed and sat down in the sand with him. After pulling out his phone and changing up his schedule, he quietly began to create mounds and mold them into hills. It became Nick's job to go back and forth to the water so they could solidify the sand.

As their lopsided castle began to take shape, his father said, "You know, I wanted to be an architect. Design, create, and build things. My father, who made me call him Brian after I turned eighteen, said that the world didn't need more people to create; we need more people to manage the people that lead the people that create. The overseers of this world. 'That's what we do, Niles,' he said. 'We sit at the top of the hill and oversee what has been created. We use our power for good and make the world a more successful place to be in. And we're the best ones to do it. If we don't sit there, someone less worthy will.'"

"Wow," said Nicholas. "That sounds very ... narcissistic."

Niles let out a loud laugh. "He was a very narcissistic man. That he was." Niles let a long moment pass by, then said, "I'm glad you're not."

"Not a narcissist?" Nick said with a laugh.

"Yes." Niles chuckled back. "Emma relishes in being a Highton, especially being the first Highton woman CEO, making her the richest and most powerful woman in the industry and forcing other powerful men to bow to her. Brian is a bit of a megalomaniac with his talented hands. He will continue to grab money, fame, status, and power. But you don't thrive in power. You've lived your life just on the outskirts of it, using the Highton name to open doors but not to hide behind. Your work and your talent speak for itself."

"I don't know what that power feels like. Because of Mother, I've felt powerless my whole life. Every decision growing up was made for me: the schools I attended, the clothes I wore, hell, even my calorie intake. It wasn't until I got to college that I got some semblance of power, of what the Highton name could do for me. And even then, there were restrictions on what I could major in and who I could love..." Nick trailed off.

"Well, you've had the power for a while now, and you don't abuse it. Honestly, until that scandal with Kierra, you were pretty quiet, an unnamed Highton."

Nick gave his father a look of confusion. "Really? Mother made it seem like my work with Deep Strokez Publications constantly embarrassed the Highton name."

"Your mother likes hyperbole," Niles said dismissively. "I didn't care. Emma confirmed none of our stocks plummeted because of it. And Brian was proud of you for stepping out on your own. I think the only one it embarrassed was her."

Nick let out a sarcastic chuckle. "That actually makes sense."

After a few hours, they stood up to admire their work. It wasn't the best, but they could make out the towers and a bridge. They even had water flowing underneath it and around the castle.

Niles smiled. "I think it's our best work together to date."

Nick smiled at his father, suddenly noticing how old he was. What little hair he had left on the sides of his head was completely white with age spots throughout his entire head and face. His eyes were crinkly and watery but held a spark at how proud he was of what they accomplished together. And Niles Highton, who was always so tall and larger than life, felt smaller than him, like he had shrunk a few inches, or decades of sitting in executive chairs had deteriorated the strong curve in his spine. Suddenly, spending time with his father wasn't just a chore to keep Madeline off his back. It was what he desperately wanted to do.

Nick put his arm around his father's shoulders and said, "It truly is, Father."

He took a picture of the sandcastle and then another picture of them. He thought of posting it on his IG page, then decided against it. This was just for him.

"So," Niles began, "next week you'll bring Mr. Matthews by, yes?"

"Rion has some family business in San Francisco to attend to, so he won't be here," said Nick. "But soon."

Niles smiled at his son. “Good. I am interested to meet the man that has captured your heart so firmly.”

Nick smiled back.

7

Rion steered the Lyft to drop him off at Muriel's job first so he could pick up BlueBird, his cerulean blue Jeep Wrangler Rubicon. He couldn't wait to drive it while in San Francisco. He flew in with Emma and Seppani on her private plane. But Emma wouldn't be meeting with his sisters until tonight, working on a Highton project and scoping out Sea Cliff Manor, so she went straight to the Fairmont Heritage where they would be staying for the week. It was fine by Rion; he wanted to catch up with his sisters first before introducing them to Nick's sister. Gabby and her fiancé Gael were hosting dinner, an adult one while all the kids were with their grandmother. Rion still had not spoken to his mother since he hung up on her while they were in Thailand two years ago and had no intention of seeing or hearing from her the whole trip.

When he got to the diner, he spotted Muriel, his African-American sister, in the corner sitting with a customer, her back toward the door. But as he came closer, he noticed that they were touching hands.

Muriel felt someone come toward her and looked up, then immediately let go of the man's hands.

"Ree!" she said excitedly, standing up to give her brother a hug.

Rion smiled at her, but across Muriel's shoulder, he frowned at the man. He had dark brown hair and hid his brown eyes behind glasses. The man came across as someone who was trying to be casual in a t-shirt and jeans, but he clearly wasn't. He glanced at Rion, took a sip of his coffee, then glanced away.

"I didn't expect to see you until later on!" Muriel exclaimed. "You were going to go right to the house."

Rion brought his attention back to his sister. "I came by to pick up BlueBird. I was going to drop my stuff off, pick up Morgan and Kate from school, and do some uncle-niece time with them." He glanced at the man, then back at Muriel.

"Oh," she said in a high-pitched tone unlike herself. "This is ... John. John Williams. He's a customer. John, this is Rion, my brother."

Rion stared at her, then smiled. "A customer, huh? You sit and have coffee with all your customers?"

The man grinned at her as Muriel blushed. "A customer and a new, special friend."

Rion nodded, then stretched his hands out. "Nice to meet you, John."

"Likewise," John said as he shook his hand back.

Rion noticed it was a strong handshake and that his hands were a bit calloused. He also took note of his tattoo across his muscled forearm that said, "Death before Dishonor." Whoever this man was, he was not someone to be played with.

"Are you joining us for dinner, John?" Rion asked.

He looked surprised by the question. "Um... No. I—"

But Muriel cut him off. "Actually yes. You should come."

Rion and John both looked at her. "I can't, Rel," said John, trying to send some kind of code with his eyes.

"Yes. You can," she insisted. "You're with me, right?"

He sighed. "Yes. I'm with you."

"Then it's settled," she said firmly. She dug into her pocket before either said another word and handed Rion his car key. "I'll see you in a few hours. My shift today ends at 4."

"Okay," said Rion. "I can swing by and pick you up—"

"That's okay," she said, interrupting him. "I'll get a ride from someone."

Rion stared at her, letting his peripheral vision glance at her friend John who was looking around the room again. "Sure, sis."

He gave her another hug and walked out of the diner. But he looked back and saw her touch his shoulder affectionately, and he touched her hand with the same affection before she went back behind the counter.

After picking up both Morgan and Kate from different schools, he took his nine- and thirteen-year-old nieces on a trip to the mall where they happily spent his money. And he happily bought them whatever they wanted from Claire's and Hot Topic and H&M. And when Kate longingly eyed a highlighter yellow leather

Guess bag from the window, he steered them there and bought them one each, to their surprise.

He knew his sisters would be annoyed at him spending so much money on a purse, but he didn't care. He had been putting a steady three thousand dollars a month in an account for Muriel, and another two thousand a month for Ava and Gabby each. Being with Nick Highton came with fame, which included his books being picked up at record breaking sales, taking him to the top of *The New York Times* Best Seller list more than once. Rion had more money than he knew what to do with, so buying two five hundred dollar bags was nothing to him. He even put an extra two hundred in cash in each of the bags for them, which made them squeal with excitement. That brought a smile to his face.

Rion drove home the long way with the three of them singing Taylor Swift songs at the top of their lungs and made promises to come back to take them to the Taylor Swift Eras concert coming to Santa Clara. But as soon as Kate opened the door, he immediately frowned. Roslyn Matthews was sitting on the couch, seemingly waiting for him. He stopped dead in the entryway.

"Mimi!" Her granddaughters ran up to her. Roslyn hugged them both but didn't take her eyes off her son as they showed her their gifts from their favorite uncle.

"Hey, baby boy," she said softly and stood up. He didn't answer.

Muriel came out of the kitchen. "Hey. You guys were gone a long time." Rion glanced at his mother, then glared at his sister. "What?" she said with an attitude. "You knew Mama was watching the kids tonight."

"In her own apartment," said Rion. "Not here. Not while I'm here."

She shrugged. "Mama stops by whenever she wants."

"You told her I was here?" said Rion angrily.

"It's been almost two years, Ree. You have to face her at some point," she responded.

He shook his head. "No."

"Rion," his mother started.

"No, Roslyn," he said to her. He turned around and began to walk back out of the house.

But Roslyn ran up, catching him on the top of the steps, and hugged him from the back. "Please, baby boy. Just give me a chance to explain everything."

"No, Roslyn," he said, standing completely still, waiting for her to let him go.

"There is so much I want to tell you," Roslyn began.

"You had twenty-eight years to tell me who my father was. Now that I know who he is, I don't need anything from you anymore."

"But if you would just—"

"No, Roslyn!" he said more forcefully and pulled out of her grasp. He turned around and said to Muriel, "I'm going to Gabby's. If she's not gone by the time I come back, I'm getting a hotel and not telling any of you where I am."

"Rion!" his sister scolded. "You're being unreasonable. Sit down and talk to Mama. Please."

"No." Rion turned around and walked down the steps to his car, leaving Roslyn standing there.

Albeit early, Gabrielle was happy to see Rion before dinner and spend some time with him. She opened the door and smiled at her sour-faced brother.

"Muriel blindsided me," he said with a frown.

"I know. She called me," she said, stepping back and letting him in. "I'm making paella with Gael's grandmother's recipe tonight." She steered him right to the kitchen, and they sat at the island together, watching the rice cook. "She's so nice. We talked on the phone for a while. She's forcing me to brush up on my rudimentary Spanish."

Rion laughed. Although her father was Puerto Rican and she spoke Spanish to him as a child, after he died when she was eight, Gabrielle had stopped speaking it, saying it made her feel sad. But Rion encouraged her to take a Spanish class when she was in college, and it made her feel connected to her culture again. Meeting Gael five years ago at work, an older man who came to the mainland from San Juan when he was in his twenties, was more motivation to speak Spanish. They began dating three years ago, and Gael proposed to her in January when they were all together for Morgan's ninth birthday at Disneyland Paris.

"Well, you were always a great cook, so I know it's going to be great."

"Thank you." She smiled at him. "You can't avoid her forever, you know."

Rion groaned. "I don't want to talk about Roslyn."

"That's fine," she said with a shrug. "Because I'm not the one you need to talk to. She won't even tell us anything, you know. Muriel flat out asked her how she ended up sleeping with Maurese's brother, but all she said was, 'I need to tell Rion everything first.' So, you know, when you're ready." She mixed around the rice and said, "I'm a little worried about her though. She started smoking cigarettes again. That doesn't mean anything. I still believe she kicked the habit for good. But you know ... cigarettes are an addiction too."

Rion sighed, really not wanting to talk about his mother. "Anyway, you're ready to be Mrs. Navarro?"

Gabby sighed too. "I don't know if I want to change my last name. I'm a Hernandez. I'm basically Gabe's junior, the only one that has his name, his only daughter. How could I give that up?"

"You could hyphenate. Gabrielle Hernandez-Navarro doesn't sound bad at all."

"Yeah..." She looked away toward the window. "He said he wants to adopt Morgan right away. Make her a Navarro too."

"That's a good thing, right?"

"It is but..." She sighed again. "Is it weird that I'm afraid of how I feel about him? That I might love him too much, you know? Steven nearly broke me when he left me pregnant with Morgan. That pain was unbearable, and I vowed never to love that hard again."

"Okay but that was literally a decade ago, Gabby," Rion reminded her. "And Gael is not Steven. He's much older, which, let's be real, you need a daddy in your life." Rion grinned and Gabby hit him with the wooden spoon in her hand.

Rion laughed but then got sincere. "Gael has been serious about you for so long. He's been patient and kind and giving. He loves you and your daughter so much. I know it feels too good to be true that you can actually be this happy with someone. Trust me,

I know," he said, thinking of his own partner. "Don't fight it; don't hide from it; don't push it away. Just enjoy it. Ride this ride into the sunset."

Gabby snorted. "You really are a writer."

Rion laughed. "*New York Times* Best Selling author, thank you," he corrected her playfully. Gabby hit him with the wooden spoon again.

8

Rion looked around the table and smiled. The big pot in the center of the table was filled with yellow rice mixed with shrimp, mussels, clams, chicken, and all kinds of vegetables. He could smell the garlic, onions, and spices coming through the steam. Emma was thoroughly enjoying herself, getting to know his family more intimately. He glanced at Gabby and Gael, who moved around each other in sync, adding other smaller dishes to the table, such as empanadas, salad, and fish balls. Gael could have been mistaken for a younger man if it wasn't for the salt-and-pepper in his beard, but his dark brown hair shone in Gabby's kitchen light.

Rion turned over to Muriel and John, who arrived not too long ago. Muriel was in a flowery wrap dress that hugged all her curves, and once again, Rion thought how Muriel could have been a model with her perfect tawny skin, 5'11" height, and long curly hair that hung inches past her shoulders. She also noticed that John's eyes never left her for a second. He held her hand, pulled out her chair, and made sure she was served before he was. Their relationship, unlike Gabby and Gael's, made him uneasy, like there was something amiss, but he kept his thoughts to himself. Instead, he took the first bite of the paella and all the flavors burst in his mouth at the same time. He listened to the conversation flowing around him as he filled his belly with the savory dish.

Toward the end of dinner, the engaged couple dropped a bomb on them. "So, we want to get married in Puerto Rico so his grandmother can attend," said Gabby.

"And we would like to do it soon," Gael said. "I plan a trip to Puerto Rico every August, and it would be a good time to do it. We just need to find a location."

"So you're getting married in two months?" Muriel said in astonishment. "Are you pregnant or something?"

Gabby laughed. "No, I am not pregnant. But I would like to be soon after." She looked at her fiancé lovingly. "Gael is forty and has no children. I would love to give him one or two, and I'm still young enough to do it. So we want to get started very soon."

But Gael shook his head. "We will not have children out of wedlock. I have a solid belief in raising strong Catholic children, starting with how they came into this world, in a healthy Catholic marriage."

Rion grinned at him. "I'm all for this. Let me tell Nick and he can look into some supreme locations."

"No," Gael said, shaking his head again. "I will pay for everything."

"Well, it is tradition that the bride's family pays for the wedding," Emma chimed in. "Rion wanting to pay for his sister's wedding seems appropriate. And you appear to be a very traditional man, Gael."

Gael looked thoughtful, taking in Emma's words.

"Let me do this for my sister," Rion said. "I promised to take her to Puerto Rico one day, and you're taking that from me. So let me do this for her, please."

Gael nodded slowly. "You are an honorable man, Rion. I will agree to the venue. But please know it will be my job to take care of her from the day you give her away to me."

Rion reached across the table and shook Gael's hand. "I know you will."

"So you're getting married in two months, becoming a Hispanic Catholic, and having a baby, all before the end of this year?" Muriel asked her sister with a smile of her own.

"*Sí*," Gabby said and grinned back.

Muriel laughed. "I think the only thing that's surprising me is the Catholic part. You never seemed to care about religion. You and Rion and Ava all scoffed at it while I was going to church every week. Now I feel like all three of y'all found a spiritual path, and I'm still treading since I stopped going."

Indeed, two years ago, Rion would have scoffed at anyone having a strong belief in any religion. But after diving a little deeper into Buddhism during their trip to Thailand two years ago, he understood how a belief in something could be strong and meaningful. It had certainly transformed his sister, Avalon, who struggled with substance abuse her whole life. Since their time in Thailand, Ava chanted in the morning and did silent mediation in the evening and found balance in her life. Nicholas was chanting at least twice a week in the middle of the night or early morning and then again midday. He told them he did his best thinking in there. And Rion, who did not consider himself a Buddhist, sporadically used a guided meditation of Buddhist principles when he felt he needed to slow down his brain if becoming overwhelmed. Suddenly, Rion realized neither he nor Nick had mediated at all since they returned from London a few weeks back. In fact, they haven't spent a lot of time together at all. It was all work with the two of them, especially Nicholas. He was going to change that upon his return.

"We go to church," said Emma. "Mostly out of habit. The Hightons are all Presbyterians. I honestly don't know what my children believe, but if you ask them, we are connected with the religion."

A thought came into Rion's head. John had been too quiet during this entire dinner, looking at his phone and seeming distracted if it had nothing to do with Muriel. So he decided to engage him.

"Hey, John, do you have a religion?" Rion asked.

"No," John said, shaking his head. "No religion. I don't believe in God."

Muriel gave him a sharp look. "Yes, you do."

John looked back at her. "No. I don't."

"Yes, you do."

"I'm an atheist."

Muriel scoffed. "Well, we're going to have to change that."

John chuckled. "Are you going to convince me otherwise?"

"I'm saying ... with all the things you have been through, you're telling me you never said, 'Oh God,' or 'God, help me,' and meant it?"

“I’m saying that I don’t believe in any god. And most people use their god to satisfy their own self interests.”

“So because people have perverted something, that means it doesn’t exist at all?”

“It means that people have made something up to suit their personal goals and fears in life. And I don’t need to do that.”

“You didn’t answer my question,” she challenged him.

John smiled at Muriel. “You seem very upset at my being an atheist.”

“I may not go to church anymore or consider myself part of any religious group, but I believe there is a God, and I do pray. And I have seen miracles happen, like my brother being cured of seizures—”

“That was modern medicine,” he interrupted.

“And my mother finally getting off drugs—”

“That was her own determination and will power.”

“And the countless times I was almost raped or killed growing up. And some stranger or my own father happened to come along and saved me.”

There was silence at the table. Then John said, “That ... was coincidence.”

“And meeting you on a dating app six months ago?” she asked. “Then you showed up in my life again two weeks ago?”

John stared at her. “That was fate.”

Rion rolled his eyes at his sister’s new boyfriend as Emma was grinning at their exchange. “I don’t think you’re going to agree on this,” she said.

But the couple was still staring at each other. Eventually, Muriel said, “He’ll change his mind.” John’s mouth curved into a smile.

"So, no Mr. Matthews again this week?" his father asked.

"No, he's still in San Francisco with his family," Nick said back simply.

"When did you know you were attracted to men?" Niles asked Nick out of the blue.

Nick turned to his father on the yacht in complete surprise at the question. They were somewhere in the Atlantic Ocean, the warm sea air providing comfort, getting served hard lemonades by the attendees. It was another Wednesday with no actual work done. Nick had decided that, moving forward, he would not have any important work-related tasks when he was with his father, who was thoroughly enjoying his retirement and pulling him deeper into a life of wealth and security and the need to allow others to work for him. But it also meant that his longer days were even longer, catching up on work missed so he could spend time with his father. And less time with Rion.

"I don't know," Nick said. "I think I've always known. You sent me to an all-boys boarding school since I was five. I liked what I saw."

"So when did you know you were attracted to women?"

"I..." Nick was thoughtful. "I don't think it's that simple for me. I liked ... people. It didn't matter what sex or gender they were. My first real sexual experience was with a girl. I was sixteen, and Arcadia Academy was doing an event with Woodcreek School for Girls, the carnival we throw every year. I was on the committee with another girl; Meadow was her name. I liked her. She was cool and smart, and she was a virgin too. The night of the carnival, we didn't even go. We ended up in the woods together; I made it special for her, blankets and chocolate and all that. But before that, I was already kissing boys. At least three by the time I was sixteen. And did some other sexual stuff with a boy named Faraday. He was the first person I ever touched in a sexual way. I don't even remember his first name, just that we all called him Faraday."

"And in college?"

"Mostly women. One or two men." Then Nick was thoughtful. "Maybe three or four men." He chuckled and Niles chuckled too.

"But you are the man in the relationship of men, aren't you?" Niles asked without looking at him.

Nick giggled. "Are you asking me if I'm a *Top*, Father?"

Niles went completely red, making Nick giggle again. He couldn't believe he was having this conversation with his own father. But Nick answered him, "Yes, I was the one giving in those relationships. But with Rion, it's different. He's the first man I opened myself up to switch roles. And I have no regrets about that."

"What made you decide to do that?" his father asked curiously.

"I wanted there to be equity in our relationship," said Nick. "I was firmly a Top, and I knew he was a Switch, but he catered to my role before his and never complained. But Rion moved across the country, leaving his family and his life behind to be with me. If he could do all that for me, the least I could do is give all of myself back to him so he would never feel as if something was lacking in his life."

"Fascinating," said Niles. "And is your relationship equitable now? You haven't felt a loss of masculine identity..." He trailed off with the irritated look his son gave him. "I feel I am treading on the offensive. I apologize for that," he said humbly.

"There is nothing unmasculine about sex between men," Nick said plainly. "It is all strength and power in any position."

Niles nodded, respectfully. "I appreciate your candor about the subject. It wasn't something I thought of until you confessed your sexuality on the national stage. It made me curious about your teenage years and if you were sleeping with men in college."

"I was," Nick confirmed. "But then I got with Trixie sophomore year and that was that."

Niles looked away and took a sip of his drink. "You really loved her," he stated.

Nick kept his anger in check. "I did. And you and Mother ruined her."

Niles did not respond, but Nick didn't expect him to. Eventually he said, "Well, it all worked out in the end, didn't it? With Mr. Matthews being the one that you've given yourself to."

Nick wanted to yell at his father but decided against it. Because the truth was it did all work out in the end for him. He wouldn't change a thing about being with Rion.

But he asked, "Are you disappointed that I'm not straight?"

Niles looked at him sharply. "No. Not at all. Don't you think it for a second." He waited until Nick nodded in agreement. "It's just that the Highton legacy is important. Having children to pass down your legacy is important. Especially a son. That is why I liked Penelope for you. She understood what was important."

"Both Brian and Emma have sons," Nick reminded him. "You don't need me to have a son, Father. You have four grandsons."

"Yes, but we're not talking about my needs. Do you plan on marrying Mr. Matthews? Having children with him? Because if you do, I'm not against adoption. But there should be one surrogacy with a child from your bloodline. That's the Highton way."

Nick hesitated. He knew Rion was his forever, and although he told his mother he was going to marry Rion just to piss her off, he wasn't sure if that was what Rion wanted.

"We haven't talked about it," Nick answered honestly. "For the record, I've never been sold on having children of my own, even when I was with Penny. It wasn't something that I needed in my life and still don't. Between Rion and I, we have a lot of nieces and nephews, which would be fulfilling enough. And having children the Highton way sounds like way too much work, all for something that I'm not sure I want in the first place."

Niles shook his head. "You really are the stubborn one." He turned to his son. "Madeline's main concern about you is that you blatantly reject our way of doing things. And we aren't sure why. Yes, you explained how growing up has affected you so. But you are an adult, and you have a responsibility to the Highton name. Yes, it's a lot of pressure, son. I've had those same pressures that you're feeling now. But you simply cannot turn your back on tradition because it suits you. You must have an heir, Nicholas. I don't care how you do it. But you must have an heir."

Nick sighed in frustration. "Here's the truth, Father. I had this conversation with Trixie. And she understood what was important too. Trixie was ready and willing to do whatever needed to be done to be accepted as a Highton. She wanted children, lots of them, and it aligned with the need for me to have a Highton male heir, so we planned on having at least three children. She talked with Lia about what it means to be a Highton wife, how to conduct herself in high society, and Lia was willing to take her under her wing, knowing how much pressure she would be under by Mother. Trixie knew I needed to go into the family business, and we talked about how that would impact her and our marriage, the long hours and lots of traveling overseas. We even talked about the possibility of affairs, and she implored me to be responsible and not have children out of wedlock. And I promised her if there were any affairs, it would most likely be with men, and I would be safe and discreet.

"Trixie would have been the perfect Highton wife, and we would have made an exemplary Highton family. But again, you and Mother ruined that for me, and yourselves, when you ruined her life. So no. There will be no Highton traditions coming from your youngest son. You have two other children for that. I will do things my way. And neither you nor Mother will get in my way ever again."

The two men sat in silence for a long while.

Rion stared at him. John stared right back.

He sipped his Pepsi as he sat across from John Williams, Muriel's new boyfriend, taking all of him in. He was in a green polo shirt and jeans, his muscled arms showing as he also sipped his coffee in the middle of the day. He could see John had more tattoos: the eye of Horus in a triangle on his neck and zig zag lines with a line going through it on both of his hands.

John spoke first. "Okay. You won the staring contest. Something you want to say to me?"

Rion sat back in the seat. "Nope."

John smiled. "You don't like me."

"Nope," Rion said again.

"That's okay. You'll come around," he said smugly.

Rion scoffed. "You're an arrogant motherfucker."

"You don't even know me."

"And that's why I don't like you."

John sat back too. "So get to know me. Ask me anything."

Rion rolled his eyes. "You have a job?"

He nodded slowly. "I'm a programmer."

"So why aren't you at work right now?"

John smiled. "I'm having lunch."

"There aren't any diners closer to your job?"

That made John laugh out loud. "You know why I eat here."

"When did you meet Muriel?" Rion asked. "Six months ago on a dating app, she said."

John cleared his throat and looked over at her serving a customer on the other side of the diner. "We met on Tinder." Then he looked Rion in the eyes.

Rion scoffed again. "Dating app, my ass. So you fucked my sister, then ghosted her?"

"Actually, she ghosted me," John said. Rion smiled at that. "Then I walked into this diner a few weeks back, and there she was. I decided I wanted to get to know her better."

"Why? You got what you wanted from her already."

He shrugged. "Why did you go back to Nicholas Highton after you got what you wanted from him?"

"Fuck you," Rion said nastily, remembering telling the world on Instagram a few years back how he and Nick met.

But John raised his hand in defense. "I didn't mean it as a bad thing. I'm just comparing. You wanted more. So did I."

"So you're falling in love with my sister?" Rion asked.

John hesitated. He glanced at her and said, "Yes."

Rion was about to ask another question when John's phone rang. He looked at it and said, "Excuse me. It's work." He got up and answered it in a low voice while walking away from the table and outside the restaurant.

"Yeah, go back to work," Rion called after him.

He sat there for a few minutes, scrolling through his social media pages, when Muriel plopped down next to her brother. "You chased him away, didn't you?"

"He said he had to work," Rion said casually.

"He's a good guy, baby bro," she started. "I think you'd really—"

"Yeah, no," he said, cutting her off without looking up.

That made Muriel giggle. Her phone rang and it was Kate. She pressed the videocall icon and said, "Hey, honey, are you home already?"

"Mommy!" she shrieked. "Reese is getting arrested!"

"What!?" she yelled.

"What!?" Rion yelled right after her.

"They said he had drugs on him, and the school police called the real police, and they won't let me in the main office to see him!"

Rion and Muriel looked at each other with wide eyes, then both stood up. "Meet me right outside the school. I'm coming."

Muriel yelled to the cook that she had a family emergency as she ran out of the door. "I'll drive," Rion said.

"Okay," Muriel said shakily.

They rushed out of the diner together as John started coming back in. "I was just coming to tell you—"

"I'm going to Teleevo. They said Reese had drugs."

They held each other's arms. "Okay. I have to go to work," he said. "I'll meet up with you later." She nodded.

He kissed her lips and walked away to his black SUV. Muriel went in the opposite direction to the jeep.

Rion was flabbergasted. He started the car and began to drive toward the high school as Muriel's right leg shook in fear.

"What kind of boyfriend is he? You're in the middle of a crisis, and he just goes to work? Fuck that dude. I knew he wasn't shit. This is why—"

"Rion, can you shut the fuck up and just drive!!?" she screamed at him.

"Okay. Sorry." He drove the rest of the way in silence.

When they got to the school, Kate was waiting out front. They both noticed the San Francisco police car sitting out front. They ran inside and were stopped by the school guard.

"Excuse me, ma'am. Who are you here for?"

"Get the fuck out of my way!" she screamed at him and ran to the main office. He chased after her and grabbed her arm, but Rion grabbed his arm right back.

"What is going on out here?" Mrs. Hill, the vice principal, said, coming out of the office.

"Where is Maurese Hollingsworth? My son!" Muriel yelled as she struggled against the cop.

"Officer Gibbons, let her go," she said. The school cop did. "Come with me."

Mrs. Hill walked them into the office with Rion and Kate behind her, past the school secretaries to the offices in the back. There was the school principal, two police officers, another school police officer, and Reese's homeroom teacher. Reese was already in handcuffs.

Muriel lost it. "Take those fucking handcuffs off my son." She started walking toward him.

But a cop jumped in her path. "I'm sorry, Ms. Hollingsworth. We have to take him in. He admitted to the crime."

"What crime?" Rion asked, pulling Muriel back. "What drugs?"

"Another student reported that Maurese was brandishing a vape pen with THC in it. When his locker was searched, he was found with a bag of delta-9 gummies."

Rion turned to his nephew, who did not look at him. He knew the gummies were his. Reese must have gone into his bag and took them when he wasn't looking. But he was slightly lifted to know that it was his nephew being stupid, not that Madeline had cashed in on her threat to plant drugs on him.

"So what?" Muriel was saying. "THC is legal in California."

"But not on school grounds," the vice principal said. "And not under the age of eighteen. We have a zero tolerance policy at this school."

"Yeah, for the white kids at this school," Reese murmured.

"That's not true," said the principal.

"Yes, it is," he argued back. "Because I already told you it wasn't my pen. I was holding it for someone else."

"But you won't tell us who you were holding it for," the teacher said. "You have an opportunity to save yourself here."

"Well, I ain't no snitch," he said smugly. "Unlike Fenton's bitch ass."

"Hey!" Muriel ran up and grabbed his face. "This isn't a game, Maurese! They are about to take you in for having drugs on school property."

"With intent to sell," the officer said.

"What!?" Rion and Muriel both yelled.

"Fenton Radnor reported to me that Maurese intended to sell the gummies on school grounds," the vice principal told them.

"Which I already told was a fucking lie!" Maurese bellowed.

"Then what's the truth, Maurese?" Ms. Hill asked.

"I already told you, there was no money involved. Someone gave me the vape pen. So I was giving the gummies to that person. That's it. Nobody was using on school grounds. And I definitely wasn't selling it."

"You were found with three hundred dollars on you," the other officer said. "If you weren't selling, where did you get the money?"

"From me," Rion spoke up. "I gave him some pocket money so he wouldn't have to ask his mother for money for a little while."

Muriel looked at her brother in astonishment. "Stop giving my kids money, Rion!" she yelled at him in front of everyone.

"I'm sorry," Rion said back. "I had already given Kate and Morgan money, so I felt like Reese should get something from me too."

"Ugh, Rion—"

"It doesn't matter. We can't confirm that," said the officer. "So we have to take him in."

"What do you mean, you can't confirm?" Rion said angrily. "I just told you I gave him money. And the gummies are mine." Rion took out his wallet and held out his medical card. "I've been using CBD for ten years to treat my ADHD and anxiety. He must have picked them up thinking it was gummy bears or something."

“Nice try,” said the officer. “But he already admitted to knowingly having THC gummies in his locker.” He took Reese by the arm. “We have to take him in.”

The officers walked Reese out, and Muriel, Rion, and Kate followed them, his sister in tears. “It’s going to be just fine, Reese,” his mother called out. “Because I’m going with you.”

The other officer turned around. “It’s not an ambulance, ma’am. You’re going to have to meet him at the 35th precinct.”

They walked with him all the way to the car, with his mother assuring him that it was going to be just fine. Several students were outside watching them put him in the police car. As the car drove off, Muriel let out an “Arrgh!!” and picked up her phone.

“Who are you calling?” Rion asked.

But she walked away from him and talked for a few minutes. Then she hung up and walked back over to him. She took a deep breath and exhaled.

“It’s going to be okay. John’s going to handle it.” She pulled her daughter into a hug, who clung to her tightly.

“John?” Rion was confused. “I thought John went to work. How is he going to help?”

“He’s going to meet us at the police station,” she said. “He knows people there. Let’s go.”

Rion was thoroughly confused. But he went back to the Jeep and started the car. Kate couldn’t stop crying, so Muriel told Rion to stop at the supermarket so that Kate could stay with their mother. Roslyn met them outside, but Rion refused to look at her. So she focused on her emotionally sensitive granddaughter.

Rion then drove to the police station. John was already there when they went through the double doors. "Hey," he said first. "I'm waiting to head back. Just wait for me here, okay?"

"Okay," she said nervously.

The door to the side buzzed and it opened. An officer stepped out and looked for John, then he motioned with his finger for John to come in. He kissed Muriel, then left them. Muriel sat on the nearest bench and began to shake her leg again. Rion sat down next to her. And they waited.

Nicholas offered to bring Niles to his office, realizing Niles had never been when he said to his son the week before, "I want to see your life, Nicholas." After giving Marcel a heads-up to get his employees in line—and banning table football—his father met him in Manhattan at his apartment that early morning, and they rode down to Columbus Circle together with the Highton driver.

As soon as he stepped out of the vehicle, he was spotted by a group of three women and two men who approached him wanting an autograph and asking about Rion. He smiled and signed the papers that they held, mostly from a fried chicken spot that was handing out flyers, but one woman simply held out the bottom her shirt for an autograph. He took pictures with them; his father graciously became their photographer. A few others approached, like two men from Kansas City who were happily holding hands in the street. Nick talked with them briefly and took a few more pics, then Nick went Live on IG with a younger group of women before he politely introduced his father and said they had to get going. He gently but quickly ushered them into the building.

"Wow," Niles said, impressed. "Does that happen a lot?"

"Depends. Some days, no one even notices me, especially if I'm not dressed up in a suit like I am today. Other days, it's a swarm. Usually if I'm with Rion, they notice quicker, which is why he and I try not to walk down the street together in any city."

"Wow," Niles said again. "I might need to correct my statement a few weeks back. You do relish the limelight. And you're very good at it. Being a celebrity."

Nick smiled at his father as they rode the elevator to the thirty-fourth floor. "Rion keeps me grounded," he responded.

The doors opened to the glass wall with the words "Deep Strokez Media and Publications" across it in white block letters. Nicholas walked ahead and opened the door for him. Mrs. Anne's petite frame stood up to greet him.

"Good day, Mr. Highton. Mr. Highton," she said respectfully. "Can I get you and your guest anything? Coffee, perhaps?"

Mrs. Anne had called him Nick or Boss since the day he interviewed her eight years ago, so to hear her call him Mr. Highton was odd. Nick also noticed she was in a dark green business suit, skirt, and jacket to match, and it made him smile.

"Good morning, Mrs. Anne," he said politely. "Two coffees: black, one cream, two sugars."

"Right this way." She scurried over to the half wall and held it open for them to walk through, then went over to the kitchen.

Nick looked out into the room and wanted to laugh but didn't. There were about fourteen people in the office. It was quiet, and everyone was hard at work, or at least pretending to be. He spotted Eddie and Dion concentrating on their laptops, while Edgar was typing away on his. He could tell Edgar wasn't typing anything but gibberish. Aspen and Barry were leaning over a monitor together talking softly, and there was no reason why the financial manager and a digital artist would ever need to be leaned over a computer together. The only person that was actually working was Nguyen, Nick was sure of it. He had a laptop and two desktops connected to a docking station and was working through an internal code.

"I thought you had a flat organizational structure," Niles asked curiously, looking around.

"I do," Nick confirmed. "Hello, everyone," he said loudly.

They all chorused, "Good morning, Mr. Highton."

Nick couldn't help it; he let out a loud chuckle. But no one moved from their pseudo positions.

Suddenly, the double doors to the only office in the room dramatically opened, startling Nick. He had forgotten it was a double door since his office was always open. Marcel came toward them in a white Prince-looking blouse and a black—*Marcel owns something in black?* Nick thought. He had only seen Marcel in fashion forward colors—half pants/half skirt bottom. He greeted them with his hand clasped and a slight bow, adjusting his cheetah print glasses on his face so they didn't slide off.

"Good morning, Mr. Highton. Your office is ready for you. There are no meetings on your calendar today, a few items on your desk that need a live signature, and a few messages, the most important being from Kitty Montgomery, who needs an answer right away."

Nick smiled while asking himself, *Who the fuck is Kitty Montgomery*? as Mrs. Anne approached with two coffees. "Thank you, Mrs. Anne. And thank you, Marcel."

Marcel bowed again. "You're welcome, Mr. Highton."

Nick laughed at how serious Marcel was being, but Marcel gave him a stern look with an eyebrow slightly raised. Nick gave him a smile and turned to Niles. "Father, this is Marcel Delacoux, my senior executive operations manager for Deep Strokez Publications. Marcel has been with me from the very beginning, starting out in Mrs. Anne's position answering phone calls, as my executive assistant until very recently, and now he leads the team in my physical absence. He keeps me structured, organized, and on task. I couldn't do what I do without him."

Marcel gave Nick a surprised look and accidentally let a smile form on his lips. But then he remained in character and slightly bowed again. "Thank you, sir. Is there anything else you need from me before I continue with my duties of the day?"

Nick grinned. Marcel looked at him innocently. "No, thank you, Marcel." He looked around at everyone else, then back at Marcel with a wink. "You've done well." He turned to his father and gestured with one arm out to his office. "Come, let's sit down," he said.

They walked through the doors, then he turned to his team. "You can all stop pretending now. You've earned your twenty percent raise. Let's make it twenty-two, shall we?"

As he closed his office door, they heard excited screams and yells, making him laugh. Niles chuckled too.

Nick showed him the projected numbers for the next fiscal year, and Niles gave him compliments and healthy advice on how to cut costs, which Nick appreciated. They talked business for a few hours before they decided to stop for lunch. When they stepped out of the office, it was seemingly back to normal, with Eddie sleeping on the green couch under the window, Edgar and Dion playing desk football over Dion's desk, Aspen, Carli, and Archer arguing loudly over color schemes, and Nguyen still troubleshooting system issues in the office.

Nick introduced Niles to his three lead reporters, kicking Eddie awake, who was seemingly embarrassed to be caught literally sleeping on the job. But Eddie explained that he was out talking to sex workers whose working area was being taken away to make room for an apartment building. He was planning a big exposé that he was going to introduce first to the online magazine and eventually make a documentary on sex workers in the city. Niles was interested and asked questions about the documentary but also about Eddie's background in journalism. While they talked, Nick went over to Martine to have her order lunch for the whole office from the restaurant Bad Ramen.

They sat at the big conference table in the middle of the room, introducing themselves one by one and detailing their education and experience to Nick's father. Niles realized working for Nick was a first job for many of them. Nick explained that he and Lionel did an open house interview and marketed it to those about to graduate from all of the colleges and universities in the city. With the exception of Barry Sorensen, who had a master's in finance and was CPA certified, and Anne Falcon, who had been working as a high school secretary for over twenty years before she retired and came to work for Nick, the entire team was all under the age of thirty-two.

"So when Nicholas decides to move his entire operation to California, are you all planning on leaving your families and lives behind and going with him?" Niles asked.

"I am," Eddie said right away. "I already told him. And my girl is coming with me."

"I'm here," Nguyen said. "My work is going to be based out of the New York office. I can do IT remotely."

"I've been waiting for an opportunity to move," said Edgar. "I wish it was moving to Amsterdam, but sure, I can do Cali."

"I have a daughter," Aspen said, "So it would be hard to leave, sure. But Nick said that he would pay the relocation expenses, and Marcel can help me find childcare out there. And with the twenty percent raise—"

Dion pretended to cough. "Twenty-ahem-two-ahem." They all laughed.

"Riiiight!" she said with a grin and gave him a high five. "With the twenty-*two* percent raise, I'll be able to afford it."

"Actually," Barry spoke up, "it would not be feasible to pack up the entire operation and move to California. We would need to keep this location open and have a

presence on both coasts. The trends of marketing and what works here may not work there. Sure, you can open up an office in San Francisco now, but the work is already fully functioning in New York City, and it fiscally makes sense to keep it functioning for a minimum of five years, then reevaluate. I've explained to Nick that we need to put together a cost/benefit analysis before making the big move. And that could take time."

Niles nodded. "Yes. That actually makes sense." He looked around and said, "You are all very impressive young people. Thank you for opening up your office and your lives to me for the day."

"Your son is impressive," said Mrs. Anne. "He's a fantastic leader and manager. And we're all proud to be working with him."

"Here, here," said Carli, raising her soda can.

"To Nicholas 'Deep Strokez' Highton!" Archer yelled out, also raising his can to him.

"And to Hump!" Eddie yelled out, making everyone laugh, but they also raised their cups and cans. And so did his father, looking at him with pride. Marcel expectantly popped Eddie on the back of his head.

Nick shook his head and raised his plastic cup. "To all of us, building an empire from the bottom up. Cheers."

"Cheers," they chorused and drank. He turned to his father, who was still beaming at him.

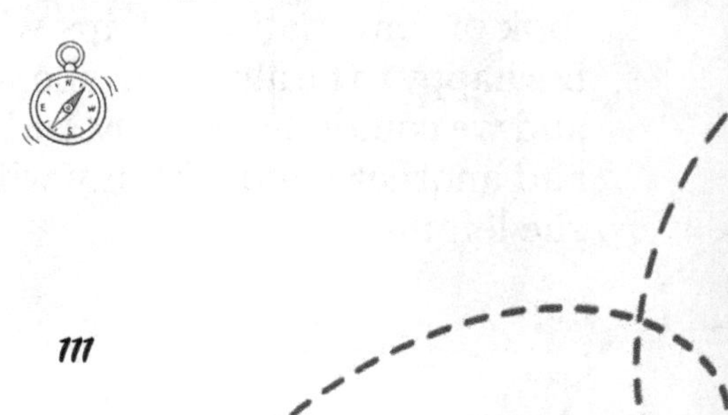

They rode back up to Nick's apartment but just so Niles could get a look at his place since, in the eight years Nick had been there, Niles had never seen his condo. Nick took Niles on the elevator to the rooftop and sat on the lounge chairs overlooking the city.

"What a great view," his father complimented him. "And a great job. And a great life you have. You've done well for yourself, Nicholas."

"Thank you, Father," he said.

"I am hoping that Mr. Matthews knows how lucky he is to have you in his life."

Nick shook his head. "I'm the lucky one, Father. It's so rare to find someone in our world that is genuine in their love for you. I am thankful every day that Rion wants me for me. Not for my name, my status, my money... Just me. I don't know many people that could say the same."

"I can," Niles said softly. "I was in love once. A very long time ago."

Nick looked at his father's white strands blowing in the wind. "Before Mother?" Nick asked.

"No... During."

"Oh," Nick said. "I knew there were other women in your life, Father. I suspected you had an entire family somewhere else, which was why you didn't come home much."

"No, not an entire family. But yes, another love that had my attention for over ten years. One that I took on international trips with me. One that made me happy to be alive. But she wanted to have children, and we couldn't together. And it devastated her that I had another child with my wife and not with her. So she left me."

"Wow," Nick said to himself. Niles was quiet, and Nick knew he was thinking of her. "What was her name?" he asked softly.

"Victoria. Victoria McDonald. She had absolutely no ties to the business world or our high society. She was a piano teacher that I met at a coffee shop of all places. She was absolutely nothing like anyone I had ever known. She was unkempt, always had a scarf around her blonde curly hair, and bright blue eyes behind her reading glasses. And we were the same age, which was a change for me. God, the first time we made love, it was in her stuffy one-bedroom apartment with her house plants and two cats staring at me." Nick chuckled. "It was the best moment of my life."

"And Mother didn't know?"

"I'm sure she did," Niles said with a shrug. "But what could she do? And I simply didn't care. Their paths never crossed, even though she became Brian, and then Emma's, piano teacher for a short stint. And she attended every Highton affair as a guest; we just weren't seen together. I bought her a bigger house in Saratoga Springs for her cats and plants and saw her a few times a week. I took her with me on every international trip, and we saw the world together. I never felt so comforted and loved in the arms of a woman as I did with Victoria."

"And she wanted to have children, you said?"

Niles sighed. "It was my fault. Two years into our relationship, I promised her I would give her one child. She was already forty-one by that time, and we tried for a year. She had two miscarriages, so we stopped trying. But I knew her desire was to have a child of her own."

"Where is she now?"

"Somewhere in Africa. She took an international job teaching music to children, and she didn't tell me where."

Nick looked at his father. "I know exactly where Trixie is. I know you know exactly where she is, Father."

Niles took a long time to answer. "She's in Matumbi, Tanzania, teaching children at a large schoolhouse. And she's happy. So I don't bother her at all. But every once in a while, I fantasize about leaving all this behind and going to her. Maybe I can now that I'm retired."

Nick scoffed. "Did you forget that you're still a married man?"

"No," he said, shaking his head. "But love has a way of drawing you in, no matter what your current circumstances are. I'm sure you've experienced that with Mr. Matthews."

Nick nodded. "I have."

"Good." Niles patted his leg again. "So now I know everyone in your life but him. Mr. Matthews should be back in time for the Midsummer Night's Dream Gala next week. Bring him. Introduce him properly to our society and to me."

Nick looked away. "Rion won't be able to make it, Father. Yes, he'll be back, but he has some other obligations to attend to."

Niles stared at his youngest son. "Pity then. We'll have to make personal arrangements for us to meet one-on-one."

"We'll see," Nick responded.

After seeing his father off, Nick decided to videocall Rion. Mostly because he missed Rion's face.

"Hey, Nicky," Rion responded as others spoke loudly around him.

"Hey, Ree. Where are you?" Nick asked.

Rion sighed. "At the police station," he told him. He got up and walked out of the double doors to talk. "But it's all good."

"Police station?" Nick said in alarm. "What happened?"

"Long story. But it's not something Madeline did. Just my nephew doing stupid teen shit like stealing my gummies and bringing them to school."

"Oh shit," Nick said with wide eyes.

Rion nodded. "And apparently Muriel's new boyfriend has a lot of connections and he's handling the situation. We're waiting out front for him and Reese to come out."

Nick was interested. "Muriel has a new boyfriend?"

"Yeah. Some ex-Marine guy that she met a few weeks back. I don't really like him, and I don't see anything they have in common, but they're probably fucking a lot, so there's that. I just hope she doesn't end up pregnant again."

"How far back did she meet him?" Nick asked. "About four weeks back? Around the same time that we came back to New York?"

"Yeah I think so. But Muriel said something about them meeting before then, maybe six months ago. Why? You think he's one of Madeline's plants!?" Rion's hand not holding the phone tightened into a fist. "I'll fucking kill him myself if he hurts my sister or any of her children."

"No, Ree, the opposite," said Nick. "I mean, yes, he could be one of Madeline's plants. Maybe she had already put things in motion. But I suspect he might be one of ours. The Nightwatch."

Rion was confused. "I thought we aren't supposed to know that they're even there."

"You're not. But once in a while, the lead will put himself right in the middle of things, just to make sure it's all going smoothly."

"In the middle of things like my sister's vagina!?" Rion yelled, then glanced around as others walked past him, looking at him strangely. He quietly walked farther away from the front door.

"I don't know about all that," Nick said. "But did you give him the code? You have to get him alone, one-on-one, and quietly say to him, 'Niion Lights Forever.' Then he knows to drop all pretenses, and you can ask him anything you want. Remember, they work for us."

"Huh," Rion said thoughtfully. "I'm going to do that tonight."

"Hey, Ree?"

"What?"

"Don't kick the shit out of him, please?" Nick deadpanned.

Rion snorted, making Nick chuckle. "No promises. If I find out he's using my sister's body as his home office, then it'll be a well-deserved ass whipping."

Nick couldn't deny that. "Well don't destroy the relationship we have with Nightwatch. They are our only protection against Madeline right now."

"Okay, fine. Hey, how're the visits going with Niles?" Rion asked suddenly.

"It's..." Nick sighed. "Hard but absolutely needed." He told Rion about his visit to the office today, seemingly impressed.

"These are all good things, Nick," said Rion. "He's getting to know you, Nicholas the man, and he's becoming proud of all your accomplishments. As he should be. You're an amazing guy."

Nick's heart melted at Rion's words. "You're always my biggest cheerleader."

"The president of your fan club!" Rion said with a grin. Then he asked, "Still haven't told him about Madeline's threats?"

"No, and I don't intend to," said Nick. Rion didn't respond. "Did you go see the house with Emma? Sea Cliff?"

"No," said Rion. "And I don't intend to."

Nick smiled. "My father has invited you to the Gala on the fourth."

"No thanks."

Nick's smile widened. "I politely declined on your behalf. But if you wanted to go and just not be seen together..."

"I don't," Rion said abruptly. "I don't think it's wise to have me in the same space with the woman that threatened to destroy me and my family. Especially if I find out the dude that's bonking my sister is one of hers."

"Yeah ... maybe not," Nick said.

But Rion noticed he looked crestfallen. "Hey. I'll be home soon. I miss you."

"I miss you too. A lot. It's so hard being without you," Nick confessed. "Two weeks is too long."

Rion agreed. "I think I might change my flight. Come home by this weekend. What do you think?"

"I think I'm going to meet you at the airport and fuck you in the car twice before we make it back to the city," said Nick with a straight face.

Rion smiled. "I'll change my flight tonight. After I have a talk with Mr. Nightwatch."

"Rion," Nick warned.

"I won't jeopardize our relationship with Nightwatch. Promise."

After they waited close to an hour, John came out of the back with Reese behind him. Muriel grabbed her son and kissed him repeatedly until he said, "Iight, Ma, damn!"

"He's okay," said John. "They dropped the charges and erased the records, like it never happened. I have a lieutenant going up to the school tomorrow to let them know the charges have been completely dropped. He probably will get suspended, but with no record, he won't get kicked out of school."

She let her son go and flew into her boyfriend's arms. They hugged tightly.

Rion turned to Reese. "You okay?"

"Yeah, Unc. I'm good."

"Good." Rion nodded. "Now I should kick your ass for stealing my gummies."

"I know. I'm sorry," his nephew said sincerely. "I haven't seen this brand out here, so I took it, and then decided to trade it for the pen. I wasn't selling anything. And I promise I'm not doing anything harder."

"Okay. We're going to have a long talk about all of this in the car. You'll ride with me." He looked over at John whispering in Muriel's ear, and she was nodding. He continued to be suspicious but turned to his nephew and said, "C'mon." They left the couple still standing there.

Rion lectured his nephew on the ride home as promised, and they arrived at the house before his sister and her boyfriend did. When they came inside, Muriel turned to her son and said, "I can't even look at you right now. Go upstairs."

"Ma, I'm really sor—"

She held up her hand. "Boy, if you don't want me to go upside your head right now, I suggest you go to bed."

Rion and John gave the boy a warning look. So Reese slowly went upstairs to his room. Once she heard his bedroom door close, Muriel sat on the edge of her couch. "I need a fucking drink," she bemoaned.

John kissed her head. "Have a glass of wine and get some rest. I have to go."

She looked up at him. "You're not staying tonight?"

He shook his head. "I have some things I need to take care of. And I have a feeling you need to have some one-on-one time with Reese tomorrow."

She nodded, then lifted her head up. He kissed her again and started out the door. Rion waited a moment, then followed him, closing the front door behind him.

"Hey, John?" John turned around. "Whatever you did in there to get my nephew out and the charges dropped, thanks for that. I appreciate it. Really." Rion held his hand out for a shake.

"It was nothing. Really," John said back but shook his hand.

As he started going down the two steps, Rion said, "One more thing I need to say to you." John turned around again. "Niion lights forever."

John stared at him blankly, then slowly began to smile. He stood up straighter and put his hands behind his back.

"Hello, Mr. Matthews, sir," he said respectfully.

"Well, I'll be damned," Rion said with a smile of his own. "Nicholas was right." He came down the stairs and approached him. "What's your real name? Because John Williams? Really?"

"It's Frank Fowler, sir," he admitted.

"Frank," he said with a slow nod. "Okay. So are you really a computer programmer? Or an ex-Marine?"

"Actually, I'm still currently active. I'm just in the reserves now, after twelve years of service, while I work full time for private security."

"But you are Nightwatch. Heading the team, right?"

"Lead security, yes."

"And as lead security, does your assignment include fucking my sister?" Rion deadpanned.

He watched Frank sigh, then look up into the night sky and sigh again. "I... I'm sorry, Mr. Matthews. I did not intend for things to go this way."

"Don't be," Rion said with a shrug. "You can just quietly make your exit out of her life now, stay in the background of this operation, and never show your face again. Goodbye, Frank."

Rion began to turn around when Frank said, "I can't do that, Mr. Matthews."

Rion turned back to him. "Excuse me?"

Frank swallowed but held his head up high. "I can't walk away from Muriel."

Rion got into his face again. "You work for me."

"I understand that, sir."

"I could fire you and your whole team right now for the shit you're doing."

"You could, Mr. Matthews," Frank said seriously. "But I don't think you want to do that. Madeline Highton has someone following you. I wasn't sure at first until today. It's an unidentified woman, brown hair, brown eyes, dressed as a teenager one day, an older businesswoman another day. You wouldn't have noticed her, but it's my job to. She was at the diner, and again at the school, pretending to be one of the many teens around. And she followed you to the police station."

Rion's mouth opened slightly. "Is she around right now?"

"Probably. Watching us. I called in another teammate to follow her. Do you want to know where she is right now, sir?"

Rion didn't answer. Frank took his phone out of his pocket and sent a text. Then he waited. The phone dinged in his hand. Frank gave it to Rion.

[JW: location and photo]

[WT: End of block, dark gray sedan, back camera with a view to the house taking pics. The UW knows RM is outside talking to you.]

Then there was a picture of someone in the backseat of the car. It was quick and Rion couldn't make out who it was, but it was definitely his sister's block.

Rion looked up with his mouth open. "Holy, holy shit."

But Frank said, "Don't look down there, sir. We don't want to give her a sign that we are onto her. I suspect she will follow you back to New York."

"Is my family safe?" Rion asked with worry.

"Yes, sir," Frank confirmed. "No signs of anyone in your family being targeted at this time. She didn't arrive until you did."

Rion sighed and handed Frank back his phone. "I don't like what you're doing with Rel. It's all lies and deceit, and she doesn't deserve that."

"It's not, I promise you." Frank shook his head. "Muriel knows who I am," he confirmed. "She figured out pretty quickly why I was always around. She has known since the first week, calling out the code just as you did."

His forehead scrunched in. "She knows you're Nightwatch? And your real name?"

John nodded. "And the entire operation, yes."

Rion shook his head. "And she's sleeping with you anyway. Great." Then he looked at Frank sharply. "When this is over, you and her are over."

Frank hesitated. "I... I can't do that, sir."

"Why not?" His eyes narrowed in suspicion.

"Because I..." Frank sighed again and stared at Rion with his mouth closed.

Rion's mouth opened instead. "Oh. You really *are* falling in love with my sister, aren't you?" Frank did not respond. "Jesus." Rion scoffed again. "Muriel's a man-eater, you know. Maybe it's you I should be worried about."

Rion chuckled as he made his way back up the stairs. "Don't call me 'sir,' Frank. Or Mr. Matthews. You're bedding my sister; we could at least be on a first name basis."

Frank smiled. "Okay, Rion."

"Oh and just use your real name. Frank Fowler sounds like a fake name anyway."

"It's actually Francis Johnathan Fowler."

Rion laughed out loud. "Francis? Holy, holy shit. Stick to John Williams."

Frank laughed too. "Good night, Rion."

"Good night, Francis."

In light of the recent information of being stalked, Rion decided not to change his flight. Instead, he took a Lyft to the bus station early the next day, then walked out of the back of the building and took a yellow cab to the airport, waiting on standby for the next flight to the east coast. He ended up getting a flight with two stops, one to Denver, the other to Washington D.C., before it landed at LaGuardia in New York after midnight the next day. Then he took a green cab to downtown Brooklyn and an Uber to Columbus Circle. From there he walked home, watching his surroundings. Between the impromptu flights and the many cabs, there was no way the stalker was able to follow him.

Rion let himself into the apartment without making a sound. It was all dark, and Izzy bounced over to him to curl around his legs and purr softly. Rion had not seen the tuxedo cat since London and suspected Zoey brought her home to them while he was away, just like she quietly brought Izzy to them when they officially moved to London a year ago. He bent down to pick her up, petting her, shushing her to be quiet. When she had enough and hopped out of his arms, he walked into the bedroom and watched Nicholas sleep for a moment. Nick was on his back on his side of the bed but facing Rion's pillow with his hand underneath it. It made Rion smile. He slowly walked back out to the bathroom, keeping the light off, and stripped naked. He took a quick shower and prepared himself. Then he made his way back to the room and climbed onto the bed.

Nick did not stir. Rion could tell he was wearing underwear but nothing else, the bedspread barely clinging to his torso. Rion crawled between his open legs and put his nose in Nick's crotch over the thin blanket. Nick still did not stir, but he could feel Nick slowly growing. Rion continued to run his face on Nick's center until he felt him get hard enough. Then he slowly began to pull the covers off him. He got as far as the top of Nick's groin when Nick absentmindedly pulled the blanket back and sighed in his sleep. Rion smiled. He waited a moment, then slowly pulled again until Nick's underwear was exposed. He put his face in the area between Nick's thighs and breathed in deeply. Nick's cock twitched. Rion silently pulled the top part of his boxer briefs down, licked up his cock, and put the head in his mouth. Nick grunted in his sleep. Rion licked around the cock head, watching it come alive but still not fully erect. After the third time, Nick moaned and woke up startled.

He gasped. "Rion."

They stared at each other, Rion bent over his groin, Nick lifting up on his elbows. Rion crawled up Nick's body and answered him with a tongue in his mouth. Nick moaned and kissed him back, laying back on the bed, running his hand through Rion's curls.

"Am I dreaming, or are you really here?" he asked groggily.

"I'm here, babe," Rion responded.

Nick moaned again and grabbed Rion's bottom tightly, pressing their groins together. They kissed and touched for a while until Rion rose on his knees and sat on Nick's stomach. He reached behind him with the other hand to adjust Nick's cock against his pucker. Then he pushed back, impaling himself. Nick lifted up his hips and slowly guided the rest in, his underwear still sitting on his own thighs. Rion put one hand on Nick's shoulder and began to ride. Nick reached down and grabbed Rion's waist, closing his eyes, getting lost in the rhythm of Rion's movement and tightness. Rion began to stroke himself at the same pace he rode, with Nick moaning loudly and freely.

"God, I missed you, Nicky... You feel so good ... so so good..." Rion murmured over and over again. "So good."

Rion began to move faster, stroke quicker, unable to control his need to cum. He went over the edge with a loud moan, depositing milky white cum across Nick's chest. Then he paused to catch his breath.

Nick raised his hands to the sweatiness of Rion's lower back and slowly turned their bodies until Rion was on his back. He took off his underwear for the freedom to move and quickly reinserted himself back inside. Rion wrapped his arms around Nick's neck as Nick began to pull back, then push in deeply. He picked Rion's right leg up so he could bury deeper and made love to Rion for a while, listening to Rion's whimpers, moans, and cries.

When Nick was ready, he lifted up both of Rion's legs and knelt before him. He began to thrust harder and faster, holding onto the back of Rion's thighs. Rion bellowed his name, and Nick forgot his own name as his orgasm overwhelmed him. He too cried out, and his body shook as he released semen, two weeks' worth that he saved for the return of his lover. He collapsed, letting Rion's legs go, and fell against him, chest to chest, his face practically buried in the pillow. Rion stretched below him but dutifully carried Nick's weight, running his fingers through the back of Nick's hair, waiting for him to return from his climax.

Eventually, Nick turned Rion sideways and kissed his face, then kissed him again and again. He kept putting soft kisses on Rion's forehead, cheeks, nose, and lips, murmuring, "I missed you so much, Ree. So much."

Rion's heart was full. "Call out of work and stay home with me tomorrow," he requested.

"Hmmm... I wish I could. But I have a six-hour brainstorming meeting with the digital and marketing teams for the rebranding. We're not leaving that room until we have some real ideas on the table."

"That sounds great, Nick," said Rion in a hollow voice.

Nick lifted Rion's chin. "I know. I've been working an awful lot lately. This year is going to be all work and no play, unfortunately. And with Wednesdays with my father thrown in the mix, which has me working on Saturdays too, it seems like we're passing ships in the night."

"So you've felt it too?"

"I have. I miss you even when you're here. But these last two weeks have been torturous." He kissed Rion again. "I couldn't get to do this."

"So what do we do?" Rion asked. "Because I don't want to be passing ships anymore."

"Come to work with me, Ree," Nick said. "The offer still stands for you to come on board full time as my VP. Come to the meeting tomorrow and throw out ideas. We can work together, build Highton media together. And we'll see each other more."

Rion sighed. He had been avoiding it, but it was logical for him to be a part of Nick's company. "Okay. I'll sign the paperwork officially. Become your VP."

Nick grinned. "You could also come to Highton events with me too. Like the Fourth of July one. My father had his mistress at every single event for ten years; he said they just never interacted. You could do the same."

"That would never work," said Rion. "I couldn't be your hidden mistress because the whole world knows we're together. The press would expect us to be side by side at these events. Also, this high society stuff... It's not my world. And it makes me a little uncomfortable."

Nick frowned, but said, "Okay. I get it."

Rion smiled. "I missed your pouty mouth." He kissed him on the lips, intending for it to be sweet.

But Nick grabbed his neck and pulled on Rion's lip with his own. "Let me cum inside of you again. Please?"

"You're so sexy when you beg for my consent," Rion said back on his lips.

"Is that a yes?"

"Ask me again."

Nick repositioned himself, licked Rion's lips, and kissed his torso as he said, "Please, please, may I put my cock in and cum deep inside of you?" He moved farther down and began to deep throat Rion.

Rion moaned, "Yessss pleeeease..."

Nick prepped and entered him. They made love again until Nick came. Then Rion moved Nick to the chaise, putting him on his knees and thrusting into him until he too came. Nick turned around to sit down, and Rion rode him again, his arms tightly around Nick's neck, Nick's hands around Rion's waist, moving together until the sun began to rise. Only then did Nick release for the last time, then reached between them to pull Rion over the edge with him. Nick carried him to the bed and tucked him in, gently running his hand through his soft curls again, holding him.

Once Rion was asleep, only then did Nicholas take his shower and head to the office. He knew he would be dead tired all day, but Rion was back, and it was worth it.

Nicholas had walked around twice, greeting guests and giving polite hellos, but mostly kept to himself, finding one corner or another to disappear into. He looked up at the moon and missed Rion. It was the first night since Rion had returned from San Francisco that they were apart, and he hated every second of being there, wishing he was wrapped up in the heat of his partner once again.

Nick realized he had been standing near the harps in the garden staring at the moon for a while, so he sighed and looked around again. The setting was once again beautiful, the theme always the same but slightly different. This time it was more starry, small twinkling lights all over the garden, the lightbulbs inside all made yellow instead of a soft fluorescent white and miniature white lights dotting the ceiling of the entire first floor. Nick never wore a costume to the Fourth of July event, and neither did Brian, who felt it was enough that their mother made them dress up every year for the October event, but so many others did.

Brian had spotted him earlier in the evening but didn't say anything about his melancholy attitude.

Nicholas began to walk back inside the house, considering slipping out quietly, when Robby approached him right in front of the accordion doors.

"Uncle Nick," he said excitedly, "I know we don't meet until next week, but I wanted to let you know I'm flying out to Missouri on Thursday. "

"What's in Missouri?" Nick asked.

Robby talked excitedly about a group of young women ranging from sixteen to twenty-six that started a small media company and moved to YouTube to put their content out there. "It's really funny stuff," said Robby. "They have a live show this weekend that they need an audience for, and I'm going to quietly vet them, then make them a pitch."

"I would have really liked to see the content before you made arrangements to vet them," Nick slightly scolded.

"Oh." Robby looked disappointed. "I'll cancel my trip and send it to you now. You'll let me know—"

"No, don't do that. I trust you," Nick said, making Robby grin. "We just need to coordinate better. Go on your trip, but send me the YouTube link."

"I will. Also, there are two others I'm looking into. One I found on TikTok, a little girl, can't be more than twelve, but she puts on skits and does impersonations. I looked into her and her whole family is in on it. They produce, direct, and edit the whole thing. And the other is a man who makes documentaries on climate change. I know he has a team, but I don't know who they are yet. He's out in Oregon. I plan on doing a lot of running around this summer and get you the ten teams to start with before I'm back at NYU."

Nick nodded. "Good work. Tell me more about the documentary on climate change."

As Robby described their content and Nick was listening, a hand slammed down on his shoulder, interrupting his nephew.

"Highton. I don't think I've seen you at this shindig in a few years." The man looked around mockingly. "Where's the arm candy?"

Nick turned around and resisted the urge to roll his eyes. Instead, he stepped to the side so that Todd's arm fell off his body and gave him a polite smile.

"Todd Porter, this is my nephew, Robert Highton-Dorado. Robby, meet Todd Porter. His family owns Porterhouse Casinos here in the US."

"And South America! We're expanding to Colombia and Venezuela, thanks to me." Todd shook his hand. "Great to meet you, Robby. Say, you're Emma Highton's son. I've been trying to get a meeting with her for years. Say, why don't you walk me over to her, kid, and do a formal introduction? I can take it from there." He gave him a smug smile.

"Robert," Robby corrected stonily, letting go of his hand. "Only close friends and family call me Robby. And no to your request. Now if you will excuse us, we were in a conversation—"

"Say, Nick," Todd said, cutting the young man off, "I heard through the grapevine that you're about to expand your media company. I have some great ideas I would like to run past you." He put his hand on Nick's shoulder again. "Picture a reality TV show with real gamblers. The ups and downs. The struggles. The wins. Great, isn't it? And being a professional gambler myself, I would star. What do you think?"

Nick moved Todd's hand off his shoulder again by taking a step back. "I think it's not the right time to talk business. Not at an event like this. But have your team call Robert's team and make the pitch. He'll vet it and see if we can use it."

He was about to turn around when Todd whined, "But I heard you talking business with the kid here. I don't want to go through the kid. C'mon, let's talk."

Nick turned to face him again as Robby grimaced. "The *kid* is Robert Highton-Dorado, and he's the Senior Executive Director of acquisitions. You'll go through him, Todd."

"C'maaan," Todd said. "Networking is part of the fun here. Let's network." He touched Nick's shoulder a third time.

Nick, who realized Todd was definitely high, dropped the polite smile and looked at Todd's hand on his shoulder until Todd got the hint and slowly slid it off.

Nick looked at him. "Thank you. Good night, Todd."

Todd threw his hands up and said, "Okay, I hear you. No business talk. Only pleasure today. Got it. But gone are the days when you're 'Mr. Highton' to me since I've stepped up into the big leagues now, eh? People call me Mr. Porter now." Todd grinned and rubbed his shoulder against Nick, who did not smile back. Todd laughed. "It's a party, Nick! Lighten up a little. Let me know if you want something to perk your spirits a bit." He gave Nick a playful punch on the shoulder. Nick just stared at him.

Todd turned to Robby and made a fake bow. "Nice to meet you, Young Highton."

"Robert Highton-Dorado," Robby corrected him again. "Next time you approach me, remember my name, especially if you want to pitch to HMP."

Todd bowed again. "Excuse me, Mr. Highton-Dorado. You may be a Dorado, but you certainly have that snooty Highton charm. I don't think you attended Arcadia Academy. I'm on the board there, and I would have remembered your name."

"No, I didn't."

Todd shook his head. "Shame. You would have done well with your name and a top-rated education." He grinned and winked at Nick, who did not grin back.

"I had a top-rated education," Robby said with a straight face. "I attended Bedford Mills International Academy in St. Catherines, Ontario. See, my parents actually loved me and wanted me close by but still have an elite education. *Je ne pense pas qu'on puisse en dire autant de toi, mon ami merdique.*" Nick grinned at his nephew.

Todd chuckled. "Hehe, French. Good one. What did you say?" Robby stared at him as a response. Todd chuckled again. "Okay, I can take the hint. Nicholas, I will catch you later."

Todd finally walked away with Robby still frowning at him. "That guy is a dipshit."

Nick chuckled. "Yeah he is. But you handled it well. I'm proud of you."

"I learned from the best, Uncle Nick." He smiled at him. "Where's Uncle Rion? For real?"

Nick frowned. "It's not time to introduce him to the family."

“Hmmm...” Robby said with his eyebrows raised. “I know what that means. Don’t worry, Grandmother will eventually come around.” He looked past Nick. “I see Sofia Coombs. She works at the movie theater in downtown Rochester, and I invited her. She’s going to be my wife, you know.”

Nick chuckled again. “Did your parents already arrange that?”

“Nah. Mother said I can marry who I want.”

Nick gave his nephew a soft smile. “Good for you.”

Robby patted his arm. “Excuse me.”

Nick watched his nephew saunter over to a pretty girl dressed as a fairy with two-toned hair, black at the roots to her ears, blonde the rest of the way past her shoulders. She smiled at him as he came closer. It made him miss Rion even more. Suddenly, his drink wasn’t strong enough to fill the absence. He walked around some, looking for something to occupy his mind until he could get on a plane back to his boyfriend’s arms.

Rion was all settled on the couch with his popcorn and Doritos mix ready to start an action movie he found On-Demand when the intercom buzzed. Rion looked at it, his hand on the remote frozen in the air, when it buzzed a second time. Rion rose from the couch to answer it.

“Hello?” he said hesitantly.

“Good evening, Mr. Matthews,” Thaddeus, who was working the front desk, said. “Ms. Kara Beaumont is waiting downstairs for you. She said you have thirty minutes to get ready, and your plane leaves in ninety."

Rion blinked at the wall. "Plane to go where?"

"Ah... She ah ... didn't say." He heard the muffled voice of the front desk clerk, then he came back to the phone. "Her driver said you are to accompany her to the Highton event in Rochester tonight, *A Midsummer Night's Dream*."

Rion shook his head. "Please tell Ms. Beaumont thank you, but I will not be in attendance."

Rion let go of the intercom and began walking back to the living room area when it buzzed again. Rion answered it. "Thaddeus, I said—"

"Ms. Beaumont wishes to inform you that you are to accompany her to the event tonight as her plus one. She is not allowed to show up alone, per the Doctor's orders. And his orders are that she is to arrive with you as her guest before the fireworks at 10 p.m., so you must make haste. The Doctor's orders are never to be ignored."

Rion groaned out loud. "Fucking Brian," he muttered. He pressed the intercom again. "Tell her I'll be down in thirty."

"Mr. Matthews," the doorman called out, "her driver is on his way up to your apartment with your attire."

"Ugh," Rion groaned again. "Okay, fine," he said into the intercom.

He waited by the door until the bell rang. An older man was standing there with a cotton garment bag with the initials BNH on it. Rion thanked the man and took the suit into the bedroom before he opened it. It was a full tux with coattails, navy blue with white trim, a crisp white shirt, and a blue silk eye mask. A note was in the pocket of the bag:

> *Nick has a pair of calfskin midnight blue Diors that would work perfectly for this suit. Brian has borrowed them, so I know they are there. Please don't be late. We have a plane to catch. -KB*

Rion groaned for the third time. Then he hopped in the shower.

The same man who brought him the suit opened the door of the black Benz GLS for him. Rion stepped in and came face-to-face with Kara Beaumont, Brian's mistress and kink partner. They had only met once before two years ago, but at that time, Kara was playing out the beginning of a Dom/sub scene with Brian right in front of him and Nick. It completely disturbed Nicholas, while it fascinated Rion. So much so that he asked to observe their entire scene, and they both consented. His last book had a BDSM scene that mimicked theirs.

Kara looked beautiful. Her makeup was perfectly done, and her straight raven hair had a tight part down the middle. Her navy blue dress was silk and lace with stones in various places, and Rion would not be surprised if each one was an actual diamond. Her sleeves were as see-through as the lace part of her dress, and she was not wearing her collar. Instead, it was a star with a big diamond in the center that sat right above her cleavage line. Kara's long legs were crossed in front of him as her tulle skirt split to the sides, and her silver open-toed shoes revealed blue painted feet, matching her blue painted nails.

"Hello, Rion," she greeted him in her soft voice.

"Erm..." Rion touched his lapels in nervousness. "Hello, Kara. Does Nicholas know about this?"

"No. He does not know that you are coming."

"Hm. Brian's idea?"

"Yes," she said. "I have a friend that I attend Highton events with, someone to help me blend in. But at Nicholas's arrival without you, Brian called me and immediately changed my plans."

"I'm sorry."

"Don't be." She reached over and touched his knee. "Nicholas will want you there."

Rion shook his head. "You don't understand. I'm not allowed—"

"I know everything," said Kara. "Brian told me everything. Remember, he needs to keep me safe too." She touched her belly.

Suddenly, her flowy dress made sense. Rion smiled at her. "How far along are you?"

She smiled and touched her belly again. "Four months. I'm due in December."

Rion smiled, then his eyes widened. "Wait, you go to all the Highton events? With his family there? His..."

"Wife present? Yes."

"Wow. The shit these Highton men get away with... Does she know?" Rion blurted out. Then said, "Sorry. That was... It's not my business."

Kara stared at him for a moment, then said, "We met once. Seven years ago. The rule was that I was to never interact with her. I got the impression that she knew of Brian's lifestyle; she knew he had a sub but didn't want to know anything more than that. But that year's masquerade ball, I was standing on the balcony waiting for Brian when she approached me. I was so scared. The last sub that spoke to his wife was immediately cut off from him, no questions asked. And she was so beautiful, confident, and intimidating. She asked me my name, then she asked me what he calls me, my sub name. She asked me how long. She asked me if I loved him. If I needed him. I answered her questions honestly. Then she reached a hand up, and I thought she was going to slap me. But she caressed my face and told me I was beautiful and perfect for him. Then she kissed me on the lips. And she walked away."

"Wow," Rion breathed out. "And she hasn't said anything to you since?"

"Not a single word," Kara confirmed. "She doesn't even look in my direction if we are in the same gathering. It's like I'm not there."

"Does Brian acknowledge you at these gatherings?" Rion could not help but ask more questions.

"Brian looks through me as well most of the night, except the one moment he finds me. Usually it's on a high balcony or a room right off the main room where the event is taking place. Then he..." She trailed off and smiled.

Rion grinned. "He takes you."

"Yes."

"Roughly."

She smiled wider. “Yes. And I’m not allowed to cry out and draw attention. It has to be silent on my part.”

“How rough does he get?”

She cocked her head to the side. “I think you know the answer.”

“I mean, he can’t exactly choke you and leave marks, right?”

Kara pulled out a white silk scarf from her silver beaded purse. Rion’s mouth dropped. “Holy, holy shit,” he responded.

“And I have a second pair of thongs in there too. And shoes on the plane. Sometimes a heel gets broken.”

“So will he take you tonight? Right on the balcony as the fireworks go off?”

“I sure as fuck hope so,” Kara said seriously.

Rion let out a loud laugh, making Kara laugh too.

13

After the ride in Brian's jet, Rion was in awe as the car went up the private road to the estate. Every tree twinkled with fairy lights, at least a hundred trees leading to the large iron gate. The driver pressed the intercom and announced, "Miss Kara Simone Beaumont and her guest."

The gate opened, and the car continued toward the massive estate with an hour to spare before the fireworks were to begin.

Rion put on his eye mask with a sigh. "Time to put on the mask, literally and figuratively."

Kara patted his leg. "It will be fine. Stay by my side until we find Nicholas."

The car was in a queue with other limos, town cars, and black SUVs. Rion watched as guests were let out and were dressed just as fancy as he was, as if they had stepped back into the Victorian era. When the driver opened up their door, Rion came out first, then held his hand out for Kara. She gracefully exited and took Rion's arm. They walked hand in hand up the stone steps, stopping at the doorman for Kara to hand over her invitation, then continued into the foyer. On each side was a winding staircase leading to the second floor. But everyone was led down the hall and to the left to the great room that could easily hold two hundred people.

Rion could not close his mouth. "Brian, Nick, and Emma actually lived here? Because this is not a house. This is..." He stopped at the large painting and could not stop staring at it. "A museum."

Kara smiled at him. "Brian is mesmerized by that one too." She tugged on his arm. "Come. The event is the garden. We'll find him there."

Kara and Rion were stopped by a waiter carrying various types of alcoholic beverages on a tray. Kara took the wine glass, and Rion grabbed a cup of dark liquor, quickly discovering it was bourbon. They walked around the backyard, and Rion noticed people were in costume as either a character from *A Midsummer Night's Dream* or dressed in evening wear, like they were going to see the play itself. Rion was in awe at the ten harpists around the gigantic fountain playing a melody together. There were lots of children there too. A couple of them ran past him with sparklers, also dressed up. Kara smiled politely but only greeted a few people.

Rion spotted Emma wearing all white with blue wings, Gary in some kind of Roman getup, and their children, Blair also looking like a fairy in a green dress and Robby in a designer t-shirt, a dinner jacket, and jeans with his arm around a pretty girl with two-toned hair. Rion was surprised at a tap on his shoulder, and Brian was there. Brian was dressed in a dark gray suit, complete with a matching vest, white shirt, and a red bowtie.

"It looks good on you," he said. "Glad you made it."

"Thanks," Rion said back.

He tapped Rion's glass with his own. "You deserve to be here, Rion. You're family. Enjoy the party."

"Thanks," Rion said again as Brian walked away. He looked at Kara, who was standing right beside him, looking around nonchalantly.

"Wow," said Rion in surprise. "He really didn't acknowledge you at all."

Kara turned to him with a smile. "I told you he wouldn't. But he'll come find me. Later."

After almost an hour of walking around the expansive yard with Kara, a thin man with a beard about Rion's age stopped in front of her, wearing a black Victorian suit with a top hat and long cane.

"Good morrow, Mistress Petit," he drawled.

She grinned at him. "Do shut up, Adolphe." She left Rion's side and walked into his waiting arms. He hugged her tightly, then she said, "Meet Rion Matthews. Rion Mathews, Adolphe Behrend."

He looked at Rion with wide eyes. "Wow. You're here. Have you seen the wicked witch of the west and east and north and south yet?" he asked with his hand covering the top hat, pretending to look for her.

Rion chuckled. "Not yet. And I plan on not being seen in this crowd of people."

Adolphe let Kara go and reached out to shake Rion's hand. "It's really good to meet you."

"Likewise. Are you a friend of Nick's?" Rion asked, shaking his hand back.

"No. Nicholas has no idea who I am," Adolphe said confidently.

Kara giggled. "Do you know where he is?"

"I saw him go toward the game room on the other side of this castle with that prick Todd that I work for now," Adolphe said with a straight face. He said to Rion, "His uncle gave him the company, and I'm the financial director and senior analyst, which means I get to clean up all his expensive messes."

Kara rolled her eyes. "Ugh. Let's go rescue him, Rion."

"Have fun," Adolphe said. "I'm pretty sure they're both coked up."

Rion looked at him in alarm. "What!?"

Adolphe gave him a bored look. "What else would they be doing in the sunroom? It's either sex or drugs."

Before Rion could respond, Kara pulled him away, giving her friend an annoyed look. "Nick doesn't typically do it; don't worry. I'm sure he's fine," she reassured Rion. But a small pit formed in Rion's belly anyway.

They walked back through the great room, across the large foyer to the other side of the estate. "Adolphe is ... interesting," Rion commented.

She smiled. "Adolphe has many sides to him. This is the 'I'm bored to death here, but I have to go to these parties because duty calls, so maybe I can stir up some trouble for fun' side of him."

"Oh." He was thoughtful. "I assume he knows all about you since he called you the name Brian calls you."

"Adolphe is in the lifestyle too," she said simply. "And he's my best friend."

"Oh, okay."

Kara turned left and pushed open the double doors to a room that had everything from pool tables to foosball tables. Rion quickly glanced around. "He's not in here."

"No. He's... Shit." Kara stopped cold. She looked at Rion with sad eyes.

"What?" Rion asked in confusion.

"Adolphe was right." She looked around then looked back at Rion. "I'm sorry."

"Right about...?" Rion said, as his chest began to tighten in anxiousness and the pit grew.

"Shit," Kara cursed again. She glanced at the glass door leading to the sunroom, then shook her head. "Come on."

She pulled Rion through the door, and it swung closed behind her. There were about ten men sitting around in dim lighting, drinking and smoking. The women were in scantily clad clothing getting fondled by them.

"What is this?" Rion asked.

Kara didn't answer but looked around steadily. "Shit," she said a third time. She led him over to the corner where two men were sitting with their heads together, laughing. She stopped Rion from walking. "Wait."

Then Kara walked up to both of them, lifted her leg, and placed her heel on the couch in between them. Both men looked up, startled. Rion saw that it was his Nicholas with Todd Porter, someone that Nick hated with a passion. It was odd seeing them talking and laughing together.

"Hey, beautiful," Todd slurred out and touched her bare leg. He slowly ran his hand up until it reached underneath her thigh.

Kara smiled and leaned in. "Go any farther, and the Doctor will remove all of your organs while you're awake."

Todd laughed and let her go. She turned to Nick. "Hello, Nicholas. I have a surprise for you. But I think you might be more of a surprise for him in this state."

"Surprise?" Nick asked.

She put her foot down and stepped to the side. Nick was still smiling as he looked over. His face contorted into shock, and he stopped smiling abruptly.

"Rion!" Nick stood up.

Rion slid the mask up. "Surprise," he deadpanned.

Nick ran up and threw his arms around him, kissing his face and neck aggressively. "I can't believe you're here! I can't believe it!"

Rion did not hug him back. "Are you on cocaine?" he asked softly.

Nick leaned back up and looked at Rion. Rion immediately noticed that his eyes were wide and dilated.

"I'm so glad you're here, Ree," he said with a smile, not answering his question. "How did you get here? And with Kara? And in this..." He stepped back and looked at his partner. "This fucking suit." He slapped Rion's chest hard. "It looks amazing on you." He grabbed the back of Rion's neck and kissed him sloppily on the mouth.

Rion pushed him back. "Are you high, Nicholas?" he asked again.

"Don't be such a Damper Dorothy," Todd said as he lit a cigar and leaned back on the chair. "Hey, remember back in the day when people used to refer to gay people as a 'Friend of Dorothy's'? That was from *The Golden Girls*, wasn't it? Still love those fucking ladies."

Nick giggled at Todd, and Todd giggled back. Rion turned around to walk away, but Nick grabbed his arm. "Hey. I'm sorry, okay? I'm just ... trying to have a good time."

"With Todd Porter? The asshole, arrogant, trust fund baby that you can't stand to be around is suddenly your best friend?" Rion asked.

Todd laughed. "I'm a better friend to him right now than you are. And I don't suck cock."

Nick giggled again. Rion walked around Nick and went up to Todd, who was still sitting. He placed his foot between Todd's legs and leaned on his knee.

"You stupid, desperate motherfucker. The only way you can get Nicholas to tolerate you is if he's coked up, huh?"

"It's true," Nick said with a chuckle. "I really can't stand to be around you."

Todd laughed. "You say that, but we've already struck two deals in the last hour. And you're a man of your word, Highton."

Nick looked at Rion and shrugged. "That's true too."

Rion sighed, then turned back to Todd. "You don't have any business deals, Todd. Because I'm the VP, and I won't sign off on anything with your name on it or tied to you. After tonight, you stay the fuck away from Nicholas. And if I catch you giving my partner drugs again, I'm going to break your fucking fingers," he said seriously.

Todd chuckled and continued to smoke. "Sure thing, Boss," he said sarcastically.

Rion put his foot down and turned to Nick, who was still smiling a goofy smile. "That was sexy as fuck," Nick said, leaning in for a kiss.

Rion shook his head, immensely pissed off, but trying to stay calm. "I'll see you at home."

He walked out of the sunroom back into the game room. "Rion, wait!" Nick yelled after him and followed. "Hey!" he yelled again and grabbed Rion's arm. "Stay with me."

Nick tried to kiss Rion again, but Rion backed up. Nick tried to touch Rion, and Rion slapped his hand away. "What the fuck!?" Nick exclaimed.

Rion was furious, but he said quietly, "We'll talk at home." He turned around to walk away again.

"I'm sorry!" Nick yelled, getting more attention from those in the room. "I know I'm disappointing you, but... I... I fucking hate being here anyway, and just knowing that I couldn't be here with you... I needed to occupy my mind. Be in a different head space. But I missed you so much, and I'm so glad you came anyway. I love you, Ree."

Rion looked around at everyone paying attention to their argument. He turned back around and said for the third time, "Home, Nick. We'll talk at home."

"So you're just going to leave me?" he said angrily. "Then what the fuck was the point of you getting all dressed up and coming out here if you were going to turn around and leave? If you really cared about me, if you don't want me to go back there and hang out with that dipshit Todd, then you should just stay. Or maybe you don't really give a shit about me."

Nick knew he was being an asshole but couldn't help himself. And he really didn't want Rion to leave, so he tried again, in his inebriated state, to make him stay. "So if you leave me like this, everything that happens next is going to be your fault."

Everyone in the room was quietly watching. Rion walked up to him, and Nick thought he had won. He gave Rion a smug smile. Rion took his time, straightening out Nick's tie, as he spoke quietly.

"You know who you sound like, right?"

"Who? My mother?" Nick said, rolling his eyes.

"No." Rion touched his chest and said on his lips, "Mine."

Nick's mouth opened slightly, finally understanding how bad the situation was. Rion turned around to walk away again.

"Rion," Nick called his name again and grabbed his arm, wanting to apologize.

But Rion forcefully pulled out of Nick's grasp and pushed him hard. Nick fell backward onto a foosball table, moving it a few inches and messing up a game that was in progress between a Hermia and Lysander lookalike.

Rion continued walking until he was out of the mansion, back to the cars waiting out front. But he had no idea which car he came in. He had no idea how he was going to get home. He was stuck in the middle of Upstate New York with people he didn't know, and he hated Nick and hated his family and hated Todd Porter and hated Brian for making him come and he hated himself for ever being in that situation.

Rion began to hyperventilate. He couldn't get enough oxygen in his lungs. He tried to calm himself down, but everything went dizzy as anxiousness rose and fell in his chest in intervals. He put his hands on his knees but almost fell over on the steps. So he sat down with his head between his knees and waited for his panic attack to pass. Telling himself that he was okay. That he was safe. That he was in control. It had been years since he had a full blown panic attack. The last thing he wanted to do was get back on Lexapro. But because he had one now, he knew they would come more frequently. And the thought that they would come back fully made the current one last longer than it should have.

As he began to regain his breathing, he heard the click-clack of heels behind him. He lifted his head and watched the beautiful Kara slowly make her way down the stairs looking like a blue silk butterfly with the way her dress flowed around her. When she got by his side, she looked down at him with concern. He stood up and took a deep breath, exhaling shakily. She sighed, looked out at the cars, and held up her hand. One of the town cars came out of the line and drove over to them.

Suddenly, fireworks began to burst over their heads. They both looked up. "You don't have to leave, Kara," said Rion as the sky lit up. "I'll find my way home."

"I'm not leaving you tonight, Rion," she simply said.

"You didn't have your moment with Brian yet. Don't let Nick and mine's bullshit mess with your fantasy night."

"Brian is aware; I sent him a text," she said. "He went to go find his younger brother and give him a scolding. And I told him I was taking you back to the city."

“I’m so sorry your night was ruined,” Rion said sadly.

“I’m sorry your night was ruined too.” Kara patted his arm as the driver opened up the door. “Come. We’ll fly back to New York City and have some fun together.”

14

Rion heard the door open from his place on the couch, and it woke him up. He sat up and slid to the corner of the couch with one knee up. He watched Nicholas walk into the living room looking disheveled, no suit jacket or tie, shirt half outside his pants. He plopped down on the couch beside Rion but didn't look at him. Rion waited.

"I'm such an asshole," Nick began quietly. "I'm so, so sorry, Rion. I can't apologize enough for my behavior last night. I shouldn't have been hanging out with that jerkoff, and I shouldn't have used. You have every right to be upset with me. And honestly I'm surprised you're here right now. I would not have blamed you if you got on a plane to San Fran last night and never came back."

"Where did you sleep?" Rion asked, ignoring his apology.

"In my old bedroom. After Brian chewed my ass out for my behavior, then invited Emma in to continue the berating, my father told me to sleep it off at the

house." He turned to his partner. "I really am sorry. I feel like such an ass."

Rion sighed. "I know I'm about to sound like a complete hypocrite since I literally use CBD and THC as a coping mechanism for my ADHD and anxiety, but..." Rion paused, then said, "You can't be high around me. Ever. Especially coke. You just ... can't."

"I know," Nick said right away, touching his knee. "I know. I'm so sorry. And it will never happen again. I told you, I'm not an addict. It's not even something I do recreationally. Literally, the last time I used was when I was with Kierra all those years ago. You know this."

"Yes," Rion acknowledged. "I know this."

"So I just won't do it ever again," Nick said plainly. "I can't even imagine how triggering that was for you to see me like that, to act that way toward you. I never ever want you to compare me to your mother when she was at her lowest ever again."

Rion stared at him. "Okay."

Nick stared back, knowing Rion would need more than just his words. "Let's go away. It's time. Let's go back to London for a while. Or travel to a new place."

"Nick," Rion said with another sigh, "that's not going to solve anything right now."

"I know." Nick took his hand. "But we've both been working so hard, been under so much pressure, and with me in Long Island one day a week and working longer hours to catch up, we don't spend enough time together. I need to get away. And I need to get away with you. Gabby and Gael's wedding is in a few weeks, so we're already planning a trip to Puerto Rico. Maybe we could stay a few days longer and rent our own space in San Juan."

"Okay," Rion agreed. "But with everyone there, we won't get to spend much time together until after the wedding, you know."

"Yes, I do. But after the bullshit I just pulled, I think you need to have the comfort of your family around you. Especially your sisters."

Rion gave him a small smile. Nick began to apologize again, "Rion, I really am—"

"Let it go, Nick," Rion cut him off. "Let's just forget last night ever happened."

"Deal," Nick said and sighed. He slumped on the couch.

Rion adjusted him so that he could put his head on Nick's shoulder and pulled the covers over them both. "I spent the night with Kara," he said.

Nick froze, then said, "Are you leaving me for her now? Should I tell my brother?"

Rion smiled. "She's actually pretty cool and really interesting. She kept me company. Trying to keep my mind off of what happened. Kara took me to one exclusive club, then another, then another, listening to music, dancing, and drinking top shelf liquor for me, club soda for her. I crashed on the couch only about an hour ago."

"I'm sure I'll get to know her better, now that she is having my brother's baby," he said with a yawn. "Rion, seriously. I'm sorry."

Rion closed his eyes. He decided that he wasn't going to tell Nick about his panic attack or how bad that moment really was for him. It was over, and they could move on from it. And he knew Nick would never make the same mistake again.

"Let it go, Nicky," he told him again. "I never want to have to think about it again."

Nick kissed his head, then adjusted so that he was laying down, and Rion laid on top of him, his head on Nick's chest. Nick patted his back, and they fell asleep together.

A few hours later, the doorbell rang. It startled them both awake. It rang again, then they heard the key in the lock, and the door opened slightly.

"It's me, Boss," Zoey called out.

Nick and Rion rearranged themselves so that they were sitting on the couch side by side again. Zoey came in with two cups of coffee and a stack of newspapers under her arm. She smiled sweetly at them.

"So. Did you boys have a good night last night?" Zoey asked.

She placed the cupholder on the coffee table first, then picked up the remote to raise the blinds and let the afternoon sunshine in. Rion raised his hand to cover his eyes, squinting at the brightness.

"I know, Zoey. I screwed up," Nick said sheepishly. "But Rion and I are okay."

"Oh, well I'm glad the two of you are just fine." She threw the papers in Rion's lap. "Because the entertainment press and the tabloids are having a feast over the push heard 'round the world."

Rion's eyes went wide. Nick groaned. "Ooooh fuck."

"Oh fuck is right," said Zoey.

Rion grabbed the first paper, already opened to the entertainment section, which was a clear picture of him shoving Nick into the foosball table. The headline was aptly named, "The Push Heard 'Round the World." He silently handed it over to Nick as he looked at the next one. It was a close-up of Rion's frown as Nick waved his arms around aggressively in front of him with the headline "Deep Trouble in Deep Strokez Waters." The third one was another of the push but farther away: "Niion Lights Have Dimmed."

"Is there a video?" Nick asked quietly as he looked through the papers.

Zoey smiled. "Of course there is, Nicholas. You're Mr. Deep Strokez. At least three people in that room sold you out. Including Dipshit Todd. Yes, Dipshit Todd is trending on Twitter, Facebook, Snapchat, Reddit, Instagram, and TikTok because he actually gave an interview to TMZ last night, saying you were drunk and high off coke, and then Rion broke up with you because of it. He thought it would make him famous in a good way, but your fans hate him for that. Now he's just #DipshitTodd forever."

"Holy, holy shit," Rion said and sat back.

"So what do we do?" Nick asked.

"I already spun it for now. Couples fight and forgive each other, it's not the end of the world, no one was using drugs of any kind, and no one is broken up. The good news is that it's working in Madeline's favor. If she thinks the two of you are on the outs, she'll leave you alone for now. But if you want to save your reputation, then you need to do something about the rumors of a breakup. I have some ideas—"

"I don't give a shit about rumors and social media," said Rion.

Zoey turned to him. "But Nicholas needs to, Rion. Because, like it or not, Nicholas Highton is a brand.

Mr. Deep Strokez is a brand. You are a part of Nick's brand. And that brand is literally what's feeding all of his employees. Nick is about to launch a huge new media corporation and needs to stay positive in the eyes of the public in all areas of his life, including his relationship with you." She turned back to Nick. "You're back in it, Boss. Full time. So let me know when you're ready to hear my ideas. You've got forty-eight hours to respond before it gets out of control."

Zoey walked out of the apartment, leaving Rion and Nick to think.

After a long moment of silence, Nick turned to Rion, about to open his mouth, when Rion put his hand up. "Don't. Don't apologize again. Just talk to Zoey and tell me what we need to do to save your *brand*."

He stood up and went to the bathroom to shower.

Nick sighed, fearful that his faux pas was widening the distance between them.

It was one of Zoey's ideas, and it was a good one. They decided to acknowledge their public fight and forgive each other publicly too. It was viewed over five million times and trended for the next few weeks on all social media platforms. It was a play off a social media stunt that Kevin Hart and The Rock had done several times, talking to the camera and bumping into each other, then talking to each other while the live camera was still rolling. And it was brilliant.

Nicholas started with his phone, live on IG, lip syncing the first four lines of Tracy Chapman's "Baby

Can I Hold You," walking backward from the kitchen to the living room. Rion began his live IG listening to the song, then lip syncing the forgive me part, walking backward from the bedroom into the living room, until their backs collided at the chorus. Nick and Rion turned to each other in surprise, then smiled, hugged, and kissed. They each held their individual phones with one hand and wrapped their other hand around the other's waist, and danced and swayed, looking into each other's eyes until the song faded away.

They both used Zoey's line as their captions: "*Couples fight and forgive each other. It's not the end of the world and not the end of us. #NiionLitesForever🌈.*"

They also threw in a few more hashtags related to couples and the #DipshitTodd for good measure.

Rion and Nick were the first to arrive at La Casa de Agua Azul, the villa Nicholas rented for Gabby and Gael's wedding. The soon to be newlyweds were already in Puerto Rico, in Marueño visiting Gael's family before they rented a bus and drove into the hills of Rincón where the wedding would take place in ten days. The sixteen-bedroom mansion sat on top of a private hill at the edge of a cliff and had a mixture of modern and Spanish décor all throughout. It took Nick and Rion forever to tour through.

As they headed back down to the massive terrace surrounded by a glass half wall, Nick said, "The staff and wedding planner will arrive in three days, move out all these chairs, and create a wedding venue overlooking the water. The reception will take place downstairs in the open space from the patio to the pool. Their master bedroom is on the west side, and while your sisters and your mother will be there for now helping Gabby, everyone moves over to the east side of the villa to sleep for that one night, then we empty out by 1 p.m. the latest on Saturday. The house is theirs for the next month. I already rented a place in San Juan for us so we can stay for a week more, then we head home."

Rion looked out at the blue sea. "It's perfect. Gabby is going to love every bit of it. I'm still surprised Gael let us pay for any of it."

"He didn't, not without a fight," Nick said, shaking his head. "The only thing we're paying for is the villa. And that was Emma convincing him again it was tradition, and me telling him that it's a wedding gift from you and I, reminding him that you promised to bring Gabby to Puerto Rico to meet her family here."

"Yeah. Fox is coming to the wedding and bringing her father's two older sons, his younger brothers, and older sister, and probably a few cousins. He'll have a full entourage of 781 members with him. Gabby said he's going to be in San Juan on some business, and at some point, he's taking her and Gael to meet Gabriel's aunt who still lives on the island. If they ever decide to leave their honeymoon villa, that is."

Nick chuckled. He stood next to Rion and looked at the water with him. "We never talked about it, you know."

"Talked about what?"

"Marriage. Kids. The future. We've just been winging it these last few years."

"Well, it doesn't matter now since we can't get married," Rion started bitterly.

"Do you want to get married, Rion?" Nick asked, turning to him.

Rion turned to him too. "Are you proposing, Nicholas?" he asked with a sly smile.

Nick stared at him. "This isn't about my mother or her threats. I'd get down on one knee right now if I knew for sure you wouldn't freak out if I asked. Marriage is ... anchoring. And you don't want to be anchored. You need your space."

Rion looked away and turned back to the water. "Do you know that I don't know any married couples? I've never seen it in real life, what a successful marriage looks like. I've seen drug addicts stay together forever, trauma bonds between gang members, couples that cycle breaking up and getting back together for decades. But actual marriage?" Rion scoffed. "And I don't think you have either, Nicky. Your parents are roommates. Brian's marriage was a business deal, and he has several other people in his life other than his wife, and Emma is—"

Rion stopped cold, remembering that Nick had no idea about her and Seppani, who would be accompanying her on the trip to the wedding.

"Emma's marriage was practically arranged," Nick finished for him.

Rion sighed. "Yeah. That."

"So you don't want to get married someday," Nick said plainly.

"I didn't say that," Rion said, turning back to Nick. "I just don't know what that would look like with us. And I also don't think it will define our relationship whether we do or don't. Madeline thinks it will. That's why she made that stipulation; maybe she thought I would be craving that type of stability in my life because of my childhood, but I don't. I'm happy and satisfied being committed to you just like this."

"Well, actually..." Nick gave Rion a sheepish grin. "Before we even got to dinner, she pissed me off by calling you my project, so I threw it in her face that I was going to marry you. I'm sure that's why she put that stipulation there." Rion chuckled. "Also, it wasn't about you. She knows it's the type of stability that I crave because of my childhood. Someone by my side to love me for life."

Rion put his thumb on Nick's cheek and rubbed it. "I love you for life, Nicholas. If you got down on one knee, I wouldn't freak out. I already am anchored to you."

Nick slowly bent down on one knee, keeping eye contact. Rion raised one eyebrow. Nick reached both hands up and began to unbuckle Rion's belt. Rion laughed out loud. Nick chuckled too as he continued to drop Rion's jeans down to his ankles, taking his briefs down too. He silently took Rion into his mouth, moving back and forth with his hands on Rion's waist. Rion placed one hand on the glass and the other on the back of Nick's neck, guiding him. He closed his eyes and let the sound of the ocean hitting the rocks and Nick's warm mouth take him to ecstasy. Nick took his time, and Rion held out for a long time, both completely comfortable and satisfied in their positions.

Eventually, Rion came with a grunt, and his body froze while Nick kept going, sliding his mouth in and out, swallowing every spurt. "Nicky," Rion moaned out as his orgasm released its grip on him.

Nick unlaced Rion's sneakers and took his socks and jeans all the way off. He stood up and lifted Rion up by his bare bottom. Rion held on, and Nick carried him to the closest blue lounge couch. He gave Rion a chaste kiss and said softly, "Don't move."

Nick went toward the front of the home to grab the lube from his suitcase while Rion stripped the rest of his clothes off and laid there with his eyes closed. He felt Nick hover over him, kissing him from his lips down to his navel, then to his pucker. After a few soft internal licks, Nick replaced his tongue with lube-soaked fingers and moistened his insides. Rion lifted his legs and waited patiently for Nick to enter him, then wrapped them around Nick's hips. They kissed and made love as Rion moaned Nick's name softly and repeatedly. Nick cried out when he came inside of Rion, grabbing onto his skin tightly, collapsing against him. Rion could still feel the pulsing of Nick's cock inside of him and didn't move his legs or arms from around his lover, holding on to the moment as long as he could.

Nick put his face in Rion's neck and kissed him, then whispered in his ear, "Will you marry me, Ree Matthews?"

Rion smiled with his eyes still closed. "Yes," he whispered back into the air.

Nicholas sighed and closed his eyes too.

Bones walked over to Rion and stood beside him, wearing a black suit and black shades, although it was already evening. Rion smiled at the gang's head enforcer, then went back to looking at his sister dancing with her husband, the happiest she had ever been. "I like your boyfriend," Bones said to Rion.

Rion smirked. "I like him too."

"I can't believe I missed it. I should have recognized him that night," he said. "I watched that sex tape so many times. Kierra got buns."

Rion laughed, remembering the night they met and Nick growling at Bones to get his fucking hands off him. "You wouldn't have known it even if he was in a suit, Bones. You weren't looking at the guy in that video at all."

"True, dat." Bones nodded, making Rion laugh again. "Nah, for real, Ree. I'm glad that you're good. That you're happy. That you didn't become like us. I would like to think that me encouraging you to stay in school had a lot to do with that."

Rion reached over and gave Bones a full on hug as a response. Bones hugged him back, then quickly let go. "Thugs don't hug," he said smugly. That made Rion laugh again.

They quietly watched Gabby and Gael dance their first dance together as a couple. "So you know Junior's your father now, huh?" Bones said.

Rion's smile froze on his face. He especially did not want to talk about that. "Yup." He took a gulp of his wine.

"He's a fuck up, a thief, and a bitch," Bones said viscerally. "I let him stay in my safe house once, and he stole $5000 from me and $10,000 worth of product. If I ever see him again, I'm gonna tie him up, cut his fingers off, then burn him alive." He turned to Rion and asked, "You alright with that, *mijo*?"

Rion stood there with his mouth slightly open, not knowing how to respond. He didn't know DJ, the one they all called Junior, his father. Junior didn't want to know him. And everyone kept saying what a bad person he was. So he shouldn't care at all.

But do I want him dead? Rion pondered.

Bones turned away. "Sorry. I shouldn't have put that on you. Forget I said anything." He smiled at Rion. "Enjoy the rest of the night, Lil Ree."

Rion watched him walk away, his mouth still agape.

Nick came from behind him and wrapped his arms around his body. "What was that about?"

Rion shook his head. "Nothing." The crowd clapped for the couple as they ended the dance. The music changed to Bachata, and others filtered onto the dance floor. "Come, I need a moment away," said Rion. "Let's go back upstairs to the balcony."

But when they got there, Kaleb, his nephew Reese, Maurese, and Frank were already there, drinking and talking. Nick and Rion joined them on the couch with Rion leaning against Nick. Reese kept trying to get them to give him alcohol—"I'm almost eighteen! And the legal drinking age is eighteen in Puerto Rico. It's not like I haven't had beer before!"—but Maurese, his grandfather, said no. So he was settled with his Pepsi, without rum or whisky.

"The wedding was perfect," said Nick, sipping his cognac.

"It was a beautiful wedding," Kaleb agreed. "Kind of have me in my feels, ya know? Thinking about the future."

"A future with Ava?" Nick said with his eyebrows raised.

Kaleb nodded. "Yeah, man. A future with Ava." He looked at Rion. "You're one of my best mates, yeah. Like a brother to me. And you're the closest thing she has to a father. So if I'm going to do this, it has to be right, innit?"

They all watched as Kaleb dug into his suit pants pocket and took out a small ring box. "Holy, holy shit," Reese said with a grin.

Nick was also grinning. "You brought that with you all the way from England just to get permission from her family?" he teased.

But Kaleb was serious. He placed it on the little table between the drinks and said, "I want you to know that I love her, Rion, and I want to make her my wife. I'll do anything to make her happy. We'll still go slow, long engagement and all, wait a little bit until she's ready to have children, but I need your blessing first. As her brother, the most important man in her life before me, and as my friend. And if you say yes, I'll ask her tonight."

Everyone was quietly watching Rion. He sat up from leaning against Nick and picked up the box to open it. Inside was a white gold ring with a triangle-shaped diamond. Or A-shaped.

Rion closed the box and stood up. He walked over to Kaleb, who also stood up. Rion handed Kaleb back the ring. "Ava's greatest fear is abandonment. If you can promise me that you'll never abandon her, no matter what, then yes, you have my blessing."

Kaleb held Rion's hand with the box between them. "I've already promised her that same thing, mate. It's nothing to make that same promise to you. Of course. I'll never leave her. That loyalty and friendship we have sustains us. The love solidifies us. We're forever too, just like you and Nicholas."

Rion nodded. "I can't wait for you to become my brother, Kaleb." He pulled Kaleb in for a hug.

As they sat down, Kaleb wiped his eyes. Reese teased, "Dude, are you crying?"

The others chuckled as Kaleb grinned at him with glistening eyes. When it became quiet again, Frank cleared his throat and said, "Well, since we're asking for blessings..."

Rion, Maurese, and Reese all looked at Frank sharply. Nick laughed loudly. "Holy, holy shit!" he said and continued to sip his glass with an amused look on his face.

But Frank was not deterred. He looked around and said, "The three most important men in Muriel's life are right here in this room. Seems like the best time to let you know my intentions."

"Dude, it's been two months," Rion said with his eyes narrowed. "And you're still on the job."

"I know," said Frank. "I don't have a ring in my pocket like Romeo over here." He gestured toward Kaleb. "But I do know that she's my forever too. I've been drawn to her from day one. I've never met a woman like her before. Besides the fact that she is stunning, she's smart as a whip, and so insightful, and she sees right through my bullshit like no one in my life has ever done before. She's so tough, but underneath all that toughness is a girl with a big heart who is ready for love on a deeper level. And I'm so ready to give that to her.

"And her kids are great." He looked at Reese. "I enjoy hanging out with you, and being there for you when you need me. You may not want a father, but you got a father figure if you need one. And Jeff and

Kate are just a joy to be around. She's done a great job raising all three of you."

He turned to Maurese. "We don't know each other that well. But I will love and protect your daughter with my life for the rest of my life."

Frank looked at Rion last. "I know we didn't get off on the best foot, but I think you know by now the kind of man I am, my character, my integrity. And I hope that you also see that I would do anything for that woman. Anything." He looked around and said, "So no, not today. Not tomorrow. Not this month. Not even this year. But I will ask that amazing woman to marry me. And I would like the three of you to give me your blessing to do so."

Reese said first, "It's cool, man. I don't mind you being around. You make my mom happy, so it's cool with me." He raised his hand, and they slapped palms.

Maurese smiled at Frank. "I want nothing but her happiness. Her mother and I put her through so much. All of Ros's children are the same way: tough on the outside, loving on the inside. They had to be; they've been through so much at such a young age, Muriel especially, being the oldest. They get that from their mother, that toughness, that thick skin. But underneath it all, they just want to be loved and accepted without judgment. It was how I fell in love with Roslyn over thirty years ago. Besides the fact that she's stunning, that brown wavy hair, those big brown doe-like eyes, that smile she does when she's happy... I was also attracted to that grit, that no-bullshit attitude she showed right from the start. First day of ninth grade, Fox said something to her about the freckles on her nose being dirt, and she kicked him right in the balls.

I think I fell in love with her right then and there. So I know what you mean when you say you've been drawn to her from day one. I know what that feels like."

He reached his hand out. "Promise me that you'll always love her the way she deserves to be loved, and you'll have my blessing."

"Always," Frank said and shook Maurese's hand.

"And fight for her, fight for the relationship, no matter what. Because my daughter is a runner," he said with a smile.

Frank laughed. "Really? I haven't seen it yet. She seems all in right now."

"Pfft," Maurese scoffed. "Just wait. She'll run at some point. She's afraid of being hurt, so if the opportunity presents itself, she'll run. She also gets that from Roslyn. You'll be chasing her, a lot. So get your running shoes on. And check in with Nick on how to deal with it because I know he knows. Rel and Ree are the runners in the family."

Nick giggled in his drink while Rion's mouth dropped. "Hey!"

"C'mon, Ree," Maurese chided. "You know you've been a runner your whole life, especially when it comes to relationships."

"I'm literally in a long-term relationship!" he implored. "I haven't run from Nick."

Nick scoffed, then caught himself. Rion turned all the way around to face him. Nick smiled. "C'mon, Ree," Nick said, mimicking Maurese. "You tried to push me away three days in, then tried to push me away the first time I left London when I came back for you."

"That wasn't running," Rion said. "That was ... not knowing where this was going."

"Then you ghosted me. For five months."

"That was... That was... Okay, I ran then," he admitted. "But I came to you! I got on a fucking plane and came to New York for you. That's the opposite of running."

Everyone snickered. Nick continued, "Then you tried to move out."

"Nooo," Rion said, shaking his head. "I just wanted to know what you would say if I suggested it."

"And if I responded in any other manner than casually, you would have moved out, and we wouldn't be living together. We might not even be together now."

"I..." Rion was at a loss for words.

"Then when Ava went missing, you tried to leave me behind—"

"That was about Ava!" Rion cried. "I had to go find Ava."

"And you told me that you weren't coming back even after you found her," Nick reminded him. "That you were going to send for your stuff. I had to follow you to San Francisco and Fresno to make sure you did come back to me."

"Alright, I'm a fucking runner!" Rion yelled, throwing up his hands, making everyone laugh. "I run when I get scared or confused or... I don't know. I'm an anxious-avoidant adult with diagnosed anxiety. I push people away if they get too close. But we've been together for over three years now, including that five-month break we took." Nick smiled at him. "I'm just saying. I'm not running anymore, Nick. I'm not."

Nick kissed Rion's lips softly, then said to Frank. "So by year three, there'll be no more running. Just hang in there." He winked at Frank, making the others laugh.

"Ugh." Rion rolled his eyes, feigning annoyance. But he leaned back against Nick's chest again. Nick slid his arm around his waist to hold onto Rion's belly.

Maurese smiled at them. "The other thing they got from Roslyn is that they know how to build solid, complementary connections. It seems like opposites attract, but really these relationships balance each other out. Gabby and Gael: older and younger. She married a replica of her father—an older, deeply religious, loyal, highly respected Hispanic man—and doesn't even realize it. And he will take care of her like no other person can. Ava and Kaleb: American and British. Ava needed a complete change and being with Kaleb, showing her the European way, has helped her grow. Nick and Rion: upper class and working class. Despite the extreme wage gap between them and the difference in upbringing, they bonded on their similarities, showing the other love, support, and protection. Muriel and Frank: fire and water. Frank is cooling that fire down in her little by little, giving her a safe space to be softer and more emotional. And it looks like she's bringing some spice into his life. Roslyn and me: Black and white. I never thought I would end up with a white girl, especially after Junior showed up with his white mother and almost destroyed my family. I had so many prejudices. But I looked past her skin color and fell in love with who she was deep inside. And she did the same with me.

"Roslyn's children gravitate toward those who truly care about them and nurture the good qualities in them. So they cling to their partners because they know the connection is real between them. Even the two that are runners." Maurese winked at Rion, making Nick giggle and Rion groan again.

"I heard my name," they heard. Everyone turned to see Roslyn coming toward them. Rion was the first one to turn away.

She slid her arms around Maurese's neck and said, "What are you all talking about?"

Nick caressed Rion's stomach as he casually drank, not looking at his mother. He had been avoiding her since she arrived days ago. Every time she attempted to talk to him, he would simply say, "No, Roslyn," and walk away from her. By day two, she stopped trying. But they all noticed, and it was getting awkward every time they were in a room together.

"Just having a friendly conversation about relationships and connections," Maurese said as he reached out and caressed her hand gently.

"Gabby is looking for you," Roslyn said to him. "She wants a daddy-daughter dance with you and Fox, as tribute to her father Gabriel."

"Well, I can't disappoint the bride," he said as he rose.

He began to walk out, but Roslyn paused and looked at Rion, who was staring off into the darkness of the ocean. Nick glanced at her and shook his head once. She ignored him.

"Rion—"

"No, Roslyn," he said automatically, almost in a bored manner.

"Rion, please. Can we just—"

"No, Roslyn."

"Rion—"

"No—"

Maurese interjected, tired of their fight. "Rion, at some point you are going to have to hear her out and forgive her. She's your mother. And she did what she needed to do to protect you."

Rion slowly turned his head to stare at Maurese. "I don't have to do a goddamn thing."

Maurese came closer. "Yes. You do. There's a lot you don't know about my brother. And—"

"Hey, Maurese?" Rion said calmly. "I'm not talking about this with you either."

"But you are *talking* to me," Maurese countered. "You didn't shut me out, and I also kept this secret from you for years. That's not fair."

Rion put down his drink and sat up straighter, getting frustrated with Maurese. "No. What you did was remain loyal to Roslyn and keep *her* secret. I know that if you knew twenty-eight years ago, you would have told me. And you and I would have had a closer relationship because you're actually my family. And I wouldn't have gone through life feeling like you were just being nice to me because I'm Roslyn's son, not because you're my uncle. And I would have learned about my lineage and roots from your side, which was all I ever wanted. And at some point, I would have found out for myself the kind of man Junior is and made my own decision about whether I needed to stay away from him or not. But I never had any of those opportunities. Instead, it accidentally comes out during a crisis, and I have to deal with the knowledge that my oldest sister is actually my fucking cousin, like we're part of some white trash, hillbilly sitcom. Roslyn's amends to you was to tell you the truth. She doesn't get to claim amends to me when it comes out that way."

"I will tell you everything," his mother said. "Even the things that I haven't told Maurese. There's so much you don't know, and if you could just—"

"No, Roslyn!" Rion exploded. "Just... Fucking... No!" Nick patted his back in an attempt to calm him down, but it didn't work. "You're a disgusting whore and the worst fucking mother on the face of the planet, and I don't want to have anything to do with you ever again. Fuck off."

It was quiet as Roslyn's eyes pricked with tears. She let them fall and said, "You know what, baby boy? You're right. I did a lot of disgusting things when I was a whore and a drug addict. And I was the worst mother for a very long time. But I'm neither of those things anymore. And I'm sick to death of trying to prove to you who I am now." She turned around and left the patio.

"Wait, Mimi," Reese called out and ran after his grandmother.

Maurese glared at him. "That was nasty and completely unnecessary, Rion. You'll regret those words one day."

Rion leaned back onto Nick and said, "Thanks for your fatherly advice, Maurese." Maurese shook his head and left them.

"Damn, mate," Kaleb said softly. Rion glared at him, daring him to say anything else. Kaleb took the hint and raised both his hands in surrender. He stood up and walked away too.

Frank, who had quietly watched the exchange, cleared his throat. "I know it's none of my business—"

"Then stay the fuck out of it," Rion snapped.

"But," Frank continued, "I understand you being upset right now, but don't slam the door on her face too hard. It may get stuck when you try to open it again." Frank stood up. "I'm going to go dance with my future wife."

As Frank started to walk away, Rion said, "Hey, Francis?" Frank turned back. "You have my blessing."

Frank smiled at him. "Thank you." He also left them on the patio.

Rion sighed, annoyed with everyone except Nick, who began to gently run his hands through the back of his hair. After a long moment of silence, Nick spoke. "White trash hillbilly sitcom, huh?"

"We are white trash," Rion mumbled. "I told you when we met that I'm white trash. My mother slept with two brothers at the same time. My sister is my first cousin. Can't get any more white trash than that."

"Except," Nick said softly, "Junior's half black. You can't be white trash because you're not completely white."

It took Rion a moment, then he busted out laughing. "Oh shit. I'm not completely white."

Nick laughed with him and pulled him closer, and Rion was grateful for his comic relief. When the laughter died down, Rion said, "Thanks for not scolding me. Or advising me. Or being disappointed in me."

Nick shrugged. "I know how it feels to be disappointed by your own mother, to not want anything to do with her, so no, you're not going to get that from me." Rion nodded. "But I agree with Frank. My mother doesn't do apologies or amends. She doubles down on her malicious behaviors, as you can see. So, you know ... don't shut that door too hard. Because I know you, Ree. At some point, you're going to want some answers about who you are. And she's the best person to gather that information from. Sometime in the future, you are going to want to open up that door."

Rion sighed again.

When Nick came into the beach house that September morning, his father was putting together a colorful Lego set of New York City. "I've been working on this all night, son. Come join me," he said excitedly.

Nick grinned and sat at the table with his father. "All night? What did Mother do while you played with toys?"

Niles shrugged. "She actually left a week ago. Back to Rochester, probably to her lover."

Nick looked surprised. "Her lover?"

Niles made a small noise in his throat. "Oh, you didn't think that I was the only one with other partners did you?"

"I guess I didn't think about that," Nick said. He started putting two Lego pieces together.

Niles shrugged. "Maybe I'm wrong. She said she needed to begin preparations for the masquerade ball. But I think she just didn't want to be in such a small space with me anymore."

Nick chuckled. "The beach house is almost five thousand square feet."

"Yes, well, the estate is twenty thousand square feet. We've gone full weeks without seeing each other while staying in the same home."

"That's frightening," Nick said with his eyebrows furrowed. "I never want to live like that."

"Hmmm... You'll change your mind after a few years. You'll want your space, even from your partner. Or he'll want space from you."

Nick shook his head. "I don't think so, Father. Our apartment now is about fourteen hundred square feet, and we're always on top of each other, literally and figuratively. Even the house in London, which has three levels; if we were in the house together, we were on the same floor, if not in the same room, unless we were working. I can't see myself ever stepping out on him or him taking another lover, even decades later. Our relationship went through a bit of a rough patch mostly because we hadn't been connecting the way we always had, but we're still very much committed to each other."

"Ah yes, the push heard 'round the world," his father commented, pushing up his reading glasses as he looked at the picture of the Empire State Building again and the two pieces in his hand. "I've heard about that. We never got a chance to talk about it. You left a week after that and just returned to New York, three weeks later."

"Yes, well," Nick quipped, sounding like his father, "I needed to prioritize Rion after all that went down. I was an ass to him. I made an ass of myself, really."

Niles chuckled. “Well, we’ve all done it, Nicholas. I once dated that young supermodel, Megan Wilkins. NutMeg, they called her. After being with her a few months, I understood her nickname. She was a bit nutty. And all we did was drink, smoke, and snort life away.”

Nick snorted as he clicked the Brooklyn Bridge together. “NutMeg is not a young supermodel. She’s older than Brian.”

“Ah, but she was twenty-four when I was fifty-six. I tried to keep up with her for about two years before I had to let her go. But not before I woke up naked and hungover in two feet of water in a Vegas pool and $500,000 stolen from me.”

“Holy shit!” Nick exclaimed, and then laughed heartily.

Niles laughed too. “Yes. That was my final coke binge. And the last model. It made me miss Victoria even more, but by then, she was gone. So I continued to indulge but a little closer to my age.”

Nick looked at his father, thinking about what Rion said about not witnessing any successful marriages. “Was your marriage ever sacred to you?” he asked. “Did you ever actually love Mother?”

Niles sighed deeply. “I loved her once, yes. But that quickly changed after we had you and Victoria left me for it.”

Nick didn’t know how to feel about that. “Well... I’m sorry my birth caused you to no longer love your wife and lose the best thing that you ever had.”

Niles looked at him sharply. “That’s not what I meant, son.”

“Well, that’s what I heard.”

"Nicholas." Niles turned his chair around completely to face him. "Why do you still treat me as if I have done some permanent damage to your life? I have no regrets about having you. And all I've done since your birth was lay the world at your feet so you would never have to want for anything."

"And yet, all I did was want," Nick said back, not looking at him.

"And you want me to apologize for that? Is that it? You want me to apologize for being in a loveless marriage and having a demanding career and falling in love with another woman, both of which took me away from my family from time to time? Because I won't. And if you ever were to have a wife and children, something you have blatantly rejected in your life, you would understand more."

"Need I remind you again of how you ruined that for me?" said Nick, turning away from his father's face.

"You know, Madeline was just trying to protect you," he heard his father say.

Nick scoffed. "Protect me. Huh."

"Yes," Niles said firmly. "Madeline's fear was that Beatrice would not fit into our society. And it would eventually cause problems between the two of you. If you would have told Madeline all you and Beatrice had talked about, how you were preparing her—"

"You gotta be kidding me," Nick said, annoyed again, this time not holding back his anger. "First, she didn't ask me. Neither did you. You both just assumed that I didn't know what I was bringing her into. And second, as if Mother would have listened or cared what I had to say. She already had her mind made up and was making moves toward pulling us apart after that first introduction. And I will never let that happen again. So that's why I kept my current relationship hidden for so long. And why I intend to still keep Rion away from the two of you."

"You have to understand," Niles pleaded. "Madeline has this vision of what she wants for her family, who she wants her children to be."

"And Trixie didn't fit into that vision," Nick finished for him. "I do understand, Father. I get it. That doesn't mean I have to accept it. Or accept what you did to her and her parents."

"Nicholas, must I remind you that they took the money?" Niles said, also getting angry. "They could have said 'No, our daughter's happiness comes before all else.' But they didn't do that, did they?"

"Father!" Nick yelled. "You destroyed their business. You took away their livelihood. Their only source of income. They had children and grandchildren to think of. And you made it impossible for them to say no. They had to take the ten million you offered them to survive."

Niles gave him a confused look. "Not ten. Sixty."

Nick double blinked. "*What*?"

"I offered ten. She said no. After the eviction lawsuit, they countered with sixty million. Ten for each of their children, including Beatrice. Nothing for them; they just wanted their business back."

"Holy, holy shit," Nick said in shock. "Beatrice asked for sixty million dollars?"

"No. Her parents did," Niles clarified. "And Madeline gave it to them. I don't think Beatrice knew the deal her parents made until it was too late. Whether she wanted to or not, she had to let you go."

Nick sat back thoughtfully. He remembered that Spring Break of his junior year when her parents said she needed to come home instead of going on vacation with him. Then she simply never came back to Harvard. He called and texted, then finally went out to Melstone, Montana to see her. Trixie was already crying and saying that it was over between them. That there was no going back. She forced him to leave the property and made him promise never to return. He found out from Emma the original paperwork said ten million into an account for Beatrice Conwell. Nick was devastated for months. He thought that was all it was. But it made sense that there would be other accounts with other names that he had no idea of, names of all her siblings. Beatrice had to choose between her relationship and her entire family's opportunity to live comfortably. She chose her family.

"I didn't know the deal Madeline made until the paperwork came across my desk," said Niles. "It was already agreed upon, so I signed it."

"You're not innocent here, Father," Nick said, his anger coming out again. "Mother might have orchestrated the whole thing, but it was your shell company that bought the building that housed their market. And your lawyers that sued the Conwells when they couldn't afford the rent anymore. And your influence in the state of Montana that took away their federal agricultural contracts. You approached her with a bribe first, and you signed off on everything Mother did, including that money in the end."

"I did," his father admitted. "I was following Madeline's lead and thought she knew what was best for you. She kept saying, 'You don't know anything about your son. You don't know Nicholas. I do. I know what he needs. You will have to trust me on this.'"

"Well, she didn't know me either. Because all it did was make me hate the both of you and pushed me further away from you."

"I know this now, son." He patted Nick's hand. "I should have discussed it with you personally. I am sorry about that, Nicholas. And I am deeply sorry for the hurt and pain we caused you by tearing you and Beatrice apart. The hurt that I caused. Please, forgive me."

Nick stared at his father. He nodded. "Thank you for acknowledging how devastating it was to me to lose Trixie in that way. And yes, it's forgiven. Especially since you are right. It has all worked out in the end. She's happy, married with three children, one more on the way. And I'm happy with Rion. He is my forever."

"It's all I ever want for you, Nicholas," said Niles. "I only want your happiness. And if Rion makes you happy, then be happy with him. I heard what you said at a previous visit. I will not make any demands on you, not even for a Highton heir. It's your life. It's your career. And it's your money. Whether you decide to get married or not, have children or not, it will be your choice. I'll make sure of that. Because I know you better now. Better than your mother ever did."

"I appreciate that, Father," Nick said sincerely. "Thank you for listening to me."

"So you don't have to keep him from me any longer."

"I'm not," Nick lied. "He really was in San Francisco with his family."

"I believe you. And I saw the plane tickets with a return flight for the 28th of June." Niles smiled and

Nick laughed, shaking his head at his father's snooping. "Not first class though. I would have thought he would be relishing flying first class because of all the times you were using your private plane, something you rarely did until you were with him."

"That's because you have no idea who Rion Matthews is," Nick said plainly. "Zoey set up the private plane without me asking, to keep us from getting hounded everywhere we went. Rion made it very clear from the beginning that he doesn't want a cent of my money, of Highton money. He bought his own plane tickets, and he pays his own way every chance he gets. He will never profit off the Highton name, not even to get him first class tickets or into the best places. He doesn't want that. He just wants me."

Niles nodded. "Very admirable. Maybe he is the one."

Nick couldn't help the smile on his face. "I know he's the one, Father. And soon, you will see it too."

Rion stared at the blank Word document. A story began to take shape in his head... *Two men working the same midnight shift cleaning high-rise office buildings...* He sighed, having no idea where to take it.

It was quiet in the apartment. Nick was in Long Island again with his father, and he decided not to go into the office today. Everyone needed something from him while he was there, and it was exhausting. Rion closed his eyes and took a deep breath, exhaled slowly, then opened them. He stared at the page

again, then decided to shift gears. A new story wasn't working. He opened up his documents to a folder that just said "Stories" and clicked on one.

He began to read:

> Eric closed John's door and came back over to the bed. He lifted up John's chin and gave him a gentle kiss. John flipped the covers so that Eric could get in them. Without breaking their lips apart, Eric crawled onto the bed and got on top of John. They kissed and grinded their erections together, then John flipped him over. He kissed along Eric's torso, moving downward and taking Eric's sweatpants off with him. He proceeded to put Eric's cock in his mouth and suck...

Rion wasn't feeling it. It felt too forced. He tried to rearrange the paragraph, then ended up scrapping it and leaving it the same. He leaned his head back and closed his eyes. It was too quiet. But the office was too noisy. New York in general was too noisy. He longed for Hyde Park or San Francisco or the forests of Thailand. He longed for Nick by his side again, just the two of them. Waves of panic began to fill his chest. He immediately put on his favorite guided meditation before it turned into a full-blown attack again. He listened to a calm man's voice telling him that he was in control of his emotions, guiding his breathing for two full minutes. Afterward, he sat there with his eyes still closed, pretending he was sitting on the back patio in his house in London with the high hedges hiding the beautiful garden.

His Teams video rang on his computer. He opened his eyes and saw it was a call from Nguyen. He pressed the intercom, and the IT manager's face popped up. "Hey, Nguyen."

"Rion. I know you wanted a day off, but you better get down here, Boss," he said quietly. "Marcel and Dion are about to go at it."

Rion sighed. "What happened?" He could hear yelling behind him.

"You know D. He's big and playful. And Marcel is ... Marcel. He's not with the shits. Nick was always the buffer between them but you know... Hump."

"Yeah. I know." Rion sighed again. "I'll be right there."

He shut down the Teams call, and the document on his computer was still there. He stared at the words on the screen.

> He proceeded to put Eric's cock in his mouth and suck...

Rion stood up, leaving his laptop on the desk and left his apartment to hail a cab.

After a short early morning flight, Nick took the car service to downtown Rochester and entered Highton Plaza. It was already bustling, the strip mall of luxury brands, Gucci to Balenciaga to Dior and a fancy South American coffee shop in between them all. He crossed the open fountains and let himself in through the glass doors of the only high-rise there, the name "Highton" shining in silver on top. As soon as he stepped in, a woman in a black pencil skirt, pink blouse, and hair in a tight bun at the top of her head came running over in her heels and a tablet in her hand.

"Good morning, Mr. Highton. I am Lita Cunningham, your personal assistant when you are on the premises. You are twenty-three minutes early for the operations meeting. I am to take you to your office and introduce you to the protocols. Would you like a beverage while you wait? Coffee, tea, a mimosa, tequila sunrise? A newspaper perhaps? A secure laptop to work?"

He smiled at the young lady eager to serve him. "Take a breath, Lita. I promise I won't be any trouble.

I didn't even know I had an office here; I just came for the meeting. Coffee: one cream, three sugars. And can you point me to Emma's office? Believe it or not, I've never been."

Lita shut her mouth and bit her lip before she opened it again to speak. "Mrs. Highton is not to be disturbed before 9 a.m. I am very sorry."

"Even for her own brother? Surely—"

"I am very sorry," she said, cutting him off. "I am so very sorry, but there are limits to even what I can do. No one is allowed on the thirty-first floor before 9 a.m." She gestured toward the elevator and swiped a card. "I will take you to your office on the thirtieth floor and then grab your coffee."

As they entered the elevator, she typed on her tablet asking, "Any Danish, scones, or bagels, sir?" She pressed the button for 30, then swiped her key-card at an empty space. The elevator began to move.

"No, thank you, Lita." He looked at the elevator and noticed that there wasn't even a thirty-first floor. "Does this not go all the way up?"

"Mrs. Highton has her own private elevator that starts at her personal garage and only opens on the first, thirtieth, and thirty-first floor."

"Huh. Interesting..." Nick muttered more to himself.

When the door opened, he saw a wall of windows overlooking the Genesee River and a small conference table that sat no more than ten people. Two men were already there in conversation. They looked up at him and the one with the sandy colored hair gave a bright smile. The other with dark brown hair did not.

"This way, please," Lita said, getting his attention. She gestured toward the right. He followed the woman to a row of wooden doors. She swiped the card again on the door at the end of the hall and it clicked open.

"Wow," he exclaimed softly.

There was a large desk in the center of the room with a high-back executive chair. On the right side was a bar fully stocked, and on the left side was a living room area with two couches and a TV. He touched his chair and noticed an open door. He went toward it and peeked inside. It was a full bathroom with a walk-in closet. The most interesting part was that there were clothes, jewelry, and accessories already there.

"Whoa," he said, touching the Italian suits.

"The Senior Mr. Highton made sure that your specific measurements were given so that your office would be ready for you."

He looked at Lita in surprise. "You could basically move into here," he joked.

"Yes, you can," she confirmed. "Mrs. Highton would spend many nights in her office before moving upstairs the first week of June."

"Oh, this was Emma's office. Interesting..."

Lita walked over to his desk and pressed a button. The wall next to the bar began to move, and Nick watched a queen size bed fold down. He went to sit on it, and it had an Egyptian cotton pillow top.

He started chuckling. "Okay, then." He went back to the desk and touched the shiny mahogany.

Lita opened up the desk and pulled out a watch-looking item, all black. She walked over to him and placed it on his arm. "This is your key fob. Just place it on any door or elevator, and it will open for you, except the other offices on this floor. It does open Mrs. Highton's private elevator, so you have access to her private garage and the thirty-first floor. She requested that you may want to use it from time to time."

He looked at her. "Take me to the thirty-first floor please, Lita."

Lita froze again. "I'm sorry. I cannot—"

"Listen," Nick said standing up. "You won't get in trouble. Just point me to the private elevator, and I'll let myself up."

"You can't guarantee that," she said with wide eyes and a bit of fear.

"I can," he said gently and touched her shoulder. "Let's go." He walked out of his office, and Lita had no choice but to follow.

As they walked past other offices, he asked. "Who do these belong to?"

She pointed to the far left. "Mr. Dorado's office is there. The two in the middle belong to Arlow Highton and Angus Highton. The one next to you is unoccupied for now."

"Brian's sons? They're only seventeen," he said in disbelief. "They already have offices?"

"Yes, and they have visited the offices a few times with the Senior Mr. Highton in the last year. They were very excited to know they have their very own space here."

"Huh. That is ... something."

She walked him through a narrow hall, and it opened to a mirrored space with only one elevator. She looked at him expectantly. "I cannot swipe my card before 9 a.m. It is an automatic termination."

"Wow," he said with a chuckle. "Emma is a hard-ass, isn't she?"

Lita's eyes went wide again. "Mrs. Highton is the most amazing human to walk these halls. Intelligent. Confident. A true and remarkable leader."

Nicholas laughed out loud. "She certainly has you all quivering." He pressed his watch to the circle, and it turned green. When the elevator arrived, he stepped in. Lita stood there. "You're really not coming with me?"

"No, sir," she said with a shake of her head. "I will be right here upon your return in..." she looked at her watch, "eleven minutes."

The door closed, and the elevator went up one floor. It opened into a large open space of windows with four connected wooden doors in front of him. He began to walk toward the doors when he heard a small cough. Nick turned around. There was a high desk with a mature brunette sitting behind it. She looked at him over her square glasses with a frown.

He smiled at her. "Good morning. I'm Nick Highton."

"I know who you are, Mr. Highton," she clipped.

He nodded. "Is Emma in?"

She stared at him.

"Tell her I'm here, please."

She continued to stare at him.

"Okay. I will tell her myself." He began walking to the door again.

"Mr. Highton," she called out sharply. He stopped and turned to her.

They stared at each other, a battle of wills. Eventually, she huffed out air, then pressed a button and spoke softly into her headset. Then she nodded.

She clicked a button and said, "You may enter, Mr. Highton."

He gave her a slight bow. "Thank you. And your name is?"

She stared at him.

Nick chuckled. "Wow." He walked to the door and pushed it open.

Emma was sitting behind her desk in a navy blue pantsuit and a tie to match with ivory white Louboutins. She smiled at her brother. He grinned back and was about to speak when he noticed Seppani sitting on the couch, looking beautiful in a spaghetti strap flowered dress.

"Hello, Seppani."

"Hello, Mr. Highton," she greeted with a soft smile.

"Just Nicholas," he said. "As I've told you for many years now."

She smiled politely back and rose from her seat. "Are you staying with us for dinner?"

"No, I have to get back home to Rion tonight."

"Of course you do." Seppani looked at Emma and gave her a soft smile. Emma smiled back. Then she walked out of the office without another word.

Once the doors closed, Nick sat down in front of Emma's desk with a thought that never occurred to him before.

"I'm so glad you're here, Nicholas," said Emma with a bright smile. "That you've officially joined the Highton team. The family legacy. How do you feel?"

"Are you fucking your housekeeper, Emma?"

She immediately frowned at him. "Must you be so crass?"

"I mean, I've always known how close the two of you are, like sisters. But maybe more like kissing cousins? Maybe I had it all wrong..."

Emma ignored his comment. "This meeting is very important, Nick. It's where I officially introduce you to the executive team. We discuss operations and projections for the next fiscal year. Highton Media is not included in this fiscal year because it was developed after the formal budget was approved. There are expectations of profit this year, and you will have to develop your financial portfolio with clear profit margins. Once we see those numbers, we'll bring your company officially into our projections. If you don't have a CPA to do that for you, let me know, and I can bring someone on your team from mine."

"I have a guy for that," he confirmed.

"Great. I trust your instincts and your people," she said with a nod. He smiled at her, grateful for her trust in him.

She looked at her watch and stood up. "Let's go. The meeting starts in five minutes." She walked him out the door, past her executive assistant, who held out her flask with the letters HOH on it. She grabbed it on her way toward the elevator. Once the doors closed on them, he turned to her again.

"You didn't answer my question," he said.

"What question is that?" she asked in confusion.

"Are you having an affair with your housekeeper?"

Emma turned away. "Stop calling her that," she said and took a sip of her coffee.

"Okay, I'm sorry. House Manager," he said, throwing the words in air quotes.

"Don't be an ass."

"Does Gary know? Are you doing her together?"

"Absolutely not!" Emma said, turning to him angrily.

Nick's eyes widened. "So you *are* doing it? Have her all to yourself, huh?"

"Shut up, *Nicky*."

He was unfazed. "All this time? It couldn't have been all this time. Robby is nineteen years old. There is no way you had an affair with your housekeeper for nineteen years and nobody knew about it."

She turned away as the doors opened. "I'm going to need you to be an adult and not a bratty little brother right now. Can you do that?"

"Of course," he said seriously.

Lita said good morning to Emma quietly, who ignored her, and handed Nick a ceramic cup of coffee with his name and company on it. He took a sip, and it was perfect. He nodded a thanks to her.

As they walked to the conference table, Nick whispered to his sister, "Just let me know if you need a stick of gum to cover the taste of pussy on your tongue."

She stopped in her tracks and glared at him. He gave her a closed mouth smile and walked over to a chair in the center of the table. She walked to the head of the table and sat down with her hands folded.

But an attendant tapped him and said, "Please, Mr. Highton, follow me."

Nick was confused, but he brought him to the other head of the table. Only when they were both seated did the other five men sit down. The two attendants and Lita moved to separate corners of the room and sat there. Another attendant sat down behind Emma at a smaller desk and waited. When Emma began to speak, he began to type.

"Thank you all for your prompt attendance. We're missing Beck Coons and Gary Dorado, but no voting will be taking place today, so we'll send them the transcript of the meeting. I'd like to formally introduce my brother, Nicholas Elliot Highton, to the team. He will be leading Highton Media and Publications as President and CEO. I am sure you all received the memo three months ago." They nodded in affirmation. "Nicholas, did you want to say a few words?"

Nick cleared his throat. "Thank you, Emma. I am happy to join this elite team of brilliant minds dedicated to our family's life's work."

He raised his cup in acknowledgment. Most of others did the same for him, but one did not; the same brunette he saw earlier just glared at him.

"Mr. Alderman, please introduce yourself to Nicholas," Emma said.

The oldest man at the table sat up straighter. "I'm Stuart Alderman. I handle international investment banking for the company, and I'm the CEO of my own company, Green Palms IBC. We're in thirty-four countries worldwide, mostly in Europe, Eastern Europe, and Southeast Asia. I worked closely with your father for over twenty years, and I am happy to see two of his children continuing his life's work and the work of his father and grandfather."

Nick smiled at him. "Do you speak any other languages, Stuart? Russian perhaps?"

His face contorted in confusion. "Um ... no."

"Then how are you conducting business in Eastern Europe and Asian countries? Like Russia?"

"Oh, I have a team for that," he said dismissively.

"Huh. That's ... interesting," Nick responded with a hint of sarcasm. Emma smirked.

Nick turned to the man next to him. "Oh, it's my turn," he said happily. It was the man who smiled at him earlier, who was still smiling at him. "Hello, Nicholas. I'm Phillip Weatherby. My family is into high-end real estate in select cities: here in New York, Los Angeles, Dubai, Tokyo, Sydney, London, and Paris. My father retired a year ago, so I'm new to the team. Like you."

Nick gave him a genuine smile back and nodded. He turned his attention to the man next to him, the one that didn't smile.

"Mick Marigold," he said curtly. "I'm the company attorney who took over for Emma when she stepped up as CEO. My firm handles all legal contracts and public relations for the Hightons. But you know that."

Nick looked at him curiously. "Cousin Mickey? *Mouse*?"

He did not like that at all. "It's Mick. No one calls me Mickey or Mouse anymore."

"God it's been, what? Ten years? You look so different."

"I grew up," he practically sneered.

"And got a nose job," Nick said. Emma snorted in laughter then composed herself. Mickey scowled at him.

Nick smiled and turned to the other side of the table. "And you are?"

"Hi, I'm Niklaus Rosseau. The original Nick at the table." He grinned and Nick grinned back. "I'm the founder and president of Gateway Vacations. We do all-inclusive resorts—adults-only and family vacations—throughout all of the Caribbean and Mexico, Colombia, Panama, and Brazil. And yes, *hablo español, Italiano, et Français*. And I'm learning Portuguese."

Nick smiled at him. "*Très bien.* It's a shame your name is Nick though. Can't have two Nicks at the table, so you're going to have to change your name now," he teased.

The man laughed. But Emma said, "Actually, he's right." Everyone turned to her. "What's your middle name, Niklaus?"

"Um... Raphael..."

"Okay. Moving forward, you will be known as Ralph," she decreed. He chuckled, but Emma's serious face did not change. So he stopped.

But Nick frowned. "Emma, it was a joke."

She looked at her brother. "There will only be one Nicholas recognized at this table. Does anyone have a problem with that?"

No one responded and averted Nick's—now known as Ralph's—eyes.

"Emma," Nick said sternly. "No."

"Excuse me?" Emma snapped, her eyes narrowed at Nick. Everyone was watching their exchange, heads moving back and forth across the long table.

"We're not doing that," he said, staring her down.

"We *do* what I say," she said seriously.

"We're *not* doing *that*," Nick said back just as seriously.

Emma was about to yell at her little brother but then changed gears. She put her long fingernails on the table, all ten of them and said, "You are the most important man at this table, Nicholas Highton. Don't you all agree?" she asked the rest of the team while still staring at her brother.

"Yeses" and "sures" were mumbled all around. Even the newly named Ralph nodded while looking at him. Nicholas immediately hated being there.

When Nick didn't respond, Emma said, "Hassan, you're last."

The tanned man cleared his throat. "I'm Hassan Asad. My division is ... less visible but no less important."

Emma raised her hand to stop the stenographer from note taking. "You can speak freely in front of my brother, Hassan."

He nodded. "My organization primarily manages trade on the black market. We broker the price of opioids for pharmaceutical companies, nicotine for cigarettes and cigar companies, and gun parts for gun manufacturers. We create space in less financially secure countries for our projects and goals and especially for real estate purposes. And we also play a bit of politics to ensure our stakeholders' goals are met and that everyone at this table is financially secured."

Nick sat up straighter and looked at Emma. "Is he for real?" he asked, pointing at Hassan.

"Of course," she said back. "We need people to protect our interests. And now your interests."

"And with every successful venture, this group gets a twelve percent kickback," Mick chimed in. "For our protection of their people and our discretion. It's win-win."

Nick looked around at all the faces. The only one that had a little bit of remorse was Philip, who cringed a little.

"Ask your questions now before we begin again," said Emma.

Everyone turned to him. Nick looked around one more time, then took a sip, wondering how many poor families were pushed out so that he could have Peruvian brewed coffee. It made his stomach churn.

"I got nothing."

Emma stared at him, then motioned with her hands to begin recording again. She explained that Beck Coons was the current CFO and Gary was the COO and that they didn't always attend these meetings, because they didn't need to. Nick nodded in understanding. Then Emma called each member of the executive team again, beginning the actual quarterly meeting. Nick sat and listened to them explain their operational plan and financial contribution to Highton Optimum Holdings for the next year. They asked each other questions and took notes but didn't pry much. Emma would look away bored if it was a project she was disinterested in and demand on the spot financial numbers if she was, berating them if it didn't match her high standards. Poor Phillip seemed to be the least prepared when Emma challenged him and embarrassed when she asked one of the attendants to put a tissue box in front of him in case he needed to cry. Nick turned to him and gave him a smile of sympathy, which Phillip appreciated. The only one that didn't discuss his current projects was Hassan, who paid attention to everyone else's. Nick watched him become very interested when the new Raphael talked about a contract to build a resort on an eco-friendly uninhabited island in the Philippines. Emma said nothing, which greatly disturbed Nick.

Then Mick informed the group that he took a meeting with the president of Porterhouse Casinos, who was interested in partnering with Highton Optimum. He wanted to bring it to a vote at the next meeting. Nick spoke for the first time since introductions.

"No."

They all turned to him. "Listen, I know you've had your issues with Todd Porter, but it's a good investment," said Mick. He turned back to their president. "Just meet with him, Emma. Let him tell you his plans. They're good ones. Picture a casino on an adults-only resort," he said to the old Nick. "Or next door to that property in Dubai, essentially paying for the taxes there," he said to Phillip. "And he has ties to a certain Colombian ... *family* in a way in which you will need," he said to Hassan. Hassan nodded. He turned back to their cousin. "And bringing him onto the executive team will quell any rumblings of a strife between the Hightons and the Porters. It's a win-win."

"You know, Mouse," Nick started, "it wasn't charming when you said it before, and it's not charming now."

"Don't call me that," Mick gritted through his teeth.

"Sure, Mouse," said Nick. Then he looked across the table. "Emma, Porter is laundering money for a Colombian drug cartel in exchange for all the coke and whores he could ever want. So, no."

"You don't know that!" said Mick angrily.

"He told me so himself while we were both high off that same Colombian coke," Nick said with a straight face.

Mick stumbled on his thoughts at Nick's candor. Then he said nastily, "You don't make the decisions here, Nicholas. It's a collaborative team."

Nick ignored him. "Emma—"

"It's fine," she said with a wave of her hand in a bored fashion. "Porterhouse Casinos will not be joining Highton Optimum on the executive level. Now if any of you want to collaborate with them directly, feel free to do so."

"But Emma," Mick whined.

"I will not be inviting Dipshit Todd to the table, Mouse," she said sternly. "Drop it." Mick sat back fuming.

Emma said, "Please have your operational plans in my inbox in sixty days to present to the next board meeting. Any other items up for business? No. Okay, thank you for your time and attention. I'll see you all next quarter." She stood up first. "Nicholas," she called and walked out of the space. Nick sighed and walked out behind her.

Lita stood up, but Emma held up her palm and Lita sat back down. He followed his sister down the hall to her private elevator in silence. When they got in together and the door closed, he turned to her.

"You are a colossal bitch."

Emma was unbothered. "If I was a man, I'd be seen as strong, formidable, determined. All the things Father called you and Brian, even though I am the one that has stood by the family legacy all this time." She turned to him. "Those men expect me to be sweet and nice so they can walk all over me. That will never happen."

Nick was about to retort when he realized she was right. "I mean, I guess you'd have to be, dealing with those shady-as-fuck characters."

The elevator opened, and she stepped out and walked straight to her office. The door clicked open as her assistant pressed the button when she approached. "It's just business, Nicholas," said Emma.

"Business..." Nick scoffed. "I'm pretty sure Stuart Alderman is hiding money for Putin in all thirty-four of his countries. And Mickey fucking Marigold? Jesus, Emma. Our cousin is one step up from being a used car salesman. And don't get me started on Hassan I've-assassinated-a-president-or-two-for-poppy-seeds Asad just to keep everyone at that table's dick hard, including yours."

She sat on her desk with her legs crossed and turned to him. "It's just business. If we don't do it, someone else will. Someone else less worthy than us."

Nick immediately remembered that his father said his grandfather said the same thing. Bile started to form in his throat just hearing it again.

"Highton Optimum Holdings make good investments in companies that give something back to the people of that land. We are not burning down rainforests, we are not displacing poor farmers, and no, we are not assassinating presidents. We move things around that benefit all of us, from the janitor all the way up to us on the executive team. Which, by the way, none of us take a salary; we all have stocks invested in the company, and that's how we make money. We're here because we believe in the work that we're doing. And I have big plans for where I want to take us, right into the heart of technology." She looked at him pointedly. "And I want you there with me."

Nick didn't want to disappoint his sister, but this was way more than what he bargained for when he agreed to merge his work with the family business.

"There can't be two Hightons at the table, Emma. This is your domain. Your puppets to pull on their strings. I don't think I should attend these meetings."

"No, you can't," she agreed, surprising him. "Not if you challenge my authority in there. Because if you continue to do that, they will look to you as the male Highton at the table instead of following my lead. So, either you sit quietly and follow my lead like you did today, or you don't show up and I'll keep you updated on Highton affairs like I do with Father and Gary."

He nodded. "Okay. I'll sit quietly. But one thing I need you to do for me."

"What do you need, Nicholas?"

"I need you to give Niklaus back his name," he said seriously.

Emma laughed out loud. "Did you see his face?" She mocked his surprised look, making Nick laugh too. "Don't worry. I'll give it back to him next month."

"You're a colossal bitch," Nick said again in laughter. "Formidable and determined. All while raising formidable children and being catered to by a husband ... and a *wife*..."

He raised an eyebrow. Emma smirked. Nick smirked back. He walked up and hugged his big sister. "You truly are the most powerful one of us all. I'm intimidated. A Highton with a dick couldn't have done any better. Well done, Mrs. Highton." He kissed her cheek.

She hugged him tightly. "Thank you, Nicholas."

Nick stopped on the thirtieth floor to talk with Lita, giving her permission to use his office whenever she saw fit, day or night, since he would not be there most of the time, and discussed how she would be fitting in with HMP. Now that Marcel was moving up to operations, Lita seemed like the perfect fit for an executive assistant. After giving her instructions and connecting her with Marcel via phone for training and consultation, Nick stepped into the regular elevator, eager to head home.

Phillip ran up and Nick pressed the button to hold the door open for him. "Thanks," he said politely.

"You're welcome," Nick said back.

When the elevator began to go down, Philip turned to Nick. "That was pretty impressive, you standing up to Emma Highton like that about the other Nick. No one does that. I fold under her pressure every time."

"Yeah, well, I can do that. She's my sister, and she can't fire me."

Phillip laughed. "True." Nick smiled at him then looked forward again. Then he realized. "You didn't press a floor."

"My office is on the sixteenth," he confirmed. "I just wanted to take the elevator down with you for a moment."

"Oh," said Nick, thinking the sandy brown haired man wanted to pick his brain about some things.

"So are you here for a few days or..." Phillip trailed off.

"No. I'm headed back to the city. Right now in fact."

"Gotcha." Philip paused, then asked, "Do you want to grab a drink with me first?"

Nick froze, then turned to him. "I'm sorry. *What*?"

"Do you want to grab a drink with me, Nicholas?" Phillip said again, staring into his eyes. "And then maybe dinner at my place. Before you head back."

Nick stared at the man. "I have a boyfriend."

Phillip nodded. "Yes. I know. Rion Matthews. Ryan D. Ryder, the author. I follow you both on all your socials. I'm sure he's great. But you didn't answer my question." Nick continued to stare at him in disbelief as he took a step closer. "I find you very interesting, and I think we have a lot in common, coming from similar backgrounds. You're someone I would like to get to know a little better. If you would want that too." He gently put his hand on Nick's chest.

Nick looked around for the cameras, thinking he was being Punk'd. He couldn't help but to smile. "Okay. Let me say it this way: I'm committed to my partner. I won't be having drinks or dinner or sex with anyone that's not him."

Phillip finally understood, and his eyes widened. "Oh! Sorry," he said, dropping his hand. "I assumed that you were ... you know ... open to other connections."

The elevator dinged at the bottom floor. Nick nodded. "I'm not the playboy the tabloids made me out to be, Phillip," he said as he stepped out. "Have a great rest of your day."

Phillip did not come off the elevator. "Well that's a shame. I was hoping we would work together on some late night projects, either here or in the city. Let me know if that changes. My office is on the sixteenth floor." The doors closed with Phillip still watching him.

Nick stood there for a moment, shaking his head. "I'm never coming back here," he muttered to himself.

Rion heard the door open and yelled out, "Hey! Right on time. I'm making burgers and fries."

Nick walked into the kitchen, stood against the island, and folded his arms. Rion kissed his lips and went back over to the stove. "How was the meeting?"

"I got hit on today," Nick replied.

Rion scoffed. "When do you not get hit on?"

"No, I'm serious. A real, honest-to-God proposition to cheat on you. Just like that. He knew who you were, who we were, and still laid it out there. Asked me if I was open to other ... connections."

Rion raised his eyebrows. "Really? Was he good looking?"

Nick smiled. "He was."

"Huh." He flipped a meat patty. "Rich?"

"Ridiculously. Old family wealth passed down, just like me."

"Wow. Sounds like you met your match." Rion shrugged without looking at him.

"On paper, sure. I'm sure we'd look very good together."

"You should give it a chance."

Nick's eyes squinted behind Rion's back. "I should. There's only one problem with that."

Rion glanced up then back down at his food on the stove. "Yeah? What's that?"

Nick moved closer to him, and Rion turned around to face him. Nick slowly went down on his knees and began to unbutton Rion's pants. "The problem is that I just can't seem to get enough of your cock. It's the only one I want in me. Like ever. So how could I go to drinks and dinner with someone else and spend the whole time thinking of your cock in me?"

Rion tried not to smile. "That does seem like a hindrance to your philandering ways."

"It's a real fucking problem," he said before he stuffed Rion's cock in his mouth.

"Fuuuuck, Nicky..." Rion said as his eyes fluttered.

Nicholas didn't stop, not until Rion's body froze, Nick's mouth filled up, and he swallowed all of Rion. He stood up, his own cock straining, but he ignored it, throwing his arms around Rion's neck.

Rion wrapped up Nick tightly. "Is this what it's going to be like when you start taking long business trips?" Rion said. "You were gone for less than a day."

"And I'm never going back," Nick confirmed, lifting up his head. Rion raised an eyebrow at him. "Yeah. That bad. I'll tell you all about it after dinner."

Nick demanded and Rion obliged. He put Nicholas on all fours in the middle of the bed with nothing but a jock strap on and rammed into him hard. Rion sucked Nick's neck, leaving a large bruise every time he teetered on the edge, slowing down to last longer than necessary. But Nick did need Rion deep inside of him, to once again claim all of him, to move with him as one, causing Nick to ejaculate without assistance. Rion grabbed him tight with all his strength, whispering Nick's name as he came.

Nick continued to moan as he stretched out his legs onto the bed, and Rion went down with him, arms still wrapped around Nick's chest. As both their heartbeats returned to their normal rate, Nick thought about his father having a long-term mistress. Even though he brought it up to Trixie as an option when they talked about marriage, he couldn't imagine ever cheating. Everything about Rion matched him so perfectly—in and out of the bedroom—that no one could ever compare.

Nick felt Rion roll off his back but kept a hand there, rubbing up and down. "What's up?" he asked softly. "Talk to me."

Nick was not about to discuss current thoughts, so instead, he turned his head and described to Rion the executive meeting and all he learned about how his family's company operated.

"Wow," Rion said in surprise. "I mean, I guess I shouldn't be surprised but... Wow."

"Yeah. I felt the same way," Nick said. "I will have to find a way to break it to my father. But there is no way I'm joining my company with my family's. It's not that I didn't know there were some underhanded dealings. But to know it and to *know* it..." He shook his head. "I can't be a part of it. I called Barry from the plane and asked him to dig deeper into the financial portfolio, to make sure there are no contingencies, that it's fully mine. My father told me he created a separate portfolio, so I think we have to actually join our company with HOH, just like all the others at the executive level did. We have a whole year before anything is expected of Hump. His initial thoughts are that if we don't sign documents and submit any official operational plan, keeping our financials separate, we technically will be okay. I just want to make sure I can't be forced to since I am a Highton."

"Emma won't force you to," said Rion. "If you want out, she'll give you an out."

"Yes but..." He sighed. "Emma was really excited for me to be a part of the family business. It's going to break her heart when I tell her I can't do it. But for now, I'll pretend like I'm all in until Barry confirms that I can gracefully bow out."

Rion nodded. "So no more meetings in Rochester?"

Nick shook his head. "Nope. I really am never going back there. Lita can handle things from my office up there. My work is here. And my life is here with you."

"I miss you, Nicky," Rion said suddenly. "I miss you terribly even though we sleep in the same bed together every night. I feel less close to you now than when we were in London and you were flying back to the States every other month. I'm having a really hard time with all of this. I miss who we were."

Nick was surprised at Rion's confession. "I miss you too, Ree." He began to caress his face with his fingers. "It's so different now that I'm all in with my family. But I'm trying to manage a new business, I'm trying to build a relationship with my father while trying to doge my mother, I'm trying to appease my brand, and all eyes are on me. I'm sorry that I've been so busy, but I am trying, Ree."

Rion sighed. "I know. You're under so much pressure. And I don't want to add to it by telling you all this. Telling you what's going on with me..." He trailed off as waves of panic began to form. But he did his best to ignore them.

"Just hang in there with me a little longer," Nick said. "It will all go back to normal for us. You'll see."

Rion wasn't so sure. But he nodded. "Okay."

When Nick arrived, Niles was sitting on the lounge chair on the back porch, staring into the ocean with a serious look on his face. "Father?" he said cautiously.

"Have you seen the paper today?" Niles asked. "Specifically the tabloids."

"No." Nick opened up his phone and put his name in the search bar, thinking it had to do with him.

Nothing came up about Nicholas Highton, but there was another Highton all over the gossip pages. "Oh. Shit."

His father grunted. "Your brother continues to disappoint me."

Nick sat down at the table and read the headline out loud, "Another infamous Highton scandal: The inside scoop of Doctor Brian Highton's pregnant mistress."

He read the rest of the article in silence, knowing his father had already done so. There were no pictures of Kara but there were rumors of him attending pre-natal visits on the Upper West Side with an unnamed woman. A "source" close to them confirmed that Brian had been cheating on his wife for the last decade and had plans to leave her for the younger woman after learning of her pregnancy. They tried to interview Idalia, but she had been in Italy at the Mercurio Villa in Tuscany for the last couple of months. Brian flat out refused to be interviewed. The article briefly tied Brian to Nick and him being caught cheating on Penny with the singer Kierra, and also to their uncle, Nolan, who had his own cheating scandal over twenty years ago where he was caught in the act at their office in Rochester with a low-level employee. It was so bad, Nolan had to resign from Highton Optimum Holdings as its CFO. Niles and his brother did not talk often, and Nick had very little relationship with his cousins.

"This won't be the same as Uncle Nolan," Nick reassured him. "Brian is smart and calculating. And I'll give him some tips on how to handle negative press."

"I just don't understand why he let this go on for so long," Niles mumbled. "And let it go this far. A baby? When he told me his plans, I explicitly told him that he cannot have a secret lovechild out there with Ms. Beaumont."

Nick looked up. "So you know who she is?"

"Of course I do. I know everything that goes on with my children."

"Oh. So you know ... everything ... about Brian and Kara?" Nick asked cautiously.

Niles turned to him. "About how deep his involvement is with the BDSM Gold Club? Yes, I know. And he is currently being vetted as a partner. One is stepping back, and they are looking to Brian to fill her spot. He doesn't know that yet; they haven't made him the offer. This might ruin it for him, however. The partners there are silent, uneventful individuals. This scandal is not silent nor uneventful."

"Oh. Wow. Okay," Nick said with a nod. He looked at his brother's face again on the front page of *The City Chronicle*. "Herring was careful not to have any paper mention her, so that's a good thing. I'm sure Brian has it all under control."

His father scoffed. "The fact that he allowed this to come out at all means he has nothing under control. Madeline is going to have to reign it all in."

Nick wondered if Brian letting the information leak out about his relationship with Kara was intentional, to keep Madeline out of Nick's hair and focused on him for a while. But his father's comment had him curious.

"Why don't you intervene, Father? Why do you always let Mother take control of these situations? Of all situations?"

"Well, that's why I chose her, son," said Niles. "The Marigolds are career attorneys, public relations and crisis management consultants. I needed someone on my team who could handle these types of situations when I was poised to take over Highton Optimum from my father."

"On your *team*?" Nick asked. Niles just stared at him. "So you married her because she comes from a family of publicists?"

"Yes. And she was young and beautiful and could conceive my children."

"So you didn't want love in your life?" Nick asked.

"Oh, I've had love in my life, remember? But that was never the purpose of our union. It was to protect both our interests, Highton and Marigold."

"To have two children and at least one male heir to carry on the Highton name," said Nick.

"Precisely," Niles agreed.

"And I ruined that when I came along."

Niles paused, hearing the bitterness in his voice. "You didn't ruin anything, Nicholas. Yes, it is true that we were separated and contemplating divorce at that time. But that night that you were conceived was the first time in over ten years that we'd had an honest conversation about what I took from her. See, I forced her father Orlando's hand to give her to me through a business deal while she was still at Juilliard. She was betrothed to me before she graduated. I allowed her a year or two to travel with a dance company, but her work was here. Producing children. Protecting the business. Managing all affairs. She told me that she resented me and how much pain it caused her to not be able to follow her dreams. Then, she danced for me. And for a single moment, I fell in love with my wife. And we made love for the first time. We created you."

"Oh, wow," Nick responded. "But when she told you she was pregnant, you didn't believe her."

Niles shook his head. "After trying for months on our own, we conceived Brian through IVF and pumped up Madeline's body with hormones very quickly afterward to conceive Emma. Then we were done; two children were enough. Sex after that was sparse and perfunctory. We had no idea that we could get pregnant naturally on our own. Not until you came along. And we had been separated for over a year before that;

she was seeing Sean Paisley, a famous contemporary dancer, and touring with him at the time. So no, I didn't believe it at first. I didn't believe it at all. Sadly, I wasn't there at your birth," he said, hanging his head in shame. "But they did a DNA test within hours of your arrival, confirming that you were my son. I went straight to the hospital and sat with you all night, in awe, in disbelief, in love."

"And then you forced Madeline's hand again," said Nick. "You forced her to stay in the marriage, to give up her lover, her career, everything she had been building the year before she got pregnant, because you had another heir to raise. That's why she hates me."

He thought his father was going to deny it, but he didn't. Niles looked up at Nicholas and said, "And for that, I am sorry. I thought that she would pour love into you in the way she didn't with Brian and Emma because she knew you were the one child conceived out of love. I thought we would be a real family. If I would have known that she was going to treat you differently and with such contempt, I would have let her go. I was selfish. And my selfishness made her the way she is toward me and toward you. I am sorry, Nicholas."

Nick turned away and stared at the ocean, taking in all his father had confessed about his relationship with his wife. And how it trickled down to his relationship with his mother.

"I wish you were around more," said Nick. "I wish you were around to be there for me when she couldn't or wouldn't. I wish we could have had this kind of relationship growing up. I wish I would have known that I had at least one parent who loved me, who wanted me."

"I am an old man who has made a lot of mistakes," said Niles. "I have those same wishes, those same regrets. I could have done better. I should have done better. I cannot make up for the past. But I am grateful that you have given us a chance to start all over and have a closer relationship in my late life. And I am excited about your future, not just with you being a part of the family business, but with your love life. And again, I look forward to building a relationship with Mr. Matthews. When you are ready to introduce us, of course."

Nick almost blurted out Madeline's threats and why he couldn't bring Rion around. But he knew he couldn't, considering how unpredictable and conniving his mother could be. Nguyen was still in the process of securing the computers, and Brian being in the forefront of his mother's wrath was a good thing for him. He did not want to bring any attention back to himself.

"One day, Father. One day."

"Well. The masquerade ball is in a few weeks. I think it would be a perfect opportunity to introduce him to our society properly. And to me. What do you think?"

"I think Mother would shit bricks if I brought Rion to one of her important social events," he deadpanned.

Niles laughed out loud. "You leave that to me. Let him know he is invited, personally, by Niles Highton. I will send a handwritten invitation to your home."

Nick sighed. But then said, "Okay, Father. I will let him know."

Two weeks later, Nick came into the apartment and put the mail on the island. "Something came for you."

Rion was confused. "From who?"

Nick didn't respond. Instead, he went into the kitchen to figure out dinner for them. It was his turn to cook. Rion picked up the yellow envelope with gold writing on it addressed to him.

He held it up. "What is this?"

"Open it."

He did, pulling out the fancy card giving him access to The Masquerade Gala by the Highton family on October 31st at the Plaza Hotel. He could see something was written on the back, so he flipped it over.

Mr. Matthews, please attend the Annual Highton Masquerade Gala as my personal guest. It would be an honor to have you.

Sincerely,
Niles Elliot Highton

Rion's mouth opened in surprise. He looked up at Nick, who smiled at him.

"No."

Nick's smile faded. "C'mon, Ree," he practically whined.

"No," Rion said, shaking his head. "Besides the fact that your mother is still out to destroy me and my entire family, that last one was a disaster, Nicholas."

"Because we didn't go together," Nick implored.

"And we aren't going together to this one," Rion said, dropping the envelope on the island.

"You cannot turn down a personal invitation from Niles Highton himself," said Nick. "No one does that."

"Well there's a first time for everything," he said with a straight face.

Nick came over to him. "Please, Rion. I do plan on telling him everything, but I want you to meet him first, in front of my mother, then tell him everything. I have it all planned out, but I need you by my side to do it."

Rion stared at him as panic flooded his chest. He turned around and started wringing his hands. "Fuck, Nicky..." he murmured.

Nick came behind him. "It will be fine," Nick said with a kiss on his head. "Trust me."

Rion closed his eyes to slow down his heartbeat before he answered. "Okay."

19

Because this was their first public event together since the Fourth of July debacle, Zoey planned their outfits. Nick was dressed as Scrooge McDuck, a red three-quarter length Mackage coat with black trim, a thick black belt, white pants, top hat, and a cane. He even added glasses to match. Rion went as Darkwing Duck, a blue turtleneck surrounded by a purple three-quarter length Mackage coat with gold buttons and white pants. Rion also wore a silk black mask, mostly for anonymity. It made him feel better. They both wore the same burnt orange Mezlan patina leather shoes.

Rion closed his eyes in the town car and counted backward from fifty to control his anxiety. *No matter what happens*, he told himself, *there will be no panic attacks tonight*.

Nick noticed and gently took his hand. "Nervous?" he asked.

Rion opened his eyes. "I have to tell you something, Nicky. Something I've been keeping from you. Something going on with me."

The car pulled up to the Plaza Hotel, and the driver came around to open up the door. Nick held his hand out to give him a minute and turned to Rion. "What?"

They stared at each other, but then Rion looked outside the car as the flashes continued. "We can talk about it later tonight."

"Tell me now," Nick said, ignoring the calls for him to come out of the car by the photographers. "What's wrong, Ree?"

But all the commotion was making it worse for Rion. "It's okay. I'm okay," Rion lied. "Let's get through the night, then we can talk, okay?"

"You sure?" Nick asked, concerned.

"Yes," said Rion with confidence. "It's fine. We'll talk tonight."

Nick leaned over and kissed him. "Okay."

He came out of the vehicle first and straightened his jacket. He smiled for the cameras, taking pictures by himself for a moment. Then he reached back out to Rion. Rion sighed and took his hand. He came out of the car and stood beside him, putting on a smile. The flashes went crazy, demanding them to look this way and turn that way.

Nick slid his hand around Rion's waist and said in his ear, "I got you, babe, okay?"

Rion turned to him. They stared at each other, then Rion leaned in for a quick, soft kiss, long enough for the cameras to catch it. The flashes went crazy again.

Someone yelled out, "Who are you two supposed to be?"

Nick answered, "Scrooge McDuck and Darkwing Duck. Two lucky ducks."

That made Rion blush and grin. Nick gave him another quick kiss, thanked the paparazzi, and pulled Rion into the hotel with him.

They went to the Fairmont La Marina Rabat-Salé ballroom, and the Highton Masquerade Ball was underway. Zoey immediately approached them, wearing a Statue of Liberty looking dress. She held up her phone and said, "Two lucky ducks. It's already beginning to trend. Well done, you two." She hugged and kissed them both. "As usual, call or text if you need me. I'll be around." She left them to it.

Nick was immediately greeted by other attendees, happy to see him there and even happier to see that Rion was by his side. Rion followed Nick around as he introduced him to several people, most of which worked for the family business or had contracts and collaborations with Highton Optimum. He smiled politely, ignoring how tight his turtleneck was around his throat, held onto his glass, and listened to them talk business until they moved onto the next person. And then the next. And the next. Rion's smile became plastic. He stayed quiet and willed himself not to fidget, listening to stock market numbers and golf statistics and money rates in other countries compared to the US. He began noticing that his shoes were too tight, the mask was becoming crinkly and uncomfortable, and his hand holding onto his glass was sweaty. He didn't want to be there at all, but he promised Nick he would try. And he was thankful that the mini squeezing of his chest had been kept at bay. He planned to hold out long enough to meet Niles Highton, then slowly disappear from the scene.

As Nick talked with another business associate, he saw through his peripheral vision a woman with long, raven-colored hair and a protruding belly walking past him slowly. He tapped Nick and said, "Excuse me," then followed her.

After a few paces, she turned around to him and smiled. "Rion."

As he got closer, Kara gave him an air kiss. "You look beautiful as always. Belle from *Beauty and the Beast*, right?" he said, acknowledging her outfit.

"Correct. And you looked like you needed an escape."

"So you walked past on purpose, knowing I would go to you?" he asked with a smile.

"I have that effect," she said slyly. He laughed. She laced their arms together. "Walk with me."

He glanced back at Nick who had barely noticed he was not by his side anymore and turned back to Kara with a nod. They began to walk.

"So is the Doctor going to distribute his medicine tonight?" Rion said in code.

"You know, I don't know. He's been doing it less and less the closer I get to my due date at the end of December. He's being very cautious and gentle with me. Very unlike him."

"Well he has to. Can't exactly lose oxygen in that state," Rion deadpanned.

Kara smiled. "How are you enjoying the gala?"

"The truth?" He gave her a weary smile. "I'm not. It's not like the other one at all. This is very... It's like one massive business meeting."

She nodded. "That's exactly right. Midsummer Night's Dream is a family event. It's fun and lively. This is very different. There are no children invited to this one. It's all business associates or people wanting to be business associates here. Brian hates it, especially since the Hightons have to come in costume. He wears his scrubs and says, 'I'm a doctor' every year. But his parents let him get away with it. It's the closest he will ever be to the business side of the Highton empire."

"So why do you come?" he asked her.

"Because Brian needs me. I'm his breath of fresh air. Even though he will never publicly acknowledge me, I will walk past him like I did just now to you, and it will revive him."

"God, you are so interesting, Kara," Rion said.

She grinned. "Come. I will introduce you to the non-business folks like us."

She brought Rion to a table near the bar. He recognized Adolphe, who introduced him to others, low-level managers invited to spend time with the One Percent for one night. Rion learned a lot about their business, some in real estate, some in finance, some in media like Nick's company. And Rion dug deeper, finding out about their personal lives, their families, allowing them to share their stories. It was the most comfortable he'd felt all night.

Kara took notice. After a while, she turned to him and said softly, "It's been about an hour. You should head back to Nick."

Rion sighed. Just thinking about it made his anxiety creep up in his chest. "Is it bad that I don't want to?"

She touched his face. "You'll be fine, Rion. All of this," she gestured around her, "is a façade. Nothing here is real. Not the clothes, not the conversations, nothing. Except you and Nick. That's real. Remember that, and you'll be fine."

Rion moved closer to her. "I don't know if I can do this, Kara. This high society, always in the spotlight, enmeshed with one of the wealthiest families in the world. I am struggling internally in ways that I haven't told Nick yet. This is beginning to be too much for me."

Kara moved closer too and touched his hand. "There are two ways to be with a Highton. Either you completely throw yourself into all of this and trust your partner, like Idalia and Gary have done. Or you live in the shadows like me." She patted his hand. "And you do not want to live in the shadows like me."

"It's too late for that anyway," he said sadly. "Everyone knows who I am and who I'm partnered with. I have to find a way to scale back from all of this before it eats me up from the inside out. I cannot do another party like this ever again."

"Talk to Nick," she advised. "Tell him how you feel. Tell him what you need. And he'll do it. He'll do whatever you need him to do to keep you safe and happy because he loves you that much. It's how Brian and I survived all these years. You and Nick will survive too."

Rion smiled at her. "Did I tell you that you're amazing yet?" She smiled back. Rion stood up. "I'll go find him." He kissed her cheek and dove back into the crowd.

Nick excused himself from talking with a music producer who was throwing out ideas of collaboration. He hadn't seen Rion in a while, but the room was big, and there were over five hundred guests, so that wasn't surprising. He spotted his father near the back, seated in a chair with Stuart Alderman smoking a cigar, and knew it was time. He walked the room to begin to search for his boyfriend.

"Nicholas," someone called out. Nick turned and watched Todd Porter walk up to him. He reached out his hand, and Nick shook it to be polite. "Todd. Good to see you."

"Likewise," Todd said as he let go. "It's been a while since we talked."

"Yes, well. We've all been pretty busy," he replied, his eyes still scanning the room.

"Right, we have. But I never received a call from your people about that business venture we talked about. In fact, Young Highton has blocked my calls and all access to him. I find that strange. I thought you were a man of your word, Highton."

Nick glared at him. But he kept calm, knowing they were in a crowd of people. "All business deals must be done with a clear head and clear mind. Neither of us were in a clear state of mind. So no, there was no deal between us. I'm sorry."

Nick tried to walk away when Todd spoke again. "I also heard that you blocked a meeting with Emma Highton. A very important meeting that would have benefited my entire company."

"I did," he said curtly. "Now if you'll excuse me—"

Todd reached out and grabbed his arm roughly. Nick looked down at his hand then back at Todd, giving him a chance to walk away. But Todd did not let go. Nick might have forgiven him if he thought that Todd was high again. But Todd's eyes were perfectly clear. And cold. He stepped closer and spoke in Nick's ear.

"I know that you and I have our differences," he said softly. "I take full responsibility for that. I was a little overeager with TMZ. But Porterhouse Casinos being a part of the Highton empire is a good business decision. Don't let our minor personal squabble get in the way of business. After all," he felt Todd touch his hip, "it just made you even more infamous. So you have me to thank."

Nick turned to him and said with a smile, their faces inches apart. "Get your hands off me, Porter. Before I end up making another infamous tape at this soirée. But this time, I'll be beating the shit out of you in front of a camera."

Todd stepped back and smiled too, throwing his hands up. "As you wish." He caressed Nick's cheek and winked.

Nick turned around and saw Rion a few paces away, staring at him, his face in a frown. Rion glanced at Todd who blew a kiss at him. Rion looked at Nick again. He abruptly turned around and walked out of the ballroom.

"Rion!" Nick yelled after him. He started running through the crowd to him, but as he made it out the double doors, suddenly his mother was in front of him.

"STOP!" she commanded loudly.

Nick was startled and stopped walking. Rion, who was in the middle of the hallway, stopped too and turned around. He saw the back of Madeline's head as she spoke to him.

"You will NOT chase after him," she commanded. "You will not. I will not allow it."

"What?" Nick asked in confusion.

"Do you know who you are?" she asked. "You are Nicholas Highton. *Highton*! You do not go and chase after anyone. Everyone in your life is replaceable, especially him. Let him go, Nicholas. He doesn't belong here."

Nick looked up at Rion over his mother's head, and they locked eyes. He looked back down at his mother and said, "If you don't get out of my way, Mother, I will forcibly remove you with my hands around your throat!" he growled.

A few people around heard him and gasped. Rion's mouth also opened slightly. It confirmed for him what he'd witnessed: Todd slipping a small tube of white substance into Nick's pocket while he whispered in his ear. And seeing Nick smile back at him was a clear indication that they had something going on. Rion wished it was sex. That would have made things less complicated. But he knew it was cocaine, the only thing they had in common. They either made a plan to get high again, or Nick was already high. But now he assumed Nick must have already been using, which was why he spoke to his mother that way. And it infuriated him.

There was no panic in Rion's chest, only rage. And he was not living in Nick's world if this was what it was going to be like.

I'm done, Rion said to himself. He turned around and walked away.

"Rion!" Nick called out again. He tried to go around his mother, but she blocked his path again.

Nick was fuming in anger, staring at her as Madeline smiled at him.

"Look at yourself," she said softly. "You have truly forgotten who you are. You have forgotten your name and your place in this world. You're now such an angry, aggressive person. I guess spending time around unsavory criminals has finally rubbed off on you, my son."

"No, the lack of parental love has rubbed off on me, Madeline," Nick said back. "I know who I am. My name is Nicholas Highton. And my partner's name is Rion Mathews. And I'm going to run like hell away from you and back to him. That's who I am, Mother. Deal with it."

He stepped around his mother and began walking toward the lobby. "Nicholas!" Nick's mother said sternly. He stopped but did not turn around. "If you run after that man, I promise you, I will strip everything from you piece by piece. You will have nothing but your name by the time I'm through with you."

Nick turned around and started walking quickly back to her. She stepped back in fear, her eyes wide. He noticed that others were around, watching the whole exchange. But Nick knew it was all fake. The beginning of her making him out to be her crazy son. So he kept his cool as he approached her.

"Take it," he said through gritted teeth. "I have him. And that's all I'll ever need."

He turned around again. "Nicholas," she started.

"Leave me the *fuck* alone, Mother!" he yelled and kept going past the hallway and through the hotel lobby.

But right before he approached the exit doors, a hand reached out from seemingly nowhere and dragged him back. He looked at who the hand was attached to. "What the hell, Zoey!?" he demanded. "I have to catch up to Rion. He just left—"

"I don't care," she said in a harsh whisper, pulling him toward the front desk. "You cannot go out the front door."

"What?"

"Todd has a plot to sabotage you somehow," she informed him. "Discredit you. I don't know. I don't have all the details. All I know is that, in the middle of the swarm of paparazzi outside, plain clothed police officers are waiting to arrest you."

"On what charge!?" he exclaimed.

"I don't know!" she whispered again. "I just know that you cannot walk out the front of this hotel."

Nick looked around exasperated, knowing that every minute that passed was a minute Rion was getting farther away from him. Zoey kept talking. "I don't know if it's a recent deal you made, someone you recently hired, anything, but they have something on you. And it's supposed to be public and really bad, not just for your company but all of Highton."

"How did you find all this out?" he asked.

"One of Todd's employees, I think his financial guy, said something to Kara, who came to find me because she couldn't approach Brian. Just trust me, Nick."

"I do trust you, Zoey."

"Then wait right here for me. I'm already making arrangements for you to be picked up in the lower-level garage. I went to find you, but someone said you ran out after Rion. I knew I had to stop you before you left."

"I'm going to murder that dipshit," Nick said darkly.

"Later," Zoey said with a nod. "We'll get our revenge later. For now, stay here. Don't leave. Get a drink and sit in the hotel lobby looking casual and don't leave." She walked away from him.

Nick sighed and did what he was told. He went back into the gala, grabbed a drink, went into the hotel lobby, and sat in one of the soft, oversized chairs. He slowly drank and waited. He texted Rion, knowing that he wouldn't respond but did it anyway. He waited and waited, watching time slip away from him.

A lanky man with a thick beard approached him an hour later and said in an Arnold Schwarzenegger accent, "Come with me if you want to live." He smiled. Nick did not smile back.

"C'mon," he coaxed. "Niion Lights Forever or whatever Zoey told me to say. You're good with me."

Nick sighed at him and stood up. They casually walked to the elevator together. The man pressed the up button, which was confusing to Nick. "I thought we were going to the parking garage. Where are we going?"

"Back to my room for a nightcap," he said. Nick narrowed his eyes. The man laughed. "You're going to have to play it cool if this is to work, Nicholas. You're being watched. Soften your face and your stance, and trust me."

Nick took a deep breath and exhaled as they waited. Upon entrance, the man pressed the second floor, the sixth, the fourteenth and the twenty-first. He smiled at Nick. When the elevator stopped the first time, they waited until the doors closed again. When it opened the second time, the man stepped out and steered

Nick toward the stairs, then they casually made their way down to the basement, through a back kitchen, and out the back doors where the food service was delivered. A white GMC XL with chrome trim was waiting for them.

The driver opened the door, but the bearded man said to Nick, "Sit in the far back. And stay out of sight."

Nick did, and the man climbed into the seat behind the driver. The driver took off through the parking lot outside of the building. But it was immediately swarmed with reporters as they exited onto the street. A Ford stopped directly in front of the SUV, blocking its path, and two plain clothed officers stepped out. Nick watched the driver roll down the window and speak to them in a calm manner for a minute.

But Nick's savior pulled the window down halfway and said sternly, "What is the meaning of this?"

The officer walked closer to his window. Nick immediately slouched down. "We apologize, sir," the officer started, "but we are looking for someone—"

"I don't care. I'm on important business for Mr. Todd Porter of Porterhouse Casinos. Check the plates if you need to. Then kindly get your squad car out of my driver's way!" he said with authority.

The officer nodded. "Right away, sir."

He stepped back and the man rolled up his windows. The officers conferred with each other and then went back into their squad car to move it. The SUV drove on through the streets of Manhattan.

After a few quiet moments, Nick said, "Thank you."

"No, thank *you*, Nicholas," the man said back. "We at the managerial level of Porterhouse Casinos are forever in your debt for the term Dipshit Todd. We use it often and frequently. We literally started a private, hidden Facebook page called 'Minions of Dipshit Todd' where we discuss all the dipshit things our asshole boss does on a daily basis. It is our saving grace."

Nick laughed out loud for the first time in a few hours. "What's your name?"

"Adolphe Behrend."

"Come work for me, Adolphe Behrend."

"I'm sorry, Mr. Highton, that would be a conflict of interest for me," he replied in an extremely formal manner.

Nick leaned closer in interest. "How so?"

"I'm not at liberty to say. Per the Doctor's orders."

"Oh, fuck," Nick said, shaking his head. "In what way are you associated with my brother?"

"I'm not at liberty to say. Per the Doctor's orders," Adolphe repeated.

"Does he know that you're doing this for me?" Nick asked.

"No. But I am sure someone close to him will tell him before the night is over."

"Kara."

"Correct."

"So are you a member of the Gold Club too?"

Adolphe hesitated, then said simply, "Yes."

"Jesus. Do I even want to know anymore?" Nick asked. Adolphe didn't respond. So Nick left it alone.

They sat quietly until the SUV stopped in front of Nick's building. "Wait," Adolphe said.

The driver let Adolphe out of the car first. Adolphe stood there vaping for about five minutes. He looked around for a moment then tapped on the glass. "Okay. It's all clear."

The driver pulled down the seat and let Nick out. "Thank you," Nick said again. Adolphe bowed his head slightly. Nick practically ran inside.

When he opened the door, he knew he was in trouble. All the lights were on. Rion's purple suit jacket was tossed on the floor, his shoes in different directions. His turtleneck in the hallway. Nick slowly walked toward the bedroom, and all the lights were on there. He could see Rion in the closet, watching him move around, throwing items into his carry-on suitcase. His stomach began to churn.

"Ree?" he asked carefully. "What are you doing?" Rion didn't respond. "Rion?" Rion went into the bathroom and came out with his shaving kit.

Nick sighed. "Look, I've had a really long and emotional night, and I just want us to sit and talk and—"

"I'm going home," Rion said, still moving around and throwing things into his suitcase.

"Home...?" Rion didn't answer. "What the fuck does that mean!?" Nick yelled. "You are home!"

"You know, Nick," Rion said with a scoff, "I'm really not in the mood for your drug-induced outbursts right now."

"Drug-induced— What the fuck are you talking about!?" Nick snapped.

"You're coked up again."

"No I am not!"

"I heard the way you spoke to your mother, Nicholas. The way you threatened her. Everyone in the hallway heard you." Rion sighed and continued packing. "You don't act like that, ever. Being high is the only explanation for it."

"I'm not using, Ree. I swear on my life I'm not high!" Nick exclaimed. Rion stopped and finally looked at him. "Look in my eyes, Ree. I'm not high." He threw his hands up.

Rion walked up to him, and they stared at each other. Then slid Rion one hand over to Nick's hip and put his hand in Nick's pocket. Nick watched his hand come out with a small tube of white powder. His mouth formed a complete O, finally understanding how Todd was going to sabotage him. If he had walked out of the hotel with coke in his pocket and it got pulled out by the police in front of the paparazzi, his whole life would have been over.

"That mother*fucker*," he growled.

"I saw the two of you," Rion said, dropping it back in Nick's pocket. "I saw him come up to you and put it in your pocket while he whispered in your ear. And I saw you smile secretly at each other. The only reason you're not high right now is because you saw me."

Nick shook his head. "You don't know what you saw, Ree. You don't know what happened after you left. That motherfucker tried to set me up. He—"

"I don't want to hear it, Nicky," Rion said, stepping back. He walked over to his suitcase and bent down to zip it up. "I'm done. I'm so fucking done with all of it."

Nick's stomach churned again. "So you're leaving me? Because of what you think I've done—"

"I need space," Rion cut him off. "I need space and time away from all of this—"

"No," Nick stepped in his face. "You can't leave. Not like this."

"Nicky—"

Nick grabbed his face with both hands. "What happened to Niion Lights Forever? What happened to RWAWN2? We're building an empire together. People are watching us—"

"You think I give a shit about any of that!?" Rion exploded, moving his face from Nick's hands. "You have no *idea* what I've been dealing with these last few months. How I've tried to hold it together, but I am falling apart. How every single fucking day my chest tightens up, and I'm willing myself not to have another fucking panic attack. I can't do this shit anymore!"

Nick was stunned, listening to Rion's confession about his mental health deteriorating. Confused why it was the first time he was hearing it.

"We're not building an empire, Nick," Rion continued. "You are. You with your family clout and money and celebrity status and adding onto the Highton empire, and I'm the shiny piece of jewelry at your side making you look good. You don't give a shit what I've been going through!"

"Rion, that's not true!" Nick implored.

"It is, Nick," Rion said back. "And I'm tired of being in the spotlight with you. I'm tired of running your company and catering to your brand and smiling for the masses and just waiting for one of your parents to fuck me over. I'm tired of being with you in this condo and not actually being with you because we barely see each other. I am tired of these waves of mini panic attacks in my chest every single fucking day multiple times a day! I'm tired of being in your world, Nick, and I want to go home!" he screamed.

"Rion—" Nick started in shock.

"Do you realize that I haven't written a single fucking word since we left London!?" Rion yelled. "Not one. I can't finish the story I had started earlier this year, and I haven't had the motivation to put any other ideas on paper. I've been so focused on you, and I need a fucking break!" He put on his yellow sweater over his head.

"From me? You need a break from me?" Nick asked incredulously.

Rion turned around to grab his suitcase. He whirled it to the front door, and Nick followed him. "Don't do this, Ree," Nick pleaded. "Don't run away. If you leave me ... I'll have nothing left to live for," he said, thinking of his mother's last words to him.

"Don't you dare fucking guilt trip me, Nicholas," he said angrily, stepping around his suit pieces and grabbing his laptop from the living room. "You have your family. Even if Madeline continues to be a bitch, you have your father now, your sister, your brother, your company, and your legacy. You're a Highton through and through now, and you don't need me anymore."

"I need you, Ree!" Nick yelled at him.

But Rion ignored him and continued. "All I had here was you and my stories. Being with you and writing my stories kept me grounded. My stories are gone. You're gone. And now I'm left with nothing." Rion walked over to the front room and put on his sneakers. "I need to go home, Nick. I need ... space."

"Are you coming back?" Nick asked. Rion didn't respond. Nick's anger flashed inside of him, and he heard himself yell, "I promise you I won't chase you, Rion Matthews. Either you stay and you fight for us and we work this out or..." Nick didn't finish.

Rion opened up the door and stepped out, not looking at Nick again.

Nick stood there, feeling numb. He put his hands into his pocket again and looked at the tube. His hand closed around it, and the heat of anger flashed again. He let it go and called Zoey.

"You're good now, right, Boss?" she asked.

"No, I'm not good," he gritted through his teeth. "Rion just left me. And it's all Todd's fault. We are going to destroy that Dipshit Todd, once and for all."

21

Rion sat on the windowsill with the window open and rolled another joint. The rain had passed, leaving a blanket of fog, and the sun was trying to come out through the clouds. He looked up for a moment and squinted at it, then resumed adding the buds to the white paper. After carefully rolling and licking it to stay put, he lit it, watching the flash of fire before it disappeared into ashes, leaving an orange glow at the end. He closed his eyes, put it to his lips, and inhaled. His mind turned back into its normal state of cloudiness, and his depression lifted slightly. He breathed it out, put the back of his head against the side of the windowpane, and inhaled again. It was his third joint of the day. He had been averaging four, thinking some random plot, scene, or story was going to motivate him to begin writing again, but all it did was leave him in despair when he wasn't high. He opened his eyes briefly and looked at his laptop, which hadn't left its case since he arrived in San Francisco over two weeks ago.

He hadn't left Gael and Gabby's guest bedroom in over two weeks either, locking the door during the day and venturing out in the middle of the night for food and water. Sweet Morgan wrote him notes and slipped them under the door, telling him good morning, letting him know what was for dinner, sending encouragement: "I'm sorry you're sick. I hope you feel better," and "You're gonna be okay. Just watch! 😊"

He wanted to open the door, but his niece could not see him like that. Sad faced. Bloodshot eyes. Depressed.

Gabby noticed, and it worried her. She called Nicholas, but Nick didn't pick up for her or return any of her texts. She called Zoey, and Zoey told her that she knew as much as Gabby did: that they had a fight and Rion asked for space, so Nick gave him space. Neither Nick nor Rion said any more about it. Nick was burying himself into a work and a personal issue while Rion was swimming in a cloud of smoke trying to write again, so they were both too busy to focus on their relationship.

But Gabby was over Rion's hibernation and smokefest, so after work on Friday, she banged on the door.

"Rion!" she yelled, taking her brother out of his nonsensical thoughts. "Open the goddamn door!"

He walked over to the bedroom door and unlocked it. Gabby stood in front of him with an N95 mask on her face. He smiled at her. "The pandemic is over. You don't need to wear that anymore."

"First of all, Covid-19 is still around. Ask Gael's sister, Arina, who just caught it again. And two, I need to wear it around you because I can't get that shit into my system. I'm pregnant," she announced.

"Gabby!" he yelled and wrapped his smaller sister in a bear hug. But then he realized the impact of what she was saying. "Oh wow... Oh shit!" He quickly snuffed out his half-smoked joint. "I'm so sorry. I won't smoke in your house anymore."

He went around the room opening up all the windows and spraying a Lysol can. Gabby watched him and rolled her eyes. "Rion, stop." She walked up to him and snatched the can out of his hand. "Even if I weren't pregnant, I would have said anything to make you snap out of this funk you're in. And if you were deep in your writing, I would have let you continue with this wake and bake shit you got going on, but you're not even doing that. You're just ... sulking. No more sulking. Call your boyfriend and go make up with him."

Rion shook his head slowly. "I can't. Because ... I don't want to."

"Uuugh," she groaned. "What does that *meaaan*? Why are you so fucking frustrating!?"

"You don't understand, Gabbs."

"Because you're not talking to anyone!" she shrieked again. "What happened, Ree?"

Rion sighed and laid on the bed. "It doesn't matter what led me to go. I can't be in his world anymore, Gabby. There are only two ways to be partnered with a Highton. I don't want to live like roommates, live in the shit day in and day out, losing myself in the process. And I'm tired of pretending like I'm okay with it all when I'm not."

Gabby sat next to him. "What is going on, Ree? Talk to me."

Rion did, starting with the first panic attack back in July and how he might need to get back on anti-anxiety medication, something he hadn't done in years. He also told Gabby about how much he hated being the Vice President of Deep Strokez Publications, having all the responsibility on him. How much he didn't want to be Nick's arm candy anymore and part of his brand. How much he missed their home and their life in Europe. How much he missed his Nicky.

"Have you spoken to him about how you feel?" Gabby asked.

Rion shook his head. "It's pointless now. He can't change it. It's who he is. I knew this when we got together, that we were from different worlds. But now that he's fully stepped into his for the first time in his life, I don't know where I fit into his life anymore. And ... well maybe I don't."

Gabby patted his leg. "You do. You just need to find a way to make your own world. Maybe move back to London? You guys were good there, right?"

"We were." But Rion shook his head again. "He can't leave now. Not until the rebranding happens officially next year at least. And I don't know if I can do another year of being his arm candy."

"Well I think you should—"

But Gabby was cut off by her phone ringing. She lifted it up, and it was a videocall from Muriel. "Hey, Rel. I'm talking to Rion—"

"Perfect!" she squealed. "Go turn on the news. Right now, before you miss it. CNN!"

They looked at each other and both sat up. "Something with Nick?" Rion asked as he took the phone from his sister.

"Not quite but maybe," said Muriel with a smile.

Gabby got up to grab the remote to turn on the TV in the room and searched for the right channel. The bright red "Breaking News!" flashed at the bottom of the screen.

Rion was confused but then started listening. "... *raid on Porterhouse Casino headquarters after an anonymous tip on money laundering for a Colombian drug cartel was given to the FBI and the CIA. Police say they found stacks of uncut cocaine with the street value of $1.4 million in the back office of Todd Porter, CEO of the company. He was immediately arrested and taken into custody.*"

The next scene was Todd being walked through his office in handcuffs with his staff chanting, "*Dipshit Todd! Dipshit Todd!*"

"Holy, holy shit!" Rion yelled.

"*Senior Financial Director Adolphe Behrend is cooperating fully with police and the FBI, turning over everything from the company's international financial portfolios to petty cash.*" The reporter cut to Adolphe's interview: "*It's so unfortunate,*" he said sadly. "*We trusted him, we believed in his leadership, and he has let us down tremendously. We just hope that the Porter family can bounce back from this. I'll stay on and do whatever I can to save this company.*"

"*Russell Porter, former CEO and uncle of Todd Porter, has come out of retirement to run the company on an interim basis.*"

"You think it was Nick?" Rel asked from the phone.

"I know it was," said Gabby. Rion turned to her. "Zoey said that Todd tried to get him caught with cocaine by slipping it to him when he wasn't looking, then calling the police and making a tip. He was trying to get him arrested the night of the Gala."

Rion looked at her sharply. "What!? I didn't know any of that!"

"Because you weren't picking up any of Zoey's calls," Gabby said factually. "She was trying to explain to you why Nick had cocaine in his pocket that night. He was telling the truth, Ree. He wasn't high."

"Well, even if he wasn't, he still embarrassed the shit out of me and himself. But he's rich and handsome and can get away with it," he said sullenly.

"Ugh, that's it!" Gabby shrieked. She looked into the phone. "I'm sending him to your house, Rel. I need to clean and air out this room, and I need a break from your depressed brother."

"Yeah, and because she's pregnant," Rion blurted out.

"Oh my God, seriously, Gabby!?" Muriel yelled.

"Rion!" Gabby hit her brother. "I was going to tell everyone next week at Thanksgiving! The only reason I told you was so you would stop smoking in the house!"

"Sorry." He giggled. "But yeah, I'm going to stop smoking. Honestly, I need to get my head on straight and figure out what I'm going to do about my relationship, my career, and my mental health. And I can't do it like this."

"Come stay and spend some time with the kids," said Muriel. "Reese is with his grandfather this weekend in Stockton, Jeff needs a video game partner, and I'm sure Kate could use another shopping spree. Frank and I can get a weekend away together while you babysit."

"God, that's still a thing?" he said, rolling his eyes. Muriel rolled her eyes right back. But he stood up and said, "Okay. I'll bring Morgan over too and have Uncle Ree's daycare. That way both of you can spend time with your partners."

"After coffee and a shower," Gabby said and hugged him. "Because you look and smell like shit. Thanks, baby bro."

"Yeah, thanks, baby bro," Muriel parroted from the phone.

Rion hugged his one sister while saying into the phone to his other sister, "Glad I'm still needed around here."

Morgan talked and talked the whole way over to Muriel's house. She went on and on about fourth grade, friendships and frenemies, and the things she was doing in the art club. He could tell that she missed him tremendously, and he missed her too.

Upon arrival at his sister's house, Muriel had met him by the door, her bag already packed, waiting for her lover to arrive. Frank didn't even make it to the porch. He opened his car door, and Muriel kissed the kids briefly before she scurried out of the house to meet him.

Rion smiled, closed the door, and faced them: a fourteen-year-old introverted girl, a nine-year-old firecracker girl, and an eight-year-old boy with ADHD.

"Wanna make nachos and watch a scary flick?" he asked.

The cheers were endless.

By Sunday, Rion definitely felt more like himself. He did whatever they wanted to do—the park, the movies, the mall, the beach—and nothing felt better to him than being around his nieces and nephew. He was no more clearer on what to do about his love life, which was stalled, or his writing, also stalled, but at least he felt like he could breathe without smoke in his lungs. Being Uncle Ree and focusing on them was a much better way of subduing his depression.

Rion came into the house with Morgan, Kate, and Jeff after their second trip to the mall, all three children loaded up with bags of clothes and toys. But he was surprised to see Maurese standing in the living room.

"Hey, I didn't know you were back already," said Rion.

"Yeah, I bought Reese back for Thanksgiving. Going to see my mom, then getting back on the road." After hugging his grandchildren, he gave Rion a hug. He pulled back and squeezed Rion's shoulder. "You're doing okay? Since the breakup?"

Rion wasn't even sure if it was a breakup. It was going on three weeks of not talking to Nick, and true to Nick's word, he had not tried to call or reach out. Nick said he was not going to chase him. And Rion wasn't sure if he wanted to be chased.

"I'm okay," Rion lied. "I know I have to talk to him at some point, and I will. Just not right now."

Maurese sighed. "Okay. Don't wait too long and let things fester. And for what it's worth, I'm hoping the two of you work it out."

"Me too," Rion answered honestly.

"Okay." He hugged Rion again, then said, "We'll talk soon—"

"Dad!" Muriel said sharply as she came down the stairs, cutting him off, glaring at her father. "Tell him."

Maurese looked at her curiously. "Tell who what?"

She looked back at him in disbelief and turned to her brother. "Junior is here, at my grandmother's house. Reese just told me. He stays in Arizona, but he was with Maurese all weekend and took the ride down here with them. If you want to meet him, now's your chance."

Just hearing the name caused his stomach to lurch. "Junior... My—" He couldn't bring himself to say the word.

"What the fuck, Muriel?" Maurese said angrily to his daughter.

"He has a right to know. To confront him, Dad," she argued back.

"This is not the right time to—"

"I want to meet him," Rion heard himself say. *Do I want to meet him?* he thought immediately afterward.

Maurese turned to him. "No. No today. He's ... not in a great mood today."

"I don't give a shit what his mood is," Rion said back angrily. "I want to meet him. I want him to meet me."

Maurese was exasperated. "Rion, he doesn't do well with confrontation. It's not the right time. I need to ease him into this."

"He's had twenty-eight years to ease himself into this," Muriel retorted. "Enough with the lies and hiding from Rion. It's time. And if you won't take him, I will." She grabbed her keys off the counter. "Let's go, baby bro."

"No, wait," Maurese said as he held both hands out to stop them from walking. He turned to Rion and said, "I... I don't think this is a good idea. But if you really want to ... then I'll take you to meet him."

"I really want to," he said, even as he could feel his stomach lurch again. "It's time to close this chapter of my life for good."

"Okay." Maurese sighed. "Okay." He turned to his daughter. "You cannot go. Just Ree. If all three of us go up there, he's going to see it as an ambush, and I don't know what he'll do. He's too unpredictable. So you stay."

He looked at Rion, wanting him to change his mind. But despite Rion's anxiety getting bigger, the rolling around in his stomach, the thumping in his chest, he was determined to get it over with. Maurese saw it all on his face.

"Okay. Let's go."

The drive was quiet. Rion considered smoking the half joint he still had in his cigarette case in his back pocket, but it was too late. And he needed to meet him with a clean mind. So he counted backward from fifty in his head as they made the ride over. He thought of a list of questions he wanted to ask Junior. Less about why he didn't accept him and more about who he was as a person. To see if they had any similarities, laugh about the things they had in common together. Maybe everyone was wrong, and they would leave there on a cordial note and continue to have a relationship. Rion could form relationships with strangers. Surely, he could formulate a good one with the man who gave him life, who also happened to be a stranger to him.

Maurese was nervous as he opened the door with his key. The room was dark, all the curtains were drawn, and the only light was from the TV set. "DJ," Maurese called out.

As Rion's eyes adjusted to the darkness, he saw the figure on the couch move slightly. "What? Ready to go?" a scratchy voice asked.

Maurese hesitated, then said, "I have someone here with me. Someone that wants to talk to you."

"Tell her to fuck off," the man mumbled, his eyes not leaving the television.

Maurese moved to the closest window and pulled back the curtain. Light flooded through, and the man shielded his eyes.

"God *damn* you!" he cried out.

"Turn around and say hello to your offspring, Junior."

Junior finally lifted his head up to see Rion standing there, in confusion then in surprise. They stared at each other. As much as he wanted to know, suddenly Rion hated that he could see his features in him: his brown curly hair more tightly coiled than Rion's but still the same, the shape of his face, his nose, his lips, all similar. His skin was slightly darker, closer to Muriel's complexion, more melanin than Rion had. Despite that, even the way his chin hairs formed were similar to Rion's.

But the man was unkempt. His teeth were rotted out from years of meth use, and his fully tattooed body, from his neck to his ankles, was blotched and sickly. His face was cratered and had several hard lines, from forehead creases to indentations around his nose, from spending years sneering at people. And yet Rion could see it. Could see himself. He was in awe, and he also hated it.

Junior sat up and grabbed his cigarettes off the coffee table. He lit one first, then moved to the other side of the couch, sitting sideways with his back in the corner of the couch and one knee up. Similar to how Rion would sit in the corner of the couch when he was feeling guarded.

He took a pull before he spoke. "Well. Sit the fuck down, *son,*" he said sarcastically. "Let's talk."

Rion did not take his eyes off the man as he slowly made his way over, sitting in the same spot Junior's head had just occupied. It was still warm. He kept his hands in his pockets, mostly out of nervousness.

Junior took another pull, also not taking his eyes off Rion. "Get lost, Grease."

"No fucking way I'm leaving you alone with him," Maurese said.

His eyes glossed over to his brother. "Go check on your mom. She was wheezing earlier."

Maurese looked alarmed, his head whirling to the staircase, then back at much lighter skinned man. "And you didn't check on her?"

"She's not my fucking mother," he said with a sneer. "Go on."

Maurese looked at Rion but started going toward the steps. "You better not do anything to him," he said to his brother. Junior smiled.

But Rion said, "He's not going to do anything to me."

Junior's eyes turned to Rion. "Brave, son."

"I'm not your fucking son," said Rion calmly. "Stop calling me that."

Maurese smiled at Rion, then said, "I'll be right back." He ran up the stairs, but neither acknowledged him as they were still staring at each other.

"Want a smoke?" Junior asked, holding out his pack of cigarettes.

"I don't smoke," Rion said. "Not cigarettes anyway."

"That's good. This shit will kill you. Hey, look at me, giving out fatherly advice," Junior said and grinned a toothless grin at Rion. Rion did not smile back. He took another pull. "So you wanna talk?" Junior said, waving his cigarette around. "Talk."

"Why didn't you want to have anything to do with me?" Rion asked first, forgetting all the other questions he had practiced in his head on the way over.

"I didn't know if you were mine," Junior said plainly.

Rion stared at him. "Then you must have been fucking blind. Because I'm looking at an older, shittier lookalike."

Junior laughed. "You got balls, boy."

"I'm not a boy," Rion said back, feeling bolder with every moment that passed. "I'm a twenty-eight year old man, and I want to know why you purposely denied me. You didn't want to acknowledge that you're my father at all."

"Do I look like a father figure?" Junior said sarcastically. "I've been a drug runner for a gang since I was thirteen. I'm nobody's father."

"You could have tried. Maurese did with Rel when he was fifteen, but also with me. Hell, even Gabriel tried with Gabby, and he killed without remorse. She was his whole world. But even Fox and Bones were more like fathers to me than you were."

Junior looked up sharply. "Does Bones know where I am?"

"How the fuck should I know?" Rion said angrily. "Did you not hear anything I just said?"

"No," Junior said with a sneer. "So tell it to your fucking therapist." Rion stared at him. Junior rolled his eyes. "I have no idea why that whore Rosebud had you. She should have aborted you the moment she found out because she already knew there was no fucking way I was going to claim you. I'm not claiming a whore's baby. The fuck do I look like?"

Rion was confused. "I thought you had a relationship with her? An affair behind your brother's back."

"*Relationship*?" Junior let out a mean laugh. "Who the fuck told you that?" He finished one cigarette and lit another before he spoke again. "I made that ho do what hos do best. It was her fault, walking around my brother's house with her milking tits hanging out, nursing that baby she had. As soon as Reese went on a product run out of town for Gabriel, I bent that bitch over and took what's mine. She had to pay for her room and board somehow."

Rion went numb, then felt a surge of anger spread rapidly through his body in finding out that his mother was raped by the disgusting man in front of him. It further explained why she never told him. He wanted to lunge over and choke him.

Junior could see the fire in Rion's eyes. He swiftly pulled out a switch blade and flicked it open. "Don't even think about it, *son*," he said seriously. "I will gut you like a fish right here on this couch."

The only thing that moved on Rion was his chest rising and falling in anger, but he stayed put. Junior smiled again. "That's what you want, right? The love story of how you were conceived? Well I'ma give you the real story," he said, waving the knife around as he spoke. "See, it involves this thing right here."

Rion looked at the knife that had a gold handle with a black star, then looked back up at the man. "My brother moved her into his house, thinking that, this time, they were going to make it. Lovesick dumbass. She already had two other kids by two different men, but he thought he was going to be a father to all three of them. I had to show him that he was wrong. You can't turn a ho into a housewife. 'Specially not a bottom bitch like Rosebud."

Junior smiled again, showing his missing teeth. Rion kept his face neutral while thinking of all the ways he wanted to hurt the man in front of him.

"They weren't fucking because she told him she wasn't ready yet since she'd just pushed out a baby. I told him that was bullshit. Hos always stay ready. So the morning Reese left, she was in the kitchen pumping out breast milk, and I pushed her down and took it. And I told her that she was going to have to pay for her stay while Reese wasn't there. When she refused, I punched her teeth in and told her that I was going to chop her kids up into little pieces with my switchblade, from the youngest to the oldest, and she would be last. She understood the rules for four days. But on day five, she fought back. Now that I think about it, that's probably when you were conceived. Because she kept trying to fight me, and I kept having to beat the shit out of her to make her stop, and we had to keep starting all over. Cut her once or twice with this very knife just to tame her. But by the third time, I stabbed her right on her shoulder, and I jizzed inside of her, she had stopped moving. She was all bloody and shit. I thought that bitch was dead. It wouldn't have been the first time that I killed a whore."

He smiled again at Rion. Rion just blinked, keeping his eyes on Junior and his peripheral vision on the blade. "I fell asleep right next to her. That bitch wore me out. That was my mistake. Let that be another fatherly lesson for you: Never, ever turn you back on a whore. The next thing I knew, she was on top of me, and do you know that bitch stabbed me in the shoulder with my own fucking switch?" He pointed to a scar at the top of his right shoulder with his knife. Rion noted that it was similar to the one his mother had in the same spot. "She had already packed up her rugrats and had them by the door. She said if I ever came near her or her children again, she would stab me to death. She left, and that's literally the last time I saw her."

He forcefully stabbed the knife into the top of the couch. "So you see, there's no love story here. Just a whore being a whore. And you're the son of a disgusting, cheap whore. Nothing more. Nothing less."

Shame washed over Rion for calling his mother a disgusting whore. He decided right then and there he would apologize profusely for that. But first, he had to settle things with his sperm donor.

"Does Maurese know that you raped his girlfriend when he was out of town?" Rion asked.

Junior laughed as he continued to touch the handle of the knife. "A good whore doesn't cry rape. That would make her a bad whore. Nobody wants a whore that's going to cry rape after turning tricks." Rion continued to stare at him. "What, you're gonna tell him? You think I give a shit? You think he gives a shit now? You're living in the stone age if you think any of this shit matters."

"Do I have siblings?" Rion asked unexpectedly.

Junior scoffed. "Probably. How the fuck should I know?" He let go of the knife handle and reached for his cigarettes again. Rion watched him light it and take a puff. Junior began to speak again. "It might be one of Black Cherry's rugrats. Now that was a good whore before she gained all that weight. I remember—"

But Junior was startled as Rion grabbed the knife and jumped on top of him, putting his knee on his groin and the knife at his throat, making Junior drop his cigarette on the floor, still burning.

Junior didn't move. "If you're gonna slit my throat, you better do it quick," he growled. "Because if you miss an artery, I will kill you, *son*."

They both heard Maurese coming down the steps, but neither turned their heads. "What the fuck!?" Maurese yelled. "Rion, let him go!"

"I didn't come here to kill you, Daniel Rion Whitman, Junior," Rion said, using his full name, staring into matching brown eyes. "I just wanted to fill in some gaps missing in my life. I wanted to know if we had any similarities. Share interests. Physical attributes. But aside from looks, I am nothing like you. I never joined the 781 and became a drug runner, rapist, thief, or killer. I got some mental health shit going on, but I'm not crazy like you. Thanks to your brother and my sisters, I went to school, got a degree, became a published author, and I'm so much better without your influence. Oh, and I'm gay as *fuck*," he sneered at him, pushing his knee into his groin to cause pain. Junior winced then growled at him. "So thank you for respecting my mother's wishes and staying away from her and her children, you shitty, worthless, motherfucking excuse for a human being. She was right to keep you away from me. And I will always love and respect her for it."

"Rion!" Maurese barked at him. "Let him go."

Junior smirked. "Better listen to your uncle."

Rion rose to a stand first before he moved the knife. But the blade was so sharp, it cut Junior under his chin anyway. He immediately started to bleed.

"Fuck!" Junior yelled and held his hand to stop the bleeding while reaching out with his other hand to try to grab Rion. But Rion jumped back from his wide arms.

Maurese quickly got between them, pulling Rion even farther back, afraid of how his brother would react. He stomped out the cigarette before it could do any more damage to the wood. He looked down at his bleeding brother. "Whatever you said to him, I know you deserved it."

"Fuck off," Junior said nastily.

Maurese turned around and said, "Let's go, Ree."

But Junior called out, "I'm going to get you back for this, you fucking bastard. The next time I see you, you're going to be a dead bastard."

Rion turned around and smiled. "No, you won't. Because Bones will get to you first." He watched Junior freeze and color drain from his face. "Yeah. Bones loves me like a son. Want me to tell you what he told me he would do to you when he finds you? All the ways he plans to torture and kill you? Imagine if I even told him a portion of this conversation. If I told him I know that you're in Phoenix."

Rion held eye contact with Junior. Junior looked away first, still holding onto his chin.

Rion closed the switchblade and flipped it in his hands. "Thanks for the souvenir. And the sperm, dickhead." He walked past Maurese out of the house.

23

Maurese got into the car and drove them both off. "What did he say to you?"

"Do you know he raped her?" Rion said right away. "Mama didn't have an affair with your brother, Reese. He raped her for five days while you were moving product for the 781."

He shook his head. "She didn't tell me that. Why wouldn't she tell me that? When I got back home, she was already gone. Junior said she didn't know where she went, but with Gabe's daughter, there was only one place she could go. When I found her, she was already using again, turning tricks in 781 motels for money. I didn't understand... We got into this huge argument, and she kept saying she's a whore, and she's doing what whores do best, and I wasn't man enough to take care of her or protect her. That was it for me and her. I took my daughter and left. The next time I saw her, she was in the hospital, and she had just given birth to you. I was her emergency contact. I didn't even speak to her then. I just took you home with me."

“Well he pushed her away from you. He raped her, abused her, and threated to kill her children. Including Muriel. And he did it on purpose to show you that a ho can’t be a housewife.”

“I’m going to fucking kill him,” he mumbled. “We were going to be a family, all of us... He ruined my fucking life.”

“Take me to her,” Rion said. “Take me to Mama’s job. I need to see her.”

“Okay,” Maurese said distractedly.

He mumbled to himself the whole way about how Junior ruined everything between him and Roslyn as he drove over to the supermarket. Rion watched buildings and cars go by in a blur, like the thoughts running through his head. He took a body scan, noticed his heartbeat was finally slowing down, no longer in danger, physically or emotionally. But his heart also ached. For his mother. For Nicholas. For himself. It was the first time in weeks that he allowed himself to feel something, and he welcomed all of the emotions inside of him.

“Want me to wait?” Maurese asked, taking him out of his thoughts.

“Huh?” Rion noticed that they had made it to the Safeway. “No. You go deal with your family. I have to deal with mine.”

Rion took his seatbelt off but turned to Maurese and threw his arms around him. “Thanks for being my father figure.” Rion quickly let him go and got out of the car, not waiting for a response. He walked into the grocery store.

He found his mother’s register and waited in line. Roslyn did a double take and stared for a moment, then continued sliding groceries of the customers along the line. She kept looking up at him in shock as she served the three customers before him. Rion waited patiently until they were all done, then he calmly put the switchblade on the conveyor belt with the star facing upward and watched it roll toward her.

Roslyn's mouth opened slightly, also watching it come toward her. When it reached the edge, stopping the belt, she continued to stare at it. With a shaking hand, she picked it up and gasped. She looked up at Rion with tears in her eyes.

"Can we talk?" he asked softly.

She nodded, then turned her light off so that no other customers could join the line. "Terry," she croaked out, the emotion all in her throat. She cleared it and said to the person next to her, "I'm taking my fifteen right now."

She didn't wait for the okay as she turned around and headed out the doors. Rion followed her. They walked to the side of the building facing the back of the parking lot. Roslyn pulled out a cigarette and tried to light it, but her hand was still holding onto the knife and it was shaking. After three tries, Rion gently took the lighter from her and held the fire steady. She looked at her son gratefully and moved her cigarette over the flame, then she began to smoke.

Rion took out his case and pulled out his half-smoked joint from last week. He lit it and began to smoke. They stood there, side by side, for a few moments and smoked silently.

"So," Roslyn began, "how is your father? Still a psychotic animal?"

"You mean my sperm donor?" Rion said back. "Because that rapist and garbage human could never be anyone's father. You were right when you told Maurese that Junior is a piece of shit even when he's sober." Roslyn looked up at him, but Rion did not turn to her. "Nicholas heard you that night we found Ava. But he didn't tell me until two weeks later when we were in Thailand."

"That night you called Maurese and Maurese called me," she said with a nod. "I figured it out that Nick overheard."

"Yup." Rion continued to smoke his joint. It wasn't enough to get him high, but he could feel the anxiety in his chest start to loosen. "I was so angry at you, at Maurese, at everyone that day. But after meeting Daniel Rion Whitman, Junior, I'm so grateful. Thank you for keeping me away from him. Thank you for being a survivor that night, stabbing him and getting away. Thank you for not having an abortion, for having me."

"Oh, Rion." Roslyn began to cry. She turned to him, and he immediately hugged her back.

"I love you, Mama," Rion said. "I'm so sorry for the things I said to you the night of Gabby's wedding. You aren't that person anymore, and you've been a good mom to all of us since you kicked the habit fully. And I'm so proud of how far you've come. Six years clean and sober this week; that's so amazing. And I forgive you for everything that you did to me or let happen to me when you weren't clean. I truly forgive you, Mama."

He held his mother, rocked her and kissed the top of her head. Roslyn couldn't talk, she was crying so hard on her son's chest. So she nodded on him instead.

All she ever wanted was the love and respect of her youngest son like she had of her other children. And now that he had given it to her, she had her family back. And had the willpower to go a hundred more years clean and sober.

After a few minutes, Roslyn said, "I have to get back to work."

"What time are you off?"

"I have another two hours left," she said, still holding on to her son.

"I'll wait for you. We'll take the bus back together. It's been a long time since I've been on a bus."

Roslyn chuckled. "Okay." She reached up and touched his face lovingly. "I'll see you at 3."

He let her go, and she went inside. Rion began to walk. He found a nearby park and sat under a tree. After about an hour thinking about his life, he realized the only person he wanted to talk to was Nicholas. So he sent him a text, hoping that Nick didn't block him.

[Rion: So many things are happening right now and the only person I want to talk to about it is you.]

[Rion: I was stupid to leave and I want to come back.]

[Rion: Can I come home?]

Rion did not get a response, and that made his heart heavy. But Rion knew the only way to make it right was to get on a plane and see Nick again, to face his fear of rejection and reconcile with his one true love once more. He decided he would, but first he wanted to spend some time with his mother through

Thanksgiving and watch her get her six-year chip, building the relationship that she so desperately wanted and he needed now more than ever.

Nick was driving fast on his motorbike on the Brooklyn-Queens Expressway. He didn't know where he was going, but he knew he needed to ride and ride fast. The curviness of the road was exhilarating, only enhanced by the cocaine in his system. A part of him wished he didn't have his helmet on, that he could feel the wind in his hair and the buzzing of the road in his ears. He needed this adrenaline rush, to replace the one he had for the last few weeks, anger burning through him from the moment he woke up until he went to bed alone, plotting with Adolphe and Zoey to bring down the biggest dipshit the world had ever known.

It wasn't hard. Adolphe let Nick into the Facebook group under an alias, where he was able to gather the intel. The money laundering. The name of the Colombian Cartel and how the shipments were done. How the drugs were smuggled into the casinos. His employees knew it all, even the code of his safe where he kept his personal stash in his office. Nick brought the information back to Emma, who reached out to the Attorney General of New York, an old classmate and colleague of hers, who set up a meeting with the FBI and the CIA. They brought Adolphe in as an informant and whistleblower, who turned over all the books and the discrepancies in the overall revenue. It took them less than two weeks to build an airtight case. Zoey tipped off the 24-hour news stations on the day of the raid, then Zoey, Adolphe, Robby, and Nicholas leaned on Nick's Camry across the street and watched Todd get dragged from his office in the Financial District and get pushed headfirst into an FBI squad car as cameras flashed and reporters yelled questions. They gave themselves high fives on a job well done.

And now that it was over, Nick felt empty. And alone. And depressed. He had spent the last few days sitting in his apartment, thinking of all he had lost. Everywhere he looked reminded him of Rion. The bed smelled like him. His towels smelled like him. The closet smelled like him.

But it all came crashing down when he finally decided to do a little housework, including finally picking Rion's outfit from the masquerade ball up from the floor and putting both of their suits together for the dry cleaner. When he dropped the red jacket onto the floor next to Rion's purple coat, the small tube with the coke in it fell out of his pocket and hit the ground, rolling over loudly across the wood and hitting the wall, spinning a few times before it stopped. And that was it.

Nicholas broke down and cried, sitting on his hardwood floor, remembering how awfully he'd treated Rion at the July Fourth party when he actually was high and had vowed then never to use it again, then how awful their fight was at the last event. Why Rion didn't believe him, he didn't know, but he used it as an excuse to run away from all they had. And that hurt, along with all the other things Rion threw at him, especially the confession of his mental health going down the toilet and not trusting Nick enough to be there for him. Everything hurt. His chest burned, his heart ached, and he couldn't get off the floor. So he sat there and cried, watching the sun go down through the picture window of his living room.

Suddenly, Nick decided there was no point in feeling all these bad feelings. Rion was gone, so there was no reason for anything anymore. He wiped his tears and reached across the wood, wrapping the small cylinder in his hand. He toyed with the tube, then decided to open it. Nick put a pile on the back of his thumb and sniffed. Then sniffed more until the tube was empty. After that, he had no more feelings. He just knew he had to get out of there.

Nick whizzed by everything and everyone in a blur, the roar of the MTT Street Fighter the only thing he heard. He almost got hit by cars twice, but that didn't faze him. He was Nick fucking Highton. Nick Highton was invincible. Nothing and no one could hurt him. *Except Rion. My Ree.* Nick felt a sting of sadness at those thoughts and pushed through it by pressing the gas, going from 85 to 98 easily. A sports car was speeding too, but Nick was faster and cut him off.

"Ha!" he yelled out loud, turning around slightly to see the car almost veer off the side of the road.

But he didn't notice the cars in front slowing down. He faced forward only to see the flood of red taillights in front of him. He gasped and pressed the brake hard, but it was too late. Nick rear-ended another car—ironically, a Toyota Camry—and went flying through the air, across the car, as his back slammed into the car next to it. He felt his body skid to a halt, and then everything blacked out.

The last thing he felt was his phone buzzing three times in his leather motorcycle jacket with text messages.

24

Rion was sitting on the couch with Roslyn, eating popcorn and watching a movie, when his phone rang. He glanced at it and saw it was from Zoey. He sighed and rejected the call, thinking he would call her in the morning. He lost so much time with Roslyn, and he didn't want to neglect another minute of it. But when his phone rang back again, and then a third time, he knew something was wrong.

"Zoey?" he said cautiously.

Zoey did not hesitate. "Nick is in the ICU. It was a motorcycle accident. We don't..." She choked out a sob as dread filled his chest. "We don't know if he's going to make it," she whispered the words as if she didn't want to say them out loud.

"What... What..." Rion felt his chest squeeze tightly at her words. "What are you saying, Zoey?"

He heard her breathing shudder, not being able to say the words again. Rion stood up. "I'm coming home."

She nodded although Rion could not see her. She swallowed and said strongly, "I know. Your flight leaves in two and a half hours from SFO. United, flight 342 to JFK, non-stop. The boarding pass is in your email. A car will be waiting for you at the airport under R. Matthews. It will take you straight to New York Presbyterian. Go to the ninth floor, and when you get to the double doors, guards will be there. Tell them your name and that you're with the Hightons. If they give you a hard time, ask them to get Brian. He'll make sure you'll be let in."

Rion was still in the same spot. "Okay. United. Flight 342. Presbyterian, ninth floor. Thank you for calling me." He had no idea why he said that so formally.

And neither did Zoey. "Rion," she said sharply, "you're family. And he needs you right now. He needs you so he can hold on. Because if he dies..." Zoey choked out another sob.

"I'm coming home, Zoey. I'm coming." He hung up and looked at his mother's concerned face.

"What's wrong with Nick?" Roslyn asked.

"He's..." It finally hit him what Zoey was saying, and his dread turned to fear. "Oh my God. Nick." He put his fist to his chest and squeezed the cotton of his shirt. Then he ran to the door and began to put on his sneakers. "He's in the ICU."

Roslyn rose up and started packing away his laptop, making sure his keys and wallet were in the front pocket. By the time Rion had grabbed his sweater and turned around, she had already approached him with his bag.

"Go to him," his mother said. "I'll see you soon."

He hugged her and said, "Thanks." Then he was running out the door, into the street to catch the next cab to the San Francisco International Airport.

It was the longest five hours and thirty seven minutes of his life, and Rion was glad to finally be off the plane. Not because of his fear of flying, but because the fear of never being able to see, hold, or talk to Nicholas again was weighing him down. He was eager to get to Nick's side. He practically ran for the exit where the taxis were. Before he had a chance to find the driver, a woman came up to him wearing a white shirt, black tie, and black pants, holding onto a tablet.

"Mr. Mathews?"

"Yes. How did you—"

"I have your photo ID," she said. "We must hurry."

"Is there news?" he said as he followed her out of the doors.

"I am to tell you to call Zoey Huffnagle as soon as you arrive," she said as she opened the back door to the black Lincoln Town Car.

Rion threw his laptop bag in first, then grabbed his phone as he sat down. He called Zoey's phone.

"He's in surgery right now," she said when she answered. "He had a small setback, a seizure, and they had to relieve some pressure on his brain."

"Jesus," Rion said as his eyes pooled. "What happened, Zoey?"

"I don't have all the details, Rion," said Zoey. "But he was speeding down the BQE on his motorcycle and drove right into the back of a car, flipped over that one, and fell against another car. He had spinal injuries, but thank God, Brian is involved. He was able to be a part of the first surgery to make sure there was no lasting damage. But even if he makes it out of this, it's going to be a long, hard recovery."

"It doesn't matter, Zoey. I'm here now. I'll be with him through his recovery. And I'm never leaving his side ever again."

"We just need to pray he'll make it out of this alive," she said and sniffed.

"He will," Rion said confidently. "He'll make it out alive, and he'll recover, stronger than ever. That's our Nicholas. Strong and self-reliant. He can get through anything."

Zoey smiled. "You're right. You're so right. Thanks, Rion, for the reminder. Nicholas is strong."

"And he can get through anything," he repeated as the tears began to fall. "I'll see you soon."

He hung up so that she wouldn't hear him breaking down. Rion reached over, grabbed the strap on his laptop bag, bit down on it, and screamed.

When he arrived at the hospital, he didn't stop until he made his way to the ninth floor. As he stepped off the elevator, the first thing he noticed was that it was quiet and deserted. He stopped at the empty nurse's station and called out, "Hello?" No one spoke back. He continued down the hall. When he turned the corner, he saw the two men sitting in chairs in front of the double doors. Upon seeing him, they both stood up.

"This is a restricted area. Please turn back," the man on the right said.

"I'm Rion Matthews," he said. They both stared at him blankly. "Nick's partner, Rion Matthews."

"We're under strict orders not to let anyone in that does not have the Highton name or is not on the close family list," the man on the left said.

"I'm not on the close family list?" Rion asked with his eyes narrowed. Both shook their heads. "Let me guess? Madeline Highton's list?"

The first man looked apologetic. "I'm sorry, Mr. Mathews. I know who you are. But we can't let you pass."

Rion rolled his eyes and took out his phone to call Zoey. But as the man spoke, he noticed the circle with the line on the front of his phone. "There is no service in this area," he confirmed. "You will have to go two floors down for reception."

Rion looked back up at them. "Call Dr. Brian Highton." They both looked at him. "Did I stutter?" he said forcefully. "Get on your walkies and get Brian up here NOW!"

"Mr. Matthews," the man on the left began.

But the man on the right picked up his walkie. "Family base to SR3, come in."

"*SR3, copy.*"

"Mr. Matthews is here. He is asking for Dr. Highton."

"*Hold please.*"

"Grant," the other guard said. "Mrs. Highton made it clear—"

"It's his partner, Ken," Grant said back. "It would be so fucked if something happened, and we were the ones standing in their way."

"We're going to get fired for this," the man named Ken said back.

"*SR3 to FB,*" the walkie croaked back. "*Dr. Highton is on his way up.*"

"Copy," Grant said into the walkie. He turned to Rion. "Dr. Highton is on his way up from the surgery room, Mr. Matthews."

"Grant..." Ken groaned at him.

But Grant said to Ken, "If the heat comes down, I'll take it on. I just know if someone were to do that to my sister and her wife, I would be furious. I can't keep them apart." Ken sighed, then nodded.

"Thank you. I'm so grateful to you," Rion said.

He went to the nearest wall and stood against it, then slid down. He brought his knees up and put his head in his hands. And he waited.

Less than ten minutes later, Rion heard the elevator ding, then heard the footsteps. He watched Brian turn the corner in maroon scrubs, a cotton hat on his head and his face mask on his chin. Brian walked over to Rion, and Rion looked up at him. It was unnerving to see the confident and steady Brian Highton look so sad and unsure. It scared Rion completely.

Brian held out his hand. Rion took it, and Brian lifted him up. Brian wordlessly pulled Rion into his chest for a hug, and Rion wrapped his arms around Brian. Then Rion clung to him and began to sob loudly, letting his fear overwhelm him. And Brian patted his back in comfort for the next few minutes, holding back his own tears.

"Please tell me he's okay," Rion mumbled onto his shoulder.

"He is for now," Brian said. "I'm going to update the family. Come with me."

Brian let Rion go and walked toward the two guards. They immediately opened the double doors and stepped to the side. Rion walked in right behind him, wiping his face with the bottom of his shirt. They passed a nurse's station with two women there. They looked up in recognition of Rion, but neither spoke to him. Brian and Rion walked down another long and quiet hallway until they reached the visiting room. As Rion passed the windows, he recognized some faces but not all. Brian opened up the door and held it open for Rion before he stepped inside.

Emma ran toward him with her handkerchief still in her hand and threw herself at him. "Rion," she breathed out. Rion held her tightly, his face composed, grateful that he had already let out tears with Brian. "I'm so glad you're here. The last time Nick and I spoke he said you asked for space and..." She trailed off.

"Yeah, we had a bad fight. But I'll never leave him, Em," Rion told her. "Even before I got the phone call from Zoey, I was already planning on coming home."

"I know, Rion," she said in a smile through her tears. "I know you were."

"Uncle Ree?" Blair said softly behind Emma.

Her mother let Rion go, and Rion came face to face with Emma's daughter, Blair. Blair hugged him tightly. "Oh wow, you're so big now," Rion said. "I know, such a corny thing to say, but really! You're like a beautiful, mini adult."

Blair grinned at him. "Thanks. I'm so glad you came."

"I'm here too," Robby said from behind his little sister.

Rion smiled. "Where else would you be, Robby?" He gave him a dap, and they pulled together for a full hug.

"Excuse me, Brian," a crisp voice spoke from the corner of the room.

Rion set his eyes on Nicholas's mother, Madeline Highton. She was thin and regal looking, her hair up in a high bun, a silk scarf around her neck. Her makeup was flawless. She did not appear to be a woman who was afraid of her son's critical condition status. Afraid of anything. Any sign of tears on her face would have been weakness, and Madeline was not known to show weakness under any circumstances.

"What is the meaning of this?" she asked sternly to her eldest son, ignoring Rion completely. "I thought I made it clear—"

"Nicholas made it through surgery," Brian said, cutting his mother off. Everyone in the room became quiet as he gave the update. "He... They lost him for about forty-five seconds on the operating table, but they brought him back and continued the surgery."

A few people gasped, including Emma, who put both hands to her face and instantly began to cry. But Brian continued talking. "The swelling went down considerably, but he hasn't woken up yet. It could be days; it could be weeks. They just don't know. But for now, he's breathing on his own."

"When can we see him, Brian?" Emma asked as she sniffed into her handkerchief.

"When I left, they were closing him up, so he should be back in the room in the next hour or so. I'm going to head back down. I'm in the gallery."

"Thank you for the update," his mother said. "Please take your friend with you back downstairs. This floor is for family only." Madeline was still staring at Brian.

"Madeline," Niles began from a chair against the wall, "don't you think you are being a little harsh?"

"No, I don't," she replied without looking at her husband. "I made my wishes very clear."

"Mother—" Emma began, but Brian raised his hand to stop her from talking.

He stood up straighter with his hands folded in front of him and gave his mother the same look he would to Kara, his sub. To her credit, she did not back down. She gave him the same fierce look right back. It was silent, the tension in the air palpable.

"Rion stays, Mother," Brian said calmly but firmly. "Nicholas would want him here. If you don't like it, you can go."

"I beg your pardon?" Madeline said back.

Emma stepped next to her brother. "He said, if you don't like Rion being here, you can go. Rion is Nicholas's family. Our family. And Nicholas needs him a lot more than he needs anyone else in this room. Including you."

"Excuse me?" she looked taken aback at her daughter's boldness. She had never spoken to her that way.

Robby stood next to his mother. "Uncle Rion stays, Grandmother," he said boldly.

Blair also moved and stood next to Robby. Suddenly, two young men, identical twins, came over to stand next to Rion and quietly faced the matriarch of the family too. Then one snapped his fingers, and their younger brother rolled his eyes and walked over there.

The boy stood next to Brian dutifully in front of Rion but mumbled, "I don't even know him." The teen was immediately nudged by one of his older brothers.

Gary, who was sitting next to Niles, stood up and passed his mother-in-law. "Sorry, Madeline," he said as he walked over to the group standing defiantly before Madeline Highton. He stood next to Emma and said, "You know I've never been a fan of your boy. But Emma's right. And if anyone can bring Nick out of this, it's this guy here. Trust me, if you love your son, you want Rion here."

Niles stood up and walked over to Madeline's side. "It's okay, Madeline. Rion is going to stay."

Madeline moved her hands to her back and clasped them. "Well. Since I have been outnumbered, there is nothing more to say, is there?" She turned around and spoke again over her shoulder. "He may stay. For now." Madeline sat down with her legs crossed and picked up her magazine.

Rion smiled. "You didn't have to do that, guys," he said quietly.

They all turned around. "Of course we did, Uncle Rion," Robby said first.

"You deserve to be here," Emma agreed. "You need to be here."

"I gotta head back down," Brian said. "Stay close to Emma."

He patted Rion's shoulder as he brushed past. Emma, Robby, and Blair went back to their seats, giving him loving pats on his back and shoulder as well.

"I'm Arlow, by the way." One of the tall young men held his hand out. "Brian's my dad."

"Our dad," the other twin said, pushing his brother's hand out of the way for a handshake. "I'm Angus. We know all about you. Nice to finally meet you."

"We followed your travel blog," said Arlow.

"We follow all your social media accounts," Angus chimed in again. "You and Uncle Nick."

"We were the first ones that discovered what relationship your acronym was," said Arlow. "And put it out there for everyone."

"Nicholas Will Always Want Rion," they chorused together.

"And it's the one that you do that helped us figure it out," said Angus.

"Rion Will Always Want Nicholas Too," they synchronized again.

It made Rion give them a smile. "Wow. You are ninety-eight percent correct." The boys let out identical laughs. "Nice to meet you both," Rion said, shaking Angus's hand, then Arlow's. He turned to the last son. "And you must be Maddox. Nice to finally meet you."

"Sure, whatever, dude," Brian's fourteen-year-old son said as he went back to his seat, leaving Rion's hand in the air.

The twins giggled. "Maddox doesn't like people," Angus said.

"We got class at NYU, but we'll be back," said Arlow.

"Stay far away from Grandmother," Angus said in a low voice. "Her word is usually law; we've never done that to her before."

"Yeah, she's too calm," Arlow said. The twins looked at her. "She's going to breathe fire and shit bricks. Just be ready for it."

Rion turned back to the seventeen-year-olds. "Thanks for the heads-up."

Arlow was about to say more when they all saw Niles walk up to them. Rion stood up straighter.

"Boys," Niles said, acknowledging them first, "don't you have class?"

"Yes, Grandfather," they chorused and quickly walked away, leaving Rion alone with Niles Highton.

"Erm..." Rion spoke first, finding his voice. He held his hand out. "Hello, Mr. Highton."

Niles took it. "Rion Matthews. I'm glad we are finally meeting, albeit under dreadful circumstances."

"Yes, Mr. Highton."

Rion let go of his hand and realized it was sweaty. He wiped it on his jeans, suddenly aware how rank he must smell after a long flight and all that running through the airports. This was no way to meet Niles Highton, one of the richest men in the world. Nicholas's father. But he said with more confidence than he felt, "I'm also glad we're able to finally meet."

"Well I had requested your presence several times, but I suspect Nicholas wanted to keep his relationship with you to himself, especially after the social media craze the last couple of years or so. And also to keep you away from his parents, understandably. We haven't been the most supportive with his previous relationships."

"No," Rion said. "Nicholas did not want to keep me from you. There were extenuating circumstances that led Nicholas to make that decision for us not to meet." Rion glanced beyond him to Madeline, then back at Niles.

Niles turned around to look at his wife, who was perusing a magazine, then back at Rion. "Yes, well. Madeline can be quite strong willed. Her word is law with us Hightons, myself included. But Nicholas was always my rebellious child. It's no surprise that he picked you as his life partner."

"Is that what you think I am?" Rion asked. "An act of rebellion? Because I specifically asked him when we first met if he was with me just to piss off his parents. He told me he wasn't. I didn't believe him back then, honestly. But almost four years later, I know I am so much more to him than that now."

"And I know it too," Niles said. "That you are not his act of rebellion. Nicholas being with you is an act of love."

Rion almost smiled, but the thought of Nick not being there anymore wouldn't let him. His eyes began to well up, but he refused to let the tears drop. Instead, he blinked them away.

Niles noticed. He touched Rion's shoulder and said, "Keep the faith. Nicholas is very strong willed too. He will come back to us. You hear?"

Rion nodded, the lump in his throat too big to swallow. Niles let him go and walked back over to sit next to Gary, away from his wife.

Rion realized he was still standing in the middle of the room. He went to the far corner on the opposite side of the space from Nick's mother and sat down. He opened up his laptop and looked at the blank Word document in front of him. Then he closed it. He began to look around the room, and a blonde woman caught his eye. He didn't notice her at first, more concerned with what was going on with Nick and the drama with Madeline, but he immediately recognized her.

Penelope Benson gave him a once over, then her eyes went back down to the book she was reading to pass the time.

Brian entered the room an hour-and-a-half later. "Nicholas's condition is stable. He's back upstairs in his room. Despite the complication, his surgery was a success. His vitals are good. There is no reason for him not to wake up now." He looked around the room and spotted Rion in the corner. "Rion, come with me."

"Brian," his mother said sharply and stood up.

Brian sighed and looked at her. "What is it now, Mother?"

"We already had a rotation of who would be sitting with Nicholas every hour. I believe Emma was next. Then Robby. Then Blair. Then Penny. And when the twins return, they will each get a chance. Your friend will have to wait."

He narrowed his eyes at her. "Are you really going to be this difficult at a crucial time like this?"

"It's fine," Rion called out. "I can wait. I'll wait as long as I need to. I'm not going anywhere."

Madeline didn't flinch at the sound of Rion's voice. She continued to act as if he did not exist.

Emma stood up. "No, Rion, you can't. You can take my hour."

"No, he cannot," Madeline said to her daughter.

"You can take mine too," Robby said. "So you have two hours."

"Three hours," Blair chimed in. "Take my hour and stay with Uncle Nick."

"I *said*—" Madeline began.

Everyone ignored her. "Rion, let's go," Brian spoke over her and walked out of the door, with the expectation that Rion would follow.

For the first time since Rion arrived, Madeline rested her eyes on him. Her expression was blank, but her eyes were cold. He turned away from her and picked up his laptop, then walked out the door to meet Brian in the hallway.

They walked down a few paces in silence, then Brian opened up a wooden door with the number 908 on it. It was a large room built to hold multiple beds, but there was only one bed there. They walked over together. Nick's head was wrapped up and bandaged. His face was sunken, and he was wearing a neck brace. His left arm was in a sling against his body and his left leg was wrapped up from his hip to his ankle. There were wires on his chest and an IV in his right hand. To Rion, he looked dead. The only thing that kept confirming his life was the steady beat of the monitor.

"Nicky," Rion whispered.

Rion reached out and touched Nick's hand. It was warm, but it did not move. Rion sat on the chair next to him and held his hand. "Tell me everything, Brian."

"The accident was Nick's fault," Brian said in a low voice. "According to the police report, he was doing at least ninety-five on the BQE on his motorcycle, cutting off cars for five miles, but he ran headfirst into stop-and-go traffic. He slammed hard into the back of a car, flew off his bike into another car, causing another accident. He broke twenty bones. The only reason he's not dead is because he wore his helmet. And the only reason he might be able to walk again is because I put his lower spine back together. That's all I've been allowed to do. So I stay in the hospital, go to his surgeries, and report back to the family."

"Oh, Nicky," Rion said again. "No, babe."

"One more thing you should know. When we did the tox screen, he had cocaine in his system. A lot," Brian said. Rion slowly looked up at him. "Madeline is keeping it off his medical records. She and I are the only ones who know. And now you."

Rion turned back to his partner, lying in front of him. "Jesus, Nicky."

"Now you start talking," Brian said firmly. "What happened? Why did you leave?"

"The night of the masquerade ball was so awful for me in ways I can't even begin to explain. But then Nick was so aggressive, to his mother, to me. I accused him of using coke that night," Rion started.

"I know that part," said Brian. "That fucking dipshit, Todd, gave it to him, hoping they would use together again or that he'd get caught with it. But Kara said Nick wasn't high. That he promised you he would not get high again."

"Well I thought he was, especially after he snapped at Madeline in front of everyone. I came home. We got into a huge argument. I packed a bag and told him that I needed space. And he didn't fight me. He let me go."

"Kara also said you were struggling with being with a Highton. You didn't want to be a part of this world anymore." Rion didn't respond. "You know Nick well enough to know that he wasn't going to fight you to stay," said Brian. "Not if you made it clear you wanted it to be over."

Rion looked up. "I had already decided I was coming back. I'm so used to running away and avoiding the hard shit because I've been through enough hard shit in my life. But I confronted some of my past demons this last week, and I know how much better it is to face things head on. I wasn't quitting on us. I love Nicholas." He looked back down at Nick. "Do you think he did it on purpose, Brian? Because he thought I left him for good?"

"I don't know, Rion," Nick's brother said. "It's the question I had been asking myself since he turned up at my hospital like this. And why he hasn't woken up yet. There is nothing wrong with him physically. He just needs to find the willpower. He has to want to wake up."

Rion looked up at Brian again. "Stay as long as you want," said Brian. "Stay the rest of the day and all night. Stay until he wakes up. I will handle Mother." He turned around and walked out of the room.

There was no other sound but the steady beating of the monitor. Rion put his head on Nick's thigh and held his hand. "Oh, Nicky," Rion said softly again, "I'm here now. Whenever you're ready to wake up, I'll be right here. I'll never leave your side again."

Nick opened his eyes and looked around. He was back in the Mandarin Hotel, Hyde Park. The sun was shining, but he could tell it was dusk. The door to the balcony was open, and a nice breeze flowed through. He looked to his left, and Rion was there, laying sideways on his pillow. Nick turned to him.

"Hi, Ree," he said first.

"Hi, Nicky," Rion responded.

"I don't remember us coming back here," said Nick. "How did we get here?"

"You've been here for a while. I just got here."

"Oh." He reached out and touched his arm. "How long are we here for?"

"For as long as you want to be here," Rion replied. "I'll never leave your side."

Nick could sense that something was off. Rion was smiling and relaxed, like he didn't have a care in the world. Even when Rion was happy, he was never that relaxed.

"Did we have a fight?" Nick asked hesitantly.

Rion reached out and touched his face. "Doesn't matter if we did. I'm here now."

"Okay," Nick said. He looked around again. "It's so beautiful here. And peaceful."

"It's where we fell in love."

"Yes. It's where we fell in love."

"Is that why you want to stay?" Rion asked.

"Yes ... because we had a fight. I remember it now. And it was a bad one. And you left."

"But I'm here now, Nicky. Wherever you go, I'll be there. You don't have to stay here."

"Oh." Nick looked around again. He heard the birds chirping and felt the breeze. "Can we stay a little longer?"

Rion moved closer and kissed his lips. "For as long as you want. I'll be right here. I'll never leave your side again."

Rion emerged from the room almost a day later when the nurses came in to wipe Nicholas down and change his sheets. When he entered the waiting area, Madeline and Niles were not there, for which he was grateful. Emma was talking to another woman, and Blair was in the corner on her laptop. But he was surprised by another face.

"Parker?" Rion said in surprise.

"There he is," Parker said, walking over to him. They clasped hands in a handshake. "They told me you were hibernating with Nicholas. As you should."

"How did you get in here? Madeline made it clear that I was not welcomed simply because I'm not family. So I know you weren't welcomed either. Although she sure had Penelope here, waiting for her darling Nicholas to wake up."

"Bah!" He scoffed. "Madeline may be the head bitch on this side of the pond, but I'm the biggest arsehole in twenty-eight countries. I go where I want when I want. And as for Penny..." Parker gave Rion a sly smile. "She took one look at me and knew trouble was coming. I simply said to her, 'Why the bloody hell are *you* here? Nicholas doesn't like you when he's well.

What makes you think he'd want you by his death bed?' She ran for the hills. I don't think we'll be seeing her around anymore."

Rion smiled at him. "You're so fucking mean."

"No, I'm an insanely wealthy, snobbish Englishman. You haven't seen mean," he said smugly. "But enough about me, how is our boy Nick?"

"He's stable," Rion said, letting out some air. "Vitals are good. He just seems to be in a very deep sleep. I've been talking with him, reading him my stories, holding his hand, things like that."

"Well, he needs to wake up," said Parker seriously. "With both of you here, I'm acting CEO of Deep Strokez Publications, and that is not a job that I want. I've basically told Marcel to run the shit and let me know if there are any problems. Honestly, I need Nicholas to wake up and take back his company."

Rion patted his shoulder. "I know. I'm worried too."

Concern flashed across Parker's face. But he looked away. His phone rang and Parker said, "Excuse me," and stepped away.

Rion took out his phone, and it still said, "No Service." He went over to Blair. "Hey, kiddo," he said.

"Hi, Uncle Ree," she said, pulling out her earpiece. "How's Uncle Nick?"

"No change. But that's also a good thing. What are you doing?"

"School work," she said. "It's all over the news about Uncle Nick, so Mother hardly had to explain to the academy why I wouldn't be physically present for the next couple of days or weeks."

"So you're online right now?" he asked.

"Yes. I'm logged into Blackboard. Why?"

"I was told this is no service zone, but Parker's phone rang and you're able to get online."

"Oh," she said nonchalantly. "There's a secret Wi-Fi, just for us. Give me your phone."

Rion gave it to her. He watched her open up her settings section and open his at the same time. After clicking on a Wi-Fi that had random numbers on it, she tapped her phone with his, then handed him back the phone.

"*Voilà*," she said with a smile.

"Thanks, Blair," Rion said back, also with a smile. "And thank you for giving me your time yesterday. You can go in if you want."

"Okay." She packed up her bookbag, books, and laptop and left.

Rion walked over to her mother. Emma stood up and hugged him, then said, "This is Idalia. Lia is Brian's wife."

Lia had a pretty, round face, caramel colored hair, and kind blue eyes. Her skin was tanned, as if she had come straight from the Italian sunshine to the hospital.

"Oh, I know that face. You are much cuter in person, that's for sure," Lia said in a strong Italian accent, kissing both of his cheeks.

"Thanks," Rion said and blushed. "I've heard so many wonderful things about you from your sisters when we were at your family's estate last year. And I met your boys yesterday, all fine young men."

"Arlow and Angus, yes. Maddox is ... a paradox." She smiled at her joke and Rion smiled too. "Brian should be done with his meeting, so I'm going to find him. We have important matters to discuss." She kissed Rion's face again. "I'm so glad you're here," she said kindly. "My advice? No matter what happens, don't react. Don't explode. Never show that woman weakness, hm?"

Rion did not need to guess who "that woman" was. Instead, he smiled at her. "Thank you, Lia."

Lia kissed his cheek again and hugged Emma before she exited the room.

After letting Emma know that she could go in as well, Rion called his mother first. She didn't pick up, but he left her a message letting her know that he was there with Nick and his status. Instead of calling his sisters, he put a text in the sibling group chat, explaining what had happened. All three expressed concern.

Then Rion called Zoey. She picked up on the first ring. "No change, right?"

"No," Rion replied. "No change."

"I speak to Brian every hour on the hour," she said.

"I'm surprised you're not here."

"I have work to do," she said. "I'm putting out general statements for Lita to present to the press as the family spokesperson, feigning off paparazzi, stopping rumors, keeping his stocks from plummeting, all while concurrent planning, getting his affairs in order in case..." She trailed off. Then she said, "I can't sit by his bedside and wait. He has you for that."

"I get it. You're doing what he needs you to do, as always."

"Yeah..." She sighed. "How are you holding up, Rion?"

"I'm..." Rion sighed too. "I spent the rest of yesterday and all night with him. He's just ... asleep. He looks like Nick when he's sleeping. And as long as I think about it like that, that he's a sleeping Nick and he's going to wake up any time now, then I'm okay."

"I believe he's going to wake up too. He has to." She sighed heavily again. "I gotta go. But I'll see you soon, okay?"

"Okay, Zoey."

26

Rion was lying across the bottom of the bed reading Nick his first book when the door opened. "Rion," Zoey called his name softly.

"Hey!" Rion closed the book as she came closer. He stood up and they hugged.

"Come with me," she said. "I have some important updates."

They walked into the hallway together, and Rion immediately saw them waiting. "Gabby! Ava! Mama!" They quickly ran up and hugged him, first one big group hug, then individually. "What are you doing here?"

"Zoey flew us out; she said you needed us," Roslyn said.

"And Muriel has all the kids, so she couldn't come, but she wanted us to keep her updated as much as possible," said Gabby.

They walked into the waiting room together. Rion immediately noticed that all the Hightons were there, from the oldest to the youngest. But so was Penelope on one side of the room, Parker on the other, and Lita and Marcel in the middle. Marcel was holding a blue folder, and Lita had her laptop, looking as if she was about to take notes in a very important meeting.

He turned to Zoey. "What's going on?" His anxiety began to prickle in the back of his neck and spread down his spine.

But it was Brian who answered. "Have a seat, Rion."

Rion looked up at him. Brian's face was expressionless, and he was the only one in the room standing, other than Zoey, leaning against the wall near the door, still in his scrubs. Rion nodded at him, then walked over to Parker's side of the room. His mother and sisters followed.

"Excuse me, Zoey," Madeline said. "I understand the basis of wanting Mr. Matthews in the room, but we do not allow guests into our family matters. Who are these people?"

"My mother, Roslyn Matthews, and my sisters, Avalon Santos and Gabrielle Hernandez-Navarro," Rion answered her. "They're here for Nicholas and to support me."

Madeline ignored him. "Ms. Huffnagle, I implore you to kindly ask your guests to leave at once. This is a private, *family* matter."

"I'm sorry, Mrs. Highton," Zoey said respectfully, giving her a slight head bow. "But I have asked them to be a part of this meeting as well. Nicholas requested that at least one member of Rion's family be present at this time."

"I don't understand—"

"I beg your pardon, Mrs. Highton," Zoey said, cutting her off but just as respectfully. "But if you will allow me to begin, you will understand, and then you will have the opportunity to ask any questions you would like."

"Begin what?" Rion asked from his seat. He did not like the temperature in the room at all. "What are we all doing here?"

"We're reading Nick's last will and testament," Emma said gently.

Rion stood up abruptly. "No the fuck we're not," he said stonily. "Nicholas is not dead."

"Someone please explain to the outsider how the Hightons handle family business," Madeline said in a bored manner. "Another reason why he should not be allowed in this room."

Rion really wanted to tell her to shove it, but Niles spoke. "We don't wait until the end, Rion," he said. "If there is even a possibility, we do an informal will reading to ensure that we know what to expect and how to prepare for the person's affairs. So there are no surprises, no arguments over estates and assets; we all simply know the person's wishes, and we respect them."

Rion turned to Zoey. "Is that what you've been doing? Instead of being by his bedside, you've been planning for his death!?"

Zoey's eyes pooled with tears. "Rion, please—"

"NO!" he yelled. "Nicholas is not dead! This is ... fucked! And I'm not sitting around to listen to this."

He began to walk toward the door. But Brian stepped in his path and yelled his name. "RION!"

Rion stopped cold. Brian walked up to him and placed one hand on his shoulder. "Look at me." Rion slowly looked up. Brian's touch was gentle, but his face did not soften as he spoke. "I know this is hard on you. But this is hard on every single person here. Look around you. Do you really think any of us want to be here?"

Rion's eyes slowly left Brian's and landed on Emma, who already had tears on her face, with Gary sitting next to her and their children across from them. Robby was staring at his feet and Blair had her head on her brother's shoulder. His eyes traveled to Brian's sons, the twins who sat with their little brother between them, Brian's wife Idalia next to Nick's parents, Penelope, who avoided his eyes, then across to Parker's stoic face, and finally settled on his own mother and sisters. He looked back up at Brian.

"You will sit down. And you will listen to Nicholas's wishes," Brian commanded. "And we're all going to respect what he has to say."

Rion never had an older brother. But suddenly Brian was the closest thing to being one, and he wanted to give him that respect. He nodded and went back over to his seat, vowing to stay quiet. Brian resumed his place against the wall.

Zoey walked over to Marcel, who handed her the folder. She opened it and began to read:

"I, Nicholas Elliot Highton, verbally dictated this last will and testament before my attorney group, Jacobsen, Pomeroy, and Jacobsen, my most trusted advisor and personal assistant, Zoey Rachel Huffnagle, my senior executive Marcel Cyrille Delacoux, and secondary witness and signature of this will, my sister Emma May Highton, Attorney at Law and CEO of Highton Optimum Holdings. I am of sound mind and body, and my current medical and psychological evaluation is placed with these documents.

"To my loved ones: If you are reading this, I am either unexpectedly dead or about to be, and I apologize for the trouble I've caused. But it is extremely important to me that my last wishes be followed without interference from any members of my family. It is my life, it is my career, and it is my money to do as I see fit.

"In the matters of Highton Media and Publications, I leave it in the hands of Parker Kenneth Madison of Parker Madison, Incorporated, as acting President, with Rion Daniel Matthews as acting Vice President, and Marcel Cyrille Delacoux as Chief Operational Officer, a title he should have been given a long time ago. Parker and Rion's salary will stay the same, but Marcel's title comes with a starting salary of six hundred thousand dollars, one hundred shares in the company, and an employment contract for ten years. Between the three of them, my company will be in good hands—"

"STOP," Madeline called out. Zoey looked up. "Highton Media and Publications is a family-owned business, and I will NOT have someone that does not carry the Highton name lead the company. This was in the contractual agreement that Nicholas signed. So no, Mr. Madison and Mr. Mathews will *not* be taking over Highton Media and Publications."

Zoey stared at her, then looked down at her paper and continued.

"Between the three of them, my company will be in good hands until my nephew, Robert Emerson Highton-Dorado, is prepared to take over as the President and Chief Executive Officer. Then a new executive team with Robert at the helm will be brought together. Under his leadership, young mind, and fresh ideas, HMP will flourish for the next couple of decades. The Highton legacy will continue."

Zoey looked up and said, "Nicholas always has a plan."

Robby looked up and said, "Surprise, Grandmother. I've been working with Uncle Nick since he took over, and he's been showing me everything behind the scenes. He said he didn't think he would have any kids, so I was the next best thing." He gave her an innocent look. "You're not disappointed, are you? I know I don't exactly carry the Highton name."

"Oh... Oh, of course not," she stammered out. "It's... It's a good decision." Robby gave her a grin, and she smiled back.

"I'm going to continue and ask that I not be interrupted," Zoey said sternly. "Now where was I?" She skimmed through and began again.

"In the matter of my financial affairs, I currently have no children to bequeath to, known or unknown, and I have no plans to have children of my own. Therefore, my four personal savings accounts and three checking accounts will be combined and split among all my nieces and nephews: Arlow Socrate Highton, Angus Giancarlo Highton, Maddox Leonardo Highton, Robert Emerson Highton-Dorado, Blair Gisella Highton-Dorado, Maurese Hollingsworth, Jeffery Hollingsworth, Katelyn Hollingsworth, Morgan Grant Navarro, and the unnamed firstborn child of Avalon Santos Mathews. At the current time, the contents of these accounts contain approximately two hundred and eighty million dollars. Any subsequent nieces or

nephews will obtain one hundred shares in Highton Media and Publications upon their birth—"

"Who are these other children?" Madeline interrupted again.

Zoey breathed out air and turned to her. "May I finish, Ma'am?"

"You will tell me who these other children are that do not carry the Highton name," Madeline demanded.

"My grandchildren," Roslyn said loudly. "Maurese, Jeffery, Katelyn, and Morgan are my grandchildren. Rion and Nick's nieces and nephews."

Madeline turned to her in disbelief and disgust as Ava raised her hand, showing off her engagement ring. "Hi, I'm Avalon. In case anyone wanted to know." She smiled around the room. Gabby pulled her hand down but suppressed a smile.

"I'm going to continue," said Zoey, ignoring them both. "To Zoey Rachel Huffnagle, you have been more than my personal assistant; you have been my best friend and confidante. To you, I leave two hundred and fifty million dollars, tax free, and ten acres of land in Augusta, Georgia, where your family is from, so you can officially retire. It is nowhere near what you deserve, but it's a start.

"And to Rion Daniel Matthews, who made it very clear from the beginning that he never wanted a cent of my money..."

Rion looked up, his heart beating faster. Once he heard that it was a will reading, he figured that Nick had included him somehow. He just hoped it wouldn't be something disastrous that would make the Highton family hate him.

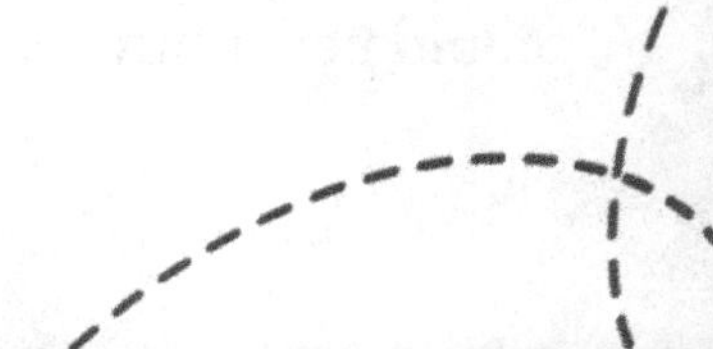

Zoey read, "To you, I leave no dollars or cents, as you wished. Instead, I leave you with assets. The apartment in New York City at 60 Riverside Drive, the apartment in Denmark, and home in East London that we bought together are all yours. So you'll always have a place to lay your head. And if my mother, Madeline Highton, ever releases her hold on Highton Estates at Sea Cliff Manor, the deed will immediately be transferred to you. All my vehicles belong to Saving Grayce except for the Toyota Camry, which is in Rion Daniel Matthews's name, without his prior knowledge. Sorry, Rion. I lied about the car. I bought it, and it's been yours. Please ensure that the cars are sold off at auction by Saving Grayce, the organization run by Penelope Benson, and Saving Grayce receive one hundred percent of the profits. It is the least I could do for her.

"And one more asset: My entire stock of Highton Optimum Holdings is to be transferred to your name, Rion Daniel Matthews. You, along with my siblings, Emma and Brian, hold one-third of all of Highton Optimum shares, stocks, and bonds. I'm sorry I made you ridiculously, filthy rich. Deal with it. In the event that my demise included the demise of Rion Daniel Matthews, my shares are to be given to his sister, Gabrielle Hernandez-Navarro, along with her husband, Gael Navarro. She is the next best thing.

"To Rion, if you are reading or listening to this, you are probably frustrated and annoyed with these decisions to include you and your family in my will. I don't care. Your family is my family too. Because you, Ree, are the greatest gift in all the world that money could never buy. My heart began to beat the day I met you. And I will forever be grateful to the universe for seating us next to each other on that red-eye flight that first day of June. No matter where I am, in life or in death, Nicky Will Always Want Ree."

Rion closed his eyes and began to count back from fifty to steady his heartbeat and to stop any tears from falling as Zoey read the remaining paragraph. He was trying to imagine his life without Nicholas Highton. All the money in the world couldn't make up for losing him, and it was tearing him apart that it was a possibility. Rion didn't want to be ridiculously, filthy rich. He just wanted his Nicky alive and well.

It was quiet, as expected. Zoey closed the folder and looked around. "Any questions?"

Madeline cleared her throat, making Rion open his eyes, and stood up. She walked up to Zoey and asked, "May I?" She held out her hand.

"Of course, Ma'am." Zoey handed Madeline the folder.

Madeline opened it, but she did not read it. Instead, she pulled out the documents, turned to Rion and his family, and tore it in half.

Remembering Lia's words, Rion gave her no reaction. But Marcel spoke first. "You do know that was just for dramatic effect, right?" he said curtly. "That was a certified copy, not the original."

"I don't give a shit!" she yelled at him. "Has my son lost his goddamn mind!?"

"Madeline, dear," Niles started to say, but she screamed at him.

"Oh, shut up, Niles! You're the one that allowed this to continue, saying he just needed to get it all out of his system. And now look! All it took was three years and we have degenerates stealing our money!"

"Hey!" Gabby called out.

"But it's not your money, Madeline," Parker said out loud. "Nicholas has earned every single fucking dime with his blood, sweat, and tears, starting from the seven hundred million dollars given to him on his twenty-first birthday. That was his consolation prize for having you as his mother."

"Excuse me!" Madeline said angrily.

Parker stood up, all 5'7" of him, and commanded the room. "You heard me correctly, you sorry excuse for a mum. As our dear old boy eloquently stated, it is his life, it is his career, and it is his money to do as he sees fit. And I know Nicholas better than you do; this will and all his assets are sealed up airtight. The funds will be distributed from the moment of his death. Nicholas will soon be free of you, but you will be forever tied to Rion Matthews and his entire family," he said with a sadistic laugh. Then he stopped laughing and said coldly, "You wield no power over him. It's over."

Madeline was shaking with fury. "You stupid little man. You have no idea the reach I have. Not one dime, not one asset, not one home, not one stock, or share, or bond will ever be placed in the hands of them." She pointed to Rion. "You think you, and you, and you," she pointed at Parker, then Zoey, then Marcel, "will get away with this!?"

She looked at Brian, who was still leaning against the wall watching her impassively. "And you, my first-born. That's not surprising," she spat at him. "You've never been the gatekeeper of this family. You've never been a real Highton man. You're barely a man, with your pregnant whore and your sex addiction. Your father was right; you're the real disappointment here." Brian continued to watch her, giving her no reaction.

She lastly turned to Emma. "But you ... my own daughter." She glared at her. "You knew about this and said nothing. You betrayed me, you bitch!"

"Hey!" Gary growled before Emma could respond. "Back off my wife, Madeline. All she did was be there for her brother and respect his wishes. Maybe you need to do the same."

"By not mentioning the moves he was making behind my back to me? Noooo that was... This is..." Madeline shook her head and pointed at Emma again. "I am done with you, Emma. From this moment on, never come to me again for anything." She turned her back on her only daughter.

But Emma found her voice. "Did you tell Nicholas that you regretted having him? That he was the son that never should have been?"

The whole room murmured and gasped. "Madeline?" Niles said to her. "You didn't!"

Ava whispered to her brother, "She didn't say that to him, did she?"

"She did," Rion said quietly, still glaring at Nick's mother for the ridiculous outburst she was making.

Madeline did not respond. Emma stood up. "And that is why I never mentioned to you what he was doing. Because you were cruel to him, Mother. You were cruel to him from the day he was born. You were cruel to him in so many ways for so many years and tried to control all of his life choices. Because at least if you could control him, it would have been worth having him. Is that right, Mother? His only use to you was to be a puppet in your show, and when he rebelled against you, you threatened to take away everything from him. What you and Father did with Trixie was unforgivable, and I would never let it happen again, not with Rion, who I love like a brother. So, yes, I helped him plan around you to ensure that his wishes were laid out in a way that you could never touch it. It's his life, Mother! His life, his career, and his goddamn money!" she shrieked.

Robby and Blair grinned at their mother for finally standing up to her own mother.

Madeline looked around the room and scoffed. "His life," she spat. "His career. His money. Well, I'm sorry to break it to you all. It's not his life. *I* gave him life. It's not his career. He would be nothing without the Highton name. And it's not his money. It's Highton money. And if you all think you can just tell me to go fuck off so he could take his family's money and throw it all away for a man unworthy to clean my gutters, then you are all sadly mistaken. I own him, even in death."

Rion had had enough. He stood up and said, "Well thankfully, Madeline, Nicholas isn't dead. You can just wait until he wakes up and tells you to fuck off all on his own."

Rion walked out of the waiting room and went back down the hall to Nick's room. He closed the door behind him and walked over to Nick's sleeping body.

"Goddamn you, Nick," he said softly. "You just had to include my family, didn't you?"

The only response was the soft beeping sound of the monitor. Rion sat in the chair and put his head on Nick's arm.

"C'mon, Nicky. It's time to come home."

"What did you say?" Nick asked.

He opened up his eyes. Rion was laying his head across Nick's chest, and Nick was running his hands through his hair.

"I said it's time to come home," Rion said. "We've been here long enough. We have to go."

Nick looked up at the sky again. It was still dusk. The sun hadn't changed, and the breeze felt exactly the same. "How long have we been here?"

"Long enough," Rion said.

"It feels like no time has passed at all," said Nick. He sighed.

"It's time. You've got a company to run and traveling to do," said Rion. "We can't stay here forever."

"Yes but..." Nick was thoughtful again. "We had a fight. And you left."

Rion turned his head to look at Nick. "I'm here now."

"But are you going to stay with me?" Nick asked.

"There's only one way to find out," Rion responded. "You take my hand, and we walk out of here together. Just like we did last time. You came back here for me, and we left together. I came back for you. Let's leave together."

Nick looked up at the sky again. The same birds singing. The same breeze blowing. "It's going to hurt, isn't it?"

"Like a motherfucker," Rion acknowledged.

"But you'll be there with me?" Nick asked.

Rion turned his head back down, and Nick resumed playing in his hair. "I'll never leave your side again."

Nick nodded. He continued to play with Rion's hair and closed his eyes one last time.

27

Nicholas could feel Rion's curls beneath his fingertips. He continued to run his fingers through Rion's hair and listened to the sounds around him with his eyes closed. It was quiet, except for a monitor beeping beside him. He tried to swallow, but his throat felt incredibly dry, like he hadn't had a drop of water in days. He tried to move his left hand, but it felt heavy. He felt incredible pain throughout his body, but his hip hurt the most.

Nick opened his eyes. The lights were dimmed around him, like it was in the middle of the night. He immediately knew he was in a hospital bed. For how long, he had no idea. He looked down to his left and saw that his arm down to his fingers was bandaged, and so was his left leg. He heard the light snoring and looked to his right. Rion was in a chair next to the bed, his head next to Nick's hip facing Nick's feet. Nick's right hand was still in his hair.

"Ree," he croaked out.

Rion didn't stir. *He still sleeps like the dead,* Nick thought, and he smiled. He kept his hand in Rion's hair, looking up at the ceiling as the accident came flooding back to him. He laid there as the room began to brighten with the sun coming up.

Finally, Rion made some movement. He turned his head but didn't open his eyes. Nick began to play in Rion's hair again.

"Ree," Nick said again.

"Hmm?"

"It's time to wake up, Ree," Nick practically whispered.

"Okay," he mumbled. Then his eyes flew open.

They stared at each other, then Nick smiled. "Hi, Ree."

"NICKY!" Rion screamed and jumped up. He forgot that Nick was still in pain and threw his arms around him.

"Whoa," Nick said softly, slowly getting his voice back. He raised his right arm as Rion sobbed into his neck. "It's alright, babe. I'm here."

"I thought I lost you. Oh my God, Nicky, I thought I lost you," he cried over and over again.

"I thought I lost you too," Nick said back to him.

Rion looked up, his eyes red with tears, snot down his face. "I will never leave you again, Nick," he said with a sniff. "I'm so sorry. I promise I will never leave you again."

Nick shook his head. "No, it was my fault. You should have left me. I was foolish and arrogant. I've been neglectful of you, of us. I didn't put you first or protected you in my world like I said I would. I'm sorry, Ree."

Rion kissed his lips gently, not wanting to talk about any of that. None of that mattered anymore.

Nick smiled then popped his lips a few times. "Water?"

"Oh, yeah."

Rion fumbled with the controls so that Nick's head was slightly elevated, then went over to his food tray and took the bottled water with a straw. He held it for Nick for him to drink.

Nick drank it all, then said quietly, "Thank you."

"Of course," Rion said. Then he stood up straight. "I should let your family know."

"Wait," Nick said and held his arm. "The last thing I remember was the red lights of cars in front of me. What happened to me? How long was I out?"

Rion sat on the bed next to him and held his hand. "It's been seven days since the accident. You've had two surgeries already, one on your spine, and your brother made sure you would be able to walk again. And then you had really bad seizures, and they had to relieve some pressure on your brain. And I think you died once on the operating table, but they brought you back."

"Jesus." Nick reached up and touched his bandaged head.

But Rion took his hand back into his own. "But you're okay, Nick. No one knew when you were going to wake up, but when you did, the doctors said you were going to be fine, no lasting damage to your brain. Brian did say that it was going to be a long physical recovery, but you're going to be okay."

Nick nodded. Rion was about to get up again when Nick squeezed his hand. "Did my family read the will?" Rion gave him a slow nod. "Shit. They really did think I was a goner."

Rion squeezed his hand back. “But I knew you were going to come back to me. Just so I could drive you home in my Toyota Camry.” Rion raised an eyebrow and squinted at him.

Nick laughed, then whined, “Jesus, Ree, don’t make me laugh, my ribs are still broken.”

“We’ll talk about the will later, you crazy *son* of a *bitch*. And I mean that literally.”

Nicholas grinned. “I take it Madeline shit bricks when the will was read?”

“Did she?” Rion said amusingly. “Madeline practically had a litter of puppies right on the waiting room floor. I was so pissed with her outbursts.”

Nick laughed and winced again as Rion told him how she reacted, interrupting Zoey, ripping the paper, berating Brian, calling Emma a bitch and Gary nearly pouncing on her for it. “Someone should have recorded it so I could watch it later,” said Nick. “I could imagine the look on her face when she discovered I was giving millions of dollars to your nieces and nephews.”

“Okay, looking back, it was pretty comical,” Rion said, chuckling too. “She started pointing and yelling at me and Zoey and Marcel and poor Emma, saying that we all conspired against her to give away Highton money to degenerates, and we just can’t tell her to go fuck off. I told her that you’re going to wake up and tell her to fuck off yourself, so please don’t forget to do that at some point.”

Nick was in so much pain but couldn’t stop laughing, tears on his face. Rion wiped Nick’s tears away and kissed his lips again. “I have to let them know you’re awake.”

“I know, I just...” Nick stared at him.

Rion understood. He slid into the bed on his side, and Nick gave him room on the small bed. They pressed their foreheads together and closed their eyes, holding hands between them.

"Nicky?" Rion whispered.

"Hmm?"

"Did you do it on purpose?"

Nick opened his eyes. "You mean did I crash my motorcycle into a car to harm myself because I thought I lost you?"

"Yes," said Rion without opening up his eyes.

"No, I didn't try to harm myself on purpose," said Nick. "But ... I didn't have anything to live for at that moment. I didn't use coke that night of the ball. I promise you I didn't. But I did use it the night of the accident. So maybe I didn't care about my life or if I died on that highway since you were gone."

"Oh, Nicky," Rion said softly. "No matter what happens next with us, I won't run away. I promise I will stay and fight for us. Promise."

"Me too," Nick said back just as softly. "I promise to stay and fight for us too. Always."

Rion walked into the waiting room. Madeline, Emma, her two children, Parker, and his family were the only ones there. He cleared his throat, and everyone turned to him.

Emma looked at Rion's bloodshot eyes and threw her hands over her mouth in fear. "Oh no! Is he... Is he..."

"He's awake," Rion said as more tears fell. "He's awake, and he's talking and laughing, and Nicholas is going to be just fine."

"Oh my God," Madeline said and touched her heart. It was the first time he had seen any kind of emotion from her other than rage.

"Oh my God!" Emma repeated. She ran up and hugged Rion. "Thank you so much, Rion."

"I didn't do anything, Emma," said Rion. "I just knew he was going to come back to me."

Blair flew into them and hugged Rion and her mother; Robby hugged on top of the three of them. Then the Dorados hugged each other. Roslyn, Gabby, and Ava hugged Rion, then hugged Emma, Blair, and Robby. The only ones that weren't hugging were Madeline, who was still standing there with her hand over her heart, and Parker, who put his head between his legs and tried to calm himself down, hiding his own tears of joy.

"Does Brian know yet?" Emma asked.

"The nurse came in and shooed me out so she could take his vitals. She paged him to the room so he should be there by now."

"Can we see him?" Blair asked. "All together?"

"I don't see why not," said Rion. "Go."

Emma and her children practically ran from the room. Madeline hurried after them, but she stopped in front of Rion. Rion waited. Her lips subtly opened, as if she was going to speak, then slowly closed into a thin line. Her head turned first, then her body followed and walked out of the room.

"You're welcome, Madeline," Rion said, although she was long gone.

Roslyn said, "We're going to go see Nick too."

"Of course," he said. "You should go. He would want to see you all too."

They hugged him again and left. Rion looked around, and it was only Parker in the room with his head still between his legs.

Rion walked over to him and sat down. He rubbed Parker's back, feeling the fast pace of his heartbeat, the slight twitch in his trembling. Rion's entire hand grazed Parker's spine until Parker's breathing had returned to normal and he was able to sit up. Rion's hand abruptly dropped and came together with his other hand on his lap. He watched Parker pull the handkerchief out of his suit pocket and wipe his eyes, fold it neatly, and stand up.

The British man cleared his throat and said without glancing at him, "If you ever tell Nicholas that I cried, I will skin you from the inside out."

"Your secret is safe with me," said Rion.

"Right," Parker said and marched out of the waiting room.

Rion sat there for a moment with a smile on his face. Then he sent a text to Zoey and Marcel, letting them know that their boss was back.

28

Rion stood in line with his hood over his head, hoping he would not get recognized. Between Nick's family, his family, and the flood of doctors in and out, Rion's anxiety was starting to take a toll on him again. Over the last couple of weeks, he had been living in the hospital without having a quiet moment to himself or a quiet moment with Nick. Regardless, he was not going to leave his side, no matter what. He was partnered with a Highton for life, and he would decide how that role would play out later; for now, Nicholas needed him more than ever.

But being with the Hightons day in and day out was starting to make him antsy. They were a bit suffocating as a group, complaining about things like the room temperature, complaining about each other, and talking his ear off. He had not spent that much time with any of them, and they all seemed to want to spend time with him, from the youngest—Maddox had come around some—to the oldest. But he didn't mind talking with Niles. Robby managed to sneak him some gummies from a local dispensary, and that helped some, a low dosage to quell his anxiety but nothing stronger. Rion wanted to be fully present. But that also meant the waves of anxiousness in his chest continued to be frequent.

He decided to go downstairs for a breather and grab something to eat. But he quickly discovered that being in a crowded hospital cafeteria was not helping either. He stared at the sun and slow falling flakes through the window as he waited in line for his sandwich, wanting to know what the air outside felt like. Rion had not left the hospital since he arrived a few days before Thanksgiving, and it was the week before Christmas.

As Rion was leaving the cafeteria, he spotted the woman with black hair and a protruding belly in the corner reading with a half-finished garden salad in front of her.

He walked over and said her name softly. "Kara?"

Kara looked up, startled at first, and then smiled. "Hello, Rion."

She looked different to him, still thin, but her body had filled out. Her face was rounder, her cheeks rosier, and her raven-colored hair was held back in a ponytail with a bow at the base of her neck. He realized what was the difference: it was the first time he had seen her without makeup or in a fancy dress. As Rion suspected, her beauty was natural, and her almond colored eyes shone as she saw a familiar face.

Kara started to rise, but Rion immediately put his hand out to stop her and bent down to give her a half a hug and a kiss on her head. "You look so great," he complimented her in her ear. Rion sat down across from her with his freshly made tuna wrap.

"Oh." She touched her belly. "I look fat and bloated," she said with a grin. "Any day now."

Rion shook his head. "Pregnancy looks good on you." She patted his hand in gratitude. "So what are you doing here? Did you want to come up and see Nick?'

She shook her head. "You know I don't engage with the Hightons at all. I'm waiting for Brian. He should be finishing up his last appointment of the day soon."

"Okay."

"But how is Nicholas?" Her eyebrows scrunched up in concern. "Brian said he's well enough to go home, but how is he really doing?"

"He's hanging in there," said Rion. "No issues with his internal organs, thankfully. The cast is off his arm, and it's in a sling. But there's still a cast going down his left leg. He hates being in the hospital and is getting restless, starting to snap at the doctors and nurses, so they're discharging him. He'll be in a wheelchair for a few weeks, then graduate to crutches while in physical therapy for another couple of weeks, but he should be able to walk on his own in three months or so. Brian said he'll always have some level of pain in his left hip bone, maybe even a limp. But if that's all it is, then we're very grateful to the universe."

"I gave Brian a list of physical therapists, colleagues of mine, that are excellent," said Kara. "I would do it myself, but I'm going to be taking a break from working for the next couple of years."

Rion cocked his head to the side. "You're a physical therapist?"

"Yes. I'm part of a team of private doctors who do intense, in-home physical therapy for expedited recovery."

"For the rich and famous," Rion deduced.

"Exactly," she confirmed.

"So you're a doctor too."

Kara smiled. "Yes, I am. A DPT."

Rion kept his voice low. "But you call him The Doctor."

Kara smiled slyly, her rosy cheeks getting rosier. "Well, that's different. Today, he's Brian and I'm Kara. When we're alone, he's The Doctor. And I'm his Petit."

"So fascinating," Rion said in awe. "Will you give it all up when you have the baby?"

Kara gave him a serious look. "It's not just something I do from time to time. It's who I am. A submissive, slutty, bratty, masochist princess."

Rion couldn't help laughing out loud, making her smile. "Okay, got it."

Kara giggled. "I obviously can't engage in anything intense right now, but after my son is born, if I need a release, I'll get my itch scratched. Or The Doctor will scratch it for me," she said with a wink. "It's a part of who we are. We'll continue to do it together, no matter how many children we have."

"Are you planning on having more children?" Rion asked.

"Well, he wants a girl, and I wanted a boy, and this one is a boy, so I agreed to try one more time after this. But if it's two boys, then it's two boys."

Rion grinned at her again. "I want to know your story, Kara."

"What do you mean?"

"There is a story there. How this beautiful young woman became a submissive, princessy, slutty—"

"A submissive, slutty, bratty, masochist princess," she corrected him. "Sometimes I add slave girl for fun."

"See? I want to know all about it. How you became each of those titles. Why Brian? Why this lifestyle? Just ... why? I want to know."

Kara smiled. "Will you write it? Tell my story to the world?"

Rion shook his head. "No. I would never betray your privacy like that—"

"I want you to write it," she said, cutting him off. She reached out and touched his hand. "I've read your books, Rion. All of them. You are a fantastic storyteller. I want you to tell my story."

"Wait, you mean like a documentary? Or like change the names and make a fictional story from your real life?"

"Whatever way you want to do it. I just want the world to know who Kara Simone Beaumont is."

That made Rion curious again. "Were you the one who leaked your pregnancy to the press?"

She smiled at him. "With Brian's permission, of course. And he got Idalia's, which was why she left a month before it all came out. But yes, I was the 'source' in my own tabloid story. It was actually pretty fun."

"Idalia just agreed to have it known that her husband had a long-term mistress?"

"Well it makes her look good, doesn't it? The poor wife whose husband had been cheating on her for years after giving up her country, her family name, and raising his children. Brian and I are the villains in her story, and I'm okay with that. She'll probably write a book, then reinvent herself and become this beautiful, famous international real estate broker. At least that's what Brian thinks."

"So you need your story out there to counter the one she will write?"

Kara shook her head. "No. My story will barely mention her. My story will be about me. My road to becoming a submissive."

Rion was thoughtful. "I'd have to talk to Brian. Get his permission. Because your story is his story too."

"I'll do that," she said. "Just tell me if you're willing to do it."

Rion was about to answer when soft-pink pointed fingernails tapped his shoulder. He looked up to see Madeline Highton behind him.

"Mr. Matthews? Can I have a word with you?"

Rion was stunned into silence. Nick's mother had not said a single word directly to him in the last four weeks they had all been at the hospital together.

Kara stood up with her plastic tray, water bottle, and book, and turned to walk away. "Kara?" Rion called out.

"Thank you for the update," she said and continued to walk away.

Before he could think, Madeline sat in Kara's place. It made him curious; there was no way she did not know that the woman whose seat she occupied was carrying her grandson. The woman she called whore to her entire family. But Madeline didn't even look at Kara once, as if she was not there. And Rion remembered how she pretended his presence was nonexistent from the moment he arrived except for twice when she actually looked at him. And it made him angry all over again.

Rion got a chance to really look at Nicholas's mother, the Highton matriarch. He had to admit, even at sixty-four, she didn't look a day over forty. Her makeup highlighted her features, and her skin was tight, the Botox doing its job at ensuring not one aging line across her forehead or near her eyes could pop out. Her hair was dark brown and had a slight wave to it; he could see it in the strain that fell loosely at the base of her neck, a defiance of her tight bun. Her eyes were wide and brown, and there was a seriousness there. Rion wondered if she had ever been happy.

An epiphany slid across his thoughts, and he almost kicked himself that he didn't think of it before. Brian, Emma, and Nicholas all chose brunettes with brown eyes as their partners, outside of what was chosen for them. Kara was a raven-haired, soft-skinned natural beauty. Seppani had a head full of thick chestnut-colored wavy hair that was always loose and had a kind smile. And from the very beginning, Nick could not stop running his hands through Rion's curly brown hair or staring into his brown eyes. It was like they unconsciously choose a better version of their mother. Softer. Kinder. More loving.

Madeline was taking in all of Rion as he did to her, in close proximity for the first time. It made him itchy, like he wanted to scratch all over, but he kept his hands still on the table. They stared and stared. Rion refused to speak first.

"Mr. Matthews... Rion," she began. "I want to apologize for my demeanor when you first arrived. It was uncalled for. You have my utmost respect for helping to bring Nicholas out of the coma. And I have watched how you have cared for him every moment of every day since. There are ... real feelings between the two of you. I can acknowledge that."

Rion continued to stare at her. He wasn't buying it.

"I know you want what's best for him, Rion. I do too, believe it or not. All the decisions I have made for his life were only to benefit him. And I will continue to make decisions that I believe will be the best for him, give him the best possible opportunity for success. But I understand that Nick is an adult and will make decisions for himself. I can accept that it is his life, his career, even his money. And for now, you are a part of that."

"Forever," Rion corrected her. "I am a part of his life forever."

"I know you believe that, Rion. I know Nicholas believes it too. And while I acknowledge the current feelings are real, I am not convinced that it is forever. I have been around a lot longer than you. I know that love fades. And when it does, the only thing you will have left to count on is yourself."

Rion sighed. "Is that what you came to tell me?"

"No." Madeline pulled out a manila envelope from her purse and put it on the table. "This is for you."

Rion looked his name on the envelope, then cut his eyes to her. "Don't you dare insult me with an envelope of cash. I'm not a farm girl named Trixie. And there is nothing you can do to destroy me."

"Oh, I know that," she said with a wave of her manicured hand. "This isn't a bribe, Rion. It's an assurance. And a thank you for bringing my son back to me. There is no cash in there. The documents are bank statements, a deed, and a legally binding agreement from me to you. There is an account with six hundred million dollars in it in your name at Sun Trust Loan and Savings in California. That is a hundred million dollars for your mother and your three siblings. You keep two for yourself. It will be released to you upon the termination of your relationship, along with Highton Estates at Sea Cliff."

Rion was confused. "I'm sorry. *What*?"

"This relationship will not go the distance, Rion Matthews. It is full of love and passion, but that is not enough to maintain a lifelong partnership, like what me and Niles have. And Nicholas needs a lifelong partner. I honestly do not care if he is gay, or bisexual, or whatever. I just want him to settle with an appropriate match in our society to carry the Highton name. And you, Rion, are not it. I know you know this. But still, you hold onto this exotic love affair, knowing, like I do, that one day it will all end. So *when*, not if, but when, this relationship between you and Nicholas finally does end, you will not leave empty-handed. You will obtain enough money to sustain you for three lifetimes and a home big enough for your whole family to move into. You can finally take care of everyone, like you've always wanted to. Be the success story in your family, as your sisters and mother expected you to be. I know that's what you always wanted. What you really want."

Rion was annoyed. She was using his words against him, things he said in his social media posts. But he kept his cool. "Do you really think I'm going to break up with Nicholas for this? I don't need your money, and we don't need the house."

"No. I think you and Nicholas are going to break up all on your own," she said, so sure of herself. "And when you do, this will be waiting for you. It's up to you how soon you will obtain it. You could leave him today, and it will be yours. He could end it a year from now, and it will still be there for you. Even five years from now. I honestly don't even see it reaching year ten, but if that is how long you are willing to put up with Nicholas, or have Nicholas put up with you, it will be completely your choice."

"I don't want it," Rion said. "I'll never accept it, even if we do end up breaking up."

"When," she corrected. "And when you break up, your family is going to want you to take the money. Especially if it was a tumultuous ending. You and I both know it will be. Your public fights have been legendary so far. One of those fights will end this relationship. They have been steadily getting worse since you came back from London earlier this year, have they not? The differences between you two are becoming clearer. You have money and status of your own, so the thrill of being with a wealthy socialite is not there anymore. And he has his family now, and the family business to run, so he's no longer looking to fill his life with extra-curricular activities. I know you left him once. In fact, I believe that if it wasn't for the accident, this relationship would have been over. So yes, it's just a matter of time. And again, when it's done, the money is yours."

"And I simply won't take it," Rion said. "Whatever game you're playing, it's not going to work. I'm not signing anything agreeing to this."

"Well that's the beauty of our little arrangement, isn't it?" she said with a cold smile. "You don't have to do anything. It will automatically be transferred in your name."

"We don't have an arrangement, Madeline," he sneered. "And I will make sure Nick knows that when I tell him of this. Because I will tell him."

"Of course you will," said Madeline, still smiling. "And because you will, it will always be in the back of both of your minds. Every disagreement. Every argument. Every time someone walks away from the other. Every time your anxiety gets the best of you and you need space from him, like it's doing right now. Yes, I've been watching you hold it together, wanting to escape from all this. And when you do ask for space again, he will wonder, 'is this the day it ends?' That would certainly speed up the process. So yes, tell him. Or you don't tell him. And he'll find out on his own and be furious that you kept it from him. Maybe that will lead to the breakup all on its own. Either way, it will have proven my point. Your Niion Lights are not meant to be ... forever."

Madeline stood up. "Nicholas will be brought to the home in Napeague tomorrow upon discharge and will be there for the next six months. Brian found a physical therapist willing to work with him daily on recovery. Don't worry. I won't stop you from moving in with him. That would defeat the purpose of this little experiment we have going on, won't it?" She walked away, leaving the envelope on the table.

Rion stared at it. Then he sighed and murmured, "This fucking bitch."

He slid the sealed envelope into his bag and went back upstairs to Nicholas's room.

29

Rion had never experienced the beach in December. The sand covered in white snow and the biting wind was enough to make him want to go back to the California sun. But he stepped out of the Camry to help Nick out of Brian's SUV and put him in the wheelchair. They quickly wheeled him up the ramp and inside. The home was already warm, and there was a hot meal in the oven of baked ziti and fresh salad in the fridge. The note on it said, *With love, from Seppani*. Rion smiled.

He turned back to see his boyfriend try to stand up and Brian hold him steady. "You can't right now," Brian said.

"I just need crutches," said Nick, but the pain in his face made it clear that he simply wasn't ready.

Rion came over to help. He wrapped his arm around Nick's waist, and Brian held firm to the left side of him. Together, they helped Nicholas hobble to the room on the first floor and get him into bed.

"Ezra will be here in the morning," said Brian. "He's the one Kara recommended the most because he's firm and gets results. You're going to need a firm hand if you want to be whole again."

Nick shoved himself up until he was sitting against the headboard. "I'm fine," he said grumpily.

Brian and Rion exchanged looks. The reality of the consequences of Nick's accident was starting to hit him hard. There were things he was going to be unable to do for a while. He couldn't stand, and even sitting too long agitated his hip. And Nick refused to be seen in a wheelchair. It was going to be a miserable few months for him, and it was already making him depressed.

Rion slid into the bed beside Nick and rested his head on Nick's shoulder. He kissed it then looked up. Nick looked down at him. "I said I'm fine."

"I know you are," Rion said calmly.

Rion took out his phone and lifted it up high for a couple's selfie. Nick was still frowning. Rion took the picture, then said, "You want your now one hundred and sixty-eight million followers to see you like this? Because I will post this pic."

Nick rolled his eyes, then took a deep breath. He looked toward the camera and gave it a small smile. Rion grinned and took the picture. He watched Rion open up his IG account and post it with the caption:

We're home. And Nick is going to be just fine. #NiionLitesForever.

Because neither Nick nor Rion had posted on their personal accounts in over six weeks, it quickly blew up, with hundreds of people sending him well wishes, asking what happened, wanting to know how Nick was, asking Rion to keep them updated on his recovery. Nick smiled and kissed Rion's head.

Brian smiled at him. "I'll leave you in Rion's capable hands. Call me if you need me; I'm an hour down the road."

As Brian left the home, Nick opened up his phone and scrolled through the messages and his DMs. He decided to go live and add to his story. He lifted up his phone to an appropriate angle and pressed the red circle.

"Hey guys. I just want to come on real quick and thank you all for the love and support. Also to clarify a few things: Yes, I was in a really bad motorcycle accident. Yes, I was in a coma for seven days until the love of my life pulled me out of it. Yes, it's my first day out of the hospital, and we've settled into a new house at a private location. Yes, I am fine, but it's going to be a long recovery. And yes, Rion will keep you updated on my progress. Now all I want to do is get some sleep in a nice warm bed next to the best man in the world."

He turned to Rion. Rion moved closer into the frame and initiated a kiss. Sweet and gentle, lips lingering together, eyes closed. Rion turned to Nick's phone and winked, then he pressed the end button.

Nick laughed. "That kiss was everything. My fans are going to think we're about to make sweet, sweet love."

Rion smiled in his face. "Your fans would be wrong."

Nick groaned. "Ugh. It's been almost two months."

"Don't be dramatic," Rion said with a yawn. "You need to rest tonight. So rest."

"Okay," Nick agreed. "Will we make love in the morning?"

Rion slid down into the bed and put his face on the pillow, turning on his side. "Go to sleep, Nicky."

Nick slowly moved down too until he was on his pillow and eye level with Rion. "You should just sit on my chest and put your cock in my mouth."

Rion's mouth and dick twitched at the same time. "Not tonight, babe."

"So tomorrow, then?" Nick reached out and touched Rion's arm. "Tomorrow, you'll flip me on my stomach like a pancake and drill me?"

"Not tomorrow either," Rion said, but the image in his head was vivid. "The doctor said—"

"The doctor said that I won't be able to do any sexual activity that involves hip action. My jaw is far from my hips. And so is yours."

Rion grinned. "You're making this really hard for me to follow the doctor's orders."

Nick took Rion's hand and placed it against his erection. "You make this hard just by being around you. We haven't been alone since the moment I woke up. I need you, Ree."

Rion was also craving the closeness, so he stopped resisting. He sat up and put his head over Nick's groin.

Nick groaned. "Just knowing you are about to blow me makes me want to cum."

"Shut up, Nicky," Rion said as he pulled down Nick's pants.

Nick went to grab it for him, but Rion slapped his hand away. Nick giggled. But then immediately stopped when Rion held onto his cock and put his mouth on the head.

"Uuuugh... Oooowww!" Nick exclaimed. He had absentmindedly lifted his bottom off the bed, causing pain in his left hip.

Rion stopped abruptly and looked at him. He shook his head. "This was a bad idea."

"No, wait! Please..." Nick begged. "You can't stop now. Look at me." Rion looked down at Nick's cock that was steadily leaking. "I'll get the worst case of blue balls if you stop. And it's not going to take me long; look how purple the head is. I don't even need you to deep throat it. Just bob a couple of times. Trust me. I'm going to cum quick."

Rion laughed at Nick's pleading. "Okay. Try not to move your bottom to meet my throat. I got you."

"Fuck... Okay." Nick took a few deep breaths, then said again, "Okay. I'm ready."

Rion resumed putting his mouth on Nicholas. He went down halfway a few times, and Nick did his very best not to move at all. But then Rion became too enthusiastic and pushed Nick deep in his throat. Nick groaned and exploded in Rion's mouth. He moved involuntarily, but the pain in his hip was nothing compared to the euphoria of cumming. Nick was breathing erratically, his hands and toes curling tightly, his eyes fluttering, and his breath caught in his throat. After Rion swallowed all of it, he touched the side of Nick's bruised hip as he hovered over Nick's body. He waited until Nick came down from his climax and opened up his eyes.

They stared at each other, then Rion kissed him softly on the mouth. "Rest, babe. I'll be here in the morning. I'll be here forever."

Nick nodded. He closed his eyes. Rion silently fell to the right side of Nick and put his arm around him. He waited until Nick was in a deep sleep, a light snore escaping him, before he closed his eyes too.

"That's it, Nick. You got it," Ezra encouraged him. "Take one more step... That's right. Then another... Another... Almost there..."

Nick held on to each bar and walked through the middle, slowly. It hurt. *Dear God, does it hurt*, he thought. But Rion was recording, and Erza was egging him on, so he kept going all the way to the end.

"Yeeeesssss!" Ezra yelled and patted his back. "You did it. Did you see that!?" he yelled at the camera. "Nicholas Highton is back!"

He patted Nick's back again and smiled for Rion's camera phone. Nick smiled too, then he said, "Turn it off, Ree."

"You don't want to say anything to your fans?" Rion asked.

Nick's smile faded. "Turn it off."

Rion pressed the off button and put the phone to his leg. As soon as he did so, Nick dropped to his knees. "Oh, no, babe!" Rion said, running over.

But Ezra was right there to grasp his arm and help him stand up. Rion came to his other side. "My crutches," Nick demanded.

Rion grabbed the metal crutches and handed them to Nick. Nick hobbled over to the couch and sat in it, lifting up his left leg. He was sweating, and his hip was aching. He put his arm over his eyes and slouched. Rion and Ezra looked at each other, then back at him.

"Hey, Nick," Erza began. "That was great. Really, really great. That's the first time you did the whole bar before."

"Still hurts like a bitch," Nick said from underneath his arm.

"But that's okay," said Ezra. "It's going to get easier the more you do it."

"Fuck that. I'm done with this."

"What?" Rion exclaimed.

But Ezra patted him. He caught Rion's eyes and shook his head. "It's fine, Nick. I hear you; we're done for today. We'll talk about it tomorrow."

"Don't bother coming tomorrow, Ezra. I said I'm done with this shit. I mean it."

Ezra didn't respond. He calmly picked up his bag and said again, "Great work today, Nick. Really great work." He silently left the house.

"Hey, Nick—" Rion started gently.

But Nick said abruptly, "Don't post that video, Rion."

"Why not? It's encouraging. Inspiring. Your fans will want to see this, and it's good for your brand."

"Since when do you give a shit about the brand?" Nick snapped.

Rion sighed and kept his cool. "I give a shit about you. And I want you to be encouraged. You're doing so great."

"Yeah? Then why am I still in a fucking wheelchair?" Nick asked moodily. "Why can't I go up the steps yet? Why is my hip still throbbing although I've been sitting for a few minutes already?"

"Because it's only been a little over a month," Rion said factually. He handed Nick a water bottle. "Give yourself some time."

Nick took it but didn't drink it yet. "I should have died on that road."

Rion quickly knelt between his legs. "Don't say that, Nicky. Please don't talk like that."

Nick shook his head. "I'm never going to be the same. I feel like a fucking loser. Like everything I worked so hard for is slipping through my hands."

"What do you mean?" Rion asked. "I'm still here."

"I don't know why," Nick mumbled and took a sip.

"What do you mean?" Rion said with an edge to his voice. "Because I love you."

"Love isn't enough though, right?" Nick said, looking Rion into his eyes. Rion stared back. "Are we going to talk about it? The fight? The things you said to me? How being with me is causing panic attacks and writers' block and how your mental health is in the shitter?" Rion sat back on his legs and put his hands in his lap. "How you don't want to be with me anymore, Rion?"

Rion shook his head. "That's not what I said. I just needed some space, some time. But I do want to be with you."

"Just not all of me, right? Conditional? As long as I'm not a Highton and part of the One Percent, we're good, right?"

"That's not fair," Rion said, trying to keep his anger in check. "Me needing some space had nothing to do with how much money you have. It had everything to do with me trying to save myself. You don't know how bad it's been for me."

"Because you didn't tell me, Rion," Nick countered. "You let me think that we were in a good place and then you exploded on me, then left me. Yes, July Fourth was a disaster on so many levels. But I thought we moved past that. I asked you to marry me, Rion."

"That wasn't a real proposal," Rion said dismissively. "Not with your dick still inside of me."

Nick scoffed out a laugh. "Okay." He took a sip and said, "If you don't want to be tied to a Highton anymore, then just go."

"That's not fair, Nicholas," Rion said. "You aren't listening to me or even trying to understand—"

"Just fucking go!" Nick yelled at him, startling Rion.

Rion stood up. "You're pushing me away. Why?" Nick wouldn't look at him. "Fine," Rion said stubbornly. He grabbed his bookbag and walked out the front door.

Nick heard the Camry start up and listened to it drive down the gravel and away from the house. He gingerly laid on the couch, slowly lifting his leg up. His body was hurting. He was hurting. And he didn't want to hurt Rion anymore either. Tears fell out the side of his eyes and slid down his face.

Rion didn't know where he was going; he just knew he needed to clear his head for a moment and give Nick time to be sullen. He parked near the boardwalk and stepped into a bar that had live music. He stopped at the bar and ordered an old fashioned, tapping his fingers to the beat the drummer was making. When he received his drink, he took a sip and looked around. He caught the eye of a man at the bar in a very expensive suit staring at him. He nodded. Rion nodded back then quickly turned his face, not wanting to give him any attention. He took his drink and found a small table to sit at. A few songs later, he ordered one more, then looked at the time, knowing he needed to get back. He hoped Nick would be asleep, and they would start all over tomorrow, avoiding the hard questions. As he thought this, the man came over to him.

"Mind if I join you?" he asked. He didn't wait for an answer before he sat down across from Rion. "I'm Dexter," he said, holding out his hand. "You look like you could use a friend."

Rion didn't take it. He was older, at least fifteen years Rion's senior, with a handsome face and a strong personality. The type of man who always got what he wanted. So Rion knew being subtle was not going to cut it.

"I'm married," he said, surprised that the lie fell from his lip so easily. And that it didn't feel like a lie at all.

"No, you're not," Dexter said with a smile. "Where's your ring?"

"I left it in my husband's asshole," Rion deadpanned.

The man let out a loud laugh. "You're hot and funny. I like that."

Rion couldn't help chuckling back. "Seriously. I'm taken. He's being a dick right now. But he's all mine. And I'm all his."

"I got it," Dexter said coolly. "I was just hoping you could use a little company. Something to take your mind off that man of yours right now."

Rion stared into the man's gray-green eyes. He decided he did need the company of a man like Dexter. Just not in the way he thought. "Hey, you're rich, aren't you? Like ridiculously rich?"

Dexter smiled. "I am. And I could show you the world if you—"

"Yeah, no." Rion cut him off with a wave of his hand and a shake of his head. "What would make a man like you want to be with a man who could barely rub two pennies together?"

Dexter sat back and was thoughtful. "If I loved him, money wouldn't matter."

"Yeah, everyone says that," said Rion. "But class does matter, right? What if he didn't fit in with the upper class? The One Percent. Your richy-rich friends and business partners. Then what?"

"It depends on how much I loved him," said Dexter. "If I was deeply in love with him, then again, it wouldn't matter. You can teach a person how to fit in. But love isn't taught, and true love is rare."

"And what if he still just doesn't fit in? What if he can't do it? What if he runs away?"

Dexter leaned onto the table and touched Rion's fingers. "If I loved you deeply, then I would chase you until the ends of the earth to bring you back to me. Or I would find you and stay where you are. Either way, it would be my job to make sure we stayed together. Because love doesn't come around that easily. And again, true love is rare."

Rion slid his hand away from him. "Thanks, Dexter." He stood up. "This has been very helpful. I hope you find what you're looking for tonight. Because it isn't me. I have a man to get home to."

"A lucky man," Dexter said as he raised his glass.

Rion grinned. He turned around and walked back out of the bar.

When the front door opened, Nick rolled his eyes and turned away. "Jesus, Ree. Just go home."

"I am home, you stupid asshole," Rion said softly and with affection. "I already told you I'm not running. And I'm never going anywhere again. So deal with it." He sat on the ottoman in front of the couch and noticed Nick's dry tears on his face. "I'm ready to talk about it."

Nicholas didn't speak for a long moment and Rion waited. "It's going to destroy you, being with me," Nick said eventually. "It was never going to be Madeline. It was always going to be me."

"Oh, Nick." Rion moved the ottoman closer to the couch. "You're not destroying me. It's my choice to be with you, to go through these struggles. I love you so much that I have battled through my own personal demons just to be with you. And I will do it over and over again just to be with you. If that's not love, then I don't know what is." He touched Nick's thigh. "And I know you love me the same way."

A tear fell down the side of Nick's face as he stared at the ceiling. "I do, Ree. I really, really do. I will go through hell and back, just to give us a chance to make it. But I don't want to hold you back. I don't want to make you feel like you don't have the space to be you while tied to a Highton. I don't want to be your anchor if it's destroying you. It's a lot of pressure. I get it. And I want to give you the room to be honest with yourself and say it's too much and walk away—"

"It's my fault," Rion said. "It's my fault because I haven't been a better partner to you. I didn't communicate fairly. I held it all inside, and I blew up, then I ran away. I did all the wrong things when you're in a relationship. But I won't do that anymore. I want to show you I can do this. I can be tied to a Highton. I can be married to a Highton."

Nick smirked. "That wasn't a real proposal. Not with my dick still inside of you."

"I'm sorry I said that. Because it was real to me," Rion said seriously. "I want that future with you, Nicky. And I'll do whatever I need to do to get it."

Nick slowly sat up. Rion reached out to help him, but he recoiled against Rion's hands. So Rion sat and watched. It took him a while. He used his right side as leverage but managed to sit with both feet on the ground, facing Rion.

"The last thing I would ever want is for you to wake up one day ten years from now and resent me because I forced you into a life you never wanted."

"Nick—"

"Just listen," Nick said. "My father did that to my mother. Twice. She didn't want to go into her family business. All she wanted to do was dance. And he took her away from that and trapped her in a loveless marriage, which forced her to play the role of family publicist. Then twelve years later, when she had a second chance at being able to live the life she always wanted, he unintentionally trapped her again by getting her pregnant with me. She never forgave him. And she hated me for it. Madeline is the way she is now because everyone took away her autonomy, especially my father. I will not do that to you."

He reached out and touched Rion's face. "I can't change who I am. I am Nick Highton. I am always going to be watched, scrutinized, followed, reported on, lied about. And anyone tied to me is going to endure the same things. I can do my best. We can strategize together on how best to keep you out of the spotlight as much as possible. But there are going to be times when things will be completely out of my control. And if being with me is hurting you in any way, then we can't be together, Rion."

Madeline words flitted through Rion's head: *You're Niion Lights are not meant to be ... forever.* And it angered him.

"Fuck that," he said out loud. "You literally risked your life and went into gang territory for me to keep us together. In those two days, I remembered how I felt, besides being worried about Ava. I knew that I had to protect you in my world no matter what. I know you will do the same for me, Nicholas. If I would have told you what was going on, you would have pivoted your entire life to make sure I was okay. So I know for a fact that we can make this work. That our Niion Lights are meant to be forever."

Rion reached out with a hand to mimic Nick's hand on his cheek. "So we strategize. We figure out the best way to keep me from spiraling emotionally. For example, I don't go to Madeline Highton parties anymore. Ever."

"Done," Nick said right away. "And you need a Zoey. She's wonderful, and she loves you so much, but she will always look out for my best interests first. You need someone objective that's going to look out for your best interests first too."

Rion thought of something else. "We have to move, Nick," he said. "As much as I love our apartment in New York City, as much as I love Emma and Brian and all their children, this city, this state, is starting to suffocate me. I have never felt so cold and so lonely being here, even with you lying beside me. It's time to go."

"Do you want to go back to London?" Nick asked, still caressing his cheek.

"Yes," Rion admitted. "But I know that's not possible right now. I may go back on my own in a few months when I know that you're better. But I know I can't stay here."

"It's not possible to be overseas right now, not with Hump starting out. But..." He leaned in closer and kissed Rion's lips. "I heard San Francisco is nice."

Rion looked him in the eyes. "Would you really move to California for me?"

"Hell yes. Besides the fact that you did it for me, I'll do anything for you, Rion. To keep you safe. To keep you happy. You're my whole world."

"Oh, Nicky," Rion said, his heart full. He pressed his lips against Nick's again.

The kiss went deeper, and Rion found himself crawling onto Nick's lap. "Is this okay?" he asked in between kisses.

But Nick was already taking off his shirt, eager to finally be inside of Rion. He kissed Rion's collarbone and licked his neck. "Let me stick my dick in you," Nick replied. "I need to be inside of you."

Rion chuckled. "Your leg—"

But Nick cut Rion off by reaching up, grabbing a fistful of hair, and saying more forcefully, "I need to be inside of you. It's been way too long."

Rion smashed his lips against Nick, no longer wanting to hold out. He hopped off Nick's lap and went into the bedroom to grab the lube that hadn't been opened since they arrived. When he returned, Nick had already taken off his sweatpants, holding onto his hardness. Rion knelt before him and kissed his hands surrounding his shaft and up his cock to the head. Nick moved out of the way and let Rion put

him into his throat. He moaned softly, but it wasn't what he wanted. Rion knew it, but he wanted to get Nick nice and silky first before he added the lubricant to make it extra silky. Once done, Rion took off his clothes and gently sat in Nick's lap while penetrating himself. He raised both hands around Nick's head and began to ride.

Nick stayed still at first, closing his eyes, moaning loudly, surrendering to Rion's power over him. He held out longer than he should have, but he simply did not want to cum. It was Rion whose breathing turned erratic, his movements no longer fluid but jerking as his climax rose. Rion let go of Nick's neck and jerked himself, calling out Nicky's name over and over again until his seed spilled out. Between the warm tightness surrounding his cock and the warmth of Rion's semen on his stomach, Nick roared and exploded inside of him, grabbing onto his waist with his head on Rion's shoulder. Rion continued to move, slow and steady movements up and down, keeping Nick hard.

"Jesus, Ree," Nick said breathlessly. "Why is it that even when you're the bottom, I still feel like I'm the one being fucked?"

Rion laughed and kissed his head, then wrapped both arms around Nick's neck again. He spoke as he moved. "I got hit on tonight."

"Really? Where?"

"Some bar on the boardwalk down the way." He ran his hands through Nick's hair. "That's where I was tonight."

"Hmmm..." Nick began to move with him, slow and steady to not aggravate his hip. "Was he hot?"

"Actually, yes," Rion said in realization. "He was older, definitely older than Brian. Rich as fuck, you could tell by his suit. He wanted to show me the world."

Nick looked up at Rion. "You should give it a chance."

Rion smiled and kissed Nick. "I told him I was married."

He watched Nick's face soften completely, his eyes so full of love. "Married, huh?" Nick said softly.

Rion kissed his lips again and whispered, "You're my anchor."

"God, that's so fucking romantic," Nick said.

Suddenly, he startled Rion by lifting him up and laying him down on the couch on his back. His hip was still throbbing, but it didn't matter. He made love to Rion slowly, ignoring the pain as Rion clung to him, letting out sounds of pleasure. He released again, then moved farther down and sucked Rion off until he also came again.

Nick hovered over Rion's torso as his heart-rate returned to normal. "Married, huh?" Nick said with a smile.

Rion looked away and laughed. "Jesus, Nicky."

"My dick's not inside of you, so if I ask you again—"

"Will you marry me, Nick Highton?" Rion interrupted, turning back to stare into Nick's eyes.

Nick's mouth was frozen open. Then he smiled. He moved back up to Rion's face and said, "Yes."

They sealed their proposal with another kiss.

In the morning, Rion woke up to Nick staring at him. Rion smiled. "Hi, Nicky."

"Hey, babe."

Rion looked at him curiously. "You okay?"

"Yeah," Nick replied. "Just thinking. About you. About me. About us. I still love us, Ree. It's not the same as it was when we first met in London. That was all love and lust and passion and ignorance mixed in together, but I still love everything that makes us who we are."

"We were a little naïve to think our worlds wouldn't tear us apart, weren't we?" Rion said with a smile.

"Ignorance is bliss," said Nick. "But we have to do better. Individually and as a couple. I want us to have a successful marriage, beat all the odds. I want us forever, like we always promised."

"I want that too, Nick," said Rion. "And we're doing that. We're strategizing, right?"

"Yes, but we need to do more." Rion looked at him curiously. "First things first. I'm going back to therapy. I'm going to call my old therapist and try to get an appointment via telehealth. I have to talk through this shit around my parents, getting closer to my father, pulling away from my mother, and how hard this physical therapy thing is on me. And I want to learn how to be better for you."

"I think that's a great idea, Nick," said Rion encouragingly. "I'm so proud of you."

"I'm glad you think it's a great idea," said Nick. "Because you're calling your doctor and getting back on meds. Actual anti-anxiety meds, not just CBD."

Rion grimaced at him. "Ugh. No."

"Yes," Nick said sternly. "And you should do therapy too."

Rion groaned louder and sat up. "God no. I'm past that."

"No. You aren't," Nick scolded. "You need to talk through the shit you just went through: meeting your birth father, getting closer to your mother, your partner almost died—"

"Stop." Rion didn't want to hear it. He tried to get out of bed as he spoke. "Nick, I am not—"

Nicholas cut him off and grabbed his arm, pulling him back into bed with him. "If I have to do this physical therapy shit for at least the next three months to get back into physical shape, then you have to take meds for the next three months to get back into mental shape. Then we'll both reevaluate if we need to continue."

"I can't, Nick," Rion pleaded. "It stunts my creativity. I can't write when I'm on it."

"Rion, you're not writing now," Nick reminded him. "And you're having daily panic attacks. Still. I see the signs. The way your body freezes up. You take short breaths then long ones trying to control your breathing. So no, that's not an excuse anymore."

"Nicky, please..."

"Ree," Nick took both his hands, "I'm so sorry that I didn't see it before. That I haven't been there for you. That I haven't been protecting you in my world. But I am now. I'm paying attention now, and I need you to do this. For us. For yourself."

Rion tried to plead his case again. "I think I just needed to wrap my head around the fact that this is my life now. I'm partnered with a Highton and with that comes the spotlight. And I'm okay with it now. As long as you're by my side. So it's okay. I'm okay now. It's actually not daily, it's been lessening... a little."

Nick was not convinced. "I'm glad it's getting better. But it's my job to make sure you stay that way. So I'm going to do my part, and you're going to do yours. When we leave this beach house in four months, we are going to be better versions of ourselves and better partners to each other. Please, Ree? I need us to do this. I need us to make it."

Rion watched Nick's eyes pool up with tears. It made him tear up too. He moved closer and put his head on Nick's shoulder. Nick ran his hand through his hair. And waited.

"Okay, Nicky," Rion said softly. "Okay."

31

Nicholas woke up on his back and absentmindedly rolled onto his side, closer to Rion so he could put his hand around Rion's waist. Rion did not stir. He moved his face closer so that his nose was buried in Rion's dark curls and breathed deeply, feeling content and satisfied. The realization hit him: he was on his left side. He did a body scan, and there was no acute pain. Not in his left shoulder or left hip. It was the first time that he didn't wake up in some level of pain. His hip felt stiff and achy, like he hadn't exercised in a while. But no pain. He smiled with his eyes closed.

It was raining, the March wind coming in strong off the water. He listened to the little taps of water hitting the deck right outside the balcony door he was facing, thinking about his last session with his therapist. Rion participated with him, which was nice, and it ended up being a couple's session. They played a game first—two truths and a lie—as an icebreaker and a warmup for what was to come. It was a childhood edition, so it had to be three statements about their childhood. That led to Nick telling Rion about some of things he and his father talked about and his sincere apology for the way his mother treated him. And Rion finally telling Nick details about what happened when he met his birth father and how disastrous it was but so important to go through. They were both in tears by the end of the 90 minute session, a traumatic bond formed over both having parents who intentionally tossed them away like they didn't matter.

Nick's therapist suggested that in addition to saying "I love you" to each other, it would be more meaningful to say "You matter to me" in their relationship. She reminded them that it was in those moments they showed the other that he mattered, all the way back to when Nick offered to give Rion a place to lay his head when they barely knew each other, that they were at their strongest. She advised them to do things to show that the other truly mattered. Rion's birthday was in a few weeks, so Nick thought about what would matter the most to Rion right now. Rion was at his happiest when he had his family around him, so Nick was already devising a plan in his head to have Roslyn stay with them for a few days.

But Nick had a more immediate issue. He was horny. As he was trying to think about Rion in a sensible way, his cock had grown stiff being so close to Rion's bottom. Sex was always the one area where they never had a problem. But since Nick's accident, he could count the number of times they were sexual with each other, and only twice was there actual penetration. Rion was caring for him with kid gloves, not wanting to hurt him, not wanting him to overexert himself. And while Nick appreciated the care, Nick's penis was over it. It was so solid it was getting painful.

Nick groaned, then moved his waist up and down Rion's cheeks with more purpose, waking him up. Rion moaned, then said, "That better be your arm."

"More like a third leg," Nick said.

Rion chuckled. "Okay. Let me—"

"Stay right there," Nick commanded. "Don't fucking move."

Rion's eyes finally opened. "Okay. What's up?"

Nick didn't answer. He lifted Rion's shirt and kissed his back, then put Rion on his stomach and slid off his briefs. He pulled his cheeks apart and tongued him aggressively.

"Ooohhh, babe," Rion moaned. He moved his knees up to his chest, his face still in the pillow.

But Nick didn't stay there long. He wanted to make sure he was nice and wet, spitting directly into his hole a few times. He rolled over to the nightstand and grabbed the lube from the top drawer. "Don't move," he told Rion again.

Rion did not. Nick prepared him, then himself, and slowly entered Rion, who moaned loudly. Rion didn't mind riding Nick and taking the lead. But it felt good to lie there and get fucked. It had been a while.

Nick worked slowly at first, but then he slammed into him hard. Rion's whole body jerked, and he moaned loudly. Nick slid back slowly, then slammed into him again. "Jesus, Nicky!" Rion screamed.

Nick kept going, an extremely slow pull out, a hard and fast push in, making Rion cry out every time. Neither of them were paying attention, or they would have heard the front door open.

"Whoa!" they heard behind them. Nick turned to see Ezra's startled face and saw him slip to the side of the doorway with his back against the wall. "I guess this is your workout today, huh, Nick?"

Nick laughed out loud. "You told me I had to get some more rotation in my hips, right?" he said as he slammed into Rion once more. Rion groaned and grabbed the sheet between his fingers.

"Yeah I did," Erza said with a smile. "But..."

"But what?" Nick said, slamming into Rion again.

"Your form is a little off."

Nick stopped moving. "What?"

"Your hips aren't lined up," Ezra called out. "You're still favoring your right side. Put more pressure on your left."

Nick turned his waist slightly and felt the pressure. "Ooof," he groaned.

"There you go. That's it."

"This shit hurts now," Nick said. His cock was still pulsing inside Rion, wondering what the holdup was.

"It's supposed to hurt a little. Put pressure on the joint muscle. Like..." Ezra was thoughtful. "Permission to enter?"

"What!?" Rion yelled below him.

Nick laughed. He pulled back and slammed into Rion, making him cry out. "Jesus!"

"Permission granted," said Nick, holding position so that their bodies were completely connected.

Ezra hesitantly walked in and touched Nick's hip. He turned it slightly more, and Nick groaned. "Slide your left knee up," he said, "so that your knees are perfectly aligned on either side of Rion. Rion, your position is perfect. Stay still."

"Thanks," Rion deadpanned with his face in the pillow.

Nick chuckled and did as Ezra suggested. "It still feels tight."

"It's supposed to. So go in at this angle," Erza said, showing Nick with his hands, careful to keep his eyes on Nick's. "You have to lean into it. And don't be afraid to move faster. Really work your hips but in a controlled way so the movement is even throughout. Concentrate on the pleasure more so than the pain. I'll have a heating pad ready for you when you're done." He patted Nick's shoulder and walked out of the bedroom.

"Okay, that was weird," Rion said, still in the pillow. "We can do this later—"

But Nick quickly pulled back and slammed into Rion again. Rion yelled out, "Fuck!"

"Yup, just like that," Ezra called out from the living room. He picked up a magazine and began to read. "Faster. I can tell by Rion's reaction how fast you're going, so pick up speed. No mercy."

Nick laughed out loud but began to fuck his boyfriend at a steadier pace. Rion hollered over and over again, and Ezra continued to yell out encouragement from the next room. "That's it! You got this, Nick! Get in there, Mr. Deep Strokez! You're doing great! Hang in there, Rion!"

"Uuuugh," Rion groaned in response as Nick pounded into him.

When he was close, Nick reached down, molding himself on top of Rion, stretching out his hands, and lacing their fingers. He moved in circles and put his lips on Rion's neck, sucking it hard. Rion shuddered underneath him as Nick let go, releasing warmth inside of his lover, moaning with his mouth still on

Rion's skin. He pulled out and fell on his back on the mattress. Rion stretched out on the bed, his own body achy from being in the same position for so long.

As they lay in silence, a slow clap echoed to the bedroom, picking up speed. Nick and Rion both laughed. When the clapping ended, Nick turned to Rion, but Rion was already watching him, his face flushed, a smile plastered across his lips.

"Sorry for using you as an exercise tool," said Nick.

Rion shrugged. "I'm not complaining. I came twice."

Nick grinned. "Whatever I need to do to get you in tip-top shape. Because, you know, you matter to me."

Nick rolled over and kissed him over and over again. "I love you, Ree Matthews."

He didn't wait for a response. He stepped out of the bed, his whole lower body sore, not just his hips. Rion watched Nick stretch, the curve of his back muscles and arms pronounced. Rion stared at Nick's labyrinth tattoo that spread from the top of his shoulder to his shoulder blade as Nick rolled his shoulders and neck around. The scars on the left side of his body were fading, and for that, Rion was thankful. His eyes followed Nick as he limped to the bathroom to shower, feeling more in love with Nicholas than he did when they first began in a hotel in London.

Nicholas and Roslyn worked in tandem so the day would be perfect for Rion. He made burgers, ground beef made from Omaha steaks, and put all the fixings in there that his boyfriend liked the best: cheddar cheese, bacon, fried onions, fresh avocado, lettuce, and tomato. And Roslyn baked a cake from scratch, something she had never ever done.

Roslyn watched Nick in the kitchen, moving slowly but still moving. He started with the one crutch but quickly realized it was getting in the way, so he leaned it against the side of the fridge and walked around without it. Every once in a while he would sit at the island to rest, but then he would get back up. As they set the table, Nick went to grab the crutch again.

"You know you don't need that," Roslyn scolded him. "Put it down."

Nick shrugged and didn't listen. "It helps. Makes me feel stable."

"It makes you feel comfortable," said Roslyn. "Not stable. I know a thing or two about doing things that feel comfortable. It's literally a crutch for you. Let it go."

Nick smiled at her and gently placed it back against the fridge. He walked over and sat at the island again. "Congratulations on getting your six-year chip. I know, months later," he said sheepishly. "And I'm sorry I pulled Rion away from that."

Roslyn smiled and sat next to him. She touched his hand and said, "You're forgiven. Rion has never seen me get a chip before or heard the story of how I got clean for good until yesterday at his therapy session. You'll hear it next year when I get my seven-year chip."

"Well, I want to hear it now. If you want to tell me."

So she told him. "I've always wanted a family. It was always me and my mom. Her mother kicked her out when she found out she was pregnant with me at thirteen, so she took me everywhere with her. She wasn't mentally well, and she did what she needed to do to survive: drugs. Sex work. Stealing. I saw a lot, I learned a lot from her, and I did what I knew how to do to survive too. Drugs. Sex work. Stealing. When I got pregnant at fourteen, she didn't yell at me or scold me. She said, 'Finally, I have a family again.'" Roslyn smiled at that, then her smile faded. "She died a year later. A john murdered her." Nick reached out and touched her hand in comfort.

"It scared me. I had to be careful after that. Maurese and Felipe were already tied in with the 781, so I inserted myself in the crew, and they became my family. The working girls took care of my baby for me when I went to work, and I was protected by the boys because I made them money. Gabriel took a liking to me real quickly, so I was treated better than the other girls. No stealing—Gabe would have killed me. Less sex work. A lot more drugs. He trusted me, so when I mentioned that the only two people I trusted out of the whole 781 were Fox and Grease, he made them two of his top lieutenants. That meant I got to spend more time with Maurese again.

"We talked about being a family, the four of us, and he was actively trying to get me pregnant again. I was sleeping with Gabe, but he mostly used condoms with me, so when I got pregnant I absolutely thought it was Maurese's, so I stopped using drugs completely, wanting a healthy baby. But Gabrielle came out looking just like Gabe. We didn't need a DNA test. Still, Maurese and I wanted to be a family. When war broke out between the lieutenants and people started showing up dead, Maurese got me out of there and moved me into a house right outside of Fresno that no one knew about because he bought it for us. But then..." She sniffed, holding back tears. "Junior..."

Nick stopped her, squeezing her hand. "I know what happened," he said gently. "You don't have to talk about it."

She nodded and wiped the wetness from her eyes. "Maurese hated me after that because I never told him what happened. It was like we were at war with each other. I felt like he kept trying to take my family away from me. He took Rel from me, but I got her back. He took Rion from the hospital, and I got him back. After Gabe died, he tried to take all three from me, so I stashed them with Bones, and by the time I got back, Ava had ran, Bones was in jail, and Maurese got Gabby and Ree from me again. We just went back and forth like that for over fifteen years. At the same time, it went by so quickly: one day Gabby was six and cleaning up my throw up, and the next day she was sixteen and cleaning up my face from when a john attacked me. My children were having children of their own, and I was a grandmother at twenty-nine. But we were still together, a family..."

Roslyn sniffed again. "Ava left first. She said she got a job in Vegas. Gabby and Ree left next. Ree had dropped out of school when Gabby dropped out to help her take care of Morgan, so when a job fair for postal workers opened up in San Francisco, they both left to work there. Muriel was still in Fresno, but she didn't talk to me at all. She sided with her father. I was alone. I dug myself deeper into the 781, managing the working girls, doing a little work myself for money, overdosing so many times... I should have died, Nick. I should have."

"But you didn't," Nick reminded her. "Because the universe always planned for you to be reconciled with your family."

She smiled at him. "Ava came to me one day and told me that Maurese had moved to San Francisco, moved his mother in because she had cancer, and was keeping an eye on Gabby and Ree for me. She said they were planning a Thanksgiving dinner, a first for us. Because we all had something to be thankful for. Everyone was healthy, and safe, and happy, and even she was on meds and feeling better about her life. Ava said that no one wanted me there, but she wanted me to try. She left the address of Maurese's house on my dresser but gave me one rule: I could not show up high. I told her I would be there."

Roslyn sighed. "I really did try. I had presents for my grandchildren with me. But two hours into my three-hour bus ride, I started sniffing the coke I carried with me. All of it. When I got to the house, Rion opened the door with the biggest smile. But he took one look at me and he knew. His smile faded and he said so calmly, 'No, Roslyn.' And he slammed the door in my face. I could hear him set all the locks and his footsteps walk away. I don't know about you, but when I'm coked up, I only feel two emotions: arrogance and rage."

Nick chuckled. "That sounds about right."

"Well I felt them both. I started ringing the bell, then banging and kicking the door, screaming at them to let me in, let me be with my family. I pissed on the doormat and threw rocks at the windows, breaking at least two of them. I yelled over and over, 'I'm going to start doing crazy shit out here, and it's going to be all your fault if you don't let me in!'"

Nick let out a gasp, remembering using similar words to Rion at the party on the Fourth. He was even more ashamed of himself. Roslyn looked at him curiously. But all Nick said was, "That must have been awful for them."

"It was," Roslyn said shamefully. "The door finally opened, and Maurese came outside. He said to me, 'Go, Roslyn. Nobody here cares if you live or die because you don't care if you live or die. Nobody wants you in there because you don't really want to be with them anyway. You care about two things: getting high and making money to get high. You don't care about them, so they don't care about you anymore. So go. You don't have family in there. You don't have a family at all.'"

"Wow," Nick said softly, squeezing her hand again.

Tears fell as she spoke. "He cut me deep with those words. He knew all I wanted was a family. I started wailing on him, kicking, hitting, punching, scratching. He never hit me back; he just threw his hands up and protected himself as much as he could. But then I looked up, and they were all at the window: Muriel holding Jeff, little Reese, and Kate; Gabby holding Morgan, shielding her face; Rion holding Ava to his chest. They were all crying except Rion. He just sneered at me. Looking just like his father. I started screaming. I just sat on the concrete and screamed and screamed and screamed. Maurese went back in the house, left me out there to scream. Someone eventually did call the cops, and they took me away from my family, still screaming."

"Jesus," Nick said sadly. "So you were arrested?"

"No, actually," said Roslyn. "They took me to a psych hospital. I was involuntarily committed on a 72-hour hold. So I was also involuntarily detoxed. On day four, the nurse came in. Connie was an older woman, around the age my mother would have been. We spoke for a long time, and she asked me, 'Do you want to have Thanksgiving with your family next year?' I told her I did. She said, 'Well, you have eleven months to do it. Can you do it?' I told her I could. I have gone clean for a year a few times. I could do it again. She gave me some tips. Go to meetings. Get a sponsor. Find a job and get off the streets. Move out of Gabe's house. That was probably the hardest. It's the heart of the 781 in a cute little cul-de-sac that was unpenetrated because so many of them lived right there."

Nick nodded. "I've been to that house."

"That's right. You were there," Roslyn acknowledged. "That was the safest place for me, a home I could always go back to. But I did it. I moved into a studio apartment. I got a job, two in fact. I cleaned hotel rooms during the day and waitressed at a 24-hour trucker stop at night. I still turned tricks with the truckers for money but not for drugs. Not even alcohol. Crack-cocaine was the hardest to walk away from, but I did it. Because my goal was to have Thanksgiving dinner with my family."

"And did you?" Nick asked.

"I tried. The first year I told them I wanted to host it at my apartment. Gabby came with Morgan. She said that Ava said she would try to make it, but Ree was living in his own place and had a boyfriend that he wanted to spend Thanksgiving with, and Muriel straight up refused. But Gabby said if I kept it up another year, clean and sober, she would make sure everyone would be there. So I was determined to make it another year. Gabby hosted at her apartment. Ava and Muriel came. I started my amends right then and there. They came with me to get my second-year chip. The third year, Muriel hosted and Rion came." She grinned. "I didn't think he would; Gabby and Muriel kept saying he was working hard on finishing up a book so he might not show up. But he did. I was so happy that at least he was there. I tried to make my amends with him, but then he asked me who his father was." Her face scrunched in.

"I couldn't tell him. Every other time he's asked me I was high, so I would say something stupid or tell him to leave me alone. But this time, I was completely sober, and he knew that I knew the answer. But how do you tell someone that, Nick?" She looked up at the ceiling. "How do you tell your son that one, he was conceived through rape, and two, that the person who raped me was Maurese's brother? Maurese is like a father to him. How could I destroy him like that?"

Nick nodded. "I understand."

She looked back at him. "Can I tell you a secret? I was relieved that you told him. At least part of it. A neutral figure in his life that could ease it to him gently. I was ready and willing to handle the other part. But then he shut me out. You know the rest." Nick nodded again. "I told him all of this yesterday. And he told me all of the things that happened to him, the physical and sexual abuse he endured because I wasn't there to protect him. And I apologized again. And he forgave me again. So I have my son back. And that's all I ever wanted: my family."

Nick stood up and pulled Roslyn with him. He wrapped his arms around her in a strong hug and kissed her forehead. "And now you have it. I'm so proud of you, Roslyn."

"Thank you, Nick. And thank you for loving my son so deeply. So completely."

"Thank you for having him," Nick said back. Roslyn squeezed him tighter.

It was just the three of them, and Izzy on the chair with one paw on the table waiting patiently for her slice. Nick leaned on one crutch as he and Roslyn sang "Happy Birthday" to Rion. He grinned at them both. "Thanks. Best birthday ever."

And Rion meant it. He was doing so much better. He hadn't had a panic attack or even a wave of anxiety for weeks, thanks to his meds. Therapy was going well. He liked his therapist, a mature woman who was more like a mother figure than a therapist the way she listened and gave strong encouragement and soft suggestions. And when Roslyn appeared two days ago, it meant everything to him to have her there. Roslyn attended the session with him the day before, and they were able to be open and honest with each other.

And he and Nick were doing better too. Nick still had moments where he was surly, mostly when either he or Ezra tried to push him to do more walking, but they were communicating better overall. Today, they made Rion leave the house so they could cook a birthday dinner for him, so Rion took the drive down to Brian's house and spent a beach day with Brian's boys. Even Maddox came out to hang with him, Arlow, and Angus.

When Rion was allowed to return, they stood side by side and sang to him. He looked at the table of homemade burgers and fries, lemon cake with chocolate icing with two number candles, a two and a nine, Hershey's kisses, and little bags of Cool Ranch Doritos on the table, and his heart swelled. They ate together and talked casually, and Rion did put the inside of the cake on a small plate for Izzy to lick up. Rion helped his mother clean up the kitchen while Nick went to find a movie for them to watch together. She casually mentioned to Rion about Nick and his crutch, and they both watched him lean on it. Rion told her he had a plan to get him to move around without it, and he invoked Zoey's help to make it happen. They settled in the living room, watching a movie until Roslyn said she was tired and went to bed.

Rion snuggled closer to Nick, both arms around him, his head on Nick's pec. "Today was perfect," he said as he was falling asleep. "This week has been perfect. It was just what I needed."

Nick ran his hand up and down Rion's back. "Well, you know. You matter to me."

Rion sighed. "Love you too, babe."

32

Niles stopped by that morning to say, "Let's go, son."

Nick's eyes scrunched up. He was standing in the middle of the living room with one crutch and eating yogurt. "Go where?"

"I'm taking you all out on the yacht. Rion didn't mention it?"

Nick turned to him. Rion grinned. He turned back to his father. "No, he didn't."

"He said you haven't left the house since you arrived at the end of December. It's the beginning of April. Let's go." He didn't wait for a response as he turned around and left the beach house.

"I'll grab a bathing suit," Roslyn said excitedly.

Nick shrugged and went to grab the other crutch. "Leave it," Rion said sternly.

Nick looked at him. "How am I supposed to get around?"

Rion raised an eyebrow. "You walk."

"How am I supposed to get onto the boat? I can't even get up these stairs."

Rion walked closer to him. "One, yes you can get up these stairs. You haven't even tried. That's why we're still in the smallest bedroom in this enormous beach house. And two, I'm sure there's a boat ramp." Rion grabbed the crutch out of reach. "Now, are you going to give me the other one?"

They stared at each other, then Nick said, "Fuck off, Ree." He limped his way out of the front door. Rion sighed, then followed him out to the car.

When they returned to the house hours later, Nick immediately noticed it. "What's this?" Nick asked.

"What does it look like?" Rion said with a smile.

Nick narrowed his eyes. "It's a Baltic labyrinth rug. The fibers are *Gossypium arboreum*, custom made in India for you."

"It's so beautiful," Roslyn commented.

"Where is the dining room table?" Nick asked, looking around.

"You don't need a table, Nicky," said Rion. "You need a labyrinth that you can walk and meditate on. Day or night. As many times as you want."

"I don't want this here," he said stubbornly.

"I know. But you need it. So it's here for you whenever you need it." Rion walked up to Nick and took away the crutch. "Now walk."

Nick glared at him. "No."

"Nicky—"

"Rion—"

"God dammit, Nicholas!" Rion exclaimed, losing his cool. "Walk, Nick. Just ... walk."

Nick sighed in anger. But then Roslyn nodded at him. "Walk, Nick."

He sighed again. But he took a step. Then another one. And another until he made it to the edge of the circular, colorful rug. He kept his head down and slowly walked through the large maze in the room. Rion and Roslyn watched him. Then Roslyn tapped Rion and pointed upstairs, giving them time alone. Rion sat on the floor cross-legged and quietly watched Nick slowly walk with a slight limp as he made his way to the center of the labyrinth.

Nick was fine until he aggravated his hip. He didn't wake up in pain, and as long as he used his crutches, the pain never came. But Rion and Ezra had been trying to get him to lean into the pain, to strengthen his muscles. He didn't want to. But he knew he had to. And Rion had gone out of his way to force him to in the most loving, thoughtful way possible. So Nick remembered to breathe in through his nose and out through his mouth as he walked, practicing mindfulness, the sound of the ocean hitting the sand helping him with the pattern. It took longer than he wanted it to, but he made it to the end. Once there, Nick sat down. He attempted to cross his legs then winced.

God, this hurts, he thought. He stretched his legs out instead and ran his hands through the cotton.

Rion stood and sat in front of him. He stretched his legs over Nick's, scooting closer until he was almost in his lap, their groins next to each other.

"Does this hurt when I sit on you like this?" Rion asked.

"No." He looked into Rion's wide brown eyes. "I've been a real dick to you about this, haven't I?"

Rion smiled and nodded. "But you've been a dick to Ezra too, so I'm not taking it personally."

"I'm surprised you haven't left me yet," Nick said out loud, then instantly regretted it. He meant it as a joke, but it came out bitterly.

Rion frowned. "I told you, Nick. I fucked up when I did that. I'm never going to leave you again. Promise."

They kissed and Nick absentmindedly began to move against him. "Rion?"

"Hmm?"

"I need you. Inside of me."

Rion moved his face back and looked him in the eyes. "You aren't going to hurt me," Nick said. "Please, Ree."

Rion nodded slowly. He stood up and walked over to the room while Nick quickly pulled his boardshorts down and off, then removed his t-shirt. Rion stepped out of his own shorts and underwear, grabbed the lube, and walked back over. Nick laid down on his back and slowly lifted his legs up. Rion gently prepared him, then entered him. Nick was tight. It had been a long while for them, so Rion moved slowly and with intention. He knew that position probably irritated Nick's left hip. But Nick didn't care. He closed his eyes and moaned Rion's name, forgetting they had someone else in the house with them.

Nick pulled Rion's face closer to him, and they kissed and made love. Nick kept squeezing him inside, and Rion had to keep slowing down so he would not cum quickly. He needed Nicholas to cum first. But it was so hard holding it together, watching Nick's

face contort in ecstasy, his body trembling, his slow-moving tugs on his own cock. Finally, he let out a loud groan and came against his own chest. Rion kissed him again, then began to move with speed, no longer wanting to hold back. His orgasm seized him before he could stop it. He froze, throwing his lips on Nick's neck as he emptied out.

It took a moment for both of them to come back to reality. Rion slowly pulled out and Nick muttered, "Jesus, Ree..." through labored breaths.

Rion chuckled and moved his face onto Nick's shoulder and threw his arm and leg around him. "That good, huh?"

Nick chuckled back. "Always that good with you."

They were quiet for a while as Nick stared at the ceiling, rubbing Rion's back. "Rion?"

"Hmm?"

"Tell me a story."

Rion hesitated. "What?"

"Tell me a story. I know you have a story kicking around in there. What's the last story you thought of?"

"Oh..." Rion closed his eyes. "Two men who work for the same company, cleaning out office buildings overnight. They get close, become friends. Then more. One is gay. The other is ... curious. He's always wanted to know but never got the nerve to explore. Until now."

"Hm," Nick replied. "Sex in the CEO's office?"

"Definitely. Right on the executive's desk." They both giggled. "But it's more than just sex. It's so bonding. Solidifying what they already had between them, which was love."

"That's beautiful."

"Yeah, it is."

"How does it end?"

"Huh? I... I don't know."

"Tell me. Do they become a couple? Does the curious one struggle with coming out?"

"Erm..." Rion was thoughtful. "No. Once he realizes what he is, it's easier for him to just go with it. And his family accepts him fully. No drama in this one. Just a sweet romance. A happily ever after."

"That's wonderful," said Nick. "We have enough stories out there with men struggling with their sexuality. He should go big and announce it on social media or something."

Rion chuckled. "Yeah, sure. Maybe get caught in a sex tape."

Nick laughed. "What are their names?"

"Oh.... Erm... I was thinking Sean, then Ron. But Sean and Ron rhymes and that just sounds terrible."

Nick chuckled. "Jesus, no. Not Sean and Ron. What other names were you thinking?"

"Something common, like Trevor. Something not so common, like Egerton. Eggy for short."

"Trevor and Eggy. I like it."

"Yeah..." Rion said softly. "Me too."

"Do they get caught ever?"

Rion was thoughtful again. "Yes. By a coworker. A female coworker."

"Ooooh," Nick said excitedly. "Is she a friend or a foe?"

"A friend. But then she—" Rion stopped talking.

"She what?"

Rion sat up and kissed Nick's lips. "You'll just have to read about it."

Nick smiled at him. "Can't wait, Ree. Can't wait."

They adjusted to where they were lying side by side, their faces inches from the other. "I know what you just did."

"What do you mean?" Nick asked innocently.

Rion smiled. "I love you, Nicholas Highton. I love you so fucking much."

Nick reached out to run his hands through Rion's curls. "I know. And I love you right back, Ree Matthews. Thank you for showing me how much I matter to you with this labyrinth."

They kissed again. As they stared at each other, Rion's eyes began to droop. "Sleep, Ree. I'll be here in the morning."

Rion closed his eyes and fell asleep. Nick fell asleep soon after, both naked in the middle of a labyrinth rug.

But when Nick woke up a couple of hours later, Rion was not beside him. "Ree?" he called out. He didn't hear a response.

He slowly stood up, his left leg achy and stiff, but he was able to stretch a little before making his way to the bedroom. Rion was not there.

"Ree?" he called out again.

No one answered him. Nick put on a pair of sweatpants and stepped outside of the room. There was only one other place he could be.

Nick walked to the stairs and took a deep breath, then he began walking up the first few steps. It was a dull ache, not a sharp pain. He continued to the top. He knew the one master bedroom was occupied, and the door was closed. But the other master bedroom at the end of the hall had a cracked door. Nick walked to it and pushed it open. He saw Rion at the desk in front of the window with his feet on the table and his laptop in his lap, typing away. He had on his Bose headphones, his head swaying to whatever music he was listening to. Probably something by Lady Gaga or Drake. Nick quietly went over to the bed and slipped between the covers to fall back asleep, leaving Rion to do what he did best.

Rion looked back over the video he recorded and edited. It was over two minutes long, but he wanted it to be perfect. He sat on the steps of the back porch and pressed play.

It started with a close-up of Nick's face, zooming out to him lying in bed in the master bedroom with nothing but a sheet to cover his midsection as he slept soundlessly. He and Rion had moved upstairs to the main bedroom a few weeks back since Nick was better at using the stairs.

Rion knew starting the video like that would attract all of their followers. The camera turned around to Rion's face as he smiled. "Now that I have your attention," he whispered, "let's step outside and take a walk."

The camera cut to Rion sitting on the beach cross-legged with the lens facing him. "First, I want to say that I love y'all Lite-heads. The outpouring of love and support you have given Nick over these last five months has been nothing short of amazing. He's getting stronger every day."

The camera cut to a video of Nick walking the line with more purpose and Erza cheering him on. Rion continued to talk about him. "Erza, his physical therapist is fantastic. I want you all to go follow him on your socials and support his work. He's @ EzraTheTrainer everywhere. Ezra knows when to push Nick to his limit, he knows when to back off and give him space, and Nick could not have gotten as far as he did without him. Nick doesn't need the wheelchair at all, and we finally got him to stop using the one crutch." Another picture of Nick leaning on the crutch while he ate a yogurt standing up.

The camera panned back to Rion talking on the beach. "But it hasn't been easy. Nothing about this last year has been easy for Nick, for me, for us." He ran his hands through his hair. "Can I give you all a little bit of truth? Share with my ninety-eight million friends?" he said with a smile. "I have been struggling while trying to figure out where I fit in Nick's world. When I met him back in London, I knew exactly who he was, and that was someone way out of my league. When it's just him and me, he's my Nicky and I'm his Ree. None of that class and money shit matters. But when I stepped into his world fully, it started to matter. Not to him but to me. It didn't matter that his sister and brother embraced me as family, that his nieces and nephews are seriously the coolest and most down-to-earth kids I've ever been around. I let it get the best of me, and my mental health went into the shitter, as Nick so eloquently said to me. And on the flip side, I think the pressure of trying to keep everyone happy—his followers, his employees, his family, me—kind of got to him too.

"For the first time ever, we weren't in sync. The tabloids got it right for once; our Niion Lights were dimming. We forgot that, at the end of the day, we still had each other to hold on to, to ground us. That we could close the door, shut out the world, and just be us, like we did at the Oriental in Hyde Park all those years ago. His tragic accident reminded us of that. I almost lost him, y'all. The world almost lost one of the most wonderful, thoughtful, talented, selfless men of our generation. But I almost lost half my heart."

He looked away from the camera and ran his hands through his hair again. Then he turned back. "It forced us to shut the door again and focus on ourselves individually and our relationship together. And we've never been stronger together then in this moment right now. That's why we've hidden away in this undisclosed location to take care of ourselves and each other. We're both in therapy. #TherapyForMen and #RelationshipGoals. We do some sessions together which has been so helpful in communication, getting us ready for marriage at some point. I'm on a low dosage of medication for my anxiety, and Nick is exercising and mediating again. He's back to work, making sure Highton Media and Publications is ready to put out great content for you. I'm writing again, so look out for new releases from me in the next year or so. And we are in a good place.

"But I need to let you know something: to continue on this path of my own mental health, I'm taking a step back from social media and public events with Nicholas Highton. Sure, you'll see me on Nick's content, the man can't stay away from showboating for y'all on IG, TikTok, or Snapchat, but as far as trying to keep up with the media Joneses... I'm officially done with that. We'll step out once in a while together, but I'm going back to being the Stedman to his Oprah.

I'll keep my travel blog; I know a lot of you liked my reviews on the places we traveled. But this will be my last official social media post. Remember, just because you don't see me doesn't mean I'm not here. I'll be here supporting Nick's career and dreams and aspirations as he supports mine. I'll be the man behind the man, loving him, encouraging him, traveling with him. And I'm going to marry that beautiful man that you all call Mr. Deep Strokez one day soon. You'll see. He is all mine. And I am his.

"So thank you. Thank you for believing in us. Thank you for hanging in there with us. I'm so grateful to all of you for your love and support of us. And I continue to be grateful to the universe for sitting us next to each other on that red-eye plane to London. Despite the haters and the naysayers, trust and believe that Niion Lights *are* forever."

Rion blew a kiss to the camera, and it cut to the picture of Nick and Rion's kiss in Thailand in front of the waterfall.

He smiled at the video, then cross-posted it on all his social media platforms with only one hashtag: #NiionLightsForever. Then Rion deleted all the social media apps on his phone.

33

Nicholas pressed the Live button on TikTok. "Hey, y'all. It's a beautiful May day out on the Island, and it's my birthday! I'm thirty-one today. It's been a rough year for me, which I'm sure if you're following the entertainment news, you already know. But I've grown so much and am so thankful to the universe, all the good and bad that I've been through. Right now, I'm feeling good, mind, body, and spirit. I got my partner, lover, and best friend in Rion, who has never left my side and never will. And after five months in seclusion, the city is calling, and I'm ready to get back into it. So you just might be seeing me soon in Columbus Circle. Thank you all for the love, prayers, and well wishes. I appreciate each and every one of you. Much love."

Nick threw a wink before he turned it off, then walked to the bedroom where Rion was throwing their clothes into the suitcases haphazardly. Nick shook his head. "I've been meaning to tell you this for years: you're terrible at packing."

"Yeah, well," Rion said, throwing their toiletries in there, "I'm just ready to go home."

"You mean five months cooped up in a five thousand square foot home wasn't your idea of a good time?" Nick said with a smile.

Rion stopped packing and came over to him. "I'm about to spend another couple months cooped up in a fourteen hundred square foot apartment with you while I finish this story and we search for a house in San Francisco. That's not the issue. I'm just ready to be in my bed."

Nick kissed him back. "Me too." His phone buzzed with a text. He read it and said, "Oh, Zoey is asking for my physical therapy discharge paperwork. Do you know where we put it?" He began walking out of the bedroom.

"It's somewhere in the bottom of my bookbag. The orange one," said Rion.

Nick went downstairs to find it in the living room and began looking for papers. His fingers closed around the loose documents, but he also brushed against a thick, closed manila envelope. Nick pulled it out and stared at it.

"Rion?"

"Yeah? Did you find it?" he called out.

"Why do you have an envelope in your bag with your name on it in my mother's handwriting?"

"Fuck!" Rion muttered to himself and practically ran down the hall, taking the steps two at a time and screeching to a halt in the living room.

Nick was still standing there, holding the bag in one hand and the envelope in the other, staring at it.

The only sound was the waves crashing against the ocean for a full twenty seconds.

"Rion—"

"I never opened it," Rion said softly.

Nick's eyes lifted up to meet his lover's. "What is it?" Nick asked softly back. "A bribe?"

"I never opened it," Rion said again.

"But you know what it is." Rion didn't respond. "How. Much?"

"It doesn't fucking matter," Rion said plainly.

Nick stared at him, then he dropped the bag and began to tear open the envelope. "Nick..." Rion said warningly.

But Nick had begun to pull out the paperwork. He read through the first page of the agreement and his mouth opened slightly. "Trixie's family got sixty million. This is ten times more than that. She basically gave you our trust fund money. That's a lot of money to make you go away."

"With the house in San Francisco," Rion said with a sigh. Nick looked up sharply, then read through the next set of papers.

His mouth opened wider. "Holy, holy shit. So that's what she's been doing with the house all this time." Nick looked up. "And it's all yours as soon as we break up. Did you know that part? That it doesn't matter who breaks up with who? The money is all yours within twenty-four hours of a confirmed break up."

"That's what she said but—"

"Do you know that she filed this in a court?" he said as the ball of anger rose in him, sitting in his chest like lead. "Signed by a judge? It's a done fucking deal. The moment you leave me or I leave you, you are six hundred million dollars richer and with a mansion that has all your sisters' names and your mother's name on the deed."

Rion walked up to him and grabbed his face. "And I told her to her face that it's never going to happen."

Nick searched Rion's face but then stepped back. Fear gripped Rion's chest. "Nick, you have to believe me. I—"

But Nick cut him off with a hand raised while he picked up his phone and called Zoey. "Did you find what I needed, Boss?" she asked.

"Call Pilot Pete. I need car service to the plane at JFK ASAP, headed to Rochester in the next three hours, immediately upon my arrival."

"On it." Zoey hung up.

Nick went to put on his shoes. Rion asked, "What are you doing, Nicholas?"

"I'm going to have one final talk with my parents," he said without looking at his partner. "With my ... *mother*. Are you coming?"

Before Rion could respond, Zoey called again. "Car service will be at your door in nine minutes. Your flight is scheduled to take off at 4:50 p.m. and will arrive at 5:57 p.m., where another car will be waiting. I didn't schedule Highton transportation, in case you didn't want anyone to know that you were coming."

Nick smiled. "You know me so well."

"I just figured it was a last-minute trip, so someone is either getting surprised or their ass chewed out."

"Both," Nick said seriously, making Zoey laugh. "Truly, you're the best."

"Let me know if you need anything else, Nicholas."

"Will do."

Rion was still standing in the same spot as Nick walked past him to gather the documents, along with a folder from his briefcase, and put them in his satchel. "Nick—"

"Are you coming or not?" Nick asked him again as he walked out the front door.

Rion sighed, then he went to grab his sneakers.

Four-and-a-half hours later, they were in a dark town car on their way to the Highton-Marigold estates. Nicholas barely said any words since they left the beach house. Every time Rion tried to start the conversation, Nick would stop him and say, "Not right now."

Rion's stomach was in knots. He was grateful that it wasn't a panic attack, the meds doing their job, but he still felt anxious. He kept thinking of Madeline's words to him, that keeping it from Nick just might be what breaks them up. So he tried again.

"I never meant to keep it from you," he said quietly, his voice quivering as he held back tears. "She gave it to me the day before you were discharged, and I swear to God, Nick, I basically told her to fuck off, that I would never take a dime from her, no matter what. She gave me two options: to tell you and have it hanging over both of our heads for our entire relationship or to not say anything and let me carry the burden on my own. She knew both options were shitty, and she predicted that either would lead to us breaking up. But I did plan on telling you. I just ... forgot about it. I was so focused on your recovery and both of our therapies and all the social media stuff we were doing and writing again that I simply forgot it even existed."

Nick was quietly looking out the window as the car turned onto the Highton path leading to the estate.

"Nicky, you have to believe me. I would never—"

"You should have told me," Nick said, cutting him off. "Because if you had, I would have done what I'm about to do five months ago. Hell, I should have done this a year ago."

Rion sighed. "Every argument, every disagreement, every time one of us needed space from the other, I didn't want you to think, 'Is this the day he leaves me and collects his money?'"

Nick scoffed. "That sounds like something she would say. Do you think I think so little of you, Rion?"

"No but..." He chose his words carefully. "I do have a tendency to bail when things get rough. I'm a runner. And in all the ways I ran earlier in our relationship, even after the masquerade ball when I just left... So it's fair to assume that those thoughts might have crossed your mind."

Nick turned to him. Even in the dark car, he could see the fear in Rion's eyes. He touched Rion's face and said, "And through all those moments, you found your way back to me, and we came out on the other side stronger than before. Even when I tried to make you go in February, you didn't leave me then. And I will never leave you now. When I wrote Niion Lites Forever that first time, I meant it. And I know you did too. So no, I know that no amount of money would be enough to make you walk away from me or make me push you away."

A tear accidentally fell from Rion's eye, and Nick brushed it away with his thumb. He dug his hands in Rion's hair and said, "This is forever."

Nick gave Rion a gentle kiss on his lips as the car pulled up to the gate. He let Rion go and rolled down the window so he could enter his six-digit code. "I told you I would protect you, protect us, and that's what I'm doing. This ends today."

Rion watched his face harden as they went farther up the road and around the circular driveway. Nick didn't wait for the driver to open up the door; when the car stopped, he immediately hopped out.

Nick walked up to the stone doors, rang the doorbell repeatedly, then began to bang on the wooden door. The door opened, and a woman in all black was standing there.

"Good evening, Mr. Highton. Mr. and Mrs. Highton were not expecting—"

But Nick brushed past her saying, "But this was my home, Marika. Isn't this my home!? My goddamn family!?" he yelled.

Rion's mouth dropped. He said a quiet, "Sorry," as he followed Nick through the home.

He continued walking through the house yelling. "Oh Mommy deeearrrest!!!" Nick sang. "Where is my dear old darling *mother*!?"

Marika ran after him. "They are having a quiet dinner—"

"Oh, are they having a quiet dinner!?" Nick yelled again. "Is their black sheep of a son disturbing their quiet night? Like I disturbed their entire lives by being born on this day!?"

"Jesus, Nicky," Rion mumbled. "Maybe this isn't—"

"Stay the fuck out of it," Nick snapped at him. Then he yelled again, "Madeline Highton! Show your conniving face! NOW!"

"What is the meaning of this!?" Niles said, coming out of the dining room into the main room with Madeline right behind them. "Are you on coke again?"

Nick scoffed out a laugh. "I have never been more sober or more clearheaded in my entire life, Father. You should try it. Start by getting your head out of Madeline's ass and see her for who she really is."

"How dare you talk to me like that!?" Niles thundered.

"How dare you have children with such a bitch!?" Nick yelled back.

"Jesus, Nicky!" Rion yelled at him. "It wasn't him! What are you—"

Nick whirled around to him. "Did you know my father's name is on the paperwork too? His signature? Cosigning this bullshit attempt to pull us apart!?"

That was surprising. Rion abruptly shut his mouth and shook his head.

Nick nodded. "Because you didn't open it. Which, honestly, I love you so fucking much for that." He turned to Niles. "Was it all lies, Father? All the time we spent together, all the things I shared with you and you shared with me... Was it all a ploy to get me to lower my guard, pulling me closer to you and the Highton legacy and into high society so that Rion and I would move further away from each other?"

"What are you talking about? Explain yourself, Nicholas. Now!" Niles said angrily.

"No, Father." Nick went into his satchel and handed his father the documents. "You explain *yourself*!"

Niles's mouth also opened in shock as he looked at the first document. Madeline stood there in her silk robe with her arms folded, her face plastic.

Nick turned to her and snarled, "You stupid, fucking bitch. You meddling, manipulative, conniving, whore of a woman. You thought that even after all this time, you would once again be able to manipulate what happens in my life. You have learned absolutely nothing about me from the moment you pushed me out of your pussy thirty-one years ago and sent me off into the world all by myself. So let me make this very fucking clear."

Nick stepped closer and towered over her. "You are dead to me. You will never see me again. You will stay away from me, my homes, my businesses, anything having to do with me. You will have your hand in nothing that has anything to do with Nicholas Highton."

Madeline's eyebrow raised. "You're acting like a petulant child, Nicho—"

But she was cut off by Nick's good hand on her throat, pushing her against the nearest wall. And this time, he began to squeeze.

"Whoa!" Rion yelled and grabbed Nick's hand.

Niles also attempted to pull his wife and son apart, yelling, "What the hell, Nicholas!?"

Rion managed to force Nick to let go. "Not the way, Nick," Rion said, pushing him back. "Not the way."

But it was just enough for Madeline to know he wasn't playing with her. Her hands immediately flew to her neck that was red with Nick's fingerprints on it as she coughed violently.

Niles stood between his wife and his son. "Let me handle it."

He turned to her. “What did you do, Madeline? Why did you do this?” Madeline was still in shock that her son tried to strangle her. She did not answer, or couldn’t, trying to catch her breath, her chest heaving. “We talked about this. We talked about no more meddling in his life, especially his love life. We agreed. That’s why we wanted him to come home.”

“With stipulations,” Nick chimed in.

Niles turned back to his son. “What stipulations?”

“That you and Rion were to never meet,” Nick confessed. “That’s why I didn’t introduce Rion to you, Father. Because your bitch of a wife threatened to put a child porn virus on my computer and the computers of my employers. And to plant drugs on Rion’s nieces and nephews. The children in his family! To destroy me and everything I care about and worked hard for and all the people that put their trust in me if I didn’t come home, spend time with you, and take the company.”

Niles slowly turned back to Madeline. “Tell me that’s not true.”

Madeline had regained her composure. But instead of answering her husband, she looked at her son. “I still can,” she said viscerally.

“Fuck you, bitch,” he said back just as nastily. “I’d like to see you try.”

“I own you, Nicholas!”

“And I will kill you, Madeline!” He began approaching her again, but Rion held on to his arm tightly.

“ENOUGH!” Niles thundered again. He was in disbelief, and furious, at all he had learned. Niles looked at the paperwork in his hands again. "No one breathes a fucking word," he threatened.

Niles stood there and read through every single page as everyone stayed quiet, his eyes widening in some areas, narrowing in others. When done, he folded up the paperwork and held it to his thigh.

He turned to his son first. "I didn't know, Nicholas. I didn't know about any of this. I meant everything I said to you at the beach house. I want you to be happy, to do the things that make you happy, and to be with the one that makes you happy. Because I know you better now. And I would never go back on my word to you." He looked down at the papers again, then back up. "I didn't sign this. I never even saw these documents. She must have gotten to Ian for my signature. But the good news is, because my name is on the paperwork, I can easily undo it. And I will, first thing tomorrow morning."

"Except the house," said Nick. "Rion gets the house. Now."

"No," Rion protested. "Absolutely not."

"You both get the house," said Niles. "As promised a year ago. The deed will be transferred to both of your names by the end of the week. And that's a fucking promise."

"Then we're moving to San Francisco by next week," said Nick, reaching into the satchel and handing Niles the folder. "I'm keeping the office in New York but buying a new building in San Francisco with my own money. And I am not joining the company with Highton Optimum. I'll keep the name, but it's my company fully, outside of the family business. No shares or stocks will be associated with Highton Optimum

Holdings. You created a separate financial portfolio, and it's going to stay separate."

Nick pointed at his mother while still looking at his father. "And you will keep her away from me. As far as humanly possible. Because I'm telling you now, Father, if I get a whiff of Madeline coming after my partner, my friends, my employers, my business, Rion's family, which is my family too, the next time I see her, I won't stop my hands around her throat until her neck snaps. And that's a fucking promise."

He glared at her and she glared back. "Congratulations. You're back to the only two children that Niles required of you. Now fuck off."

Nick turned around and began to walk out. Rion looked at Niles helplessly. Niles gave him a solid nod. He glanced at Madeline once and ran out behind his partner, grabbing Nick's hand as they walked back to the car.

"You're ready?" Maurese asked.

Rion chuckled nervously, readjusting his white tie. "I mean, yeah. It's just a piece of paper at this point. Nothing's going to change."

Maurese put one hand on his shoulder. "It's not just a formality. And everything is going to change. You were tethered to him, but now you'll be officially with Nick for the rest of your life. So I'm asking, are you ready, son?"

Rion looked up at his uncle. "Are you trying to make me run?"

Maurese laughed and pulled him into a hug. "No, the opposite. I want your feet to be steady when you walk down the aisle."

Rion looked over at the picture on the dresser that they blew up. The one of him and Nick taking a selfie in Hyde Park five years ago. "Yeah. I'm ready."

Maurese let him go and patted his shoulder. "Then let's go."

They walked through the expansive estate together. It was quiet. Everyone was downstairs, waiting for him. As he made it to the top of the stairs, Nick was waiting at the bottom of the staircase in a similar all-white suit. He was clean shaven, the sides of his hair shorter than the middle that was slicked back. He reminded Rion of how he looked when they first met. Nick smiled, watching Rion come down the stairs. When Rion stood before him, Nick straightened out his lapels, although they didn't need to be straightened; he just wanted to touch him. Rion also had a haircut, his curls much shorter to his head, but he had also grown a thin beard. Nick wanted to run his hands through Rion's hair so badly but knew he couldn't mess up his look. And Rion looked perfect.

"Ready?" Zoey said behind them. Maurese silently left the vestibule to find his seat in the great room that overlooked the Pacific Ocean.

They turned to her. "Yes," they chorused and grabbed hands.

She smiled at them, then said into her walkie, "Cue music." She turned to the wedding party. "Start walking."

Morgan and Jeff went first. Then Kate with Robby, and Blair with Reese. Then his sisters with their partners. Roslyn and Niles were last. They hugged their children one last time before they made their way through the double doors, arm in arm.

They didn't look at each other. Instead, Rion and Nicholas squeezed hands tightly and walked through the hall of less than a hundred guests for their private ceremony at Sea Cliff Manor. Not until they stood before an officiant and turned to each other did their eyes meet. And simultaneously, the tears began to flow. They read their vows to each other, long and emotional, and waited patiently for the final proclamation of "I now pronounce you husbands. You may kiss—"

Nick moved quicker than Rion, grabbing his face and pulling on his lips. Rion moaned and tongued him first. They kissed and kissed and kissed, ignoring the excited screams and hoots and flashes that wouldn't stop flashing. Eventually, they slowed down and turned to face all of their loved ones that traveled from New York and Fresno and London to San Francisco to celebrate their special day.

The reception was held in the garden as the sun dipped low, with the Golden Gate Bridge as their backdrop. There were no speeches; everything that needed to be said had been said a long time ago. Instead, their guests mingled and danced. It was nice to see Emma and Muriel sitting together, Brian and Frank toasting on drinks, Kara and Gabby sharing motherhood tips, bouncing their babies on their individual laps as Ava rubbed her protruding belly and listened intently. And it was really nice to see that all of the cousins had pulled two tables together, getting loud and excited as they talked about whatever their generation was talking about.

They tried to leave quietly, leaving their guests to enjoy the flowing food and alcohol, to dance all night or have any pick of the twelve bedrooms the estate provided. But as they stood in the vestibule giving Zoey last-minute instructions on selling their wedding photos to *People Magazine*, and all the proceeds going to a Thai orphanage that they picked, Robby yelled loudly, "They're trying to escape!"

Suddenly, they were swarmed with hugs and well wishes, making them laugh and blush. "We'll take good care of the house for you," Ava said with a wink as she hugged them both.

Frank hugged them right behind her and whispered in Rion's ear, "Didn't want to outshine your day, but now that you're leaving, tonight's the night." He patted the pocket of his suit jacket.

Rion grinned and patted his back. "Good luck. And congratulations."

When the hugs began to lessen, Nick reached over and gently took his husband's hand. "You ready to go, Mr. Matthews?"

Rion grinned, knowing what he wanted to hear in return. "Yes, Mr. Highton-Matthews. I'm ready to go."

Nick kissed his face and pulled him out of the home. The guests followed, throwing lotus petals at them as they made their way to the car. They kissed a lot on the way to the private jet, then kissed a lot on the jet on their way to their destination, both eager for more but determined to wait just a few hours more. They made it to Koh Samui, where another driver was waiting to take them to The Ritz-Carlton, where they booked out a pool villa and all the surrounding villas for privacy. They sent one last text to their family members to let them know they arrived safely, then gave their phones over to the front desk and were escorted to their room.

As soon the door closed, they didn't even look around. Nick lifted Rion up and carried him to the king-sized bed. He stripped Rion bare first, leaving hickeys from his neck to his calves. Rion returned the favor, taking off each article of clothing and kissing every part of Nick's body. He grabbed the lube and got on top first. Nick laid there as Rion rode with vigor, calling out his name, stroking himself until he came on Nick's dirty blond chest hair.

Nick, who was still hard, grabbed hold of Rion's hips and gently leaned over to the right, rolling them both over until he was on top. Rion simply lifted his arms and connected them around Nick's neck, his ankles on Nick's lower back, and held on. Nick began to move, slowly and deliberately, watching Rion's face scrunch up, listening to him moan and sigh Nick's name every so often.

They made love for hours.

"You're so sweaty and delicious, Mr. Matthews," Nick said, licking his neck again before sucking it when they had exhausted themselves.

Rion chuckled. "I still can't believe that you're taking my last name. You're a crazy sonofabitch."

Nick turned Rion's face to him. "I'm just a man in love with his husband."

Rion touched his face. "I love you back, Nick Matthews."

Nick rose before the sun and gave Rion a gentle kiss. He quietly left the room and met up with a guide, and they silently walked out of the resort together to walk the forty minutes to the Big Buddha Temple. He made an offering and was allowed to sit and chant with the morning monks and meditate for a while before the tourists came. He decided to take a cab back since it was too hot to walk by then, and he wanted to get back to Rion quickly.

When he arrived at the room, Rion was naked in the infinity pool. Nick grinned at him and silently took off his clothes to join him. Rion swam up to him, and they hugged and kissed.

"Where did you go? The temple?"

"Yeah. I wanted to see it, be able to use it, before anyone else could."

Rion nodded. "But I don't want to wake up any more mornings without you. So you can't do it again."

Nick smiled and pushed the wet curly hair off his forehead with a finger before he kissed it. "Don't worry, Ree. We'll have a lifetime of waking up next to each other. This I promise you."

Rion responded by putting his arms around Nick and holding on to him.

The couple enjoyed every moment of their honeymoon, having complete and total privacy for fourteen days. They snorkeled in the reef, discovered their love of Muay Thai together, and visited Fisherman's Village at night, picking up gifts for their family. They made love in every corner of their room and on the sand in broad daylight. Food was brought to them three times a day. No phones. No internet. No laptops. No work. No family drama. Just love and laughter and meditation and sunshine between them.

Rion was quiet on the last day as they rode back to their plane. Nick noticed he was affectionate but not as talkative. Rion had dreamed of Hyde Park the night before. They hadn't been back to England in over two years, even though they planned to go. But they had spent the last year packing up their apartment in New York and officially moving to Sea Cliff, taking over one wing of the expansive estate. The only one of his family members that moved in was his mother, saying it was closer to the supermarket. But he knew it was because she wanted to be close to him. And he didn't mind at all, wanting them to spend as much time together as possible. Maurese too stayed in her wing of the estate, also wanting to spend as much time as possible with Roslyn. The high school sweethearts and teenage parents found themselves together again at their mature age.

Rion had resigned as VP of Highton Media and Publications, and Nick hired his old roommate, Lionel Degrassi, instead, and they were happy to be working so closely together again. Nick sold the building that Niles had given him and bought a large warehouse in Fisherman's Wharf, where Robby gave the media companies he found and vetted a choice to either move to California or New York to be a part of the company. Rion hired Lennox Parry as his personal assistant and publicist, who was all too thrilled to move to America with Sonny and get paid to hang out with Rion and handle all his affairs. Nick was still extremely busy running back and forth from New York to California, but when he was home, he catered to Rion all day and every night. And Rion finally finished the book he started in London and completed the second story he had been trying to start until Nick inspired him again. They were good together again, and the wedding and honeymoon felt like a fresh start.

But it had been so long since he touched the grass in Hyde Park. He realized that it was five years to the date that he and Nick were laying side by side under the sun, and Nick had asked him, "*How does our story end?*" Rion would have never imagined their story would end like this. From strangers on a plane to husbands. It made him chuckle a little as he looked out onto the tarmac, seated across from the love of his life.

"What are you smiling about?" Nick asked him.

"Nothing," Rion said and looked over at him lovingly. The plane began to move and Rion flinched. Nick grinned and Rion grinned back.

"I don't think I'll ever get completely used to going up in the air, no matter how many times I've done it."

"And that's okay," Nick said gently. "Because I'm going to be right by your side. Forever and always."

Rion nodded slowly. Then he said, "Nicky? I want to go home. Our home."

It took less than a moment to figure out what Rion meant. He touched his hand again. "Okay, Ree. Let's go home."

He pressed the intercom next to his seat and said, "Pilot Pete?"

"Yes, Mr. Highton-Matthews?"

"Change of plans. Take us to Heathrow Airport in London."

"You got it, sir."

Nick stood from his seat and sat next to Rion. They clasped hands and kissed as the plane rose in the air to take them home.

BOOK CLUB QUESTIONS

1. Rion and Nick created a home and a life in London, where it all started for them. If you have ever been to the city of London, what were your favorite parts? If not, what areas would you like to visit?

2. Nicholas and his father Niles had some pretty intense conversations. Which one stood out to you the most?

3. Should Nick have told Niles about his mother's malicious threats?

4. Was Rion's treatment of his mother before he met his birth father justified?

5. What do you think of Ava and Kaleb's relationship? Of Gabby and Gael's? Of Muriel's and Frank's? Do these relationships have what it takes to go the distance?

6. The Hightons and the Matthews were finally in the same room during the will reading. If you were in that room, how would you respond to Madeline's outbursts?

7. What are your thoughts about Nick requesting that he and Rion do therapy, both individually and a few sessions jointly?

8. In the final installment, you learn more about Madeline and Roslyn's individual history. Describe your thoughts about them. Did your opinion of them change?

9. How different do you think their relationship would have been if Rion had told Nicholas of his panic attacks and writer's block?

10. At the end of book 2, Nick made promises to Rion to protect him in his world. Did he live up to his promise? Why or why not?

11. If Rion were to write a book about Kara's life, would you read it?

AUTHOR BIO

Wife, mother, partner, daughter, sister, friend, social worker, life skills coach and part-time erotic romance novelist, Eskay Kabba finds the complexity of human nature and creates romantic and erotic love stories. The characters reflect the notion that no one is all good or all bad, but we are all just trying to find love in hard places. Eskay pens erotic romance novels that celebrates the LGBTQ community, people of color and interracial relationships. When not writing about the throes of passion, Eskay finds joy in spending time with her family and loved ones, reading dystopian and fantasy series, and binging popular shows from a streaming app. Eskay.Kabba@gmail.com

More books from Eskay Kabba

Hidden Love
Not So Hidden
Signs of Affection
Deeply Devoted to Him
Honest Love
A Plane and Simple Connection
A Familiar Family Connection

Discover more at
4HorsemenPublications.com

10% off using HORSEMEN10

Printed in the USA
CPSIA information can be obtained
at www.ICGtesting.com
LVHW042038251124
797601LV00004B/40